TRIAL BY FIRE

Books by Terri Blackstock

Newpointe 911

Private Justice
Shadow of Doubt
Trial by Fire
Word of Honor

Sun Coast Chronicles

Evidence of Mercy
Justifiable Means
Ulterior Motives
Presumption of Guilt

Second Chances

Never Again Good-bye
When Dreams Cross
Blind Trust
Broken Wings

With Beverly LaHaye

Seasons Under Heaven
Showers in Season

NEWPOINTE 9 1 1

TRIAL BY FIRE

TERRI BLACKSTOCK

BOOKSPAN LARGE PRINT EDITION

ZondervanPublishingHouse

Grand Rapids, Michigan

A Division of HarperCollins*Publishers*

This Large Print Edition, prepared especially for Bookspan, contains the complete, unabridged text of the original Publisher's Edition.

This book is lovingly dedicated to the Nazarene

Trial by Fire

Copyright © 2000 by Terri Blackstock

Requests for information should be addressed to:

ZondervanPublishingHouse
Grand Rapids, Michigan 49530

ISBN: 0-7394-1314-7

Published in association with the literary agency of Alive Communications, Inc., 7680 Goddard Street, Suite 200, Colorado Springs, CO 80920.

Interior design by Jody DeNeef

Printed in the United States of America

This Large Print Book carries the
Seal of Approval of N.A.V.H.

Acknowledgments

Special thanks to three good friends and fellow novelists who shared their expertise with me for this book. Dr. Harry Kraus Jr. helped me with my medical facts, as he has done many times before. Lawana Blackwell shared her husband's experiences in a burn center. And Rev. Alton Gansky — former firefighter — gave me personal insights about fighting fires.

I also must thank the Christian novelists of Chi Libris, all of whom I consider dear brothers and sisters, who constantly challenge and edify me. We came together as a group in 1999 because of our common calling. We stay together because of our common love. Thank you for being my co-workers in Christ's Harvest, instead of my competitors in publishing.

What a mighty God we serve!

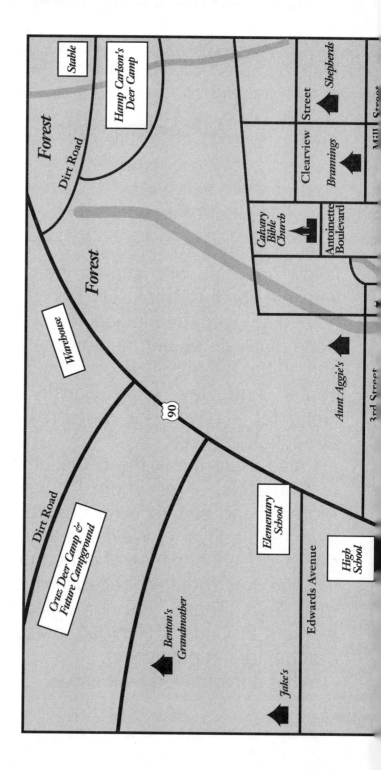

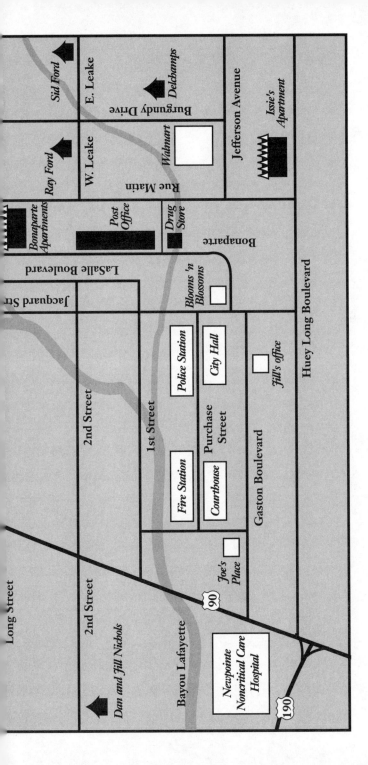

Chapter One

● ● ●

The fire alarm blaring at four A.M. jerked Nick Foster from a sound sleep. He swam through his groggy stupor and sat up, slipping his feet into the turnout pants and boots scrunched together next to his bunk. Mark Branning and Dan Nichols stumbled into their own gear and raced out of the room.

Adrenaline snapped Nick to attention, and his heart rate, which had gone from sleep to sprint in a matter of seconds, brought him fully awake. He grabbed the radio mike. "Midtown to Simone," he said to the dispatcher who sat in an upstairs room at the police station next door. "It's Nick."

"Nick, the church is on fire. Sounds bad."

"What church?"

"Your church, man! Calvary Bible Church."

Nick froze as the words filtered through his consciousness, then settled hard in the pit of his stomach. He forced himself to think clearly and grabbed his helmet from its hook. Pulling it on, he bolted out to the truck bay.

"Where to?" Mark yelled from the driver's seat of the pumper.

"The church." Nick grabbed his turnout coat and helmet and leaped onto the truck. "My church is on fire!"

Mark didn't comment that it was his church too, and Dan's as well. He turned on the siren, chasing away any remnants of sleep that might have dulled their senses, and drove into the warm October night as fast as reason would allow. A faint yellow glow lit up the night sky in the distance, and Nick could see the smoke billowing through the air as the fire truck approached Calvary Bible Church.

"Faster!" Nick shouted, but he knew Mark was driving as fast as he could. Maybe it was just in the rec hall, he thought. Maybe they could save the sanctuary.

But as they reached the street, he saw that the building was fully engulfed. Every wall was in flames, and the roof was a stage on which the fire did its wicked dance. The truck stopped and Nick leaped out, pulled on his tanks, and snapped on his mask. As he unwound the hose from the truck, he broke into warrior mode.

He heard the other fire truck from across town coming up Jacquard Boulevard, and behind their truck, the rescue unit screeched to a halt. The hose opened, blasting the way in front of him. As he entered the building and saw how thoroughly the fire had taken hold, he forced himself to think like a fire-fighter and not a preacher.

The fire had already consumed the west side of the building where all the children's Sunday school classes were held just yester-day, and the north side where they had fellow-ship and ate dinner together on Wednesday nights. He sprayed his way into the sanctuary, searching for the origin of the flames. The sanctuary was engulfed as well, and the air billowed with black smoke. It was tangible evil, blinding him to the source of the fire. But he would not give up. He was David facing down Goliath. His hose was like a few small stones, but if he aimed it well, he could knock Goliath to the ground. God would help him.

The gates of hell would not prevail against this church!

l l l

Stan Shepherd — Newpointe's only police detective — arrived on the scene just as the firemen began fighting the flames. As if he were watching his own home being consumed, he sat paralyzed behind the wheel. How had this happened?

Not so long ago, he and Celia had made the decision to lower their lifestyle so they could donate money for the building now going up in flames. All that money wasted . . . all those hours of work sanding and scraping and painting . . .

Stan tried to shake off his shock and got out of the car. A crowd of people was gathering in the street.

"Back up," he told them. "All the way across the street." Slowly, they did as he said.

"Stan, are they gonna save the building?" Mildred Buford asked.

He didn't want to pronounce the building dead, but it didn't look good. "I don't know, Mildred. Now get back."

"But I had some fish and a hamster in my Sunday school room. The kids'll never get over it if they can't save 'em! If I could just run in and get 'em —"

"You can't go in there. Now, come on,

Mildred. I need you to get across the street."

"But could you tell the firefighters to look for them?"

"No! They're trying to put the fire out, Mildred. They don't have time to look for your pets."

He could tell that she was offended, but he couldn't worry about that now. As several more police cars came to the scene, he yelled for the uniformed officers to block off the street so that no other cars or curiosity-seekers would be able to come this way. Then he headed into the crowd reassembling on the opposite side of the street. "Did anybody see what started the fire?" he yelled. "Who made the call?"

"I did," Zeb Fox said. He was the old man who lived next door to the parsonage — Nick's home — across the street from the church. Zeb worked the night shift, seven to three, at the Mason Dean steel factory. "I seen smoke comin' up out the roof when I got home," he said, "then it started comin' out from under the doors and I knowed I'd better call somebody. I was just fixin' to call the police when I seen the flames comin' from 'round the back."

"But did you see anybody nearby?" Stan asked. "Was there anybody in the church or any cars around?"

"I seen somebody," Thelma Fox piped in. She was Zeb's wife, and kept up with everything that happened in the community. She had mounted a rearview mirror at the perfect angle on her sink window, so that she wouldn't miss a thing while she was washing dishes. "I was fixin' breakfast for Zeb, and I seen a car full of young'uns over there just before the fire started. Three or four of them, and when I seen 'em in the parking lot, I knew they was up to no good."

"Did you get their tag number?" Stan asked.

"Why, no, I didn't think to do that," she said.

"Well, what about the kids? Did you recognize any of them?"

"No, but I believe it was a red car."

"What kind of car?"

"All I know is red."

"I seen those kids too," Cliff Breaux said. "I was rollin' my newspapers when they screeched around the corner and like ta hit me."

"Could you see them well enough to identify them?"

"No, it was too dark. But like Thelma said, they was young folks." He tapped his pockets for a pack of cigarettes and shook one out. He pulled it out of the pack with his lips. "Oh, I almost forgot. There was some bumper stickers on the car. One o' them Nazi symbols."

"A swastika?"

"Yeah, that's it. And they had a KKK sticker too."

Stan gathered the rest of the information the bystanders had to give him, then hurried back to his unmarked car and radioed the dispatcher.

"Simone," he said, "put an APB out on a red car full of kids, with a swastika sticker and a KKK sign on the bumper. Possible suspects in the church burning."

He looked out through the windshield and saw that George Broussard and Cale Larkins, as well as several other off-duty firefighters, had arrived on the scene to help. Most of them kept turnout gear in their trunks in case they were called from home.

For the first time, he wished he was a firefighter so he could go in there with them and take on this raging enemy.

Chapter Two

● ● ●

Ray Ford, the fire chief of Newpointe, had heard the call on his scanner as he got ready for work that morning. He hurried out the door without telling Susan goodbye, and sped to the scene.

He got out of his car and reached for his boots and gear, gaping in horror at the building that meant so much to him. But like the others, he shoved his emotions down. There was no time for grief or shock now. He had a job to do.

He saw Mark and Dan emerging from the building, and bolted toward them.

"What happened?"

"Looks like arson," Mark said. "I don't know how else it could have gone up so fast. The place wasn't locked, so anybody could have walked in."

They heard yelling from inside. Ray recognized Nick's voice, but he couldn't make out what he was saying. He headed for the door, when something cracked overhead. "Get 'em out!" Ray yelled. "The roof's cavin'!"

* * *

Inside, flaming roof beams fell, missing Nick by inches. He jumped back, almost tripping on something under his feet. He bent down and tried to see through the smoke. It was a body, lying facedown. He had stepped on a hand.

"Over here!" he yelled. "I've got a victim!"

He saw the fluorescent stripes of two turnout coats as firemen headed toward him, but he couldn't make out their faces through their masks. "Unconscious, unresponsive!" he yelled.

"Is he alive?"

He bent to check, but another beam fell, cracking around them and spreading across the carpet.

He turned the victim over to lift him, but froze when he saw his face. "Aw, no . . ."

Another beam dropped, just missing the four of them. "We gotta get outta here!" George Broussard said.

Nick slung the victim over his shoulder as George and Cale headed out. A beam cracked overhead, and the front half of the flaming roof caved in. Nick screamed as beams and sheet rock knocked him to his back, the victim on top of him. Pain shot through his chest and legs, and he fought to throw off the beams that lay across them both. The tanks under his back must have been damaged, and his mask had been knocked askew, so he could no longer get the air that they had provided. He managed to move one of the beams from his chest, but one on his shins was flaming, burning through his fireproof clothes, melting his skin . . .

He tried to kick it free, but his legs were trapped.

More of the roof caved and bounced on the floor behind him. He'd have to get out of here on his own. No one could come in after him. Smoke seeped under his mask and filtered through his lungs.

With one adrenaline-filled, panic-driven kick, he got the flaming beam off his legs, and wincing at the pain, tried to get up with the victim. But he couldn't do it. Collapsing in a fit of coughing, he fell back.

◦ ◦ ◦

When Ray saw George and Cale emerge without Nick, then saw the roof cave in, he broke into a run. Mark was right behind him.

They heard muffled screaming, and behind them, Dan came in with the hose, spraying a path through the flames. George and Cale followed on their heels. "Where's Nick?" Dan shouted.

"He was right behind us when the roof caved!" Cale shouted.

"He found somebody hurt," George said. "I couldn't see 'im in all the smoke."

Ray yelled, "Broussard, Larkins, go out and surround and drown. The fewer of us in here, the better." George and Cale hesitated, obviously reluctant to leave Nick again.

"Nick!" Mark yelled.

"Over here!" they heard, then coughing, and they fought their way to where Nick lay.

Cale threw off his mask and shrugged out of his tanks, handed the gear to George, then ran out, holding his breath until he was in fresh air.

Ray saw from the soot around Nick's nose that he was breathing smoke instead of oxygen, and it was clear from the scald marks on his torn turnout legs and boots that he had been burned. Mark got on his knees, and working fast, threw off Nick's dysfunctional mask and replaced it with Cale's. "Help me get him!"

They got Nick to his feet and threw him over Mark's shoulder, knowing he could be doing terrible injury to his spine if there was a break, but there was no time to hesitate. They would all be dead if more of the roof fell.

But Nick yelled something incoherent, then pointed frantically toward the pile of flaming beams. Dan soaked it down, temporarily extinguishing the flames, until they could see the victim lying under them.

Ray and George attacked the beams. Ray managed to lift the victim, but the smoke was so thick that he couldn't see his face. "Outta here!" Ray cried. "Everybody! *Now!*"

As they burst out into clear air, Ray checked the victim for a pulse. He couldn't find one.

He put him down to try again, and only then saw his soot-covered face.

It was Ben, Ray's only son.

The sound that shrieked out of Ray's mouth seemed unnatural and foreign. Life seemed to screech into slow motion as Ray took his son from George and carried him further from the flames and the smoke and the yelling firefighters and the tumbling, fiery roof, to the paramedics waiting just out of the perimeter of the smoke. It was as if his spirit stood back in shock and looked on, helpless to save his child's life. But his body continued to do as it would do for anyone they had found in a fire, and his mind ran through practical facts about Ben's condition. He was burned badly on his legs and back, worse on his hands. His legs looked broken where the beams had crushed him. The smoke alone would have been enough to kill him, and Ray knew he had probably been inhaling it from the beginning. The paramedic pushed him out of the way and fell to Ben's side, urgently searching for a pulse.

And then he saw the worst injury of all, the one that made all the others seem like nothing at all . . .

"Noooo!" he shouted. "His head!" he wailed. "A bullet hole. *Somebody put a bullet into my boy!*"

Not able to accept the verdict Issie Mattreaux was about to declare, Ray threw off his mask and fought his way back to his son. His face dripped with sweat as he pressed a finger against his neck, waiting for some hope, any hope at all. *"Please, God,"* he whispered, *"please . . ."*

When he felt nothing, he shook his son, then gritted his teeth. "You listen to me, Ben Ford. You better not be goin' nowhere! *You listen to me!"*

Issie tore open Ben's shirt. "We need to defibrillate, stat!" she yelled, and opened the megaduffel to hand Steve an oxygen cylinder. "Ray, do compressions while I get the defibrillator!" she ordered, and Ray began compressing his son's chest, desperately trying to force his heart to beat. As Ray worked, Steve put an oral airway down Ben's throat, then pressed the mask against Ben's face and began administering pure oxygen.

Issie pulled the two pads out and peeled off the backing. She attached one at his ribs and another under his collarbone. She looked at the small screen of the monitor and yelled, "Stop!"

Ray rested a moment, streams of sweat and tears dripping into his eyes. He heard the whine of the machine charging, then the automated voice, "Press to shock."

"Clear!" Issie yelled. Steve and Ray got

back, and she pressed the button. A 200-joule jolt shook through Ben, and Ray held his breath, praying for a pulse. But there was none.

The machine whined again, recharging, and they repeated the process. "Come on, Ben!" he shouted through his teeth, his eyes as hot as the flames swallowing the building. Issie pressed the button to shock him again. "Fight! Don't leave me, son!" But, again, there was no pulse. Someone behind him pulled Ray away as Steve and Issie made last-ditch attempts to revive him. Ray was shaking and could hardly stand on his legs. He felt as if his knees would buckle and he would collapse like a marionette. He thought he might throw up.

"Nooooooo!" The word ripped out of his heart with the same violence as if he'd torn off a part of his body.

Chapter Three

● ● ●

Nick threw his hands over his face, elbows in the air, as Ray's anguished cry told him all he needed to know about Ben's condition. Ray's firstborn child and only son was dead.

He wailed out his own lament, oblivious to Karen and Bob, the paramedics who worked quickly to swap Cale's tank for their own oxygen mask. He sat up, clutching the mask, straining to see the boy.

He saw Ray fall onto his son's body and lift him up, as if by holding him he could bring him back to life. Issie's smoke-stained face twisted with momentary despair. Then, wiping her tears, as if rolling up her sleeves, she abandoned the body and ran over to Nick.

"Is he all right?" she asked Karen, as if Nick couldn't speak for himself.

"Smoke inhalation," Karen said. "Airway doesn't seem patent. Nasal hairs are singed. Carbonaceous residue in the nose and mouth. He needs immediate transport. Also several pretty bad abrasions . . . Second-degree burns on the legs . . ."

"Let us take him," Issie said. "Nick's a friend of mine. You take care of Ben."

Nick couldn't take his eyes from Ben, limp in his father's arms. "He's dead, isn't he?" Nick managed to croak out.

She seemed to ignore him as they lifted his gurney into the ambulance. "There was nothing we could do," she said in a dull monotone, as if he hadn't already seen the tears streaking through the smoke stains on her face. "He was probably dead before the fire."

"What do you mean?"

"There's a bullet hole through his head."

"Bullet hole?" Nick tried to sit up again. He hadn't seen a bullet hole, not with all the smoke and soot and rubble covering Ben. He wanted to ask where it was, but he couldn't make his voice function, and as Issie hung the bag and began to examine his legs, pain shot through him, clearing his mind of anything but that.

Steve Winder jumped into the unit. "Ready to go?"

"Yeah," she said. "Radio in, Steve. I need

permission to intubate before the airway closes."

"Intubate?" Nick choked. "No, I don't —"

"Nick, let me be the medic, okay?" Issie said. "I have to do it to keep it open, or it'll be so edematous that I can't get a tube in. But I'll do the nasotracheal."

He heard Steve talking to the receiving physician, and the doctor giving them the go-ahead. He tried to hold himself still as Issie threaded the painful tube into his nose and down his trachea. "I know it hurts," she said as she worked rapidly. "But I have to use as big a tube as I can get in, just to keep the way open. That's good. Don't try to talk."

But Nick had so many questions. If Ben had a bullet hole through his head, who had shot him? Had Ben started the fire, or had the killer?

He arched at the pain as she checked his burns again.

"Second degree, partial thickness, Steve. Eight percent. He feels it, all right."

As Steve radioed that into the receiving physician, Nick tried to remove his mind from the pain. She opened his clothes carefully, trying not to peel any cloth from the burns. "Nick, where else are you in pain? I only see burns on your legs."

He pointed to his right side. She began to palpate him. "Feels like broken ribs," she yelled to Steve. "Possible internal injuries."

But Nick's mind wandered from his own injuries to the fire chief and deacon in his church, who had just encountered one of the worst tragedies of his life.

Chapter Four

● ● ●

Susan Ford ran two stop signs and a red light, then screeched around a corner. The smoke billowing above the trees on Antoinette Boulevard was her target. She didn't know who had called to tell her that her son had been found in the fire. She couldn't remember if the caller was a man or a woman, or whether it had been someone she knew. All she remembered were the words, hitting her like a cruel blast of evil.

She heard a siren and saw an ambulance heading the opposite direction, and her mother's heart almost made her turn around and follow. But something told her that wasn't Ben.

Maybe it was the voice on the phone, the finality of the tone, the very words they had chosen . . . *It's too late, isn't it, Lord? Don't let it be too late.*

Her brown hands trembled as she punched on the scanner that Ray kept in the car. She tried to tune to the police frequency for information, but all she got was static.

She ran another red light, then peeled around a corner. The church came into view and she saw the flames that had devoured it, saw the firefighters still spraying it, saw the emergency vehicles parked in haphazard fashion wherever they had found a place on the street.

Paying no regard to the yellow tape blocking off the road, she drove right through it and came to a halt in front of the pumper truck.

She threw the door open and bolted out of the car. Another ambulance was parked at the curb, but there was no light flashing and no siren blaring. The paramedics were not hurrying.

She looked around for someone who could help her, then screamed, "Ray!"

Mark surrendered the hose to another firefighter, then jogged to be at her side. She didn't like the look on his face. "Susan . . ."

"Where's Ray?" she demanded, unable to ask where her son was. She didn't want to know yet, didn't want to hear the words. Somewhere in the pit of her stomach, she already knew.

"He's in the ambulance," he said, "with Ben."

Something about the way he said that gave her hope. She turned and ran to the ambulance, tried to get the door open. When she couldn't, she just banged on it, screaming, "Ray! Ray, let me in!"

The door came open, and she looked up and saw her husband slumped inside.

And next to him she saw a body with a sheet over it.

Her head was suddenly cloudy, her vision blurred, and she collapsed onto the asphalt. Ray leaped out of the rescue unit and gathered her back up.

"My baby." Her words, couched in pain and brokenness, were barely audible.

"He's gone," Ray said. "Shhh. He's gone." His voice was hoarse, high pitched, and she could feel the pain coursing through him as he held her.

"What was he *doin'* here?" she asked through her teeth.

"Nobody knows."

Not satisfied with that answer, Susan pulled out of Ray's arms, straightened with determination, and climbed into the rescue unit. She went to the body, grabbed the sheet and pulled it back, saw his face and his charred arms, the hair singed on his scalp . . .

Then she saw the hole through his forehead. Another anguished scream ripped out of her. "He was shot! Ray, he was shot!"

Ray nodded, but couldn't manage to speak a word.

"Who shot him?" she screamed. "Who shot my baby?"

He tried to guide her away from the body. She wailed in rage and despair, as if her very cries could bring him back from the dead.

▪ ▪ ▪

Outside the ambulance, Mark and the other firefighters began to realize the hopelessness of the situation. Already, most of the building had been consumed, and it was obvious that nothing was going to be salvageable. The roof had continued to cave in, little by little, and now some of the walls were beginning to crumble. Whoever was responsible for this had done a thorough job.

Mark ran to the truck to switch air tanks. Dan was already there doing the same.

"It's gone, man," he said. "The church is history."

Mark shook his head and stared back at it. "I can't believe it. In the blink of an eye it's totally gone."

He didn't have the heart to fight the fire anymore, but still he put his mask back on and plunged back into the smoke. He had a job to do whether it looked possible or not, but he knew as soon as the fire was put out, the real work would begin.

Chapter Five

● ● ●

Issie couldn't get Nick off her mind as she finished her shift that afternoon. In an uncharacteristically busy day, she had transported another fireman for smoke inhalation, then Miller Henderson over on Spencer Circle had gone into cardiac arrest. Apparently, he had been the carpenter who'd made the pews and pulpit for the church, and had keeled over at the thought that his work had all been destroyed. She'd revived him before she had gotten him into the ambulance, and the last word was that he was stable. Then there'd been a wreck over on the highway, and a teenaged boy escaped with his life.

It had been one of those days. But it was precisely because of the busyness of the afternoon that Issie found herself too tense to rest now. She was filled with nervous energy, and her thoughts kept gravitating back to the preacher. Nick had been diagnosed with smoke inhalation, bruised ribs, and second-degree burns that would keep him in the hospital overnight. The receiving physician had dealt with his airway first. Because both sides of his lungs sounded good, he was able to rule out a collapsed lung and determined that he was ventilating and oxygenating properly. He rushed him into the X-ray room and saw that there was no significant damage to the lungs. He had decided to take the tube out and administer oxygen through a mask. The medics had done the right thing, he told them in a rare compliment passed from doctor to paramedic. The chances of his airway closing en route had been high.

Because the doctor seemed reasonable, she had bucked protocol and stayed with Nick while he debrided the top, blistery layer of his burned skin. She'd made sure they gave him pain medication before they started the excruciating scrub-down with the antibacterial solution. He'd clung to her hand, his grip almost crushing her fingers, and yelled without inhibition as they ministered to his wounds. She had stayed, talking him through it like a Lamaze coach, until they applied the Silvadene, an antibiotic ointment which gave some relief. She had left him as they were dressing the wounds, knowing that someone back in Newpointe might need her again.

All the way back, she and Steve had been quiet. They'd kept the usually loud radio station off, and had both been lost in their thoughts. She couldn't get Ray and Ben out of her mind. Daily, they witnessed tragedy, sometimes were active players in it. It rarely made sense, and this made the least sense of all. Tragedy and death were no respecters of persons. They happened to good and bad people alike. Living the "good life" was no protection against life's blows, she thought, so what was the point in walking the straight lines?

She wasn't hungry enough to eat when she got off duty, and it was too early to go to Joe's Place, the bar where so many of the protective services employees hung out, so she decided to go back to the hospital in Slidell to see how Nick was doing. She donned a pair of blue jeans and a pink blouse. Her uniform was so colorless and bland that she tried to wear bright things as often as possible when she wasn't on duty.

As she took her hair out of its binding and

shook it out, she wondered why she was making such a fuss. It wasn't like she was trying to impress Nick Foster, of all people. He was as different from her as the east was from the west. That was a quote from the Bible, she thought with a smirk, though she had no idea of the context. She doubted it had anything to do with personalities.

She touched up her makeup and applied lipstick to match her blouse, then stood back and took a look. She was still a pretty woman. She knew that because men's heads turned wherever she went. Only recently had she realized that was not necessarily a good thing.

The men who turned *her* head were nothing but trouble. For years that hadn't bothered her. The more trouble the better, as far as she was concerned. If they were married or ex-cons or escaped cons, or drinkers or druggies, or daredevils, or irreverently charming or roguish, they were her type.

But it was only lately that she realized the domino effect her own behavior had on other lives. She didn't live in a vacuum, and nothing she did affected her life only. There were wives and children, jobs at stake, even her own physical well-being . . . and she had found lately that she was known by the company she kept.

She wondered why it was that once you got on the wrong track it was so hard to get off. You just kept going, hoping somewhere the road would turn. But it never did.

She tugged herself away from the mirror, telling herself that she didn't need to stroll down this dark lane where she started hating herself and counting regrets.

She hurried out of her apartment as if fleeing from the thoughts pressing down on her, and dashed out to her car. She turned the radio on as loud as she could stand it. All the way to Slidell, she listened to blaring rock music, as if the volume could chase any random thought from her mind. The music kept her from thinking too hard about herself and her regrets. It always worked. If she just drove fast and kept busy, stopped thinking, hummed along to the music, she would eventually forget those thoughts that haunted her, and get back to living her life, without indictment, guilt, or apprehension. By the time she got to Joe's Place tonight, she'd have a clear mind and be able to start all over again, drinking what she liked, meeting whom she wanted, going home with whomever caught her eye.

The other paramedics would arrive there with various degrees of fatigue, ready to swap stories about their medical adventures that day . . . whose lives they'd saved, whose they'd lost, disgusting things they had dealt with, funny things patients had said . . . And then there were always the stories about the hospital personnel — young doctors who didn't even know how to properly intubate a patient, grumpy nurses who treated the medics like inferiors. Tonight she would tell of the doctor who'd admitted Nick, and how he'd treated her like someone who knew what she was doing. He was rare enough to make a good story.

They were her family, even more than her own family had ever been. Her mother had died two years earlier, but she hadn't grieved, for the woman had left her to fend for herself long before it was civil to do so. She had worked at a bar in Slidell until the day she died, chain-smoked, and never rebleached her hair until the black roots were two inches long. Issie had been ashamed of her.

When she'd needed a woman's ear, Issie

had turned instead to Karen Insminger, the thirty-year-old medic they considered something of a matriarch in a young profession. She had a lot more miles on her than her age would suggest, and had managed to keep from burning out like so many other paramedics did. She thrived on the thrill of saving lives, of leaping giant obstacles, of doing what others could not do. She had seen things that normal humans should never see, had patched up gore and prolonged both life and death. She always had a story to tell.

When Issie couldn't talk to her father, an alcoholic who had abandoned her and moved to Las Vegas to strike it rich when she was eight years old, she talked to Steve Winder, her wiser, married, slightly older partner who shot straight with her. He dispensed advice to her, welcome or unwelcome, like he dispensed IV bags and epinephrine, and didn't mind telling her if she was stupid when, in fact, she was. He had never shown a romantic interest in her, which was why they worked well together. Instead, he seemed slightly amused and a little disgusted at her life, though his didn't seem that appealing to her, either. Since he left his wife at home with the kids while he hung out at Joe's Place almost every night, she figured his credibility was slightly impaired. Yes, he was like her father in many ways, except that Steve did occasionally show interest in Issie's life.

And then there was Bob Sigrest, the jokester of the group, who turned every horrible, ugly call into a stand-up routine, and had them laughing over their beer when they could just as easily have been crying. He was the great stress-reliever, the one who helped them keep things in perspective. He was the one who forced them to stop dwelling on death and gore, and kept them functioning. The two of them had shared a couple of trysts over the last couple of years, when night bled into morning and the alcohol had properly dulled their good sense. It usually took weeks for their friendship to recover, but eventually, it always had. The times following those "mistakes," as she called them, were some of the loneliest she had ever spent. There was nothing worse than having to avoid someone's eyes because you'd done things in the dark that you would never have done in the light. If the lights could just stay perpetually off, if she never had to look in the mirror in daylight, her life might be easier to live.

But regardless of their past, she still enjoyed being around Bob, and Frenchy, and Twila (built like a linebacker and able to restrain the most combative patients, though her name made her sound like a petite blonde), and all the medics who showed up at Joe's Place every night. Sometimes a couple of firemen or cops would join them, and they'd try to outdo each other, implying that the other occupation was for wimps and old ladies, and that only theirs was the noble profession of heroes and champions.

They were a family, all right, not always a happy one, but they served their purpose much better than her real family did. Issie didn't waste her time trying to explain that relationship, or her need to spend each evening at the bar, to people who judged her. No one but another medic could really understand. She supposed firefighters and cops had the same relationship, that they, too, suffered stress unequaled in regular jobs.

She didn't know how Nick Foster managed to get through an ordinary night without a stiff drink and comrades who'd seen what he'd seen that day. Mark and Dan, she could understand. Being married, they had companions waiting at home, though she couldn't imagine how Allie had any understanding at all of Mark's job, when she did nothing more dangerous than pricking her finger on a rose thorn at the florist. Jill, Dan's wife, was a lawyer, so she wasn't exactly sheltered from the things they encountered. But it still wasn't the same. That was why, for a while, Mark had come to Joe's Place at night to sit around the table and swap stories and insults. As the alcohol filled their bloodstreams, the talk inevitably grew more serious, until Issie and Mark would be left there alone, in deep conversation about his marriage and her singleness.

But Allie had straightened him out somehow, and now he avoided both Joe's Place and Issie, as though either of them had the power to cast a spell on him that would lead him right back to destruction.

Or maybe it was Nick casting the spells. The preacher did seem to have a strong influence on those who attended his church. Like the pied piper, he had a charisma that she didn't understand, charisma that led people to do as he said. She wondered if it had anything to do with his blue eyes under those glasses he always hid behind, or his teddy bear look that made women want to hug him. He seemed harmless enough, yet he sure kept his people marching straight.

She got to the hospital in Slidell, got his room number from information, and headed up. His door was wide open, and she stepped over the threshold. Nick lay in bed with an oxygen mask over his face. He was attached to an IV replacing critical fluids in his body, and he lay staring out the window overlooking the parking lot. She rapped lightly on the door.

He turned, and she saw the shadows under his eyes. He wasn't wearing his glasses, and it was clear from the strained look on his face that he was in a lot of pain. He pulled the mask down. "Issie," he said, but his voice was damaged. He wouldn't be singing tenor for a while.

She grinned and came inside. "I've been upset all day that they undid my hard work and took the tube out, so I came by to put it back in."

He smiled weakly and held out a hand to stop her. "Don't come near me with any tubes."

She laughed and came to the bed. "You're not mad, are you?"

He shook his head. "I owe you a big one. You looked out for me. Thanks."

She shrugged off the gratitude. "I sure wouldn't recognize that voice over the phone. I'm surprised you're not worse off. Smoke inhalation can be deadly. Your nasal hairs were singed, you know. That's a bad sign."

"It was only seconds between my tanks failing and the guys bringing me oxygen. Seemed like a long time, but I still had my mask on and had that little pocket of air. I wasn't inhaling any more than I had to."

His voice just about cut out. Issie saw the ice chips on his table and offered him some. He lifted his mask and let her feed him.

"Thanks," he whispered when his throat was wet again. "I don't even know why they're keeping me here overnight. I'm fine. I have too much to do to be stuck here."

Issie dropped her purse on a chair and set her hands on her hips. "Don't kid me, Nick. Smoke inhalation, second-degree burns, bruised ribs. They have to keep you on this IV at least overnight, and get you set up on the dressing care program. In the

morning, they'll probably get you to physical therapy for a whirlpool cleansing of the
burn. And you know, you could still have internal bleeding. They have to watch you and
make sure your stomach doesn't start
swelling up and that you keep breathing
normally. Not to scare you or anything."

"Thanks," he whispered. "You give me
great peace."

"Hey, medics don't do peace. We give
great pre-hospital care, but peace is
where we draw the line." He smiled, and
she turned her attention to the bandages
on his legs. "So how are these feeling?"

"Ever been fried in a cauldron of hot oil?"
he asked.

"Not that I recall."

"Well, it's something like that."

"Ouch," she said. "That's gotta hurt. So
are you using the painkillers?"

"Morphine." He held up the pump. "I just
click here if I need a dose. I'm trying to use
it as little as possible. Don't want to get
hooked."

"Use it if you need it, Nick. You won't get
hooked."

"My point is, I can hurt just as easily at
home as here. Except for the fact that they

haven't finished torturing my legs yet, and the infernal internal bleeding . . ."

She grinned again. "At least your sense of humor is holding up better than your voice. So why are you in such a hurry to go home?"

"I have to take care of things with the church," he said. "It's gone, you know. The whole building . . . gone."

She knew, for she had gone back by the site several times during the day. There was nothing left of the building. They would have to clear the land and start completely over.

"You'll rebuild," she said.

He shook his head. "Don't know if I've got it in me."

Issie pulled a chair close to the bed and sat down, trying to look relaxed. But she didn't feel relaxed. "Come on, Nick. Where's your faith?"

He grinned then. "*My* faith?" he asked. "Coming from you . . ."

"Yeah, kind of a left-field question, huh?" she asked. "I just thought I'd throw you off guard a little."

He smiled again, and this time the smile made it to his eyes. He looked at her for a minute, and she realized that he was seeing her, not as a colleague who'd just shown up at the hospital, but as a pretty woman sitting in his room.

Something about that satisfied her. Yes, she still had it. She could turn men's heads, even if they were preachers. "But really," she said finally. "There's not much you can do for the church tonight."

"I have people to see," he told her. "I need to talk to my church members, maybe call a meeting."

"Where would you meet?" she asked.

"That's another thing," he said. "I've got to find a place to hold services. And there's a funeral coming up." His voice cracked, and he put his hand over his face. "Susan and Ray . . . have to . . . bury their child. Got to figure out where to hold the service. Got to talk to them, got to apologize."

"Apologize?" Issie asked. "For what, Nick? You didn't do anything wrong."

He turned his head and looked out the window again. "I left the church unlocked. I thought we should have an open-door policy, twenty-four hours a day. I didn't know somebody would die —"

Issie reached out to touch his shoulder, but stopped her hand before it made contact. "Nick, there's more to this story than we know," she said softly. "There was nothing you could have done."

"I don't know that for sure," he said. "If I'd listened to the deacons and locked the church, maybe it would have never been burned. Maybe Ben would be alive. Maybe none of this —"

"Stop it," she said.

He turned around and looked in her eyes. She hadn't seen him without his glasses very often, if ever, and she hadn't realized his eyes were quite that blue. They glistened with moisture from the pain he had endured today. She could still smell the smoke in his hair.

"You can't do this to yourself," she said. "You and I, we rescue people all the time. For every life we've lost, there's a hundred that we've saved. Some things just happen, Nick. We can't control them."

"Have you talked to Ray and Susan?" he asked.

She shrugged. "Susan and I aren't very close, and I figured Ray didn't want anybody around. Word is he's taking it really hard."

" 'Course he is," Nick said. He closed his

eyes. "Ben had just been home from LSU for the summer. A friend of his, who was spending the summer on a special job in London, had offered him his apartment while he was gone. Ben had gotten a job and was doing construction work for the summer. Even though he'd eaten almost every night at home, he'd seemed to enjoy having his own place. He was happy. Right on the cusp of so many things."

His voice broke, and he cleared his throat, reached for the ice chips again.

Issie sat there for a moment, silence hovering between them. He was, after all, the kindest man she knew, and it didn't seem right for kind, gentle men to suffer so much guilt. Before she realized what she was doing, she touched his shoulder.

He didn't seem to notice. "I failed the church," he said. "It was under my care."

His guilt made her angry. "Nick, look at me."

He met her eyes. His were red, tired.

"You didn't fail that church. In fact, you're probably the only one who's going to hold it together."

"I don't know if I can," he said. "Now that we don't have a building, the church could just disperse and go to other congregations where their preacher isn't so distracted with fires and shootings and domestic quarrels."

"Oh, so now you're beating yourself up because you're bivocational? Like that's your fault? You're right, Nick," she said with sarcasm. "If you'd been demanding a full-time salary, none of this would have happened."

"I might have been in the church when it happened," he said. "I might have been there when Ben needed somebody."

"Even if you were full-time, you wouldn't have been there all night. It's not your fault. I want you to say that after me. 'It's not my fault.' "

Nick couldn't say it. He just turned back to the window.

A knock sounded on the door, and Issie turned to see Stan Shepherd leaning in. He nodded at her, then moved closer to the bed. Nick took a deep breath and wiped his eyes. He grabbed his glasses from the night table and shoved them back on. "Hey, Stan," he said in a rasp. "How's it going, man?"

Clearly, Stan couldn't make light of such a horrible day. "Been better," he said. "I hear you've been better too."

"Me? I'm fine," Nick said. "I oughta be home." He studied Stan's face for a moment. "Have you talked to Ray and Susan?"

"Briefly."

"How are they taking it?"

"Just as you'd expect." Stan took a chair across the room and sat down with his elbows on his knees. "Nick, I've got to crack this case before anything else happens."

Nick started to sit up, then remembered his bruised ribs and dropped back. "Something else?"

Stan stood up and paced across the floor, his head down, then stopped and turned back to Nick and Issie. "If you want to know the truth, my gut feeling is that this was some sort of hate crime, racially motivated."

Nick's mouth fell open. "No way."

"Think about it," Stan said. "Our congregation is mixed. We have blacks, whites, Creoles, Indians, Chinese, Hispanics. We never discouraged anybody from walking through our doors. We're right at the beginning of this investigation, but I got to tell you, Nick. It's all pointing to that."

"But who?" Nick asked.

Issie shook her head. "Does Newpointe really have people like that? People who are hateful enough to destroy the building people worship in because their skin is a different color?"

"The KKK group in Newpointe has been quiet for several years. But you can bet I'm gonna be all over them to get as much information as I can."

Nick looked thoughtfully at Stan for a moment. "It could very well be what you think," Nick said. "But a thought keeps nagging me, and I can't let it go."

"What thought?"

"Remember that kid who was coming to our youth group, stirring things up? Him and his sister?"

"Yeah. Cruz and Jennifer Somebody."

"Well, just a few weeks ago, when I broke up his party at that gay ball at Mardi Gras, he threatened to get even."

Stan got to his feet and began to pace as he rubbed his chin. "I had forgotten all about that."

"What?" Issie asked. "Who is this kid?"

"Well, it's kind of a long story," Nick said. "See, back around the first of the year, he and his twin sister started coming to church. Everybody called this kid Cruz. They were eighteen, pretty popular, instantly likeable. Seemed like good kids. Claimed to be Christians. They seemed real interested in our doctrine, but they started challenging the Sunday school teachers. The teachers got frustrated and asked me to talk to them. So I did. I went out to their house, hoping to answer some of their questions so they wouldn't have to keep interrupting their teachers. But as soon as I got them alone, I started to realize they weren't quite the up-standing, likeable kids I thought. They had an authority problem and didn't think I had a thing in the world to teach them. Their mother was just as much of a smart aleck as they were. Said they knew the Bible in-side out and didn't need the likes of me snooping around trying to change their thinking. I left there kind of baffled.

"But I started noticing that the kids were following this boy around like he was their leader or something. I mean, the pied piper kind of thing. They started missing youth group functions because they were with him. It was almost like this ingenious re-cruitment effort, you know? Like he was only there to win our kids over one by one."

"Win them over for what?" Issie asked.

"Well, that's what I wasn't sure of. When I

tried to get to the bottom of it, I got vague answers about how he was mobilizing them to win Newpointe for Christ. Sounded fine, except it didn't ring true. The kids I had tried to get through to weren't the spiritually conscientious types. And then I heard through the grapevine that he had rounded up a group of them to go protest during Mardi Gras, outside one of the gay balls. I got worried and decided that I'd show up and see what this was about. And lo and behold, there they were. Most of my youth group were following this kid around in circles like puppies on leashes, and they were holding some of the most contemptible signs I've ever seen."

"What did they say?" Issie asked.

Stan slid his hands into his pockets. "They were vicious, hateful signs that claimed God hated homosexuals."

"That's right," Nick said. "And I lost my temper."

Issie was confused. "Why? I thought you Christians believed that."

"Well, you thought wrong. God doesn't hate anybody. He may hate their sin, but he hates mine too. So I got out of my car and stormed to their picket line and started grabbing those hateful signs out of the hands of my kids. I was so mad that I smashed them against a brick wall and broke them. Then I told that Cruz fellow that God didn't hate anyone, and I wouldn't allow him to fill the minds of my youth with lies and hate." Nick stopped and went for the ice chips again, coaxing his voice into finishing. "I told him he wasn't welcome back in my church if all he wanted was to lure my kids into this kind of activity. I loaded all those kids into my van, and it was a real tight fit. He cursed at me and yelled threats as I got them in. Before we drove off, he yelled to me that it wasn't over. He told me he'd get even, that my 'heretical' church and I would be sorry for what I'd done."

"Maybe I'd better see what I can find out about this kid," Stan said.

"I'm not saying he did it. He was mad, not crazy. I can't see anyone burning down a church and murdering somebody just to get back at me."

"Stranger things have happened," Stan said.

"Yeah," Issie agreed. "It sure wouldn't hurt to look into it."

Chapter Six

● ● ●

When Issie returned to Newpointe it was still too early to head over to Joe's Place, so she went home. The phone was ringing when she came in, and she snatched it up. "Hello?"

"Issie, it's Mike." Her brother sounded irritated. "Do you know where Jake is?"

Issie hadn't seen her sixteen-year-old nephew in a couple of days. "No. Why would I know?"

"Well, we thought maybe he had dropped by your place."

She knew where he probably was, but wasn't about to tell them. She and Jake had a special bond. He was just like she had been at his age, and she knew that his occasional tastes of the wilder side of life were harmless. She had even aided and abetted them on occasion. "I haven't seen him," she said.

"Well, if he does happen to drop by your place, give us a call, will you?"

"If I see him, I'll call." She hung up the phone, knowing she had no intention of doing any such thing.

She thought about it for a moment and realized that her brother did have a right to know where his son was. She supposed that was a father's prerogative, though she couldn't rely on her own experience, since her father had never cared about anything she had done.

She checked the clock and saw that it was only eight. Where would Jake be at this hour? He could be at one of his friends' houses, but usually they didn't go there until after the parents were all in bed.

No, if she had to guess where he was, she would start with the old vacant house over off the highway. The grandmother of one of his friends had died, and his parents had kept the house until they could get the place cleaned up enough to sell it. That was where he and his friends liked to hang out when they wanted their privacy. She knew because Jake had taken her there a time or two. The kids felt independent sitting out in the backyard or in the stale rooms, smoking cigarettes, cursing and necking where nobody could stop them. He'd recently gotten into a band and told her they used the house for practice.

She went back to her car and drove to the wooded outskirts of town to the vacant house, and as she pulled into the driveway, she realized that she'd been right. Jake's ten-year-old Escort sat in the garage, and some of his other friends' cars were on the street.

Since the front of the house looked dark, she walked around to the back. There was a bonfire back there and three guys stood near it, but inside she could see a light.

"Hey, guys," she called down to the bonfire, "is Jake here?"

The kids all turned, but none of them answered. One of them stepped out of the crowd.

She tried to see his face, but he was silhouetted against the bonfire. "Who are you?" he called.

"I'm Jake Mattreaux's aunt," she said. "I'm looking for him. Is he here?"

He came closer, looking her over. As the dim light from the house caught his face, she realized she had never met him before. He looked like a lifeguard and wore a tank top and a pair of camouflage pants. He came too close, squinting down at her with blue eyes that might have mesmerized her if she'd met him in a bar. "How long have you been here?" he asked.

"I just got here," she said, puzzled by the suspicious question. "Do you know where he is, or do I need to go in?"

He didn't answer, just kept looking down at her, as if wondering if she was friend or foe. "This could be very serious," he said, and a chill went through her at his tone.

"What could?" She was beginning to feel like she had stumbled into a national security meeting.

"She's awright, Cruz." Instantly, she recognized the name. This was the guy Nick had told Stan about. And her defender's voice was familiar. She looked behind Cruz to see Peter Benton, Jake's best friend and the one whose family owned the house. He was draped in shadows, as the kid behind him was. Only Cruz had come close enough to separate from the light of the fire.

Around this Cruz person was an aura of respect, a held-breath kind of anticipation, that seemed to keep Benton and the other kid a few steps behind him.

She stuck out her hand. "I'm Issie Mat-treaux. And you are . . . ?"

He glanced down at that outstretched hand but didn't take it. "Benton, go in and get Mattreaux out here."

She watched as Jake's friend retreated into the house. She looked up at the life-guard/leader and tried to keep things light. "So what's the bonfire for?" she asked. "Roasting marshmallows?"

He grinned then, and she saw a perfect row of bleach-white teeth. "Didn't you hear us singing 'Kum Ba Yah'?"

She breathed a laugh, and tried to sound unconcerned. "Really, what's it for?"

"Call it a pep rally," he said.

"Oh?" She glanced at the fire, wondering if anyone was watching it. She hoped no sparks flew into the nearby trees. They hadn't had enough rain lately.

The screen door opened, and Jake bolted down the back porch steps. A tall girl with long blond hair sashayed out beside him.

"Issie!" Jake came toward her. "What are you doing here?"

"Looking for you."

The girl stepped up next to Cruz with an authority that set her apart from the rest.

Issie noted that she stood as tall as he and had the same compelling eyes. She wore a cross around her neck, but her neckline scooped too low, and her shirt was at least two sizes too small.

Issie realized Jake would be mortified if she acted like an older aunt who had come to tell him his mommy was looking for him, so she tried another tact. "I didn't have anything to do so I wanted to hear your band practice. But I didn't know about the pep rally." She grinned and shoved her nephew playfully. "Since when have you had school spirit?"

He looked a little confused, but one look by Cruz seemed to set matters straight. "Yeah, well. We didn't practice tonight, so —"

"Bummer." She shrugged. "Oh, well. Guess I'll find something else to do then. See you guys later. Oh, Jake, you might want to give your folks a call. They're looking for you." She gave a flippant wave, then ambled back to her car.

She drove away without a look back, but she had no intentions of leaving. Something about the way that Cruz guy had looked at her, and the way Benton and the other kid had stayed silently behind him, and the look of anger and fear in Jake's eyes, all added up to something being wrong.

That was no pep rally.

She made a U-turn and headed back to the Benton property, but this time stopped before she got to the house. There were no houses for a mile or so on either side of the vacant house, so she doubted she would be seen as she slipped quietly out of her car. She cut through the pine trees and wild azalea bushes, stepping over fallen branches and tangled vines. She wished she could use a flashlight. She looked out at the bonfire and saw Benton and the kid she didn't know standing on the north side of it. Cruz, Jake, and the girl had apparently gone into the house.

She steadied herself on tree trunks and tried to push through the brush as she headed toward the fire. She had to see what they were burning. Kids didn't start bonfires, then stay inside. No, the two who were guarding it were watching something burn. What it was, she couldn't see.

As the ground cleared into overgrown grass that needed to be mowed, then dirt farther toward the back of the property, she stayed in the perimeter of the trees and made her way closer to the fire. She heard the popping, crackling sounds she had heard this morning at Nick's church. She hoped these kids didn't start a forest fire.

Afraid to get closer, she tried to see what they were doing, when something in the flames caught her eye. She strained to see it, but wasn't close enough.

Slowly, she inched closer . . . closer . . .

It looked like rolled up carpet, and a big dark spot stained it. She hunched over and ventured out of the trees, moving closer, until she was satisfied that it was, indeed, carpet. The stain was the color of blood.

What had Jake gotten involved in?

She retreated before they spotted her and went back the way she had come, but curiosity drew her to the house. She went to one of the back windows and peered inside. She saw a dozen kids sitting on a concrete slab.

The carpet had been pulled up.

In front of them, one hip resting on a wooden stool, sat Cruz, talking as if he was the teacher and they were his pupils. His tanned face was lit up in a smile, and his expression was warm, animated, nothing like the closed expression he'd worn when he stood face-to-face with her just moments ago.

Jake sat among those on the floor, next to the tall blond, leaning into her as if the mere brush of her shoulder warranted lies and secrets.

He had it bad for her, Issie realized. At best, the girl looked merely tolerant of Jake.

Issie stood at the window for a moment, trying to sort through the barrage of images and impressions. The bonfire, the bloody carpet, the way Cruz had blocked her from coming closer, the charismatic way he spoke to the group . . .

What was going on?

"Hey!"

The voice behind her spun her around, and she saw one of the kids from the fire running toward her. "What are you doing? Hey!"

She took off running back along the trees, back out to the street. She heard the screen door slam, heard voices yelling, heard them getting closer. She made it to her car and jumped in, quickly jabbed the key into the ignition, and screeched away before they had crossed the street.

She was over a mile away before she caught her breath and realized she might have been in danger.

She needed a drink.

Still shaking from the scare, she headed to Joe's Place.

The parking lot was full, as always, and as she walked in, the haze of smoke assaulted her. The bar didn't have the appeal that it usually held for her. The faces here were the same every night, and tonight the Cajun music grated on her nerves. Fiddles and accordions were not calming enough after a day like she'd had. She looked around for the other medics who usually showed up here around nine, but none were here yet. She went to the bar, took a stool, and looked up at Joe, the bartender.

"Where y'at?"

"Awright," she said, returning the Cajun greeting as if it was second nature. She ordered her drink, then spun around slowly on the stool and scanned the customers. Already she'd caught the eye of several of the men across the room. There was no one here who particularly thrilled her.

R.J. Albright, one of the cops of Newpointe, sat at the end of the bar in his usual place.

"You heard anything about Nick?" he asked.

She nodded. "Saw him a little while ago."

"How's he doing?"

"Worse than he'll admit," she said.

Joe brought her the drink and she took a sip. Someone tapped on her shoulder, and she looked up to see one of the new electrical workers who'd come to town recently. She'd met him on a call when he'd been shocked on a job, and she had stabilized him and had rushed him to the hospital. It was amazing the number of people she met each day, and most of them never forgot her even though their faces became blurry in her memory. This guy looked better standing up than he had on a gurney, and she decided that the night had promise after all.

Chapter Seven

● ● ●

It was after eleven before the visitors all left the Fords' house, with their empty casserole dishes and emptier platitudes about the death in their family. A few relatives remained, and Susan had spent hours trying to figure out where she would put them for the night. Usually, she let guests stay in Ben's room, but tonight she wanted to keep that room closed off until she could go in there alone. She didn't want the evidence of his life to be disturbed. She wanted it left untouched, just as it had been the last time he'd stayed at home.

Vanessa, her brokenhearted teenage daughter, needed her room. The girl was distraught and exhausted, and Susan wanted her to have a good night's sleep in her own bed. Susan would have given up her own bed, since she doubted there was much sleep in her future, but she knew that Ray needed rest.

So she made pallets on the living room floor for her sister and her husband, her nieces, and Ray's parents. Sid, Ray's brother, had graciously taken some of the other relatives into his home.

But now that the house was winding down and people were getting quiet for the night, she found that there was no place she could go to be alone. She had some things to say to God, and she meant to say them alone. She didn't want anyone standing over her telling her that there was a purpose in all this, that God would comfort her, that Ben was ready to be with God. She didn't *want* him with God, and she didn't want God's comfort. She wanted Ben, her first-born, whom God had given her, never warning he would snatch him away.

She waited until the clattering in the kitchen stopped as her sister found creative places in the refrigerator to store the food, waited until she heard no more sniffing from Vanessa's room or the living room, waited until the silence from Ray's side of the bed finally settled into a light snore. Then she went to Ben's room, quietly slipped in, and closed and locked the door behind her.

The lamp was shining. She wondered

who had been in here to turn it on. She looked around at the baseball memorabilia on the wall, the trophies he had won growing up, the framed certificates and ribbons. His childhood was trapped, frozen in this room, but he had moved on. He had become a man and moved into an apartment, had excelled in school, had forged dreams and plans that would have made her proud.

The pain wrapped around her, sharp tentacles of grief that cut into her flesh, straight to her heart, and threatened to immobilize her. Rage spiraled up inside her, like the grief from her heart making a pilgrimage to her head. Someone had to pay. Someone had to suffer. Someone had to explain to her why her son, her only son, had been chosen.

She muffled the grief moaning out of her mouth and squinted her eyes as her hands folded into fists. She looked up at the ceiling as if God was there, and thought of taking the lamp and flinging it at the Sheetrock, lashing out at the God who would allow such a thing.

"How could you, God!" she whispered. "How could you take my baby?" She sat on the bed and pulled her feet up, hugged her knees to her chest, and rocked back and forth, back and forth, as if recoiling from the touch of the Lord who could comfort her.

Explain it to me, God! I don't understand this. I need to understand.

She had known people who'd lost children before, had even visited them in their home the day of the tragedy, had taken food and mumbled things that sounded wise at the time. Some of those had been sick; others had died in car accidents.

But none had been shot, or left in a fire to die. None had so much mystery surrounding their last hours.

What had gone through Ben's mind before he died? Was he tortured? Tormented? Had he suffered?

"I can't do this, Lord!" she cried. "I can't. Let others do it, who are stronger." She thought of the pain she had endured after being shot in the chest a couple of years earlier, left to die in a fire much like the one that had taken Ben. Ray had found her in time and saved her, and the Lord had allowed her to have a second chance at life. "Did you save me for this?" she asked. "So's I could grieve my son?"

So many today had told her she would get through this, that they would help her and love her, that God would give her what she needed. "No," she said now. "I *need* my son back! That's all that would help me. I don't want to live . . . I didn't survive so I could learn to get along without him." She shook her fist at the ceiling. "Do you hear me, God? I cannot do this! Just take me too. Take me on outta here. Take me home, 'cause I don't want to stay."

But she knew he wouldn't. For some reason, he had given her life back, and he had taken Ben instead. Not an even trade, she thought. She would never have agreed to it. But God hadn't asked her.

She didn't know if she could forgive him for that.

She pulled the pillow from under Ben's bedspread and buried her face in it as her anguish wailed out of her. She wanted to break things, kick things, scream and rant and rave . . . even hurt herself. But then the family would come, and they wouldn't leave her alone again. The cycle of being surrounded would continue, and she wouldn't have time to think . . .

So she didn't throw anything, didn't break

anything, didn't scream or hurt herself. She just lay on Ben's bed, moaning and sobbing into his pillow as her mother's grief dragged her through the worst night of her life.

Chapter Eight

● ● ●

Though Issie was sometimes gullible and reckless, she wasn't naive. She had been around the block a few times and knew when things weren't right, and lately, she'd made a point of raising her standards. It had taken her a little over an hour to figure out that the man hitting on her was married. There were subtle signs, like a white stripe on the ring finger of his left hand. She didn't know why men didn't realize that it was obvious when they took their wedding rings off.

While this wouldn't have bothered her in days past, she found that it irritated her now. She didn't like being treated like a fool. Twice during the conversation he'd gotten a call on his cell phone, and he had kept it short and sweet. She felt like grabbing the phone and saying hello to his wife, telling her to come get him before he made a victim out of some girl who wasn't as smart as she was.

When she'd finally been able to shake the guy, she'd decided that she needed to go home. Maybe Joe's wasn't the place for her tonight. Anyway, it wasn't doing the trick. Her spirits were just as low now, and her nerves just as shot as they had been when she'd left the Benton property.

She paid her tab, said her goodbyes, and headed out to her car.

The night air was cool, and a breeze whispered through the Mimosa tree next to Joe's Place. A couple of college-age kids were standing at a truck on the perimeter of the parking lot.

The wind picked up their laughter and carried it to Issie, making her almost jealous that others found smiles after a day like today.

She got into the car and jammed her key into the ignition, turned it, and shifted the car into drive. A loud rap song beat out its morbid message, and she changed the station as she stepped on the accelerator. The song changed to a softer, more harmonic song by a popular boy band. But the car stalled.

She gave it more gas, and the wheels began to turn slightly, but they fought the movement. Frowning, she shifted back into park and got out, leaving her door open, and looked at her tires.

All four were flat.

Anger roiled inside her. She punched the button to open her trunk and pulled out her flashlight. She shone the light on one of the tires and went closer, looking for the source of the problem. Had she run over something big enough to deflate all four tires?

Then she saw the slash, and realized that someone had taken a knife to the tire. She went from wheel to wheel, shining the light, and saw that they had all been slashed.

Who would have done such a thing? Had she been chosen randomly, or was it a deliberate act?

The autumn breeze whipped through her hair, fluffing it into her face, and she pushed it back and looked around, first to the right, then the left, hoping whoever had done this was still in the area. She had visions of catching and restraining them, and somehow getting them across the street to the police station. There she'd have them locked up and the key thrown away until they bought her four new tires and gave her an apology.

But there was no one in sight.

The college kids still laughed and horsed around, oblivious to the rage coursing through her. She stormed over to them. "Did any of you see someone around my car?" she demanded.

"No," one of them said. "Why?"

"Because all four of my tires are slashed. You didn't see anybody?"

"Ma'am, we just got here," one of them said. "There hasn't been anybody in the parking lot since we got out of the truck."

She muttered something under her breath and stomped back to her car. Not knowing what else to do with her rage, she kicked at the tire. This was all she needed after a long day.

She looked across the street and saw the lights of the fire department and some of the firemen milling around in the truck bay, and next door the police department with its squad cars parked out front. At least there was someone over there who could take her home.

She headed across the street to the fire department, went inside the truck bay, and saw Dan Nichols lifting weights. "Issie," he said, setting down a barbell. "What are you doing here?"

"I was at Joe's Place," she said, "and somebody slashed my tires. I need a ride home. Can you take me?"

Dan hesitated. "Why don't you ask somebody else?" he said. "No offense, Issie, but I'm a newlywed and I don't want to start rumors."

That made her even madder. "Oh, no, of course you wouldn't want to be seen with a piranha like me."

She bolted into the fire station, slamming the door behind her. She saw Mark Branning sitting in front of the television watching a ball game. George Broussard was sprawled out in the recliner across the small room. "Mark, I was just over at Joe's Place and my tires were slashed. Can you take me home?"

Mark just looked at her for a moment, and she could see that he was trying to come up with an excuse.

"Oh, come on, Mark," she said. "It's not like I'm going to attack you in the car. Give me a break."

Mark shrugged. "Allie and I are doing real well, Issie. I don't want to rock the boat."

"Would Allie want me to walk home at

night?" she asked. "Come on, I'm a lady in distress. You're a public servant."

Mark grinned. "Nice try, Issie, but I'm gonna pass. Get George."

She looked at George. "George, surely you can do it."

The big Cajun was a young widower, left alone with a little boy. He looked up at her as if it pleased him to be asked. He dropped his feet and got up. "I'll brought you home," he said, and looked down at Mark. "I got the scanner in the car. Won't be long, no way." He bowed with a flourish and said, "After you."

Issie started out without saying goodbye to Mark or Dan.

When they were on their way home, George grinned over at Issie. "Sorry 'bout them attitudes back there."

She shrugged and looked out the window. "I guess I deserve it. But Mark doesn't have to be scared of me. We never did anything wrong. And I have no idea why Dan Nichols would have to worry about Jill. The whole time he was a bachelor he and I never went out once. We weren't each other's type."

"What type you like, Issie?" George asked.

She sighed and shook her head. "I have a broad range of types, George. I'm not that specific."

"Maybe ya ought to be, pretty girl like you," George said.

Was he hitting on her? She glanced at his double chin and his Santa Claus paunch. He was the last one she'd be attracted to. She looked out the window, quiet until they reached her apartments. "Thanks, George," she said. "I really appreciate it."

"So how ya gon' get to work tomorrow?" he asked.

"I don't know. I'll call Steve or somebody. Guess I'll have to get AAA out to change my tires. My insurance doesn't cover tires, so it's going to cost a small fortune, which I don't have at the moment." She groaned and dug through her bag for her keys. "I've got to get a better-paying job."

"You can do like me," he said, "save lives one day, sell smoke alarms the next."

"Yeah, I'll have to consider that," she said without much enthusiasm. "Thanks again."

She got out of the car and trotted up the steps to the apartment on the second floor. She put her key in but found that the doorknob turned too easily. Normally it took a little effort unless it was unlocked.

She turned the doorknob and pushed inside, quickly flipped on the light, and looked down at the knob again. Had it just been her imagination, or had the door really been unlocked? That wasn't like her. She never left it without locking it. Maybe the stress of the day had distracted her into forgetting.

She locked it now, then dropped her purse on an end table and headed for her bedroom. She kicked off her shoes toward the closet as she rounded the corner.

Then she saw it. Written in red spray paint across her wall were the words, "Ignorance is bliss."

She gasped and stepped back, and quickly ran for the gun that she kept hidden in her closet. Her hands trembled and her heart raced as she tried to load it, then she went around the apartment from room to room, looking in closets and behind doors and under things. Someone had been in her apartment, and they had left her a message. What did it mean, ignorance is bliss? What kind of ignorance? Ignorance from what?

She had no idea what it meant, but as shivers coursed through her, she realized that it had something to do with the four slashed tires.

She got to the bathroom, turned on the light, pulled back the shower curtain. There was no one there. She was sweating now, and she stumbled out of the bathroom, still holding the gun, and grabbed the telephone next to her bed.

She picked it up and started to dial 911 when she noticed a small lump under her comforter. Aiming the gun at it as if it was a live thing that would jump out and grab her, she peeled her comforter slowly back. She screamed as she saw the dead cat, brutally slain.

The sight backed her against the wall, and she stayed there, pushing against it as if it would let her slip through. She saw a note attached with a rubber band around the cat's torso. Still holding the phone and the gun, she forced herself back to the bedside, pulled the note out from under the rubber band, and unfolded it.

"Tell the police about anything you've seen and you're as dead as this cat."

There was no signature. No need of one. The message was clear. Issie didn't know what things she knew or what they were referring to, but the fact that she had picked up the phone to dial 911 reminded her that someone was looking in on her thoughts, figuring out her moves just before she made them.

She slammed the phone down. It was those kids with Jake, she thought. He and his friends were worried that she was going to tell something.

Did it have anything to do with the carpet that she'd seen them burning in the bonfire? Was this about the church burning? Had they killed Ben?

She was shaking so hard she could hardly grab the phone again, but she picked it up and dialed her brother's number. He answered quickly. "Hello?"

"Mike, it's me," she said, her voice wobbling. "Some weird stuff is happening around here and — can I come and bunk at your house tonight?"

"What's wrong?" he asked.

"I've just got to get out of here. Somebody slashed all four of my tires, so I don't have a car. I'll need you to come get me."

"Slashed your tires?" he asked. "Who would do that?"

"The same person who'd put a dead cat

in my bed and leave me threatening mes-
sages!" she shouted.

"Issie, what have you gotten yourself
into?"

The question would have enraged her if
she hadn't been so exhausted. She rolled
her eyes and shook her head. She didn't
have the heart to tell him that it very likely
had something to do with his own son. "I
don't know," she said. "That's the bizarre
thing."

"Have you called the police?"

"No. They left a note telling me not to,
and frankly, I don't think I want to mess with
them right now. Will you come get me or
not?"

"I was asleep, Issie. I'm not even
dressed."

"What don't you understand?" she bellowed. "Someone has been in my apartment. You're my brother! I don't have anybody else to call!"

"All right, all right," he said. "I'll be right
over."

"Can you put Lois on the phone until you
get here? I'm a little spooked."

"Let me see if I can wake her up." She
knew he expected her to tell him not to

bother, but she was too frightened to be selfless right now. After several moments, Lois came to the phone. "Issie, what's going on?" her sister-in-law asked irritably.

Blinking back her tears of frustration and indignation, Issie told Lois what had happened while she waited for her brother.

Chapter Nine

● ● ●

When they got back to her brother's house, Issie spent two hours convincing Mike that they were not to call the police. She didn't want to provoke whoever was after her, she said. She needed a few more clues before she went to them.

But the truth was that she didn't want to implicate Jake.

When Mike and Lois finally went back to bed, Issie stayed up waiting for Jake to come home. She didn't know what had gotten into her brother, raising a teenage boy without a curfew. He should know better. If not from his own teenage days, then from hers. She had been a wild one, staying out sometimes all night, watching the sun come up with her dates, then sleeping all day. It wasn't a very productive life, she knew. It hadn't been until she started showing her own self-imposed discipline that she'd even been able to get through her paramedic training. Now she saw Jake following in her footsteps, and the thought worried her.

He rolled in about 4:30. When she saw his car drive up, she went to his bedroom and sat on his bed. She wanted to surprise him.

It worked. He came in and flicked his light on, saw her on the bed, and sucked in a breath.

"Issie, what are you doing here? You scared me to death!"

"I couldn't stay home tonight," she said through her teeth. "My tires were slashed at Joe's Place, and then when I went home, someone had been in my apartment."

She could see the guilt on his face, but he straightened and tried to look innocent. "Oh, really? Did you call the police?"

"No," she said. "You can tell whoever it is that I didn't call them. But I won't be manipulated by a criminal. I want to know what you know right now."

Jake threw up his hands as if he couldn't believe the accusation. "Issie, how would I know anything about this?"

"Because in my mind it's no coincidence that after I came to your playground and saw what you were up to, my tires get slashed and a dead cat turns up in my bed!"

"Dead cat?" he asked. "Gross!"

She nodded. "Yeah, it's gross, all right. Thank goodness for your father. He came over and got it out of my apartment, but I'm afraid the mattress is ruined. So now I'm stuck for four new tires and a new mattress if I want to sleep in any kind of peace, not to mention the fact that I don't know how they got into my apartment. But I was thinking that maybe someone who had a key let them in."

"I don't have a key to your apartment, Issie."

"No, but your dad does, and it's hanging in the kitchen on a hook. It doesn't take a genius to know which key it is."

He swallowed and turned around, putting his back to her.

"And incidentally, I've already checked. It's not there right now."

He turned back to her. "What did you tell Dad?" he asked.

Her laughter was dry and brittle. "I didn't tell him that I found you in the vandalized house of some old lady who died. So you don't have to worry just yet. He doesn't know anything."

"That's good," he said, "because there's nothing to know."

The obvious lie made her livid, and she got up, crossed the room, and put her face inches from his.

"I know I'm not a whole lot older than you, and I know that I don't have any authority where you're concerned, but so help me, Jake, if that was more than cat blood on the carpet I saw in that fire, you'd better cut yourself loose right now before you wind up in prison. The police need to know about that bonfire and that carpet."

Jake's eyes hardened. "I wouldn't do that if I were you, Issie."

"There you go, threatening me again. What'll it be this time? A dead snake in my bed? A *live* one?"

"I'm not threatening you," he said. "I'm warning you. I don't have a lot of control over some people. I can't be held responsible for what they might do."

"Then you are threatening me," she said. "I thought so." Her eyes began to fill with stinging tears, but she blinked them back, refusing to let them fall. "I'm warning *you* of something," she said. "You get out of this group or this gang or whatever it is that you're calling it. You get out of it, you re-move yourself from those friends, and you save yourself while it's not too late, be-cause, so help me, those kids are going to go down if I have to take them down my-self."

With that, she went back to the guest room, closed the door, and locked it. For the first time in her life, she didn't trust her nephew. She didn't even know who he was.

Chapter Ten

● ● ●

The fact that Nick was single rarely bothered him, though he had expected to marry by now. Most of the time he was so busy that he didn't have time to think about his loneliness, but on days like today when he was getting out of the hospital with no one to take him home and care for him, he inevitably wondered why God had not answered his prayers for a helpmeet.

Though he had only been here one night, it would have been nice to have a wife come from home and bring his toothbrush and his shaving kit, a change of clothes. Last night he had been barraged with visitors, but no one had thought to bring him the necessities that a wife might have thought of.

Now as he signed the papers and prepared to leave, he thought how nice it would have been if his wife had been there to fill out the paperwork for him, to fuss over him and make sure the nurses gave the proper instructions for caring for his burns and his broken ribs. It would have been nice to have someone look at him with concern in her eyes, and maybe even pamper him a little when he got home.

He didn't like to admit it, but it had been nice having Issie stay with him through the worst of the treatment yesterday. She had held his hand, talked him through the agony, pleaded with the doctor on his behalf. He wasn't used to that, but he had appreciated it.

A knock sounded on the door. He looked up and saw Jill and Dan Nichols standing in the doorway.

"Hey, guys," he said, his voice still raspy from the smoke inhalation. "Thanks for coming."

"We were glad to do it," Dan said. "Somebody's got to get you home, man."

Jill came in and hugged him. "How are you feeling, Nick?"

"Sore," he said. "I'm not liking these burns too much, but it could have been a lot worse. Voice is shot, but that's no big loss. Some people will love having me shut up for a while."

She looked around the room. "Where's your suitcase?"

He chuckled. "What suitcase? They brought me here in an ambulance."

"But no one brought you any clothes?"

He stood up carefully, showing her the T-shirt and gym shorts he'd been wearing when he was brought in. It was what he'd slept in at the station, and he had pulled his turnouts over them. "If I'd had a change of clothes, do you think I'd be wearing this?"

Jill tried to muffle her laughter.

"It's you," Dan said. "I really like the look."

"Hey, buddy, you were wearing the same thing when we got called to the fire. But you got to change." Nick grinned and went back to signing the papers. "I'm expecting the fashion police to arrest me in the parking lot."

"Hey, why didn't you get one of us to go by your house and get you some clothes?"

"Last night I didn't think of it. It never occurred to me until this morning that I didn't have anything to wear. I'll be fine. If you can just get me home without anybody seeing me, then I can change clothes and go visit Ray and Susan."

"Visit Ray and Susan?" Dan asked. "Nick,

you need to be in bed. You don't need to be out visiting people."

"I'm not visiting 'people,'" Nick said. "They lost their son. I'm their preacher. I have to go see them."

Dan shot Jill a look that said they weren't going to be able to change his mind.

"Well, use your own judgment," Jill said quietly. "I hear they're taking it real hard."

"Of course they are." Nick's voice caught, and he shoved the papers away. "I never thought I'd be burying one of their children."

He got up and drew in a deep breath. It caught in his bruised side, and he winced. And putting weight on his legs made his burns hurt worse. "Let me just go find the nurse and get these forms turned in and we can go," he said.

He walked carefully as he stepped out of the room. But it wasn't his wounds that were keeping him down now, he thought. It was the heaviness of his heart over a destroyed church, a broken family, and a sense of failure that had enshrouded Nick since the fire yesterday.

Chapter Eleven

● ● ●

Stan and Celia were waiting at Nick's house when Jill and Dan got him home, and he was grateful to see that Celia had vacuumed and dusted and put away the few scattered things that he had left out. Already, at least a dozen casseroles lined his countertops. Someone had loaned him a freezer, and had delivered it to his carport this morning. Celia was trying to figure out what dishes could be frozen and which could not.

They'd moved his furniture around slightly so that he could rest more easily in the recliner and still reach reading materials and coffee on the table next to him. He hadn't thought of arranging the furniture quite that way before, but the woman's touch certainly added something. He gave Celia a hug and thanked her.

"Now sit down," she said. "Let me get

you something to eat. You must be starved. I know how that hospital food can be."

"No, I can't. I've got to go visit Ray and Susan."

Celia's silence spoke volumes. She had been trained well, being married to the one detective in town. She knew better than to lecture him about taking it easy or being careful. Stan never listened.

"I'll go with you," Stan said.

Nick frowned. "It's not necessary, Stan. I can do it myself."

"No, you can't," Stan said. "I've been kind of putting it off. I need to talk to them about the case anyway. I think maybe we can answer some of their questions."

"Okay," he said, "but let's not wait much longer. I feel like I should have been there yesterday when they were going through the worst part of it. I just need to change clothes."

Celia grinned. "You sure you want to? Your gym shorts make a nice statement."

Nick looked down at his bandaged legs and the shorts he'd slept in at the station. "Yeah. It says, 'I'm an idiot.' " He shot her a grin and limped back to the bedroom.

He sifted through his drawers, looking for

a pair of khaki shorts. Were they dirty? It was October, but it was still shorts weather most of the time in south Louisiana. He'd worn them just a couple of days ago. He began to feel overcome with weariness, and he sat down on the bed and tried to think. Had he washed them? If so, had he folded them, or did he need to go look in the dryer to see if they were still there? He dreaded the walk back in there. The scorched skin on his legs was covered tightly with bandages, but every flex of the muscles seemed to stretch the skin and cause undue agony. Just standing was an ordeal.

He forced himself to get up and look in the next drawer. He found them there, carefully folded, then sat back down to put them on.

Is this how it's going to be? he asked the Lord. *Is every movement going to wear me out?* He was going to have to do these things for himself, because soon he would be alone.

He could do this, he told himself. Carefully, he stepped out of his gym shorts and stepped into the khakis. The seam hit his bandage on the way up, and he winced. But he got them up, then sat there a moment, trying to catch his breath. His lungs felt as if they'd trapped half the heat of yesterday's fire in them, and his throat and trachea felt parched. He needed something to drink but didn't want to take the time.

His mother would come to take care of him if he asked her. But that wouldn't work, because she might bring his dad. The last thing he needed was his military father rummaging through his things and lecturing him on the need to do something with his life. No, he didn't need his father calculating what rank he should be, had he joined the military, or what income bracket he would be in. He didn't want him reminding him what kind of house and family he should have at age thirty-two.

No, he wasn't up to that now. He could handle this himself. In just a minute . . . he would catch his breath . . . and the pain would cease, and he could go visit Ray and Susan.

He slipped on a pair of flip-flops, and as he did, he thanked God that the burns hadn't been over his joints. At least he still had mobility in his feet and knees. It could have been so much worse.

He trudged back into the living room.

Stan was ready to go, and he leaned over and gave Celia a kiss. "Pray for us," he said.

Celia nodded. "I will. You know I will. I've been praying for Ray and Susan all night. You too, Nick."

"Thanks," he said. "I needed it." He didn't know why he got choked up as he walked out to the car.

Chapter Twelve

● ● ●

Nick had hoped he and Stan would be able to visit with Susan and Ray alone, but he was surprised to see that the house was full of people when he got there.

Susan's parents were in the kitchen organizing the food that people from the church had already brought over. He figured they had doubled the recipes, and he had the counterparts at his house. Vanessa, Ben's sister, sat in the living room with her eyes swollen, talking on the phone in quiet tones. Several cousins and aunts and uncles milled around the small house. Susan was nowhere to be found, but they discovered Ray in the backyard hammering nails into a trellis he had been building during his time off.

Grief was a funny thing, Nick thought. Some people kept busy, some withdrew, some chattered. Some curled up in bed and cried, while others ate. He never knew what he would find.

After the introductions, Nick stepped into the living room to speak to Vanessa. He gave her a hug and she burst into tears. He told her how sorry he was. She nodded, suddenly unable to speak even with the phone next to her face.

"Where's your mother?" he whispered.

She shrugged. "I don't know. Probably in the bedroom. Mama's not feelin' well."

That didn't surprise him. He looked around and found Stan at the back door, saw that he was about to go out and talk to Ray. Nick crossed the room and followed him.

When they stepped out into the yard, they saw that Ray was hammering with more strength than was necessary. He didn't look up as they came out, just kept hammering as if his life depended on finishing this trellis and making it stand.

Next to the trellis, Susan had already planted jasmine, and Nick supposed that within a year the fast-growing vine would be covering the whole structure. Life went on.

They crossed the yard and finally caught Ray's eye. Nick put his hand on his shoulder, but Ray just kept hammering. "Thought you was in the hospital," Ray said.

"Just got out."

"You s'posed to be out and about?"

Nick shrugged. "I figured this was important enough."

"You didn't have to come." Ray stood back, surveying the trellis. "I was lookin' for a weak spot that needed a nail."

Stan looked down at his feet and saw some of the nails that Ray had already dropped. He bent down and picked a couple up, rolled them around in his hand.

"Do you think we could talk to you and Susan?" Nick asked. "Is there someplace we could go?"

Ray dropped the hammer to his side and looked down at it. "I don't know if Susan wants to talk. She's in the bedroom feelin' sick." He gave Stan a thoughtful look. "Is it about the investigation?"

"Yeah, it is. I wanted you to know where we are on this."

"Okay," he said. "I can go get her. I know she'll want to hear that." Ray dropped the hammer onto the fence next to the trellis, dusted off his hands, and started back into the house. "Let me just give Susan some warnin'," he said, "and then we can go talk to her in the bedroom. It's the only private place in the house right now."

"We'll just wait out here," Stan said.

Ray went into the house, and Stan sank down onto a patio chair.

Nick sat down next to Stan and looked out across the yard, thinking how miserable it felt to come here like this, to minister to a couple who had lost a child with no explanation, no warning. It was the part of his job he liked the least.

They sat in silence until the back door opened and Ray stuck his head out. "Come on in," he said. "Susan's waitin' in the bedroom."

Nick got up, trying not to wince when his legs protested, but he headed in and Stan followed him. They cut through the crowd of people meandering through the house and made their way back to the master bedroom. It wasn't a big room, just large enough for a full-sized bed and dresser, but one of the uncles had brought some chairs in so they could all sit together and talk.

Susan was already sitting in one of them, looking out the window.

"Hey, Susan," Nick said softly. He bent

over to give her a hug, but she didn't respond at all. He squeezed her shoulders and backed away. Stan didn't even try.

Ray took the seat next to her and held her hand, and Stan and Nick sat on the bed across from them. Nick had never seen Susan like this. Her eyes were dull, and her face was as lifeless as Ben's had been.

"What you got to tell us, Stan?" Ray asked.

Stan leaned forward, his elbows on his knees. "Ray, Susan, we think this killing was racially motivated. Witnesses saw several people in a car leaving the scene, and the car had a swastika and a KKK sticker on the bumper."

Susan's face twisted as those words sank in. "My son was murdered because he was *black?*" She pressed the heels of her hands against her eyes and shook her head. "God help me! God help me!" she whispered.

"I think it's possible," Stan said. "The church burning could have just been a way of disposing of the body, or it could have been racial. We are a mixed congregation. If the KKK was involved, I'd say it was some kind of statement against us."

Ray's lips stretched tight across his teeth.

"What statement could they have to make with my son?"

"I don't know," Stan said quietly. "They've been pretty quiet for a number of years. Sidney Clairmont, the grand wizard, is in his seventies. Probably doesn't have the venom he used to. Recruitment's way down. On the other hand, this could have been his way of letting us know that their activities are starting up again."

Ray got up and started walking around the room. Susan's dismal eyes followed him. "All these years," he said, "I've raised my children not to think of theirselves as bein' a different color. I told them that you could be anything you wanted to, that God had plans for everybody, no matter the race. Here I am, fire chief of Newpointe, and my son was a year away from havin' his marketin' degree at LSU. He was gon' be somebody. And you're tellin' me that because of the color of my skin, somebody come along and shot my son, burned down my church, all for some kind of sick statement he wanted to make?"

"I don't know for sure," Stan said. "But it's a lead."

Ray's face turned marble hard as he met

his wife's eyes. "I'm gon' go out there and find 'em, Susan. I'm gon' find who did this and I'm gon' kill 'em with my bare hands."

Nick drew in a deep breath. "Ray, I know you feel that way now, but you can't go off half-cocked and try to do something about this. You have to let the police handle it."

Stan shifted in his seat. "Ray, we're not going to let this go. I have a personal interest in it. I don't take it lightly when friends of mine are murdered. Calvary was my church too. I'm going to find who killed Ben, and we're going to put him behind bars and he's going to stand trial and suffer for what he's done. You've got to let us do it."

Ray sank back down into the chair. Susan touched the back of his head. "He's right, Ray. I don't want to lose both the men in my life. Let Stan do it."

Ray began to weep, and Nick found himself staring at a spot on the carpet, making a valiant effort not to break down himself. When Ray had pulled himself together, Nick tried what he had come for.

"Ray and Susan, I need to talk to you about the funeral, if that's okay."

Ray drew in a deep breath and wiped his face roughly. "We didn't know if you'd be up to it," he said, "so we asked Susan's Uncle Thomas to do it."

"Oh, a relative?" Nick was not sure whether to be relieved or offended. Truth was, he really *wasn't* up to it, but he could have mustered the strength for them. He told himself this decision wasn't rejection of him. He didn't have time for wounded pride. "Well, that's understandable. I can see why you'd want him."

"I gotta tell you, Nick," Susan choked out. "We're mad at God. Real mad."

"I understand," he said. "That's normal. I think God understands that too."

"I want answers," Susan said through her teeth. "I want to know why — with all the violent, hateful, malicious people in this world — why did he take Ben?"

Nick met her eyes. He had always loved Susan. She had been a dynamo in the church, was always the encourager and the one to bring food when someone needed it, the one to baby-sit kids or take in a family who was down on their luck. She was always willing to give. Now she needed for someone to give back. He wished he had the answers for her. "God allowed this to happen for a reason," he said. "We may never know why, Susan."

"Don't matter *why*," she said. "There was no *reason* good enough to get my baby shot through the head and left in a ragin' fire to die. None! You hear me, Nick? And God and I won't be on speakin' terms till he convinces me otherwise."

She looked out the window again as tears rolled down her face. Nick dropped his eyes. Her child was gone and she couldn't hear reason. There was no rationale, only questions that couldn't be answered.

Chapter Thirteen

● ● ●

Nick was silent all the way home, but Stan kept lecturing to him about the fact that Susan and Ray had been through trauma, and that their reaction was only temporary. But Nick would rather have them blame him than God.

When they got to Nick's trailer, he saw the arson inspector from Slidell across the street sifting through the rubble. Several of the firefighters were on fire watch, to make sure that nothing ignited into flames again. Several members of his congregation were sitting in a circle on the lawn, holding hands and praying. The sight didn't evoke the usual paternal pride he felt when he saw his flock acting without him.

"What are they praying for?" he asked in a dull voice.

Stan shook his head. "There are a lot of things to pray for right now, Nick. Every-body feels real vulnerable. Our hearts are tender. Maybe this is just where God needs us to be."

Nick went in and watched from behind the screen door as Stan drove away. The trailer smelled like a celebration, with the different scents of lovingly cooked dishes. Ordinarily, he would have let the scents draw him and comfort him, but he had no appetite. And looking at those prayer warriors across the street, praying right out in the open, where anyone who drove by would see . . . that should stir the spirit in him. Were they praying for the people who had done this to their church? Were they praying for Ben's killers? He hoped they were praying for Susan and Ray, or for him.

But somehow he felt those prayers were falling on deaf ears.

"How does it glorify you, Lord," he whispered, "to see our church in a heap of ashes? How does that work to the good of those who love you?"

He closed and locked the door before anyone could cross the street to speak to him. He had nothing to say to them, nothing to give. Nothing at all.

He sat down and tried to get comfortable. He realized that since the church was no more, maybe he was no longer a preacher. He didn't have a funeral to preach, didn't have a pulpit, and his library of books which he kept in his office in the church had been burned away.

Every hope and dream had been consumed. And if Nick was no longer a preacher, then who was he? Maybe being a firefighter was enough. But the truth was that he had even been a failure at that. The irony overwhelmed him, that here he was a preacher and a firefighter, and his own church had been destroyed by fire.

The doorbell rang, and he closed his eyes tight and decided not to answer it. He couldn't see anyone right now. He couldn't talk.

His stomach told him it was lunchtime, so he ate a dinner roll. He was too tired to get up and serve a plate from one of the dishes in the kitchen. Sometimes a person needed to just lie there and stare at the ceiling. There seemed to be no alternative.

He tried to nap for a while, but sleep wouldn't come. When the phone rang, he let the machine get it.

The call from Stan telling him the elders of his church had called a meeting to discuss what needed to be done hit him like a dull thud between his eyes. He wasn't ready to meet with the elders, not until he'd managed to drag himself out of this melancholy.

But he didn't know if he'd be able to do that. Despair had never weighed so heavily on his heart. There was nothing left. Someone might as well admit it.

For some time he had been insecure about his calling. Every time he failed a church member by saying the wrong thing, saying too much, not saying enough, he wondered if he should be a preacher at all. Every time he lost a member, every time he saw one backslide, every time he couldn't address their needs, he realized how much better a full-time preacher might do. Maybe being bivocational was his downfall, but he couldn't afford to live on what they paid him at the church. Maybe someone else could.

He went to his computer in the tiny living room and turned it on. He sat staring at the screen, wondering what he would say if he composed a letter of resignation and gave it to the elders tonight.

But his resignation seemed almost moot at this point. What was there to resign *from*, after all? Still, he felt he needed to make the

gesture just for the purpose of offering closure to the congregation who depended on
him. They would all be free to scatter in their
own directions. Some could go to the Baptist church that worshiped on Jacquard.
Others would decide to try the Presbyterian
church over on Second Avenue. Methodists
worshiped on Rue Matin, and then there
was, of course, the Catholic church on the
west side of Newpointe. Nick supposed
that he would find a place to worship, where
it wouldn't be so uncomfortable being a
sheep instead of a shepherd.

He typed a letter that was straightforward
and to the point, then punched the key to
print it out. He watched as it scrolled
through the printer. In a few seconds it was
a done deal. The elders would have to accept the demise of the church, put the land
up for sale, and move on with their lives.
Somehow, he would get over the Lord's re-
moving his calling. He had to fight the bitterness welling up inside, and this debilitating
sense of failure. He had to get rid of the
pride that was making him bitter.

Somehow, he had to swallow it all and
find a way to look up to the Lord with his
hands open and say, "What next, Lord? You

tell me. I'm yours." He was a jar of clay, and some jars of clay were meant to be used for noble purposes. Others were not. Maybe he was one of those instruments of mediocrity, one of those common vessels with no significant purpose. Maybe he'd just been kidding himself, thinking that the Lord had marked him for special service.

Fighting back the tears in his eyes, he bathed himself as best he could without getting his bandaged legs wet, and tried to wash the pain and regrets away.

● ● ●

Nick was a few minutes late for the meeting, which was being held in the kitchen at the fire station. He went in and saw that most of the church leaders were there. Mark and Dan, still on duty, Stan Shepherd, Frank Dupree from the hospital lab, Jesse Pruitt, retired schoolteacher, Vern Hargis and Sid Ford, cops, and Andre Bouchillon, who owned most of the apartments in town, were all at the table, waiting. Aunt Aggie, as comfortable in the fire station's kitchen as any of the firefighters there, was cutting pieces of cheesecake and pouring coffee. They were already engaged in discussion when he arrived, but the room got amazingly quiet the moment he limped in.

He stood in the doorway, looking from one man to the other, wishing he didn't feel so vulnerable and broken. He felt like telling them there was no point in going on with this. They didn't have to pretend anymore. It was over. They could just pronounce the church dead and move on.

"T-Nick, you get off 'em feet and prop them legs up, you!" Aunt Aggie cried, pulling him toward two chairs. She had fashioned an ottoman out of one of them. "I tried tellin' 'em you didn't need to be out runnin' around with burned up lungs and fried legs. Want some cheesecake, *sha*?" The Cajun forms of *petite* and *chere* rolled right past him.

"No, thanks." He was too tired and out of breath to refute any one of Aunt Aggie's claims about him, so he just lowered to the chair and propped his legs up.

"So how are you feeling, buddy?" Jesse Pruitt asked him gently.

"Fine," he said. "Really, I'm fine. I'll be good as new in a few days." Each man reached across the table to shake his hand, and as he greeted them, he realized that one of the deacons was missing. Ray Ford. Of course. A man preparing to bury his son didn't come to church meetings. Especially if he blamed his son's death on God.

His heart twisted with as much pain as his bandaged shins. When the greetings were done, the men sat back, giving the floor to him, as if he would open the meeting and lead them in some enlightened discussion about the state of the church, making them all feel better.

He could hear some of the firemen — probably Slater Finch, Marty Bledsoe, and Jacob Baxter — working out in the truck bay. Today was truck cleanup day. They would have their work cut out for them, after yesterday. Tomorrow they would do yard work when they weren't on a call. The next day was housecleaning day, when they scrubbed toilets and mopped floors. Despite all the menial chores that kept them busy, fire fighting was an important job, nothing to sneeze at, nothing to make him feel deprived. At least he'd been properly trained for that. It was preaching he wasn't adequately educated for. Taking seminary classes at night wasn't the kind of training that made one a great pastor.

He shifted in his chair, wondering if the fatigue brought on by his damaged throat and lungs, the stress from yesterday, the burns and bruises, might be making him feel extraordinarily defeated. Maybe he needed to sleep on it, pray on it, and wait a little while before handing them that letter.

But he didn't have the energy to wait. The sooner this door was closed, the better. He didn't have what it took to see them through the life-support efforts when the church was nothing but a corpse.

He cleared his throat. When they kept waiting, he knew he should open with a prayer. But he was too tired. He needed to economize his words, save his voice. "I want to thank whoever called this meeting," he said finally. "As you might imagine, I've been a little shaken up and haven't really been thinking too clearly. But we do have some decisions to make."

He pulled the letter out of his pocket, his hands shaking. He looked down at it, ran his fingers over it. After a long pause, he put it on the table in front of him. "I guess this can be the first decision we take care of."

The deacons stared at it as if they didn't know which one of them should read it first.

"What is it, Nick?" Sid asked.

Nick drew in a deep, raspy breath and pulled it back. "Well, I guess I'd better read it out loud," he said. "It's my letter of resignation."

There was a collective gasp around the room, and Mark slapped his hands on the table. "Nick, you've got to be kidding."

"No," he said. "I have to do it. God took my church away from me. I have to accept that."

"God didn't take your church away," Dan said, in a tone that suggested Nick was delirious. "Some maniac did. He didn't *fire* you, for heaven's sake. *We* didn't fire you. We still have a congregation, Nick. We need a pastor."

Nick fought the tears in his eyes, but they were stronger than he was. "Maybe I've led us wrong," he said. "Maybe I haven't been everything I need to be."

Stan sat at the end of the table, watching him with tired, serious eyes. "This is about Ray and Susan, isn't it, Nick?"

Nick met his eyes. "No, Stan, it's nothing to do with that."

"Of course it is," Stan said. He looked around at the others. "Nick and I visited Ray and Susan today. They said some things about being mad at God. Nick's taking that as a personal failure."

"Look, my brother's hurtin'," Sid cut in gently. "The whole family is."

Nick pinched the bridge of his nose.

"The point is," Stan said, "you can't base your decision on emotion after a tragedy."

"I'm basing my decision on a lot of things," Nick said, sliding his hands down his face. "I've failed the church. I've failed it miserably. When a kid is found murdered in your sanctuary and it's burned down before your eyes, you have to ask what God is trying to tell you."

"He's not trying to tell you anything," Dan said. "Nick, you've taught us a million times in a million different ways that sometimes God brings suffering to purify us. We've prayed for revival. Well, maybe this is it. Maybe this is really an answered prayer."

"An answered prayer?" Nick asked. "How in the *world* do you figure that?"

"Maybe people will get closer to the Lord through this. Maybe he can use it."

Stan leaned forward on the table, his arms crossed in front of him. "Nick, I think I can speak for all of us when I say that we won't accept your resignation. You need to pray about this. You don't need to do it the day after you've been through such serious trauma, both physical and mental. You need to give it some time. I guarantee you, when you're feeling better and stronger, when you've had time to rest and heal, when you see what God is going to do with the church from here on out, you're going to change your mind."

"No, I'm not, Stan. I'm not going to change it."

"Fine," Dan told him. "Then if you still feel this way in a month or so, you can always quit then."

Nick sighed heavily, then began to cough. When he stopped, he felt soul-weary and too tired to fight them. "I'll think about waiting," he said. "I'm not promising anything."

"Fine," Sid said. "Now then, we need to talk about where we gon' meet till we get that church rebuilt."

"I was thinking," Dan said, "of asking the mayor if we could use the courtroom. It's probably big enough, and it's empty on Sundays."

"Good idea," Stan said. "You get her to agree to it, and we can start calling people to let them know. If she doesn't agree, we can try the high school auditorium. Third choice might be the Ritz Theater. We might have to sweep up popcorn and drink cups before the service, but it's better than nothing."

"I'll find us a place," Dan assured them. "Leave it to me."

"Well, that's one problem solved," Sid said.

"Now we need to get the insurance adjuster out," Jesse Pruitt said. "Nick, you give me the information on the company, and I'll place the claim."

Nick hadn't even thought of that. Maybe they were right. Maybe he was too sick to make rational decisions. "Okay, Jesse," he said. "I appreciate that. I'm sure I've got a number or something at home, even though the policy itself probably burned in the fire."

Mark touched Nick's shoulder. "See, Nick? It's all gonna be okay. We're gonna take care of what we can, and God will take care of the rest. And I just have a feeling about Sunday."

"What kind of feeling?" Nick asked.

"A feeling that the Holy Spirit is going to do some mighty things," Dan said, as if he had the same feeling. "You wait, Nick. This is not the end of our church. It may just be a fresh beginning."

Chapter Fourteen

● ● ●

Because there was always the chance that a smoldering ember might blow into a flame again, Mark, Dan, and George took the evening fire watch the day after the fire. They hacked at parts of the wall still standing, making sure that every spark had died. There would be someone here around the clock for the next couple of days.

When members began showing up to see the charred structure, they kept them back. So the members congregated at one end of the property, far enough away from the debris not to get hurt, but close enough that they were still on the property.

Someone brought a guitar and they began to sing praise songs together, and slowly the crowd grew. From the way they sang and praised God, one would think that he had swooped down and struck them with a glorious gift instead of a devastating fire.

Mark didn't want Allie to miss it. He went back to the truck, got his cell phone out, and dialed his home number.

"Hello?"

"Hey, hon. How's it goin'?"

Her sigh told him she hadn't gotten over the shock of the tragedy. "Okay, I guess. I just got back from Susan and Ray's. It was bad, Mark."

"I know something that might make you feel better. They're holding a bona fide church service right on the church grounds. Singing and praising God, just like Nick taught us."

"You're kidding."

"No. It's really amazing. Jacob Baxter has his guitar, and people who drive by to see the damage keep stopping and getting out. I think it's a great testimonial to the community. Don't you want to come?"

"Do you think it's too cool out for Justin?" she asked, referring to their toddler.

"I think it's fine. He'll probably sleep through it."

"Then we'll be right there."

He clicked off the phone and leaned back against the truck, watching the spirit of his church declare that it had lived on, even if the building was gone. He wondered if he should go knock on Nick's door and give him the chance to join in. Then he thought better of it. If he wasn't aware of it already, it probably meant he was so wiped out that he needed his rest.

Allie arrived with little Justin, and the child slept on her shoulder as she sang and swayed in worship. Staying near the debris, Mark began to sing with them, and soon Dan and George joined in. Like the others, they began to feel a sense of hope rather than a sense of mourning. It was just as Nick had taught them to react to trials. "Consider it joy," he'd said time and time again. "Thank God when he refines you like silver."

Soon the praise songs turned to prayers, and the members prayed one by one, lifting up the Fords and their family and friends, lifting up Nick for healing both inside and out, lifting up the church body, which had challenges ahead, lifting up the community that still had so much to learn.

People began to weep as they prayed, and one by one, some dropped to the ground, with no concern for the dirt on their knees. Eventually, others fell to their faces, wailing out their combination of confession and repentance, mourning and thanksgiving, prayers of intercession and prayers of hope for the future.

As night fell over the group, the singing began again, interspersed with more prayer. The group grew, as if word had traveled that a prayer meeting was going on, and no one wanted to miss it. It was loud and heartfelt, passionate and private, purging and purifying, a tent revival without a tent or an evangelist.

Something was happening in the church, something Mark had never seen before. The Holy Spirit was here, his power brighter than the fire that had swallowed the building. They could set fire to the church and destroy the building, but their lampstand still stood.

● ● ●

It was about nine o'clock when a 1986 model Ford van drove by too slowly, its rattling engine disrupting the church, and its loud rap music blaring at eardrum-shattering level. The dirty white van slowed as it passed the worshipers, then it screeched off, running a stop sign. Sid Ford, who had joined the group halfway through, left the circle and went to his squad car, parked on the side of the road. It took him a couple of blocks to catch up to the van with the half-deaf occupants. He knew he had no grounds to arrest them, but at least he could shake them up a little, make them stop disturbing the peace while driving through town.

He turned on his lights and gave them a block to pull over. Holding his flashlight, he got out, walked toward the van, and saw a swastika sticker in the bottom corner of the rear window. An alarm clanged in his head. Hadn't a witness claimed she'd seen several kids leaving the church before anyone noticed the fire? But she'd seen a red car, with two stickers on the bumper, not on the window. Still . . . had these four had something to do with murdering his nephew?

The radio volume lowered as he continued to the driver's door, staying back as he'd been trained. He shone the light into the window.

"We didn't do nothin'," the driver said.

In the flashlight beam, Sid saw three white guys and a girl. They all looked relatively clean-cut. The driver was blond and more tanned than normal for this time of year. He had the look of one of those action-movie stars who hit celebrity overnight.

"Can I see your driver's license, please?" he asked through his teeth.

The driver pulled his billfold out and thrust his license at him. "What did you pull me over for?" He sounded weary and fed up.

"For going sixty in a thirty-mile zone, runnin' a stop sign, and disturbin' the peace."

"Disturbin' the peace?" the driver asked. "You've got to be kidding me. And I wasn't speeding."

"I say you was. And since I'm the cop, it's my word that counts. See, they listen to me down at headquarters, not to a vanload of punks with hate signs stuck on their windows. Besides, I got a couple dozen witnesses back there. Stay right here."

The driver opened his door and started to get out.

"I *told* you to stay there," Sid said.

The kid continued to get out of the van. "I don't take orders from people like you."

Sid laughed bitterly, thinking how much he would enjoy putting this kid in his place. Yeah, these white supremacists were superior, all right, with their smart mouths and

stupid rebellion against authority. Real intel-
lectual.

It occurred to him that he could show this
little coward who he'd take orders from, but
he decided to savor the moment. He
needed backup, just to make sure he didn't
lose them. Since they very well could be the
killers and arsonists, he wanted to keep
them here as long as he could. He put his
hand on his weapon. "You got a choice. You
can either get back in your van until I say
you can get out, or you can stand here,
provin' your superiority with a pair of handcuffs on your wrists, or you can come sit in
the back of my squad car with those handcuffs on, since that's probably where you
gon' wind up, anyway."

After trying to stare him down, the kid
slowly got back into his car, as if it was his
idea and had nothing to do with Sid's sug-
gestion. Sid grinned and leaned down into
the window. "There now. You are an intel-
lect, ain't you? A veritable genius. Now you
just stay there while I go back to my car for
a minute, because if you so much as start
your engine, you won't have to worry about
gettin' arrested. I'll take care of you myself,
before you even have time to turn that

steerin' wheel. Now why don't you give me your driver's license?"

He left them sitting there and went back to his car. Keeping his eyes on them, he radioed in. "Three-three-two to Midtown. I just pulled over four punks for speedin' and disturbin' the peace, but I have reason to believe they could be suspects in Ben's murder and the church burnin'. Witnesses saw a swastika sticker on the getaway car, and this one has one. Need backup and a search warrant, fast as I can get it. And run this name through, see whatcha got."

After a moment, the dispatcher radioed back. "Sid, that Jason Cruz is the one Stan's been looking for. He said to tell you he's the one threatened Nick Foster."

"Score!" Sid sat still for a moment, feeling no joy that his nephew's murderer might be in that car in front of him.

"We have a search warrant on the way. Judge DeLacy was still at the courthouse. Vern Hargis is bringing it."

In moments, they had all four kids out of the van being frisked, while Sid and the others searched it for any clues that they had played a part in the burning or the murder. They found stacks of white supremacy and

Aryan nation propaganda, but no gas cans or guns, no blood on the seats or in the carpet, no drugs or alcohol, nothing that would make it appropriate to impound the van and throw them in jail.

Nothing, except for the hunch that Nick Foster had had about Jason Cruz getting even. They had been looking for him, wanting to bring him in for questioning, but hadn't caught up with him until now. Sid Foster wasn't about to let him go.

"Okay, now, here's how it's gon' be," he said, trying to temper his voice so he wouldn't sound like a vengeful uncle. "Jason, here —"

"Cruz," the kid cut in. "They call me Cruz."

"Okay, *Cruz.* Cruz here's gon' come to the station with me. We got a few things to talk about, like where he was in the wee hours of yesterday mornin', what he knows about Ben Ford's death and the church burnin' . . ."

"Wait a minute," Cruz said. "I ain't goin' nowhere."

"Well, now, you can come peaceably, or I can handcuff you and drag you in. I prefer the latter, but we'll let it be your choice."

Cruz swallowed and looked back at his sister. "Jen, go back and tell everybody that we're being persecuted. That they ran us down on the road without probable cause and are taking me in without an arrest warrant. Tell Granddaddy to call his lawyer."

The girl flung her hair back over her shoulder and took a bold step toward Sid. She was almost as tall as he, and as skinny as a runway model. He could see that she didn't have much fear in her. "You ain't got anything on him."

"We have witnesses," Sid said. "Witnesses who saw some punks comin' out of that church just before they noticed the fire. Witnesses who saw a swastika and KKK emblem on the bumper. And the curiosity that had you drivin' by the church grounds tonight, what with the sticker on your van and your smart mouth, make you prime suspects, as far as I'm concerned. Maybe you'd like to come in with your brother and answer a few questions too." He pulled out his pad as if to write. "No problem to add Cruzette to our little party tonight."

"I go by Jennifer," she bit out.

"You can see how I'd be confused. That's J-e-n-n —"

"No," Cruz cut in. "Jen, you go back and tell them. Tell Granddaddy. I can take care of this until he gets there."

Jennifer didn't like it, but she nodded to the others and went to get in on the driver's side. Before she got in, she gave him a worried look over the door. "Cruz?"

"It's okay," he said, almost gently. "Don't worry. Just do what I said."

As Sid escorted Cruz to the backseat of his squad car, he watched that van drive away. He wished he could lock up the whole bunch. Eventually, he vowed that he would, if they had anything at all to do with Ben's murder. As soon as he took care of Cruz, he'd get a rap sheet on each of them, assign someone to tail them, find out who else they hung out with, what they did in their spare time, where they worked, what their agendas were. If they were involved in the killing of his nephew, Sid Ford was going to make sure they paid.

Chapter Fifteen

● ● ●

Because the Cain and Addison Funeral Home expected record numbers of mourners for Ben's visitation, they convinced Susan and Ray to have a four-hour visitation. That would help with traffic in the parking lot and through the building, they were told. It was simply a matter of convenience.

There had been some debate as to whether to open the casket, but the undertaker had promised that he could cover the bullet hole. There had been no significant burns to Ben's face, so Susan saw no reason to deprive his friends of the closure the viewing would bring them.

By the third hour, Susan and Ray were still on their feet, hugging tearful friends who'd lined up to pay their respects. Susan wasn't making sense anymore, and Ray wished he could call a halt to the rest of it and take her away where she could sit down and take her shoes off and let go.

But as many words of comfort were offered to them, Ray found that Susan was trying to offer just as many in return. She clung to each mourner, as if she knew their hearts were broken with hers. She told them each what precious friends they'd been to her son, even if she'd never seen them before in her life. She made them each feel that their presence here had made all the difference in her level of grief. He didn't know how she did it. He knew she had not slept last night. He had heard her sobbing in Ben's room, and had gotten up to see about her. The door had been locked, so he'd respected her need to be alone. He had gone out to the backyard then and wept his heart out under the stars. He wasn't sure anymore if God heard.

Someone whispered something to her, something Ray hadn't heard, and Susan burst into tears again and clung to that person as if he were Ben's best friend. She wept openly, without any stoic acceptance, without that glow that some were able to have in the face of tragedy, declaring God to be sovereign and all-knowing, and trusting in him. Instead, he knew that trust would be a long time in coming. She would have to work that out with God on her own . . . just as he would.

Lord, I can take the pain, he thought. *But help her with hers. She's so fragile. She can't take it, Lord.*

He watched, broken and weary, as they came one by one. And each time someone approached the casket, he saw Susan stiffening slightly, looking that way, as if desperately wanting to tell them not to touch him, that she didn't even want them looking at him long. He knew how she felt. He felt it too. It was all he could do last night not to come to the funeral home and insist on sleeping on the floor next to his son.

The fact that Ben was in heaven, and not lying in that casket, provided little comfort. He had searched his heart for all the Scripture he had ever learned about heaven and death, but it failed him now. He needed someone to quote it to him, remind him what it said. But he didn't want to hear it from Nick, because part of him blamed the preacher.

He blamed him and Mark and Dan, and all the guys who'd fought the fire that morning.

He blamed Stan and the police force for letting lunatics run the roads and kidnap innocent victims and murder them. He blamed the paramedics who couldn't bring him back to life, and he blamed the coroner who must have seen Ben as just another job, even though it hadn't been obvious.

And if he were honest, he had to admit that he blamed everyone in line here, for not being aware enough of the evil in their community to call it what it was and purge it from their town. If someone, anyone, had seen them take Ben . . . if one person had made a phone call . . . turned someone in . . . Ben might be alive.

He knew it wasn't rational, but he didn't care. And now he blamed the funeral home for a visitation that stretched beyond human endurance, and for the mourners who dared to smile in the halls and talk about things other than death and Ben.

And most of all, he blamed himself, for not being there when his son needed him, for not coming to his aid, for not protecting him as he had always tried to do. The big fire chief of Newpointe, the big rescuer, who couldn't even save his own son.

The irony almost buried him.

But still the people came, and whispered, and wept, and Susan kept clinging and crying and chattering empty phrases over and over . . .

Ray just wanted it all to end.

Chapter Sixteen

● ● ●

Jennifer bolted into the house, all fury and rage, and slammed the door with an authority that silenced the dozen kids there. "They arrested him. Took him to jail without probable cause."

"Who?" Jake asked.

"Cruz, that's who!" she shouted like he was a fool. "Took him in handcuffs like a criminal, when he didn't do nothing wrong. We were just driving through town minding our own business . . ."

Jake decided it wouldn't be a good time to point out that Cruz *had* done something wrong. There was that little matter of murder, but everyone seemed to have forgotten it.

"I got my granddaddy to call his lawyer in Slidell, but the idiot is out of town and won't be back until morning. So Cruz has to sit there all night, in a jail cell, and he ain't done nothing wrong!" She waved her arm at the group as a thought came to her. "You know what this is about. It's about who we are. The grandchildren of the grand wizard of the KKK. But you know what? This is a free country, and you don't get to arrest somebody just because they're related to somebody you don't like."

"Did they say anything about the fire and the shooting?" Benton dared to ask.

Jake was proud of his friend's courage. He wished he'd managed to get that question out.

"Oh, yeah, that came up," Jennifer said. Her cheeks looked as if they'd been slapped hard, and she paced back and forth, back and forth, in front of them, like a caged tiger trying to find an escape. "We've got to intervene, that's all there is to it. We have to do something to divert suspicion."

"We should pray for him." The guy who came up with that was what Jake would have called a fanatic. Roy Decareaux had dropped out of high school in the ninth grade and worked at the Burger King for minimum wage. His dream had been to be an evangelist, until Cruz gave him a greater purpose.

"Okay," Jennifer said, almost as if humoring him. "Let's pray."

"On our knees," Roy said.

"Right. On our knees," Jennifer said, then flashed her eyes to the others. "Get down, everybody. Now!"

Jake looked around, feeling awkward, and realized that everyone else did too. Some of them stood on their knees, with hands clasped in front of them like toddlers beside their beds. Others sat back on their heels, balancing themselves with a hand on the floor on either side of them. Only Jennifer failed to kneel, but she stood at the front of the room with her hands raised high, and began to yell her prayers, as if God was hard of hearing.

Jake wondered if a real God would like to be talked to like that. Would he really want some raving girl, pretty as she was, spouting out confusing things like "confound the enemy" and "curse those who persecute us"? Or was that just what God wanted from them? Did you have to know his language to approach him? What if some ordinary Joe like him ever wanted to pray, and didn't know those phrases? Would God still hear? Would he hear now?

Jake looked up at Jennifer from his crouch on the floor, and saw the tears

streaming down her face. His heart softened, and he realized her prayers were gen-
uine. It broke his heart. He didn't like seeing
her cry. He fought the urge to get up and put
his arms around her and let her cry on his
shoulder. It probably wasn't a good idea.

So he kept pretending to pray, wondering
if there really was a God up there who was
listening to their pleas to hide the murder
they'd committed, and helping them get
away with burning one of his churches. Was
it true that God really favored white people?
Wasn't Jesus from the Middle East?
Wouldn't his skin have been dark?

But Jennifer seemed to think God was listening. Who was Jake to question it? After
all, he knew nothing of God. She'd been
raised from birth to believe. She knew tons
of Scripture by heart, and Cruz, the most
spiritual person he had ever known, had
memorized the entire New Testament. If
anyone knew God, he supposed they did.

He thought about the first time he'd seen
Jennifer Cruz, a couple of years ago when
he was fourteen and she was sixteen. She
and Cruz had been at the ballpark after a
game one night, when kids congregated on
the dark field to smoke cigarettes and drink

wine coolers. They had walked onto the field like some kind of rock star and super model, and had gotten everybody's attention. Especially Jake's.

He'd had a crush on Jennifer ever since, and unless he was mistaken, the feeling was mutual.

After all, she'd recommended him as drummer for their band, hadn't she?

Plus, Cruz was the most likeable guy he'd ever met, and had accepted Jake right into his group. What a relief to be taken for who you were after being labeled an outcast in high school, since he wasn't a jock or a junior politician. Jake felt like he was part of something important. The Twelve Disciples, Cruz called them, leaving himself and Jennifer out of the count. Jake and Benton had nothing but respect and admiration for all of the "brothers and sisters" of the group, from the illustrious "inner circle," consisting of Cruz, Jennifer, Redmon, and Graham, to Grayson and LaSalle who constantly lobbied to be among the favored few. And he respected the couples — Decareaux and his girlfriend Blair, Butch and Meg, and Drew and Kaye. They were all unified in purpose, and accepted without question.

When Jake and Benton had told Cruz about Benton's dead grandmother's house, they had suddenly become heroes. They needed a place to gather until they could start converting Cruz's grandfather's old deer camp into a compound in which they could all live. Cruz told them that God had sent them, because he knew they needed a place to hold their meetings and their band practices. Since this house was vacant and Benton's family had no plans to sell it for a while, it was perfect.

Suddenly, life got interesting. Though Jake still drifted home for a couple hours of sleep each night, he had bought his way into Cruz's following by donating anything he owned that they could sell. It seemed to be for a good cause. Cruz and Jennifer had goals, and he was part of them. He didn't think he'd ever had a goal before.

But now he wondered if it was getting out of hand.

Jennifer finished praying, then wiped her face and took the stool that her brother usually occupied. "It came to me during prayer," she said. "God revealed to me that we have to do something to divert attention from Cruz. If they think he was involved in the church burning and the killing, and that the others of us were . . . me and Redmon and Graham . . . then we have to give ourselves an airtight alibi tonight, and do it all again."

"Do what again?" Jake asked.

"Another church burning, and another black killing."

The crowd of kids roared out its disapproval, but she raised her hands and quieted them. "Just listen. This is a holy war. *Rahowa.* Say it with me."

All twelve followers muttered the word that had become a chant, symbolizing the racial holy war that Cruz said they were engaged in.

"Again!" she cried.

"Rahowa!"

"Like you mean it!"

"Rahowa!"

"We've had one taken captive," she went on. "If we're really what we say we are, then we can't stop now. We have to prove that Cruz ain't the one responsible for the killing. Something has to happen while he's in police custody, and while we're busy somewhere else. We have to throw them off. I need volunteers to do this for us. For

Cruz . . . for me." She waited, and no one came forward.

An alarm blared in Jake's chest. She was asking him to be involved this time, to kidnap some kid and beat him to death or shoot him, to throw him into a fire and let him burn to death. She was asking him to get his own hands dirty, not to just stand back on the perimeter while somebody else did the dirty work.

He began to sweat as the silence in the room lingered. What if she chose him, as Cruz had chosen the ones who'd helped him with Ben Ford?

"Cruz ain't made disciples of cowards, has he?" she asked. "No, he's chosen only the best. The loyal ones. And when he comes into his kingdom, those of you he's counted on will reign with him."

Jake hadn't been with the group long enough to understand all of the things they believed about Cruz. This "coming into his kingdom" stuff still baffled him, but he knew there was something different about this genius who could memorize the Bible and build a compound and plan the security to protect it. He wasn't an ordinary man. Whether he was some kind of higher being,

Jake wasn't sure, but he supposed he had more belief in Cruz than he had in God. He just wasn't ready to gamble his life on him.

When his best friend, Pete Benton, got to his feet, Jake froze.

"I'll do it," Benton said with a half-grin. Jake knew he didn't fully understand what he was volunteering for. His bulb had always been a tad dim. Jake thought he just had bad genes, since his father was an unemployed construction worker who only got a job when he ran out of drinking money. His mother supported them fixing hair twelve hours a day.

Jennifer's face blossomed into that charismatic Cruz smile, and she gave Benton a my-hero look and slid her arms around his neck. As she raised up to press a kiss on his lips, Jake felt a stab of jealousy that almost made him volunteer. But even the thought of Jennifer's attention wasn't enough to make him volunteer for murder.

But it was enough for Roy Decareaux, who was next to volunteer. Jennifer laughed with delight, as if he'd just asked her to the prom. Then Jack LaSalle, rumored to have a coveted relationship with Jennifer already, offered himself.

Jake was flooded with relief.

Jennifer turned all three around to face the group. "I always knew these three were chosen, that one day I'd need them, and that I could count on them. Now, here's the plan. The band plays at the Viper Pit tonight. I'll talk to Butch and set it up. We're all there, making a lot of noise. Meanwhile, our three heroes find another victim, take care of him, start another church fire, then rush back to the Pit, where we'll swear you've been all along."

She pulled her hair back from her face, and let it slip back down. "Of course, the cops will come looking for us first thing, but we'll have all been there. They won't have no choice but to start looking for some other group. With Cruz in jail and us at the Pit, how could we have done what they say? And then they got no choice but to move on and look for somebody else."

Everyone cheered, and Jake wondered if these poor idiots could really pull off such a thing. Chances were, they'd wind up in jail. Would they talk then? Name names? How would she keep them from it?

As the band members began loading up their equipment to take to the Viper Pit,

Jake tried to shake the swirling doubts in his head at what they were all getting into. Another kid was going to die, and what was it all about? To purify the culture, by getting rid of those who were ethnically inferior?

Things were getting hazy, and now it didn't seem about any cause at all. The first death had been about getting even with some preacher guy who'd insulted Cruz. This second one was about diverting the police.

It was hard to get behind a cause that wasn't really a cause.

As they dispersed and headed for their cars to the Viper Pit, he moved slowly, thinking of speaking up, questioning what they were about to do. Jennifer approached him near his car. "Hey, Jake," she said in that sweet way that made him feel favored above all the others.

"Yeah?"

"I was thinking about your aunt. How safe do you think Cruz is with her out there?"

"I don't know what you mean."

"I mean, she was snooping around here last night. She saw things. Her apartment was hit. What if she goes to the police and tells them about the carpet in the bonfire? What if she identifies my brother?"

"Identifies him as what? She doesn't know anything."

"She could cause trouble, is all I'm saying."

"But she won't. If she did, she'd get me in trouble, and Issie won't do that."

"But she's mad about her apartment — the cat and everything. Maybe she's scared and won't feel safe till she exposes us."

He wanted to ask her why they didn't think of that before they'd terrorized her, but he managed to keep his mouth shut. "You don't have to worry about Issie. I talked to her last night, okay? She's cool. She doesn't want me to get tied up as a murder suspect, so she won't say anything."

"I was just thinking that . . . maybe we need to make sure."

Anger tingled in his face. "So what are you suggesting? Kill her too?"

"Jake!" She smiled and took his hands, pulled him close, and clasped his hands behind her back. He hadn't been this close to her before, and he smelled the strawberry scent of her hair. His heart was on overload, hammering out a maddening beat. He hoped the others saw this. "Of course I don't mean kill her. What kind of person do you think I am?"

He thought of saying that she was the kind of person who would order a murder just to throw people off of her brother, but the words seemed broken, incomplete in his mind. He couldn't think clearly when she was this close.

"I'm saying that maybe she needs to be watched. Maybe she needs to be a little more afraid than she is."

"She's plenty scared. She slept at my house last night because she was afraid to stay home."

"Excellent," Jennifer said. "Really, that's excellent. Then you talked to her?"

"I told her to stay out of it."

"Do you think she will?"

"Like I told you, Issie's kept my secrets before. The last thing she wants is to see me thrown in jail. Really, Jennifer, you can trust me and my family."

"I thought I could," she said, gazing down into his eyes. He saw adoration there, infatuation so deep that it almost mirrored his. She liked him too, he thought. It wasn't just his imagination. He wasn't one of those geeks that she was manipulating into committing crimes. This wasn't like that.

She leaned down and kissed him so suddenly that it startled him, and then he gave into it and gave back. Just when he thought his heart would leap out of his chest, she stopped. She released him and stepped back, looked down at the ground, swept her hair behind her ear. "I didn't mean to do that," she said, looking embarrassed.

His throat was suddenly dry, and he rasped out, "No, don't apologize. It was . . . it was good." He laughed then at his own poor choice of words. "Excellent."

"Yeah, it was excellent, wasn't it?" she asked. She leaned into him and whispered, "Just like I thought." Then, as if she couldn't bear to face him after saying that, she turned and headed back to the van.

Jake stood there watching her, his heart beginning to hurt. It wasn't just his imagination. She *had* singled him out.

How had he gotten so lucky?

Forgetting the doubts that had swirled through his mind earlier about the cause not really being a cause, he finished loading his drums.

Chapter Seventeen

● ● ●

So you're the grandson of Sidney Clairmont, the grand wizard of the KKK?" Stan asked Jason Cruz as he sat across from him in the interrogation room.

"That's right," Cruz said, thrusting his chin up as if they were talking about a former U.S. president.

"So what was his part in this murder and in my church burning?"

"My granddaddy had no part in this. He's an old man. The KKK ain't hardly even active in this town anymore. You're the cop. You ought to know that."

"Looks like we might have a new generation of hate mongers."

"Hate mongers?" He leaned up on the table, getting closer to Stan. "Hey, man, you're white. And if that was your church, then you're Christian. Don't you want your country back? Don't you want to take care of your own?"

"Some of my own are black," Stan said.

"Right." Cruz leaned back in his chair and leveled those hypnotic eyes on him. "Come on, be straight. Don't you ever imagine what our country would be like if every culture under the sun wasn't here?"

"I'm sure the Indians used to think that, when we whites were moving into their land."

"But they're inferior too. God gave the land to the people with the brains, man. The ones who could make it fly. And we have, except that the gays and blacks and Latinos and Jews and Muslims and who knows who else are in here corrupting everything and turning it into hell."

"Actually, it's people like your group turning it into hell," Stan said. "If it weren't for people killing each other and destroying each other's property, it might not be a bad place to live."

"But *they're* killing each other and destroying property."

"So you feel justified in killing them?"

Cruz sighed, as if Stan was too dense to understand. "I told you, I didn't kill nobody. That's not what we're about."

"Then what *are* you about?"

"We're about being left alone to worship

and work and live together. We're about protecting ourselves from Big Brother."

Stan was getting weary, and he looked down at the boy's file. He had little on him, but much on his grandfather and mother, and even on his father who'd become an informant just before he vanished from town. He'd had many suspicions, himself, about what had happened to the man, after the first black mayor of Newpointe was murdered. Terrence Cruz had become an informant, but without any evidence of a body, they'd had to let the matter go.

He tried to find an approach somewhere in the file, but finally he shut it and slid it away from him. "I'm just gonna be honest with you, Cruz. I've known about your family for years. When your father vanished a few years ago, I spent a long time looking for him. I had my suspicions that something had happened to him."

Cruz seemed unduly interested in a spot on the table. "My father is dead."

"Who killed him?"

"God, according to my mother."

Stan narrowed his eyes. "God killed your father?"

"My daddy was eat up with sin," Cruz

said, bringing his eyes back to Stan's. "He was an immoral traitor, and God rained destruction down on him."

Stan sat back in his chair, staring at the boy. "I think I know why your mother might call him a traitor. But why do you call him immoral? I thought you people thought everything you did was moral."

Cruz's jaw began to pop. "What has my daddy got to do with that church burning?"

"I'm just saying that one day he talked to the police about the murder of our first black mayor, and the next day he vanished."

"That was years ago."

"Sticks in my memory," Stan said, shaking his head. "I don't like having unsolved crimes."

"It's not unsolved," Cruz said. "I told you, he's dead."

"And God did it."

"That's right."

"But God hasn't struck your grandfather for burning people's houses down, terrorizing them into leaving town, killing the mayor . . ."

"My granddaddy was never convicted of nothin'."

"No, but some of his cronies were. If I remember, some of the informants who told us what happened mentioned that you and your sister were involved in some of the crimes the KKK committed. You must have been little then. What? Eight? Nine?"

"They weren't crimes," Cruz said. "They were battles. Little battles in a big war."

"Then you admit that you've been involved with the KKK since you were a kid."

Cruz breathed a laugh. "You know I have been. I was practically raised in their headquarters. I stuffed envelopes, answered phones, went to meetings."

"And you were with your father and grandfather when crosses were burned in people's yards . . ."

"I never did nothing wrong. The Klansmen are soldiers in a war, and war is not criminal. It's necessary."

"So was it war last night when you killed that kid? Or was it just getting even with Nick Foster for what he did to your picket line at the gay Mardi Gras ball?"

Cruz slammed his hand on the table. "Is that what that sleazebag told you?"

"He said you were angry. That you'd threatened him. Is that true?"

"Threatened him? I hardly even knew he was there!"

"He said he broke your signs and took home the youth from his church."

"I still had plenty of supporters, and we made new signs, okay? Nick Foster isn't going to stop me. And there is a thing in this country called freedom of speech. Picketing was perfectly legal. It's my duty as a Christian to point out to those people that they're bringing God's wrath upon themselves."

"But to tell them God hates them? I'd be interested in seeing where in the Bible it says that. Wanna show me?"

"I don't wanna show you nothing," the kid said. "You're as much the enemy as Nick Foster is, embracing those people and pretending to worship with them, like God can even hear you when you're such an abomination."

"Then you do consider Nick Foster your enemy?"

"I didn't say that."

"Where were you yesterday morning between the hours of four and six A.M.?" he asked suddenly.

Cruz seemed thrown by the sudden shift. "I was sleeping."

Stan began to write on his legal pad. "Where?"

"At home, of course."

"Was your sister there?"

"Yes."

"Then why did your mother say she hadn't seen you in a couple of days?"

"Because she hadn't. She was asleep when I got home, and gone when I got up."

"But she *said* you hadn't been *home* in a couple of days." Stan made a point of turning the pages in his legal pad, looking for his notes he'd taken when he'd gone looking for Cruz earlier. "She said, and I quote, 'Them kids never tell me nothing. They stay out all night and sleep all day, and sometimes don't come home at all.' "

"So you jump to the conclusion that I must be a murderer?"

"Actually, the conclusion I've drawn is that you must be a liar. You just told me you were home."

"Well, my mother misses a lot of things. She never has seen half the things going on in our house."

"I thought she home-schooled. Aren't most home-schooling moms real attentive?"

"We're both eighteen. We don't need

home-schooling no more. But when we were young, a lot went on that she didn't see. Truth ain't one of her passions."

Stan looked down at the legal pad again, and he began to wonder what kind of childhood these kids must have had, with every adult in their lives engaged in criminal activity against anyone they saw as different. How many murders had they witnessed? How many lives had they terrorized? How could any child come up with a healthy view of society when they'd been taught nothing but hate?

And when they slapped the label of Christianity on that hate, it got even more confusing.

No wonder so many Americans thought Christians were hateful zealots with murderous agendas and evil hearts.

He looked across the table at the kid who had probably grown up too fast. What were the secrets he harbored about his father's immorality and his mother's blindness to it? What immorality had he borne as a child?

If murder wasn't considered immorality, he could only imagine what was.

The door opened, and Chief Jim Shoemaker leaned in. "Stan, can I see you a minute?"

"Sure." He got up and stepped outside, closing the door behind him. "What is it?"

"There's been another church burning," he said. Stan caught his breath. "Bayou Missionary Baptist Church. And there was a victim in this one too. My understanding is that this one isn't dead yet."

"Then maybe he can tell us who did it." He spun around and looked through the glass. The kid was sitting there with his face in his hands. Stan was pleased he had gotten to him. "Pick up his friends," he said. "And his sister. They had to have something to do with it."

"We have cars en route. Sid located them at a bar called the Viper Pit. We've had problems with them before for serving to minors. It's the teenage hot spot."

"I gotta get over to that church," Stan told him. He nodded toward Cruz. "Can we keep him here a little longer?"

"Yeah, I'll get somebody else to question him for a while, just to mark time until you've worked the scene. It's over on Briarson and Catalpa Street. I'll meet you over there."

Stan took off without a look back, hoping another kid wouldn't have to die.

Chapter Eighteen

● ● ●

Jennifer's three chosen ones were a wreck by the time they got back to the Viper Pit, after doing what she had ordered. They came in, soaked with sweat and trembling, and instantly split up to get lost in the crowd. Jake tried not to miss a drumbeat as he looked for his best friend. Benton looked like he'd been in a fight. He had blood on his shirt and scratch marks on his face. His eyes were wild as they darted east to west. He came to the edge of the stage and looked up at Jennifer as she banged on the keyboard. She nodded to him that she would come down, and quickly announced that they were taking a break.

Jake followed her off the stage and watched her usher Benton into a back room.

Benton was hysterical by the time she had the door closed. "We found some kid out ridin' his bike and LaSalle runned him down and he put up a fight when we tried to get him in the car and we started the fire and left him there unconscious . . ."

"Hush!" Jennifer said, jerking his shirt over his head. "Get this shirt off immediately."

He looked down, noticing the blood for the first time, and obediently pulled the shirt over his head. She rolled it up in a ball. "Let me look at the rest of you. You look like you were caught in a stampede. You didn't leave any witnesses, did you?"

"No, of course not!" Benton was trembling, like he was about to snap. He started to cry. "He put up a fight and started hollering and begging and I thought about my little brother and him pleading for his life and I couldn't really remember why we were doing this and what it meant except that it was something about throwing the cops off . . ."

"Stop it!" Jennifer ordered, taking him by the bare shoulders. "Now stop it!"

"You don't know my name, do you?" Benton demanded. "Tell me my name."

For the first time since he'd known her, Jennifer was at a loss for words. She looked at Jake for help.

"Benton," he said, and Jennifer's smile returned.

"Benton, you know I know who you are. I wouldn't have chose you if I didn't know and trust you."

"We did this for you and we don't even know why and now the police are gonna come and they're gonna question us and figure out that we did this . . ."

"No, they won't," she said. "It's gonna be fine." She pulled him against her, and he dropped his forehead on her shoulder and began to sob. Jake stood back, wishing he could just take his friend and get out of here. But they had to be here when the police came. "Come on, it's okay," she said, stroking his hair maternally. "You're heroes. All three of you. People will be talking about what you did years from now. You'll be legends. They'll write songs about you. Now, you go out and get a beer," she said. "You need to calm your nerves. Tell Butch at the bar I said to give you all you want on me. Don't worry about him asking for your I.D. He never gives us a hard time. He's one of us, remember."

Benton pulled back and studied her face. He tried to calm his breathing. "Okay. I just . . . need to know that this is gonna pay off, you know? That you ain't just gonna forget."

Jennifer's face softened, and she turned back to Jake. "Jake, leave me alone with him for a while, okay? I just need a few minutes."

Jake's stomach took a dive, and he got sick at the thought that she was doing to Benton what she had done to Jake just hours ago. She was using his crush on her to manipulate him, and she was good at it. He found himself seething with jealousy. He didn't want to leave them alone.

But as he headed back into the crowd, with the stereo music playing until they could get back to the stage, he noticed a buzz around the door. He pushed through and saw that police were swarming in.

Quickly, he dashed back to the room. "Cops are here," he said.

Benton looked as if he might as well be dead. "They know," he said. "They already know and they're coming after me and I don't want to go to jail . . ."

She slapped him and made him look at her. "Stop whining! You've been here the whole time with us. Nobody's left. You have fifty witnesses out there who'll swear to it.

We all have alibis. If they ask you about the cuts and scrapes, you tell 'em you were fighting with LaSalle and . . . who was the other one?"

His face twisted in deeper dread. "Decareaux! Man, you don't even *know* us."

"You were fighting with *them*, okay? They have scratches and scrapes too." She went to a shelf and grabbed a folded black Viper Pit T-shirt, set aside for bar employees. "Here. Put this on. Now go out there and get lost in the middle of that crowd, and so help me, act like a soldier instead of a whiny little girl."

He stumbled out. Jennifer got back on the stage and signaled for the other band members to join her as the police made their way through the crowd.

Chapter Nineteen

● ● ●

Nick Foster was lying in bed, staring at the ceiling and listening to the scanner, when the call came through that the Bayou Missionary Baptist Church was on fire. The pastor was a friend of his, and he knew he had probably been called and would be heading to the fire with as much dread and despair as Nick had just days ago.

He got up and decided he had to go and provide whatever support he could. He got dressed as fast as his injuries would allow and headed toward the blaze.

▪ ▪ ▪

The boy who'd been found in the fire was still alive, but just barely.

"I will not lose this one," Issie said through her teeth. She had worked for eight hours already — the three to eleven shift — but when the call came at eleven o'clock, she and Steve had answered it. "He's alive. We've got to stabilize him."

Steve Winder was busy intubating him since his airway had obviously closed.

"Issie, who is he?" Nick asked.

She cast a glance up at Nick. "I don't know. He's burned so badly he's practically unrecognizable. No identification, no nothing. But he's young, thirteen or fourteen. Pulse rate's dropping, guys!"

"He's gone," Steve yelled. "No pulse. Come on, get the defibrillator." They attached the probes to his chest, and as they pulled back to allow the shock to jolt him, Issie prayed to a God that she didn't know that this kid would not slip through their fingers like the last one had. He had a mother and father, as Ben had. He might have brothers and sisters, friends, relatives.

The heart didn't respond. She got down on her knees and began to pump furiously on his chest.

"Clear!" Steve shouted, and she pulled back and waited as he sent the jolt again.

Nothing.

"No!" she shouted. "We can't let him die!" She kept pumping.

"Clear!" Steve shouted again, and she

stopped and pulled back. The jolt shook his body again, and she held her breath as she waited one second, two seconds . . .

"Beat, you stupid thing!" she screamed to his heart. "Don't you give up!" She began compressions again, pumping as if her own heart was connected to his.

"He's gone, Issie," Steve said. He stopped pumping air into his tube and wilted in defeat.

"No!" she shouted. "We can't stop! Don't stop, Steve." She kept pushing on his chest, trying to force the heart to beat. Had Jake had anything to do with this? Had that smart aleck Cruz thrown this kid into the fire?

Nick bent down and touched her shoulders. "Issie . . ."

"No!" she screamed. "I won't let 'em do it!"

"Let who do it?" Nick asked her.

She didn't answer, but the tears rolled down her face and she pumped his chest with fierce urgency, pleading with him to come back to life. "Pray, Nick," she cried. "Do what you do!"

He was silent behind her, and she wondered if he had closed his eyes, if he was sending up those prayers to God. Prayer was all that could help the boy now, but she wasn't sure that bringing him back was going to do him any good, not with the flesh dissolving on his body in horrible third-degree burns, and months, even years — possibly a lifetime — of excruciating treatments, not to mention the disfigurement that would come upon him if he lived.

She finally gave up and fell back, sobbing. Where was Jake? Was there another carpet rolled up in a bonfire with this boy's bloodstains on it?

She felt hands on her shoulders. She fell back, and strong arms came around her, embraced her, held her.

"It's okay." She recognized Nick's deep whisper against her ear. "It's okay. You did the best you could."

"He's dead," she sobbed. "Another kid is dead just because he's black."

"You don't know that," Nick said.

"I *do* know it!" she bit out. "How could they do this? How could they be so cruel? This kid has a mother, just like Susan." She slapped the tears on her face and got to her feet, pulling out of the security of Nick's arms. She didn't want to feel that security.

She didn't want to feel any comfort right now. She just wanted to hang on to that anger and soak in it and wallow in it. She wanted to find her nephew and grab him by the throat and shake him until he told her who was responsible for this and why he was a part of it. But she couldn't leave the scene yet, not until the fire was out and all the firemen were safe. Someone might get hurt like Nick had the other day. Any number of things could go wrong. She had to wait this out.

Meanwhile, she prayed once again to the God she did not know, that the efforts of the kids who had done this thing would be thwarted until she had the chance to stop them herself.

Chapter Twenty

● ● ●

Due to lack of evidence, the police were forced to let Cruz go after they'd worked the fire and interviewed his followers at the Viper Pit. Cruz was able to reach Jennifer at the Viper Pit, and she told him she was sending someone to get him. She herself couldn't leave, she said, because there had been some new developments, and one of them needed to be there.

He trusted her, and told her he'd meet her back at the Benton house.

Sye Redmon — one of the members of Cruz's inner circle — came to get him. He seemed nervous, and Cruz wondered what was going on.

They were quiet until they got to the car. "Tell me everything," he said.

He got behind the wheel, even though it was Redmon's car. Graham got in on the passenger side and tossed him the keys. "There was another fire," Redmon said as they pulled away from the police station. Cruz glanced into the truck bay of the fire department and saw that it was empty. "Another church."

Cruz frowned. "Copycat?"

"No," Redmon said. "It was a ploy Jennifer came up with to prove you weren't involved. We were all making a big ruckus at the Viper Pit, so we've got alibis. It ought to throw them off."

"Like they don't know we could lie for our own?"

"Man, they interviewed us. They talked to dozens of the kids at the Pit, and didn't come up with anything."

Cruz was quiet for a moment as he drove. "Who did it?" he asked finally.

"Benton, LaSalle, and Decareaux."

"Why them?"

"Volunteered. Plus, they're expendable. If they have to take the fall, it's no great loss."

"We don't hardly even know them. What if they talk?"

"And get theirselves thrown in jail?" Redmon asked. "I don't think that'll happen. Besides, Jen has things under control. She has them eating out of her hand." Redmon chuckled. "She's good at this."

The comment sent a tide of anger rising up inside him, but Cruz held it back.

By the time they got to the Benton house, everyone seemed to be there. Cruz got out, slammed the car door, and headed into the house. The stragglers, still out at their cars, cheered for Cruz and high-fived him, as if he was MVP of the toughest game of the season. "Everybody inside," he said, bolting up the porch steps and into the house.

Jake was just inside. "Cruz!"

Cruz shot him a look. "Where's my sister?"

Jake hesitated to answer.

"Where is she?"

"She's in the back with Benton."

"Benton?" he spat out.

"Yeah," one of the others piped in. "He's freaking out and threatening to stop letting us use the house. She's trying to calm him down."

Jake looked as if he realized how dangerous Benton's instability could be. "Benton's all right. He's just worried about his parents finding out, that's all."

Cruz shoved past him and went into the kitchen, reached up over the cabinet, and pulled down a switchblade he'd hidden there. He engaged the switch, making the blade fly out.

"Cruz, what are you —?"

Cruz's head was beginning to ache, and his stomach burned, just like it had when they were kids and he'd heard Jen crying when her father was in her room . . .

He stormed back through the house, his angry step shaking the walls. He found the closed door and flung it open.

He saw them standing with their arms around each other, Jen with her back against the wall and Benton with his fingers all tangled in her hair.

Rage like that he'd experienced as a child crashed through him, blinding him to anything but that picture of his father using his sister . . .

He flew across the room, switchblade flying, but Benton reacted just in time. The blade missed.

"Cruz!" Jennifer screamed. "Stop it!"

He spun around and headed for Benton again and slashed the knife through the air, slicing into his leg. Benton screamed in pain.

Then Jennifer was on his back, crying and screaming that this wasn't their father, that Benton wasn't hurting her, that Cruz was confused . . .

Slowly, his rage deflated, and he tried to catch his breath. She whispered childhood memories into his ear. "It's okay, Cruz. It's okay. You've always been my rescuer. It's okay."

He swallowed and turned around and pulled her into a fierce, fraternal embrace. "I'm sorry, Jen," he whispered, sweating and breathing hard. "I'm so sorry. Did I hurt you?"

"No." She was out of breath too. "But I think Benton is in trouble."

He turned back to the kid he'd cut and saw him writhing on the floor as the puddle of blood beneath him grew bigger. "Get a towel," Cruz ordered Jake, who stood at the door, dumbly gaping in.

Jake ran out, then came back with a towel and fell down next to his friend.

"We have to stop the bleeding," Cruz said, taking charge again. "Put pressure on it."

"Cruz, he needs a doctor," Jake said. "We need to call somebody or get him to the hospital."

"He's okay," Cruz said. "He'll be okay as soon as the bleeding stops."

"But you can bleed to death in five minutes!" Jake said. "Cruz, we have to do something."

"I told you, he's all right!"

"I'll call my aunt," he said. "She's a paramedic. She could help Benton, and I swear she'll stay quiet. She cares about me and wouldn't want to get me in trouble."

"She's already been snooping around here," Cruz said. "We can't trust her." He got down beside Benton and held the wound. "It's all right, buddy. You're gon' be all right."

Jake was getting frantic. "He's my friend, man! He needs help!"

"He's my friend too," Cruz said more calmly now. "All right. I care enough about this man to risk calling your aunt. But only because he's indispensable. He's a courageous foot soldier, and when this is over, I'm goin' ta make him one of my lieutenants."

In spite of his pain, Benton looked at Cruz with pride in his eyes.

Jake ran out to find a cell phone so he could call Issie.

Chapter Twenty-One

● ● ●

Issie felt defiant enough to return to her apartment that night when she finally turned her shift over to Frenchy and Bob. Earlier today, the manager had painted the wall that was written on, but had tacked an extra hundred bucks onto her rent to cover it. She had dragged the bloody mattress to the street. She didn't know when she'd be able to buy a new one. The four new tires on her car had cleaned out her meager savings. With her gun within reach, she took a shower and washed off the residue of the smoke that soiled her face and uniform. She watched the water swirl down the drain and wished that her anger and fears would go with it.

She got dressed, dried her hair, then sat looking into the mirror. How would she get through to her nephew? Jake thought she was no different than he, and if she was honest, she had to admit she wasn't. At his age she had been following an equally dangerous crowd, except her friends had been threats to their own bodies, not those of others. She'd spent all her nights making and getting into trouble, but no one had ever suggested burning down a church or murdering a kid because of the color of his skin.

But what if they had? she wondered. Would she have followed along blindly like Jake was doing now? Would she have been needy enough to do whatever she was told in the interest of belonging? She hoped not, but she wasn't sure, and she knew Jake wasn't sure, either.

Even now, she teetered on the edge of risk in most of her relationships. Even her job was a risk, a constant jolt of adrenaline. She liked to live dangerously, and she was easily bored. Jake was just like her.

She decided to try talking sense into him again and picked up the phone to call her brother's house. His wife, Lois, answered.

"Hello?"

"Lois, it's Issie. I'm sorry to call at midnight, but it's important. Where's Jake?"

She sighed. "He's out, as usual. You know that boy never stays home."

Her heart sank. "Any idea where he is?" she asked.

"Your guess is as good as mine," Lois said. "He doesn't tell us anything."

"Okay. Maybe I can find him."

"What's this about?" Lois asked.

Issie thought of telling her what Jake seemed to be involved in, but something told her it was too soon. She needed to give Jake a chance. She needed to talk to him first.

"Nothing," she said. "I just had a message to give him."

"There isn't anything wrong, is there?"

Issie hesitated again. "Not that I know of." She sat there a moment longer, then finally asked, "Lois, what do you know about the kids he's hanging out with?"

"Not much," her sister-in-law said. "It's not like he brings them home for dinner."

That made her angry. Her own mother had never demanded to meet her friends. She had never held her accountable. "Then why do you let him hang around with them? I mean, what if they're dangerous or something? What if they're leading him down the wrong path?"

Lois chuckled as if the questions were incompatible with Issie Mattreaux. "I've never heard you talk about the wrong path before. You told me once the only path was the one you paved."

Issie knew that was true. She wished she could eat those words now. "Well, I used to think that, but I'm starting to wonder."

"Is there something Jake's doing that I need to know about?" Lois asked.

Again, Issie thought that one over. "I don't know, Lois. I just don't like his friends much. They look like trouble to me."

"More trouble than the ones you used to go out with?"

"Yeah, even more trouble than that," Issie said. "Maybe you need to get more involved in his life."

"Get more involved? How? He's hardly ever home, and he doesn't want to talk about anything when he is."

"You're his mother. Maybe you need to make him."

Lois was offended. "Issie, just a few years ago *you* were the one staying out all night and getting into trouble. Mike complained about you all the time. Your mother *never* knew where you were."

"Mama never cared."

"Well, maybe that was true," Lois said. "But Jake knows I do. And now you're telling me that I need to demand that he make me a part of his life?"

"I don't mean like that," she said. "I just mean, don't take things for granted. Don't assume anything."

"Anything like what? Jake's a good kid, Issie."

"Maybe that's exactly what you don't need to assume."

She heard Lois breathe her surprise, and realized she might have gone too far.

"Issie, if you have something to tell me about Jake, then go ahead and tell me."

Issie closed her eyes. She knew her sister-in-law was right. She needed to either spit it out or shut up. "I'm sorry. I'm just worried about him."

"Well, if you want to let me in on what you're worried about, I'll worry with you. I am his mother."

"It's nothing, really. Just a feeling."

"A feeling about his friends?"

"Yeah."

"Which ones?"

She shook her head. "I don't know for

sure, Lois. That guy Cruz kind of gives me the creeps."

"Cruz? Is that his first name or last name?"

"I don't know. Last, I think."

Her sister-in-law was quiet, and Issie imagined the wheels turning in her head as she tried to figure out what she could do as a mother. She knew that her brother and his wife were both good parents. They had just abdicated their power.

"Believe it or not," Lois said, "I love him. Just because we're not real close right now doesn't mean I don't care about him. I'm just trying to give him a little more space as he gets older."

"Maybe space is the wrong thing to give him," Issie said. "Maybe you need to ride him . . . just stay on his back."

"And if anybody had told your mother to do that just a few years ago," Lois said, "you would have packed your bags and disappeared, never to be heard from again."

"Maybe," Issie said.

"I have certain parameters I have to work in as a mother," Lois said. "I have to give him his space and let him go and hope that maybe by doing that, I'll be able to hold on to him a little longer."

Issie was suddenly glad that she wasn't a mother herself. As she hung up the phone she told herself that she wasn't thrilled about being an aunt right now, either.

She went to the window and peered out on the parking lot, looking for a sign of anyone who shouldn't be there. She had found the key to her apartment hanging back on the hook in her brother's kitchen this morning, and she had taken it in case Jake tried to get into her apartment again. Still, she felt uneasy.

Though she was exhausted, she was afraid to sleep, so she lay down on her couch with the gun on her coffee table and turned on some mindless infomercial about skin care. Slowly, she drifted off to sleep.

She didn't know how long she had been asleep when the phone shrilled, waking her. She grabbed the gun and sat up. Her stomach tightened as she went to the caller ID and looked to see who it was. It looked like a cell phone number. Slowly, she answered, "Hello?"

"Issie?" It was her nephew's voice.

"Jake, it's you! Did you have anything to do with —"

"An emergency," he cut in. "Issie, we need your help."

"We?" she asked. "Who's we?"

"Me and some of my buddies," he said. "Look, we're in a lot of trouble. Benton got hurt, and we can't take him to the hospital. I need you to come over and see what you can do for him."

"I'm a paramedic, not a doctor," she said. "Jake, what's going on? How did Benton get hurt?"

"He cut himself," he said. "Can't you come look at it, try to stop the bleeding?"

"He's still bleeding?" she asked.

"Yeah, and it's bad."

"Where are you?" she asked.

"We're at the house. You know, Benton's grandmother's house?"

Issie closed her eyes. "Jake, I don't want any part of this. I've already told you."

"He cut himself, Issie. That's all. It's not illegal to cut yourself."

"I don't trust your friends," she said. "How do I know that if I come over there I'm not walking into a trap?"

"Because *I'm* here," Jake said. "I

wouldn't let anything happen to you. Issie, I wouldn't have called you if you weren't the only one who could help us. Come on. The guy's bleeding."

She recognized the panic in Jake's voice. He wasn't faking, and the last thing she needed on her conscience was another death. "All right," she said. "Where is the wound?"

"On his thigh," he said.

"Well, then you need to wrap it and apply pressure to it. Have you done that?"

"Yeah, we wrapped a towel around it, pretty tight."

"That should help the bleeding to slow down until I get there. Jake, how did he get the cut?"

"It's a long story," he said. "I'll tell you when you get here."

She knew it was a story that she was better off not hearing, but quickly she got dressed, grabbed some dental floss and scissors, a bottle of alcohol, and a few other makeshift supplies from around the apartment. She threw them into a bag and lit out as fast as she could to her car, still clutching her gun, just in case anyone lurked around waiting to jump out and ambush her.

Chapter Twenty-Two

• • •

Jake was waiting nervously for her in the front yard at the vacant house, smoking a cigarette. She pulled her car into the driveway and quickly got out. He dropped the cigarette and stubbed it out with his toe.

"Thought you quit smoking," she said.

"I did," Jake said. "Cruz doesn't like it. But I'm a little stressed right now. This way, Issie."

He led her into the house to a back bedroom, and she saw the boy lying on the floor in a back bedroom. The tall blond girl sat against the wall with a worried look on her face. Cruz stood at the center of the room like a traffic cop. "Before you touch him," he said, "I need to warn you that you can't breathe a word about this to anyone. It was an accident. He was drunk and playing around with a knife . . ."

Issie fell to her knees beside Benton and tried to uncoil the boy. "Let me see, Benton. I can't help you until you give me your leg."

Cruz was getting impatient. "One word, and the next injury won't be an accident. Are you hearing me?"

Issie had coaxed Benton out of his coil and saw that the towel pressed against his cut was soaked. "Benton, I'm gonna move this towel. I need to see how bad the cut is."

"I'm talking to you!" Cruz yelled.

Issie shot a fiery look up at him and yelled back, "Do you want me to help him or not?"

Jennifer grabbed Cruz before he could react. In a soft voice, she said, "Come on, Cruz. Let's go to another room, and we can fill each other in about tonight."

He didn't want to leave, but he finally let her coax him out. Jake stayed behind.

"What is his problem?" Issie peeled the towel off the wound, and Benton groaned and tightened up, starting the bleeding again. She winced as she saw the depth of the cut.

"This is not a cut, Jake," she said through her teeth. "This is a stab wound." She looked up at him. "Isn't it?"

"No," he said. "He was just playing around with his knife, that's all. He got drunk and was playing around."

"You're trying to tell me that the guy was

drunk enough to give himself a cut three inches long and at least an inch deep?"

"Yeah," he said weakly.

She shook her head. "I can't do anything with this. He's going to need lots of stitches. He needs to be in a hospital."

"Issie, he can't go. That's all there is to it. We need you to help him."

She got on her knees and tried to see if he was lucid. He was half-conscious. "Benton, can you hear me? I need to get you to the hospital."

He shook his head. "No, can't go," he slurred.

She groaned and looked up at Jake. "What is it with you people? I'll do what I can, but I'm going to need your help."

Jake nodded and got on his knees.

"You're going to have to hold him down. I'm going to have to clean the wound first, and it's gonna hurt. If he was drunk, maybe he won't feel it."

"Hope he drank enough," he said.

"Me too. Now, hold him down."

As Jake tried to keep him from writhing and recoiling, Issie began to do the best she could to take care of the wound.

• • •

Later, when she had sterilized it and stitched it up, Cruz came back in.

"We need to get him to a hospital," she said.

"But that isn't an option," Cruz bit out, dismissing the subject by leaving the room.

Issie started to object, but she caught Jake's eye, warning her not to pick a fight with him. Benton had passed out long ago, whether from blood loss or alcohol, she wasn't sure.

"Jake, you've got to figure a way to get him treatment," she said. "He lost a lot of blood. He needs fluids. Antibiotics."

"I can't," he said. "Cruz knows what he's doing."

Issie didn't doubt that for a moment. "What is their draw, Jake? What do they have that you want?"

"Nothing," he said.

"You're risking prison to hang out with them. I want to know why. Is it that girl?"

He glanced toward the door. "It's a lot of things. I'm somebody with them. Not just a freak who gets in the way. And they've given me something to believe in. Something important to *do*. We're all gonna help build the compound where we're all gonna live. And Cruz, he's special. There's something *different* about him. He's on a higher level than we are. Like, if there's a God, maybe Cruz has an in with him."

Issie couldn't believe what she was hearing. "So he's setting himself up as some kind of Messiah figure?"

"Yeah, kind of," Jake said. "Only it's not his fault. He was chosen, just like we are."

Issie brought her hand to her forehead, trying to puzzle this out. "Jake, have you quit school?"

"Well, not officially, but I haven't been there in a couple of weeks. Mom and Dad don't know. Since they're both at work during the day, the school hasn't been able to fink on me yet."

"Jake, you're sixteen! What are you gonna do without a high school diploma?"

"I won't need one," he said. "We're all gonna live together in the compound when it's built. We'll take care of ourselves and mind our own business."

"Where is this compound?" she asked.

He shook his head. "I can't tell you that."

She wanted to throttle him.

"They're good for me, Issie."

"Jake, another kid was killed in another church fire tonight. Did you have anything to do with that?"

He looked down at the crude stitches on his sleeping friend's leg. "Issie, I don't know what you're talking about. My band played at the Viper Pit tonight, until just a while ago. Since then I've been right here with Benton, trying to figure out what to do about his leg."

"Well, there's a lot of secrecy around here, Jake, and a lot not being explained. Where was Cruz?"

"At the police station, being questioned about the other church burning. So see? He couldn't have done it. The rest of us were all at the Pit. None of us could have done it. And the cops can verify it. They were there, giving us all a hard time." He met her eyes and seemed to read her doubt. "Why won't you believe me?"

"Because there are too many secrets. Scary secrets. The kind that get people like you killed."

Jake got quiet.

Her eyes stung as she stared at him. "You know, you remind me a lot of myself when I was sixteen."

"You're not that much older now."

"I'm eight years older than you," she said. "I know you think that's not very much, but there's something I've learned in the last few years that you apparently haven't caught on to yet."

"What?"

"I've learned that the kids I hung around with when I was your age, the ones who got into trouble and came up with mystery wounds and committed petty crimes . . . they're all either dead or in prison right now."

"Yeah, right," he said.

"I'm not kidding, Jake. I have three friends from high school who are dead. One died of an overdose and one in a drunk driving accident. He was the drunk. Another was shot in the French Quarter on the south shore."

"Your point?" Jake asked her.

"My point," she said, "is that two other friends wound up in prison. These were the people I counted as my closest friends, the ones I depended on for everything, sometimes even my life. This Cruz guy is not going to get you anywhere, Jake, nowhere but maybe dead or in prison, and I don't want to see you in either place."

He pulled out a cigarette and lit it. His eyes narrowed as he inhaled. "You know, you're right," he said on the exhale. "You are a lot older than me. You're already starting to sound like my parents."

"Your parents don't want you dead or in prison either," she said. "These friends of yours don't care. If your parents had any idea what I've seen the last couple of days, this house you've vandalized, the bloody stain on that carpet I saw you burning the other night, the stab wound tonight . . ."

"Come on, Issie," Jake said. "You need to just keep your nose out of it. We appreciate what you did tonight, but these things are still none of your business."

"Hey, Ray Ford is a friend of mine. If you had anything to do with his son's murder —"

"Of course I didn't," Jake cut in. "You really think that about me?"

"Don't act so hurt," she said. "You know I hardly even know who you are anymore. You used to be this sweet kid I loved to be around, and now you're turning into . . . I don't even know what."

Jake looked hurt. "You were never so high and mighty when it was you that wanted to party."

His words were like a slap in the face. "I don't do dangerous things, Jake. I don't step over the line."

"What line?" he asked. "You don't have any lines!"

"I make better choices," she said. "You don't see me breaking and entering, committing arson, murdering innocent people."

"Give me a break," he said. "You live just as dangerously as I do, Issie."

"How do you figure that?" she demanded.

"Everybody knows you like dating ex-cons and married men, and spending every spare night at Joe's Place. You live on the edge, just like me. You just found a way to make a living at it."

"How dare you?" she flung back. "Don't you *ever* talk to me that way again!"

"Why not?" he asked. "You talk to *me* that way all the time."

"I'm trying to save your life, you little fool," she said. "I'm trying to keep you from going the wrong way."

"Well, when you figure out what the right way is, why don't you come tell me," he said, " 'cause I don't see your path bein' all that different. At least these people have a purpose and a plan that lasts longer than one night. At least they stand for something!"

"You want to stand for hate and lies and death?" she asked. "Does that make you feel important?"

He made a face as if he couldn't believe she was cornering him this way. "I haven't done anything! Just because a church burns down doesn't mean I know something about it."

"Well, you knew something about the first one."

Again, he looked shocked. "What makes you say that?"

"The carpet I saw with the blood on it. The conversation we had when I brought it up."

He looked at the doorway, as if worried that someone was listening. "Issie, I'm going to tell you this one more time. You need to keep your mouth shut and get out of here now."

"Or what?" she asked. "Are you threatening me, Jake? Because I'm your flesh and blood, and those people in there aren't. You can pretend ignorance, but you need to know that tonight I tried my best to save that kid's life. We defibrillated him three times. I pumped his heart for twenty minutes. His skin was bubbled up like melted rubber. Even if he had lived, he probably never would have walked again, or moved, or had any of his organs function properly. If you're involved, I want you to know that his death was probably horrible, and you'll pay for it some day. And if you're not involved, then I want you to look around and figure out which one of your friends might have done this, because you might be next."

She had her nephew's attention now. He was staring at her, his face serious. She knew that he really was in over his head. "Who was the kid?" he asked.

"Some kid named Frankie Sardis who lived over on Twenty-third Street. He was thirteen years old. Seventh grade. What kind of coward goes around killing boys too small to even defend themselves?"

Again Jake kept staring at her. "We were all at the Viper Pit," he whispered, as if that was the story he was sticking to.

"Look, I don't know what any of you are involved in," Issie said, "but as a member of Newpointe's protective services I'm obligated to tell what I know."

"You don't *know* anything," Jake said.

"I do know some things," she said, her voice low. "I know what I've seen, and I'm going to tell it. I know that after I saw that bloody carpet, I had someone break into my apartment last night and put a dead cat on my bed. I know that I've had my wall written on and my tires slashed. I know that your friend was stabbed tonight."

"So what are you going to do?" Jake asked.

"I'm going to go to the police," she said, "and I'm telling you this, Jake, because I don't think it's too late for you to get out of here. I suggest you surgically remove yourself from this group of friends and make sure that you never become a part of this cancer again. Maybe if you go with me to the police, tell them what you know, this will have a better ending than it looks like it's going to have now."

He swallowed hard. "Issie, don't do it."

"I have to do it," she said. "It would be stupid of me to just sit here and keep my mouth shut, knowing that tomorrow another church might burn down and another kid might be found dead. And I'll be called to the scene and I'll have to try to save his life.

Have you ever tried to do that, Jake? Have you ever tried to keep somebody alive who's slipping away, knowing that somebody in your family might have had something to do with killing them?"

"I had *nothing* to do with that," Jake bit out. "You have to believe me. I wouldn't do that."

"It's a sickening feeling," she said. "It makes you vomit. It makes your head ache, and it fills you with so much guilt that you don't know what to do."

"You don't have any reason to feel guilty," he said.

"Tell me about it. But you do. And you and I are related and I love you and I don't want to see you follow the path that these guys are following."

"Issie, I'm telling you. Don't go to the police. It's not a smart thing to do."

"Well, since you have such bad judgment about what's smart and what's not, I think I'll follow my own."

She left the room with Jake following behind, and they cut through ten disciples in the living room. Cruz seemed to be giving a lecture to the rest who were there. He had relaxed now and was sitting on his stool, and the group was laughing at something he'd said — oblivious to Benton on the floor in the back room. They got quiet as she came in. "If he doesn't take that kid to the hospital, then don't any of you believe that he cares about you," she said. "You could be next, hurt however Benton was and left to suffer."

Cruz got to his feet, his stance suggesting that she had crossed the line.

Issie bolted out of the house, and Jake followed her. "Issie! *Issie!*" She got into her car and slammed the door hard. She turned the key and flipped on her lights. Her nephew stood in the circle of headlights, and she could see the confusion and fear on his face. She wished there was some way she could talk him into coming with her, but she knew it wasn't going to happen. Something about that brother and sister was pulling him back toward the group.

She started backing out slowly, hoping he would run after her and get in the car with her, go and tell the police everything he knew, but he just stood there. Tears came to her eyes as she put the car in drive and set out down the road.

Chapter Twenty-Three

● ● ●

Cruz came out of the house and watched her car pull out of the driveway. "What was that all about?" he demanded.

"She just got upset," Jake said.

Jennifer came out with some of the others behind her. "Where is she going?"

Jake felt sick. He didn't know if he should tell them what she'd threatened to do. If he did, they would chase her down, and there was no telling what they might do. But if he didn't, they would all go down. "She's just upset because of the fire tonight. She tried to save the kid, but he died. She's a little suspicious."

"Did you tell her about my being in police custody when it happened? Did you tell her you and all the rest were at the Viper Pit?"

"Yeah, I told her."

"So what did she say? Where is she going?"

"I don't know."

Cruz stood there for a moment, just staring at him, then suddenly, he launched forward and grabbed Jake by the throat. *"Where is she going?"* he bit out.

Jake grabbed Cruz's wrist and tried to disengage it. "I don't know."

"She's going to the police, isn't she?"

"No!" he lied. "No!"

That grip on his throat tightened, and Jennifer stepped forward. "Cruz, stop it. Let him go!"

Cruz didn't. His thumb and forefinger cut into the skin of his neck, and Jake thought he would pass out.

"Let him go, Cruz!" she shouted. "Cruz, do it! Let him go!"

Finally, Cruz loosened his grip, and Jake fell on the gravel driveway. "I'm going after her," Cruz said.

Jennifer headed for their car. "I'm coming with you."

Jake watched from the ground as they got into their car and screeched out after Issie.

Chapter Twenty-Four

• • •

Issie hadn't gone five miles when she saw the headlights behind her. The car was moving up too close, right on her bumper, and she did what she always did to make it back off. She tapped her brakes and slowed, hoping the car would either pass her or slow down, but it stayed locked on her bumper. Someone was pursuing her, she realized.

Fear rushed through her and she slammed her foot down on the accelerator and jolted forward, but the car was right with her, not allowing her to get away. She made the next turn onto a street just as desolate as the one she'd been on, and looked for a public place where she could pull over and cry for help.

She reached for her cell phone, tried to dial the number for the police station, but it fell out of her hand and onto the floor. She bent down to grope for it, but couldn't feel it. She looked in the rearview mirror and saw that the car was coming up beside her. It was a red Camry, but she couldn't see who was inside.

A gunshot exploded the window next to her head, whistled past her ear, and shattered her windshield. She swerved and felt her wheels leave the road and sink into the dirt. Her car tilted, and the wheels skidded into the grass. Her headlights flashed a sequence of bushes and branches, tall grass and wildflower. Then a telephone pole loomed in front of her. She screamed and tried to avoid it, but her hands seemed frozen on the steering wheel, and her foot on the brake pedal made no difference in the skid. Metal crashed and glass shattered as she hit and fell forward, jamming her knee into something and crushing her sternum into the wheel. Her seat belt cut a diagonal line across her from shoulder to hip.

She sat there, dazed for a moment as her mind slowly cleared. She saw the car make a U-turn and start back for her. She reached clumsily into her glove compartment, felt for her gun. Her fingers closed over the metal.

♦ ♦ ♦

Cruz made a U-turn and stood on the accelerator. "The gun," he shouted. "Give me the gun!"

Jennifer thrust it at him.

He slowed as he reached Issie's smoking car and rolled down his window. He aimed his pistol and fired. The bullet went through her shattered window and burst through the passenger side.

He slid into a U-turn again, and thrust the gun at Jennifer. "She's on your side. Don't miss."

He slowed, allowing Jennifer the chance to aim.

But before she pulled the trigger, a bullet whistled past his head. He cursed. "She's got a gun!"

Another bullet shot through their back windows, and he punched the accelerator again.

"Get out of here!" Jennifer cried.

"No, we have to go back. We can't leave her alive!"

"But she's shooting at us!"

"Not for long! Give me the gun!"

She handed it to him and ducked as they skidded past the wrecked car again. Issie fired before Cruz could aim the gun.

Jennifer jerked, and blood hit the dashboard. Cruz almost ran off the road. "Jen!" he yelled. "Jen!"

Another bullet whizzed past, and Cruz dropped the gun and reached for his sister.

She looked up at him, her forehead covered with blood. "Get out of here, Cruz! Please don't go back!"

He didn't need any more incentive than that to make him speed away from the scene.

Chapter Twenty-Five

• • •

Issie clutched the gun in a tight-knuckled fist, trembling as she waited for the car to come back. Her heart pummeled out a deadly rhythm.

She only had two bullets left, and she knew they had no intention of leaving her there alive. Keeping her eyes on the road, she groped for her cell phone on the floor and finally found it.

Then quickly, she stumbled out of the car, slamming the door behind her. Pain shot through her chest, and her knee threatened not to support her.

She limped down the grassy embankment and into the trees skirting the road.

She prayed that the phone would pick up a signal. Quickly she dialed 911.

Simone, the dispatcher, came on. "Nine-one-one. May I help you?"

"Simone, this is Issie," she said, breathless. "I'm on Meadow Road out in that wooded area. Car's wrecked. They've been shooting at me . . ."

"Who has?"

"Cruz somebody. Send police, Simone. They'll come back." She knew she wasn't making sense. "Please hurry!"

"Issie, are you hurt? Do you need an ambulance?"

"No. Just . . . please . . . It was a red Camry and they're still in the area."

"We'll get somebody right out," Simone said. "What's your cell phone number?"

Issie spouted it off, then clicked the phone off and dropped down behind a tree. There was no sound of a car coming and she wondered if they were just waiting, trying to make her sweat, giving her a chance to get good and scared before they came back around again. She kept the pistol up, waiting to use it.

She had never felt more tragically alone. There wasn't anyone in the world she could lean on, except perhaps her brother, and Jake's part in this confused things. Overcome with despair, she began to cry. She pulled her good knee up to her chest and dropped her face on it. There was no loneliness like that of sitting in a black night by yourself, knowing that any minute wheels could screech and bullets could fly. And there wasn't really anyone who cared.

Her car sat just yards away, still smoking from the accident that wasn't an accident. She might die before the police came. With only two bullets left, she might not be able to defend herself. The need for human contact overwhelmed her, and her mind drifted back to the fire earlier tonight, when she'd wrestled with the dead boy to make him live, and Nick Foster had held her and whispered in her ear. *It's okay. It's okay. It's okay.*

She dialed information, got Nick Foster's phone number. It was one-thirty in the morning, and she knew she would wake him.

He answered on the third ring. "Hello?" It came out too loud, as if he'd been startled awake.

"Nick, this is Issie."

"Issie." He sounded surprised.

"I'm so scared!"

"What is it?"

"Nick, somebody just tried to kill me," she said in a wobbling, high-pitched voice, "and they ran me off the road and I hit a telephone pole. I'm sitting on Meadow Road waiting for the police to get here, but I'm afraid they're going to come back and —"

"Issie, where on Meadow Road are you?"

She heard a siren in the distance. "About halfway down the wooded block."

"I'll be right there," he said. "Will I be able to see your car from the street?"

"Yes," she said, "but I'm not in it. I got out and I'm sitting off the road. Hiding in the trees. I only have two bullets left, and I know they're coming back."

"I'll be there in five minutes," he said.

She clicked the phone off and wondered what was taking the police so long. She wondered if anyone was chasing down the car, and if her nephew had been in it. She wished she could jog back to the Benton house and see who was still there. She wondered if she had shot anyone.

For the second time that day, she found herself praying.

◆ ◆ ◆

Cruz took the back roads on the outskirts of Newpointe and cut down a dirt road near his grandfather's deer camp. When he knew he was hidden, he stopped the car and groped for his flashlight.

"Jen, let me see."

"I'm okay." Blood rolled down her face and into her eyes. She smeared it away.

"That's it. I'm taking you to the hospital!" He put the car in reverse and tried to turn around.

"No, wait. I don't think I was shot. I think it's glass."

He stopped the car again and shone the flashlight more carefully on her face. "It is. It's not a bullet, Jen. It's glass from the window." He shoved his fingers through her hair to hold the back of her head still, and picked a fragment out of her forehead. "Man, the blood . . ." He pulled his shirt off, wadded it up, and pressed it against her wound. "You still may need to go. I'll take you, Jen, if you need a doctor."

"No," she said. "We've got to hide. She'll send the police after us. Just drive. I'll be fine."

He drove down the dirt road, then over the old swinging bridge near the place where he and Jen grew up. He threaded down the road until it came out near his grandfather's house.

"We'll go home," he said. "Mama can patch you up and make you good as new."

"I'm gonna scar up like a freak," she said.

"At least you're alive. That could just as

well have been a bullet as glass. I never shoulda let you come with me."

"We're in this together, Cruz. I hate being left out. You know I do." She pulled down the visor mirror and shone the flashlight on her forehead. "The bleeding's stopped. Maybe the cut's not so bad. Maybe I won't have a Frankenstein scar. Should we tell Mama about the killin's and all?"

"Maybe," he said. "Only don't tell her it was revenge against that preacher. Let her think we were takin' up the cause."

"Ethnic cleansing, we'll tell her," Jen said. "She'll be proud of us. Mama always did get into the fight. It made her feel all patriotic."

"I'm not through with that preacher yet. Won't be through till he's as dead as them other two. And Jake's aunt with him."

"We've got to do somethin' about the car, Cruz. She'll describe it. And the shot-out window won't help matters any."

"I'll drop you home, then I'll take care of the car. Remember that old stable on the edge of Grandpa's land? I'll hide it there till we can get the window fixed and change the color."

Jen actually smiled, filling him with relief. "I knew you'd have a plan, Cruz. You always take care of everything."

Chapter Twenty-Six

● ● ●

Issie didn't emerge from her hiding place until two squad cars had stopped and R.J. Albright and Anthony Martin had stepped into the circle of light created by the street lamp. Then, on shaky legs, she'd limped back up to her car.

She had finished filling them in about her chase and the gunfire, when Nick screeched up to the curb. She didn't know why the sight of him drew her to tears again.

He was still limping and moving carefully, and those bandages on his legs reminded her how serious his own injuries had been. She felt guilty for getting him out tonight.

"Issie, are you all right?"

"Yes," she said. "Nick, I may have shot somebody . . . I'm not sure . . . but they were shooting at me . . ."

His arms came around her and pulled her against him, and she pressed her wet face against his chest. His hand cupped and stroked the back of her head. "Anybody looking for the car?" he asked over her head.

"We put an APB out, but no one's found it yet," Anthony said.

"They will," Nick assured against her ear. "They'll find them."

"I want to get out of here," she said. "Please, can Nick take me to the police station? I want to talk to Stan. I have . . . information . . ." The words filled her with terror, as if a spray of bullets would come from nowhere to shut her up. "Before I lose my nerve, I have to stop them. That's why they were trying to stop me."

"You can give *us* that information," R.J. said. "Right here, right now."

"No. Not right out in the open. Please. I want to talk to Stan. It's about the church fires and the killings. I know who did it, R.J. Stan will want to talk to me."

"We'll have to wait for backup," Anthony said. "There's some strange things happenin' in this town, and if you don't mind my sayin' so, I don't want to be caught in the middle of 'em."

"Both of you stay, and I'll take her in," Nick said.

R.J. shrugged. "Reckon that'd be okay, since you're practically one of us. I'll notify Stan you're comin' so he can meet you there."

Nick released her, and she felt that cloak of security jerked away. He ushered her to his car, helped her buckle in, then went to his side.

"Nick, I appreciate you coming," she said. "I don't even know why I called you. Of all people, you're injured yourself and don't need to be rescuing damsels in distress."

"I like rescuing damsels," he said. "I'm glad you called."

She looked out the window, her eyes searching the streets for a red Camry that might come from nowhere and start shooting again.

"Issie, what's going on? What do you know?"

"I know who did the church burnings and committed the two murders. I think it was my nephew's friends."

"You've got to be kidding."

"No. It's exactly who you thought. That Cruz kid and his sister. Last night, right after your church burned down, I went to this house where they hang out, and I found them burning a carpet with bloodstains in a bonfire."

Nick gaped at her. "Why didn't you say anything then?"

"I didn't want to implicate Jake. But then my tires were slashed, and I tried to convince myself there wasn't a connection. I got home and there was a dead cat in my bed, and somebody had been in my apartment and written on my wall. And tonight Jake called and had me stitch up a kid who'd been stabbed."

"Stabbed?"

"Yes, and I warned Jake I had to go to the police, so next thing I know I'm being chased and shot at and run off the road."

"Issie, you really think he could have been involved?"

"I know his friends were," she said. "He's with them all the time. I can't see how it could have happened without his knowledge. My brother's going to have a heart attack when he finds out. My sister-in-law's heart will break. She just doesn't deserve it."

"But you can't cover for him if he's guilty."

He reached the police station and pulled up to the front curb. "No, I can't," she said.

"But, Nick, when I tell what I know, my life is going to be worth about as much as Ben's was to them. They won't stop until I'm dead."

He stared at her across the darkness. "You're a brave woman, Issie."

"I'm not brave," she said. "I've just run out of choices."

He sat there for a moment, his eyes locked into hers, as if his mind worked on the puzzle of Issie though some of the pieces were missing. After a moment, he opened his door. "Well, let's do it."

He came around and opened her door, then put his arm around her shoulders as he walked her up. She wondered why he made her feel so protected. Was it his size, or just his character? She decided it was his character, since she knew so many strong, tall men who gave her more to be insecure about. She remembered earlier today when he had pulled her back against his broken ribs and held her as she'd wept over losing the boy. It was a feeling so different from that of men's lustful arms around her, hands groping instead of stroking, grabbing instead of calming.

He opened the door for her and they

stepped inside. The lights in the squad room made her feel safer, and she looked around and saw the buzz of activity. She didn't see Stan, but she knew that R.J. had called him at home and asked him to meet her there. At least she was marginally safe here. Surely those kids weren't stupid enough to come firing into a police station, no matter how desperate they were. Again, she wondered what kind of damage her bullets had done. What if she had killed one of them? What if Jake had been in the car?

Her knee hurt and her chest ached. She would probably have a bruise in the shape of her steering wheel, and no doubt her neck would ache tomorrow. But at least she was alive.

She looked up at Nick and realized he was probably in much more pain than she was. It was selfish of her to keep him here. "I appreciate you getting me here, Nick. You can probably go on home now. I know you're not feeling very well."

"No. I'm staying," he said. "You called me, and you're stuck with me."

"But you really don't have to. I can take it from here. I mean, if I'm safe anywhere, it's in the middle of a police station."

"I just want to stay here," he said, ending the discussion. "If it's all right with you, I'll just stay."

She nodded, thankful that he didn't want to leave. Truth was, she was petrified, and even sitting here, she worried that her killer might return. Nick's calming presence was what kept her from cowering through the station. She wondered if this was what it felt like to have a father — someone who counted it his responsibility to walk ahead of her through the land mines. No, she thought. These feelings toward Nick had little to do with father hunger, but there were things about him that fed that, anyway. Until now, she'd spent her life trying to rewrite the ending to her father-story, with men just like him — detached, lustful, selfish, unavailable. Her heart had expected every love to fulfill itself better than her father's love had. But it always came out the same.

Now she wondered if her heart had been as clueless as her mind.

Don't look at it too hard or it'll go away, she told herself. *Good feelings never stay.* So she thought, instead, about the land mines dotting her personal landscape as she bolted across it.

Chapter Twenty-Seven

● ● ●

It was almost four A.M. when Stan and Sid went to make arrests. Issie stayed behind at the conference table in the interrogation room, staring down at her hands splayed out in front of her. Directly across from her, Nick watched the emotions pass across her face.

"You okay?"

She cleared her throat. "No."

He set one of his hands on top of hers and tried to get her to look up at him. "What is it?"

"I . . . I'm wondering if I should warn my brother . . . you know . . . that Jake might be arrested."

"I don't think you should," Nick said. "He might tell Jake, and Jake might tip off the others . . ."

"You're right," she cut in, trying to blink back tears. "I know you are. It's just . . . he's only sixteen, you know . . . He's been brought in before . . . disturbing the peace, drunk and disorderly conduct . . . I bailed him out. I don't think I can bail him out this time."

"Issie, they would have killed you tonight. He's *with* them."

"But . . . what if he's just gotten in over his head? That slimeball apparently stabbed his friend. What if he's afraid he'll be next?"

"It doesn't matter why he's doing it, Issie. If he's involved — or even if he knew about it — he's accountable. He has to pay."

"But you're supposed to be all about forgiveness, aren't you?" she asked, looking up at him. "Loving the sinner but hating the sin."

He had to look deep inside himself to find the answer she needed. It was in there somewhere, way down, covered over by anger toward the people who had killed Ben Ford. "You're talking about two different things, Issie. God's forgiveness, and the world's consequences."

Tears filled her eyes, and she stared down at her hands again. "What do you mean?"

He swallowed. "Paul the apostle killed Christians. He told himself he did it in the name of God. But it didn't matter why he did it. He killed people. He murdered them. Later, when he realized how wrong he'd been, when he repented, when God forgave him . . . those Christians were still dead."

"But . . . I thought Paul was one of the good guys."

"He was. He was one of the greatest Christians who ever lived. He wrote most of the New Testament. He was responsible for spreading the gospel throughout the world. But those Christians he killed . . . he could never undo it. God forgave him completely. He even forgot. But their families were still missing loved ones. They couldn't forget."

"Then what good is forgiveness? How does it help anybody?"

"It takes away the guilt."

"But if they still have to pay . . ."

"The world still makes you pay for your crimes," he said. "God doesn't."

"Even when you die?" she asked. "He doesn't punish people who've been involved in murder? They get off scot-free?"

"In heaven, God still requires payment for your sins . . . all of them, great and small. That payment is death. But he provided someone to make that payment. Someone to take your execution, just as surely as if he'd walked onto death row, unlocked the door, and taken your place. But no one can sit through your execution unless you let them. He doesn't force you to take the pardon."

He could see from her eyes that she was turning it all over in her mind. He wondered if she was processing it for Jake, or for herself.

"What if you don't deserve a pardon?" she asked.

"That goes without saying," he said. "Nobody deserves it. But the offer still stands."

The door opened, and LaTonya Mason stepped in. "Sorry, folks. I need to use this room."

Issie nodded and got to her feet. "We're leaving."

Nick wanted to turn around and beg LaTonya for ten more minutes. Issie was close. So close. But still so far from embracing the truth.

She came around the table and took Nick's arm. She was still shaking. "Come on. Let's go."

He followed her out into the noisy squad room, with telephones ringing and printers buzzing. Perpetrators and complainants cursed and yelled.

He watched that hard look flood back over her face, as if the reality of a fallen world had wakened her from a deep sleep. "Thanks for staying with me, Nick." She looked down at his bandaged legs. "I know you can't be comfortable. I forgot all about your injuries, I was so wrapped up in my own problems."

"Well, go easy on yourself," he said. "They're pretty tough problems."

She sighed and shook her head help-lessly. "I don't know where I'm going to go," she said. "I can't stay at home, and my brother's is kind of out of the question. Maybe I need to get a hotel."

"No, you'd be too nervous in a hotel by yourself. You wouldn't sleep a wink. Look, there are a number of places you could stay. I could call several different families in my church. Usually I call Ray and Susan first, but under the circumstances I don't think they're up to taking any guests tonight."

"No, I hate feeling like an intruder. I don't want to stay in someone's house, especially if I don't know them that well."

He drew in a deep breath and tried to think. "I have an extra bedroom, but it wouldn't be appropriate for you to stay there with me."

She gave him a smirk. "Can't you just see it now? The tongues would be wagging for years. Issie Mattreaux and the preacher. Wouldn't that be a hoot?"

He didn't find it amusing. In fact, the thought had already occurred to him too many times. *Issie Mattreaux and the preacher.* No, she couldn't stay at his place. He frowned as an idea came to him. "You know, there is somebody who would probably be glad to put you up, and you know her really well."

"Who?" she asked.

"Aunt Aggie. She's got plenty of room, and she likes you."

"Yeah, I could stay with her. Do you think she'd take me?"

"Let me call her and we'll see."

As he took one of the spare desks with a telephone, he propped his legs up, wishing he'd brought his painkillers. But the pain was worth it to walk Issie through this process. She needed someone, and the fact that she'd chosen him filled him with an inexplicable pride.

Nick let the phone ring several times, for it

always took Aunt Aggie a little longer to get all the way down the stairs to the one phone she kept in her foyer. He didn't know why no one had ever been able to talk her into putting a phone upstairs, but the old woman had her ways, and no one was about to change them now.

She finally picked up the phone. *"Hola."*

"Aunt Aggie, it's Nick. I know I woke you up. I'm sorry to call so late . . . or, so early."

"Hey, Nick," she said. "How them burns are?"

"They're okay, Aunt Aggie. Did you hear about the latest church burning?"

"Yep," she said, "and I hope you see that it ain't just your church burnin' down. It got nothin' to do with you so you can quit that down-in-the-mouth stuff and jus' get on back to preachin'."

"I plan to, Aunt Aggie," he said, "but we've got a problem. I need your help. Issie Mattreaux just named some people that she thinks might have something to do with the murders and the church burnings, and we think she's in a little trouble. She was shot at on the way to the police station, and she's afraid to go home. The police are making arrests right now, but if they don't round everybody up . . ." He hesitated, trying to get to the point. "Aunt Aggie, she needs a place to stay, and I wondered if you'd take her in."

"That girl can stay with me anytime," she said. "Only I ain't too crazy 'bout havin' bullet bait in my house."

"Bullet bait?" he asked.

"Yeah. If people out shootin' at her, I don't want her here, me."

"But, Aunt Aggie, she doesn't have any place else to go."

"Well, she can brought herself here, all right," Aunt Aggie said, "but I ain't got a man to protect us. I'll take her if you come too."

He frowned. "Me? I have a house, Aunt Aggie."

She didn't seem to find any relevance in that. "I'll put you downstairs in the guest room. Anybody comes in this house, they go by you first."

He sat back, thinking it through. Aunt Aggie had never been the frightened type, so her fears now didn't ring true. "Aunt Aggie, is this a trick? Are you just trying to get me in your house so you can hover over me?"

"You want me to take that girl in, or not?"

He grinned and met Issie's eyes. "Aunt Aggie, you're a sneaky little thing, aren't you?"

"You call it sneaky, I call it smart, me. If I got bullet bait in my house, then I gon' have a man to protect me. And if I have to cook and do for you to return the favor, then you'll jes' have to let me, you."

"All right, Aunt Aggie. You win."

"I'll take good care o' you, *sha*," she said with delight. "You ain't been pampered in a long time, you, so y'all come on over, we'll pass a good time."

He hung up the phone and sat there a moment, wondering how he'd been snookered into that.

Issie approached him. "What did she say?"

"She said you're very welcome to come." He looked up at her, wishing she wasn't quite so pretty . . . wishing he wasn't quite so happy about staying in Aunt Aggie's house with her. "There's just one little catch," he said.

"A catch? What catch?"

"She wants me to come too."

"What do you mean? To spend the night?"

"Yeah," he said. "She said that she

doesn't feel very safe without a man there and she'd like for me to come."

"Well, if you don't mind my saying so, she's probably right. I'm not the safest person to be putting up right now. But that doesn't mean that you have to take a bullet for me."

"I'm not going to take a bullet," he said. "Nobody's even going to know where you are. I'll just take you by your apartment and we'll go in and get your stuff, get whatever you need for tonight, and then we'll go by my house and I'll get my stuff. I'll just forward my calls to Aunt Aggie's. Oh, and I've got to try and change these bandages. I put it off all day, dreading it, but I guess I can't put it off any longer."

She looked down at his legs. "I'll be happy to do it."

He couldn't stand the thought. He wanted her to think of him as strong, invincible. Not wounded and disgusting. "No, that's okay. It's not very pleasant."

"Hey, I do unpleasant things all the time. I can do a lot better job than you can, Nick. When we get to Aunt Aggie's I'll change your bandages and apply the medication, and make sure everything looks all right."

The thought of doing it himself was almost more repulsive than the thought of getting her to, but he couldn't decide between the worse of two evils as they drove to her apartment to get her things.

Chapter Twenty-Eight

• • •

Cruz and Jennifer's mother let a string of curses fly when she saw Jennifer's face. At that, their grandfather had wakened and shuffled into the kitchen, his big paunch protruding like that of a pregnant woman.

"What are you two tied up in?" Sidney Clairmont demanded.

"It's them church burnings, ain't it?" Hattie Cruz spouted as she doused Jennifer's forehead with hydrogen peroxide. "Reminded me of the old days."

"Except for the bodies!" Clairmont boomed. "Whatsa matter with you two? You don't kill somebody first thing! You leave a warning, then you burn a cross. You make sure they know the KKK acted, but they can't narrow down who done it."

"We ain't like you, Granddaddy," Cruz said. "We ain't the KKK. We have different ways."

"Use the ways that work, fool!" he bellowed. "That way you don't get shot at and chased and put in jail before you have a chance to make a difference."

"They know how to do it," Hattie said. "Daddy, they was raised with this. They been follerin' you since they was knee-high to a grasshopper."

Cruz went to the refrigerator and got a beer out. "I hear the police been snooping around here."

His mother made a derisive noise. "Come wanting to talk to you, but I ain't seen you in days."

"We found a house we could use till we get the compound done," Cruz said. "When it's done, I want you two to come live there with us. We're gon' have massive security to keep the Feds out, and you can help us recruit older soldiers who have money. We need a cash flow, and the younger ones ain't got much."

"I ain't movin' nowhere," Sidney said. "I'm fine right here."

"But they'll come after you to get to us. I can't promise your protection if you ain't with us. When we get moved in, we'll have a supply of food for a year, an arsenal of weapons, and won't nobody be able to touch us. Just think about it. Think of all we can accomplish with the resources our recruits bring with 'em."

Hattie put a big Band-Aid on Jennifer's forehead and winked at her son. "I'll work on him," she said. "Time it's ready, we'll be set to go. Now ya'll ain't going back to the group tonight, are you? You gotta hide. They'll be back lookin' for you again."

"We'll need to hide the car for sure," Jennifer said. "They'll be lookin' for it. We put it out in the shed near Granddaddy's deer camp. You think it'll be all right?"

"Yeah," Sidney grunted. "And you two better stay at the camp. It's empty right now. They won't look there."

Cruz liked the idea. "Thanks, Granddaddy. I knew you could help."

By the time they got their things and set up at the deer camp, they were ready for a few hours of sleep.

Chapter Twenty-Nine

● ● ●

Aunt Aggie's house was one of the biggest and oldest in Newpointe, and was situated on one of the last undisturbed stretches of land in the center of town. The center point of her acreage dipped down into a valley that flooded when it rained, but her house sat half on a hill overlooking her well-tended garden in front, and half on pilings in back that protected her from rising waters. The driveway swung down and around to the back of the house, and she parked her huge, fifteen-year-old Cadillac underneath. Nick parked next to her car in the garage, and he and Issie carried their things up the steps and into her massive kitchen that smelled of cayenne pepper.

"Come right in, you," she said. "Issie, you look wore out, *sha.*"

The old woman was wearing a hot pink satin robe and fresh red lipstick on her thin, wrinkled lips. "T-Nick, you takin' care of her?"

"Yes, ma'am, Aunt Aggie."

"We sure appreciate you taking us in, Aunt Aggie," Issie said. "I don't know where I would have gone if you hadn't. I've never been so scared in my life."

"Jes' let 'em try gettin' you here," Aunt Aggie warned. "Nick'll show 'em, won't you, *sha*?"

"They won't come here," he said. "My guess is they're hiding from the cops as we speak."

"So d'yeat?" she asked, going to a pot on the stove and taking off the lid. The smell of jambalaya wafted across the room. He wondered if she just kept a pot on 24/7, or if she had thrown this together at the last minute.

"I'm not really hungry," Issie said, and Nick shot her a sharp look. She cleared her throat. "But it smells so good . . . I'll have some, anyway."

"Gettin' too skinny, *sha*. You ain't one o' them anorexics heavin' in the toilets, is you?"

"No, ma'am, Aunt Aggie. I wouldn't do that."

She spooned out the jambalaya and handed Issie a bowl, then started dipping Nick's. "I ever tell you I was Miss Louisiana in 1938? We needed curves then, not the bones and angles like today. Ma Dugas, he liked ma shape. Never did have nothing for them skeleton types. But I does try to keep ma figure. Ain't no excuse for letting yourself go. Who trying to kill you, Issie?"

Nick grinned at the sudden shift in thoughts as he took his bowl and sat down.

"I think it's the same people who killed Ben Ford," Issie said.

"Like t'get my hands on 'em," Aunt Aggie said. "Yellow-livered murderers."

She ranted and raved for a while longer before she began to wane. Finally, she retired to her bedroom, and Nick found that he felt awkward being here alone with Issie. He wondered what his church members would think if they learned he was spending the night in this house with Aunt Aggie and Issie Mattreaux. Was it really much better than putting Issie up in his own home? But he couldn't worry about that now. Issie's life was in danger until the police rounded up all those who were responsible for the church burnings and the murders.

He carried Issie's things up to her room, then came back down and found her standing in the dark, peering out the window.

"They don't know you're here, Issie. It's gonna be okay." He came up beside her and closed the blinds, then turned a Tiffany lamp on. The darkness fled.

Issie took Nick's hand, making his heart jolt. "Okay, let's have a look at those burns," she said.

He shook his head. "It's okay, really. Now that I think about it, I can do it. It's really not that hard."

"Then why have you been putting it off all day?" she asked. "You know, you really should have done it this morning."

"They're feeling fine. I just —"

"You *have* to change the bandages," she said. She pulled him toward a chair and got too close, setting a hand on his shoulder and giving a little shove. She was such a flirt, and she was so good at it. He sat down.

"Come on." Her voice was gentle as she lifted his feet onto an overstuffed ottoman. "Let's put your feet up on this and I'll see what I can do. Where's your stuff?"

He nodded toward the guest room. "It's in there on the bed. In the little black bag."

"I'll get it." She took off toward the bed-room, and he closed his eyes and leaned his head back and prayed a silent prayer that he would keep this in perspective. He wasn't used to being alone with women or having one address his needs. Oh, occasionally someone would bring him a meal or come clean up his house when he was particularly busy, but usually it was one of the married members of his church. He had a few single women who had targeted him for husband material, but they weren't women in whom he was interested. And Aunt Aggie's ministrations didn't count.

Issie Mattreaux was someone he had spent too much time thinking about. He wondered if she was aware of just how attracted he was to her . . .

. . . And just how much he didn't want to be.

She came back, her black hair shimmering in the lamplight, and he wondered if she took any special care of it or if it came easy to her. He didn't think he knew any other women whose hair looked quite that silky. It was midnight-colored satin, and he told himself that it probably didn't feel as soft as it looked. In fact, it was probably coarse to the touch, and probably smelled like sauerkraut or old gym shoes . . .

Yeah, right.

She brought the bandages and the Silvadene cream that he was to put on the burns. He tried not to wince as she peeled the bandages off. Instead, he chuckled, amused that he would be concerned about impressing her with his toughness.

"What's so funny?" she asked as she worked.

"It's not funny," he said. "I was just thinking how big and strong I'm supposed to be — since I'm ostensibly protecting you and all — and here you are, making me coil up like a toddler about to get a shot."

She grinned. "Am I being rough with you?"

"No, it's okay." He chuckled again. He watched her work on his legs and she did it quickly, competently, and he realized that she was very good at what she did. The pain was making him sweat, and he tried to get his mind to shift gears.

"What would you have been if you hadn't been a paramedic?" he asked her.

"Oh, I don't know. I'd probably be in jail."

He hadn't expected that, and he laughed. "Jail? Come on."

She grinned. "I'm half serious," she said.

"I really only decided to be a paramedic for the money. It looked pretty good, and there's a lot of time off. A lot of time on too, though."

"Give me a break. You love what you do."

"Sometimes," she said as her grin faded again. "But days like today . . . I think I'd opt for jail."

He wished her eyes were easier to forget. "Tell me you didn't have any feelings of wanting to help people, wanting to rescue them."

"I think I kind of liked the idea of the adrenaline pumping through my veins. You know what I mean?"

He nodded. "Yeah, I know. But I saw you today. You weren't trying to save that kid's life for the money or the adrenaline rush. You really cared about him."

She seemed to concentrate harder on the burns.

He winced. "And besides that, the money isn't that great," he said. "You could have been a nurse or a doctor and made a lot more money."

"Yeah, can't you just see me as a doctor?" she asked. "I couldn't care for patients long-term. I don't do anything long-term. I'm not like you, Nick."

"What do you mean, you're not like me?"

She kept her eyes on his burns. "I'm not the commitment type."

"And I am? You haven't ever seen me commit to a woman, have you?"

"Well, you've committed to a lot of other things. Your church, the people you're friends with. People rely on you. I, on the other hand, am not one that anyone relies on."

"Hey, if I was in a fix and needed rescuing, you'd be the one I'd call."

She gave a weak smile. "Thanks, Nick. I appreciate that, and obviously the feeling is mutual since that's exactly what I did tonight."

His face sobered, and suddenly he felt very vulnerable. It wasn't a bad feeling. "Why *did* you call me, Issie?" he asked quietly. "Me, of all people?"

She sat back then and looked a little embarrassed. "I don't know. I really don't."

She wouldn't meet his eyes. She just kept looking at his legs as she worked, and he forgot the pain and watched the pink color climb in her cheeks. He'd never seen her blush before. She wasn't the type. He wondered if it had anything to do with today when he had pulled her back against him and held her. It had been instinctive, something he probably shouldn't have done. He was a preacher, after all, and had to maintain a certain amount of decorum. But she had been so distraught . . .

He couldn't forget how small she had felt in his arms.

She finished bandaging his legs, then stood up. "Almost good as new," she said.

"I appreciate that. You just don't know how much." He carefully lowered his feet to the floor, then set his hands on his knees.

He was nervous, he realized, and that was so silly. He was almost always nervous around Issie. He didn't know why. Sometimes it felt as if she was playing with him. Other times he felt a fierce, overwhelming sense of protection toward her. He didn't know why he would think that God might appoint him protector over her. Surely, there were plenty of other men who wouldn't mind guarding her, men who were more her type.

She got up and sat facing him on the ottoman, her knees just inches from his. She had something on her mind, he sensed, something she didn't want to say from across the room. He expected coy flirtation, but instead, her face was serious as she looked into his eyes.

"Nick, can I ask you something?"

"Sure," he said. "What?"

She looked down at her hands, and he saw that she was fidgeting. Her voice was quiet, as though she didn't want Aunt Aggie to somehow overhear. "Sometimes . . . I look at my life . . . and it's not exactly the way I thought it would be. And I see my family . . ." She swallowed. "My father's an alcoholic . . . not that I would know it first-hand, since he's never been around. Before my mother died, she worked in a bar in Slidell and had very little interest in anything I did. She had . . . weird priorities, you know? Always did. And then I see my brother and Lois standing back at arm's length while Jake gets involved in such a mess. I start to wonder . . . what things might have been like if we were different."

He knew that she was leading up to an important question, one for which he needed an answer, and he silently prayed that God would give him the wisdom to answer it in the right way. It was tempting, sometimes, to tell someone what they wanted to hear, just to make them feel better. But Issie's life might depend on the truth. Her eternal life, anyway.

"Different how?" he prompted.

"Different, you know. Religious maybe. I mean, sometimes I look around at the people who go to church, people like you and Mark and Allie . . . Dan and Jill . . . Susan and Ray . . . and I think how together they all seem to have things. Sometimes I just look at them and think it's harder for them, you know? Like when Mark and Allie were having problems. Other people might have just gone for divorce, moved on, taken the easy way . . . but it was harder for them because they had this standard to live by. In some ways I felt sorry for them because of that. Angry even. But that's another story."

Nick couldn't meet her eyes on that one. He knew that she had been in love with Mark and wanted to see that marriage break up. The fact that it didn't happen had probably surprised her.

"But then I look at them now and I see how happy they are, and they've got the baby. They're a real family. And Dan and Jill. You know all that time when Dan was single,

I used to watch the women line up for him. And frankly, I would have gone out with him in a second if he'd asked. He just never did, and I think I know why."

Nick met her eyes again.

"I wasn't his type," she said. "I was a little too loose and free. And, of course, most men like that, but Dan was of a different ilk."

Nick grinned. "You can say that again."

"But he was," Issie said. "He had that standard, that different set of rules he lived by."

"They're not rules," Nick said. "Really, Issie, they're not."

"Well, the Ten Commandments are rules."

"Issie, the only reason Christians live by a different standard is because they trust that God wants what's best. God gave those commandments for their good, not so they couldn't have any fun. He knows how sin hurts people. It really does, Issie. Look at what's happening to Jake. Look at the murders. Look at the church burnings."

She nodded. "Look at my life."

She was coming around, he thought as his heart rate sped up, like it always did when someone started to see and understand the truth. He wondered if Jesus had gotten that racing heartbeat when someone finally got it. He took her hands, as if to hold her there and keep her from backing away. "The cycle doesn't have to go on," he said. "You could stop it right now."

She was quiet for a long time, staring at a button on his shirt. "I don't know, Nick. I'm not the type to start living by rules. And besides that, I can't imagine a God who would care a thing about me. Some stupid medic who drinks and parties too hard . . . who has a past like I have."

"He does care, Issie. You have to believe that."

"Well, I wish I could believe it. I really do. It serves the people who believe it. Kind of a placebo effect, maybe. If they think it, then it makes things better for them. Maybe it's all psychological anyway. Maybe I just need to get my mind thinking right."

"Mark and Allie's marriage wasn't healed because of any psychology," Nick said. "It was because God worked on their hearts and changed them. Trust me, Issie. If there was a woman alive who could have lured Mark from Allie, it would have been you."

Her eyes rounded in surprise, and he realized the spiritual talk had given him solid

footing and made him forget his awkward-
ness.

"Funny coming from you," she said.

They were too close, and he never should
have taken her hands. He needed to get up,
put some distance between them. But he
couldn't seem to do it. He kept his eyes
boldly locked with hers. "I have the same
impulses you have, Issie."

Her eyes were the softest brown, almost
hazel, and he felt he could see through
them right into her heart. The air between
them was charged with electricity, and he
feared he would feel the shocking pop,
telling him that the voltage was too high.

"I never would have figured," she said.
Now he heard the expected flirtation in her
tone.

"Yes, you would," he whispered.

It was clear by the grin in her eyes that
she relished the power she had over him.
"So you're telling me that even preachers
have temptations?"

"They absolutely do," he whispered. He
swallowed hard, trying to get his bearings.
"But the Bible tells us there's no temptation
too great that God won't give us the means

of escape. And I've found that to be true every single time."

The pleasure seemed to fade from her eyes, and he sensed her disappointment. "Haven't you ever wondered what it would be like if you didn't escape it?" she asked. "Just once? If you gave in to something that you wanted to do?"

He wanted to say yes, that he was struggling with that now, that it would have been so easy to let her have that power over him as she sat knee to knee, holding his hands, grinning into his eyes. It would have been so easy to just lose himself in that moment, to taste of Issie Mattreaux and learn what he was missing.

But then there would be tomorrow, and the emptiness would set in, and when it did . . . where could he run for comfort? How could he turn to the Savior he had betrayed? She would never understand.

"I *want* to please God," he said. "That's my first priority."

She sighed, as if disappointed. "I don't even know why I like you," she told him. "There are a million other people I could have called tonight. I could have called Joe's Place and just asked for somebody and ten people would have come to the phone wanting to help me. Ten medics, like me, sitting there unwinding together. We have a bond, you know. We're close. I could have called them."

Nick smiled. "But you didn't call them," he said. "You called me. Isn't that interesting?"

"So what are you saying? That that's a God thing?"

"I think maybe."

She lifted her chin high and leaned closer. Her eyes sparkled. "Maybe it was a chemistry thing," she said defiantly. "Maybe I called you because I'm attracted to you, God-only-knows-why."

He felt the blood rushing to his face and pulled his hands away. Had she just admitted she was attracted to him? Issie Mattreaux, to the preacher? He didn't know where to go with that.

"Maybe God's telling us that you and I are supposed to be an item," she went on, chiding him. "How would you feel about that, Nick, with all your rules?"

His mouth suddenly felt dry. "I don't know, Issie. I don't think that's what happened."

"Of course it's not," she said, "because a pious person like you could never get involved with a wretch like me, is that right?"

She was too close to him now, looking up into his face, daring him to back away. He smelled the scent of her hair. It was nothing like sauerkraut or gym shoes. Strawberries, maybe. He liked strawberries.

She turned her face up to his, her lips too close to his. "I'm not good enough for you, am I, Nick?"

He looked down at her, feeling her breath against his own lips, and wondered what it would be like to kiss her just once. He wanted to feel that sprinting of his heart and that sweet relief and urgent desire warring inside him. He wanted to tell her that he thought about her more than any other woman he knew, that her image was constantly on his mind.

But escape lingered there in the back of his mind. He could take a step backward, break this spell she seemed to have over him. He could close off the vision he had of holding her and kissing her, and focus back on the Christ who would not have orchestrated their coming together for the purposes of becoming a couple, not when they were so unequally yoked. Christ would want someone for him who could share his passion for the kingdom. Christ would have chosen someone who shared his passion for the Lord. A woman who had the same goals and purpose that he had, someone who understood the grace of the Cross, someone whose heart was broken over it.

Issie was not that woman.

He took that step back. "I'm going to bed, Issie."

"Did I scare you, Nick?" she asked, almost angrily.

"No," he said. "Let's just say I'm taking that escape." And before she could dare him further, he went into the guest room and closed the door.

Chapter Thirty

● ● ●

Jake woke to the sound of moaning. He opened his eyes and squinted at the light pouring in through the window. He had come home after Cruz had run out after Issie last night, and had brought Benton with him. The rest of the kids in the house had scattered, for fear that the latest killing, and Cruz's actions if and when he caught Issie, might bring police. Jake's parents were in bed when he got home, and now, at nine A.M., he hoped they were both at work.

He had called Issie's house at least twice an hour all night long, and she had never answered. His stomach burned. What had Cruz done to her?

There had been no news. His parents hadn't gotten a phone call in the middle of the night, and Issie hadn't shown up here in desperate flight.

So what did that mean? Had they gotten

to her, shut her up? Or had she gotten to the police first?

He sat up in his bed and admitted to himself that his association with Cruz and his group wasn't working out to his advantage. Playing drums for their band was definitely a perk, and the idea of living in a commune without school or parents, growing their own food, and following a charismatic spiritual leader like Cruz had been cool enough . . . but he hadn't counted on murder and seeing his friends and family abused.

He heard the moan again, and squinted up to see Benton writhing on the twin bed across from him, his leg exposed where Issie had cut open his jeans last night. The dental floss stitches she'd made were crude and looked like something out of a Frankenstein movie. He wondered if the muscle beneath would heal without deeper sutures, or if Benton would have a limp for the rest of his life.

He got up and went to Benton, reached out to shake him, and felt that his skin was burning. "Benton?" he said. "Wake up, buddy. You're burning up with fever."

Benton's eyes barely slit open. "I'm f-f-f-reeezing."

"Chills," he said, grabbing a blanket to put over him. "Man, we need to get you to a hospital. You may need surgery or something."

"Cruz said no."

"I don't care what Cruz said," Jake threw back. "He's not the one with the gash up his leg."

"Don't even know what I d-d-did."

"Something about Jennifer. He sees red when anybody touches her. Goes ballistic, man. Like a total personality change. Jekyll and Hyde."

"She didn't do nothin' wrong, Jake. You're just mad 'cause she was with me instead of you."

"We need to get you to the doctor, and while we're there, we need to have our heads examined for hanging out with people like Cruz and Jennifer in the first place."

"You better sh-sh-shut up," Benton said. "He might kill you if he hears you talking like that."

"He's not even here. We're at my house." He bent over and touched the swollen place around Benton's stitches. "Come on, man. We've got to get you to a hospital before Cruz comes looking for us."

"B-b-but what'll we tell 'em?"

"We'll think of something on the way there. Now, come on."

Benton tried to sit up but was too weak. Jake bent down and helped him. "Man, you lost a lot of blood last night. No wonder you're weak. Wouldn't hurt to get you some food too, and something cold to drink. You're hot as fire. Here, lean on me and try to get to your feet."

He managed to get Benton up on one leg, and they limped out the door. With each step on his hurt leg, Benton moaned and winced. Jake looked down at his leg and saw that the stitches were pulling as the wound swelled, and the cut was beginning to bleed again.

"Here, just stop. Don't put any more weight on it, man. Just stand here against the house, and I'll back the car around. Can you do that, man?"

Benton seemed to be dizzy, but he managed to nod.

Jake ran to get the car, drove up in the yard, turned around, and put it in reverse. He backed up to just a foot or two from Benton, then got out and helped him into the passenger seat.

As Jake got back into his car, he realized that if Benton hadn't been so scared of Cruz, he would have gotten him to the hospital before now. At least he could have taken him home, where his parents could care for him . . . if they felt like it. But Benton's dad sometimes got a little crazy himself, and Jake wouldn't put it past him to beat Benton for coming home wounded, as if he'd miraculously heal if his dad gave him enough other injuries to concentrate on.

"What are we gonna tell 'em?" Benton slurred as he leaned his head back against the seat. "We can't squeal on Cruz."

"I know, I've been thinking about that," Jake said. "Let's tell them that we were out last night, and we got really drunk at the Viper Pit, and you fell on a broken bottle and it cut your leg."

Benton thought that over for a moment. "Does a glass cut look like a knife wound?"

Jake wasn't sure. "You got a better idea?"

"No."

"Okay, then."

"What about the stitches? Do we tell them about Issie?"

"No, man. We can't get her in trouble. We tell them that I did the stitches. That we got paranoid about coming in 'cause we were so drunk . . ."

"Yeah, okay." Benton closed his eyes, thinking it over.

Jake tried to measure for flaws in the story, and decided it was okay.

Benton began to laugh. He threw his wrist over his eyes and shook his head. Jake glanced over at him, grinning. "What's so funny?"

"They'll probably lock us up to protect us from ourselves," he said. "Man, we're gonna look stupid."

"I don't care how stupid we look," Jake said. "Just so they take care of you."

Silence filled the car as they both ran the scenario through their minds. "It makes me sick . . . Cruz doing me like that," Benton said. "I didn't do nothin' to him. I trusted him, looked up to him. Look what I did for him!"

"He turned on us, man. He's not the person he wants us to think. Cruz's dangerous. He doesn't tell us anything, but he expects us to jump in with both feet, no questions asked. Well, I don't work that way."

"We've both been workin' that way lately," Benton said. "I worked that way last night. That kid we killed . . . He reminded me of my kid brother . . ." He got quiet for a moment, his eyes closed and his head leaned back on the neck rest. "Man, you think I might go to prison?"

"Of course not," Jake said. But as he navigated his way to the Slidell hospital, he realized that prison was a secondary problem. First they had to keep Benton from losing his leg.

Chapter Thirty-One

● ● ●

Dan and Jill Nichols sat in the waiting room in Mayor Patricia Castor's office. They knew she wasn't busy. They had heard her through the wall talking on the phone to her daughter about what to get her grandchild for Christmas, but she always liked to keep people waiting for meetings, just so they would know who was in control. The only time she was prompt was during election years. Then she made a career out of being courteous and polite.

This was not an election year.

Jill checked her watch and gave a disgruntled sigh. "You know, I've got a lot of work to do. I probably ought to just let you handle this and get on back to the office."

"No, wait." Dan slapped down the bodybuilding magazine he'd been scanning and got up. "I've had enough. I'm going in."

The mayor's secretary looked alarmed. "You can't do that, Dan."

"Watch me." He went to the mayor's door and threw it open. "Pat, I'm sick of waiting. Now if you can get off the phone and quit talking about Christmas presents and grandkids, maybe we can get down to some of the town's business."

Pat Castor looked up at him, disgusted. "Where is my secretary? Why didn't she keep you —"

"I'm here, Mayor," the woman said, scurrying to the doorway. "I'm so sorry. I tried to keep him from comin' in, but —"

"Come on, Pat," Dan said, motioning for Jill to follow him as he bolted in. "It's not her fault. I sat there patiently listening to you talk about Beanie Babies and Play Stations until I was sick of it. Jill needs to get back to the office, so can we please get on with this?"

The mayor looked indignant, but she made her apologies to her daughter and got off the phone. "What do you want, Dan?"

It occurred to him that they hadn't gotten off to a very good start. This didn't bode well for the favor he had come to ask her. "I want to talk to you about our church."

She shifted in her seat and crossed her arms. As far as anyone could tell, Pat Castor didn't go to church, though she claimed affiliation with the Methodists on every campaign flier she had printed up. If she attended a Methodist church, they could only assume it was one out of town, since no one at Newpointe's Methodist church had ever seen her there. "Yes, that church burnin' was such a tragedy," she said. "And poor Ray. I've been meanin' to get a card out to him, expressin' my condolences."

Dan started to say that a card should make up for everything, but Jill anticipated the sarcasm and pinched his leg. "Pat, we appreciate your time," she said, though Pat hadn't given it willingly. "We're really upset about our church and the fact that it's completely devastated and there's no place for us to worship."

"It was a tough break," Pat said, "and I'm trying to get to the bottom of it. I won't have people in my town going around burning down institutions. Next thing you know, they'll be burning down the courthouse and the police station and my office, so's you're not safe anywhere. I'm thinking about getting a bodyguard. You just never know what you might run into."

Jill nodded sympathetically. Again, Dan

bit his tongue to keep from expressing amazement that she'd managed to twist the conversation back to herself.

"Mayor, we wanted to ask you a favor," Jill said. "We want to ask if you would allow us to use the courtroom to have our services on Sunday."

The mayor just stared at her for a moment, then laid her head back and let out a laugh.

Now it was Jill's turn to be angry. "Would you please tell me why this is so funny?" she demanded.

"Because I can't believe you'd ask me that. You, a lawyer and everything. You know I can't let you have church services in the courtroom. Whatever happened to separation of church and state?"

Dan pinched Jill's knee, figuring that either of them had grounds for going across the desk and throttling the woman. "The separation of church and state," Jill said in her best legal voice, "had to do with preventing our states from telling us how, when, and where we had to worship. It had nothing to do with congregations using municipal buildings paid for with taxpayers' money to hold their services. In fact, they did it all the time in the early days of our country. Our founding fathers even worshiped in them."

"Well, if I let you," Pat said, "I'd have to let the Muslims and the Hindus and the Buddhists."

Dan shot her an are-you-crazy look. "First of all, there aren't any of those in Newpointe to my knowledge, and if there were, they'd have their own places to worship. Ours, on the other hand, was burned to the ground the day before yesterday. Every one of us is a taxpayer. We're asking to use this facility for a public assembly. We have the right to worship."

"But you don't have the right to worship in my courthouse," the mayor said. "Sorry, folks. I just can't let you do it."

Dan gave further consideration to lunging across the desk. "Pat, what is your problem? You've let us have meetings here for everything from planning the policeman's ball to organizing a fund-raiser for the public schools. You've even let Aunt Aggie cart food in here when people were meeting. It's one of the few rooms big enough for our whole congregation to fill."

"There've got to be others," she said. "Try

the hotel. It probably has a conference room."

"A conference room is not big enough, Pat. We have two hundred members. Besides, we don't have a lot of money, and the hotels want us to pay for those rooms."

"So the city is supposed to give you a handout?"

"Not a handout," Jill said. "A place to meet. That's all."

Dan stood straighter as an idea came to him. "Pat, do you realize how many of your voters go to our church?"

That got her attention. Her eyebrows came up as she considered that fact. "Since I won by a landslide, I guess you're right. My constituency is everywhere."

"But if word gets out that you wouldn't let us meet here, how do you think they'll vote next time?"

"It'll blow over by then." She preened, patting the back of her short hair. "They have short memories. Anyway, they'll probably understand because they all know about the separation of church and state."

Jill stood up and went into attorney mode. "You mean, they're all *deceived* about the separation of church and state.

As you are. You know, it really chaps me that our own elected officials don't know the Constitution any better than that."

"Well," the mayor huffed. "Insult me all you want, if that's the way your church operates . . ." She got to her feet, dismissing them. "I appreciate you stoppin' by," she said. "Wish I could help. I hope I can still count on your vote in the next election."

"My vote?" Jill asked. "I was actually thinking of running against you."

Her face hardened instantly. "Run against me? You?"

"Why not?" Dan asked. "She's younger and smarter and has more character. Better looking too. I think she could win it hands down."

They both knew they were bluffing, but Pat's reaction was amusing. Her face was turning red, and her lips were compressed as she looked at them. "Well, you just do that," she said in her saccharine drawl. "May the best woman win."

Dan and Jill left, still fuming, and headed to the school superintendent's office to see if they could use the high school auditorium. When they saw the man's reaction, Dan wondered if Pat Castor had already warned the superintendent.

He told them that he had enough trouble getting federal aid without turning the school into a church. One move like that and he'd be on a street corner trying to raise funds to pay teachers.

Then they tried the theater in town, but the owner told them that the first scheduled movies on Sunday were for eleven o'clock. If he allowed them to have church there, he wouldn't be able to start the movies on time.

Feeling defeated, they left there and went to the fire station to tell Mark and some of the others that they had struck out. Aunt Aggie was there serving lunch to the men.

The old Cajun woman was almost ninety years old, yet she still insisted on cooking for her boys every day. The habit had started decades ago when her own husband had been a firefighter and she'd been known as the best cook in town. Aggie, rich from her investments, had pitied her husband for having to eat their cooking, and had started bringing meals from home for him. When there was enough of an uproar from men asking to share what she'd brought her husband, she had started bringing her groceries to the station and cooking it all up there. She had been doing it ever since. It was one of the joys of her life, and theirs too. They'd had to start a strenuous workout program for the firefighters, to offset the extra calories they took in while on duty. Today they were having Cajun popcorn, which was really fried crawfish claws, and homemade seasoned French fries for lunch.

As Dan and Jill walked in, Aunt Aggie motioned for them to hurry. "Did ya eat yet, *sha*?"

"Not yet, Aunt Aggie," Jill said.

"Then sit yourself down. Hurry up. I gotta get this on the table while it's still hot, me."

"That's okay, Aunt Aggie," Dan said. "I'm off duty. We're not eating."

"I don't care if you off duty. You here, ain't you?" She pulled out a chair and ordered them to sit down. They both took their seats obediently as the firemen filed in.

"Well, what you two doin' here on your day off, Dan?"

Dan shrugged. "I was just coming by to tell Mark that I didn't have any luck with finding a place to worship. Pat Castor won't let us use the courthouse, and Dennis Fournier won't let us use the high school. The theater manager refused too. I can't think of any other places, but I thought maybe somebody here could."

"How 'bout my house?" Aunt Aggie asked. Mark was just coming to the table, and he looked up at her.

"Your house, Aunt Aggie? Your house is big, but it's not big enough for two hundred worshipers."

"I meant outside," she said. "We can get folding chairs and sit out in the yard. I got plenty of land and plenty of shade, *sha*, and it ain't too cold yet."

Jill and Dan looked at each other. "You know, that's an idea. We hadn't thought of meeting outside."

Aunt Aggie was a new Christian and was still a little green about the things of Christ, but she knew how to solve a problem. "I'll cook and we can have food and —"

"No, Aunt Aggie," Jill cut in. "You don't have to cook. If we use your property, that'll be enough. We'll be so grateful."

Mark's eyes were widening as he looked at Dan. "I think that's the answer. We can have services Sunday morning, can't we, Aunt Aggie?"

"*Mais oui,* you bet we can. I'll get Bradford over to the rental place to brought us the chairs. You boys can help set 'em up. We'll have us a church 'fore we even know it, right there under God. He'll be smilin' down at us."

Mark was getting excited. "And the neighbors around will hear us singing and praising the Lord. It might turn out to be a good witness. Maybe our numbers will even grow."

"I like it," Jill said. "I like it a lot. Aunt Aggie, are you sure?"

"I'm sure, *sha,*" she said, "and I'll be insulted if you don't do it, me. I ain't never had much to give that church 'cept money, and that don't mean nothing now that the building's flat on the ground. If I can help keep the church goin', then that's what I'll do, me."

Chapter Thirty-Two

● ● ●

Sunlight shone through Nick's window as he lay in his own bed, staring at the ceiling. Issie had gone to work today, so he had gone home to catch up on some things. He hadn't slept well in Aunt Aggie's guest room, so he tried to rest now. He'd had several visitors today, all with food, but hadn't had an appetite. He had finally felt so exhausted that he'd put a note on the front door that he was sleeping, and had gone to bed. The soreness had settled in, but the pain was not as great as the depression cloaking itself over his soul. Issie's lure last night, along with the state of his church, had driven his spirits to ground level.

He heard tires on his gravel driveway and pulled up enough to look out the window. Dan Nichols was getting out of the car. He hadn't seen the note yet. Nick dropped back down on the bed. Should he go to the door? he wondered. Dan, after all, was more than part of his flock. He was one of his closest friends.

He got up and limped to the front door and opened it just as Dan started to turn to leave. "I'm up," he said wearily. "Come on in, Dan."

Dan came in and closed the door behind him as Nick went to his recliner and slowly lowered himself into it. "You don't look so good," he said. "You need to be in bed."

Nick almost laughed, but he didn't find it very funny.

Dan sat down on the couch across from Nick. "You looked pretty rough at the station yesterday, but you look worse now. Are you all right?"

"I'm okay," Nick said.

Dan cocked his head. "Come on, Nick. You can be straight with me. You look like you're in pain."

"I'm fine," he said, irritated. "My side is kind of sore, and the burns aren't feeling so great. Throat hurts. But my real problem is that I stayed at Aunt Aggie's last night and didn't sleep well." He chose not to mention that Issie had been there too.

"So Aunt Aggie's been taking care of you?"

"Some," he said.

"Good," he said.

"So what brings you by?"

"I thought you could use some good news."

"Good news," Nick said, as if that was a concept he hadn't thought of in a while. "Yeah, hit me with some good news."

"We have a place for you to preach on Sunday."

He moaned. "Dan, I'm not up to preaching."

"Then we'll get a guest preacher, or one of us'll do it. We were a church before we had that building, Nick. We're still a church. Remember, we used to have worship right here in this trailer when there were only ten or twelve of us that came."

Nick looked around and remembered all the places they had found to cram chairs. It had worked for a while until they'd been able to put up a makeshift structure on the church property, then raised enough money to build the permanent one. It was all wasted, he supposed.

"So where do you plan on having this service?" Nick asked.

"In Aunt Aggie's yard. We're renting

chairs from Buzz Brady, and we'll sit out there and worship in the breeze under the sun, and people up and down the streets are going to hear us and want to join in."

Nick breathed a laugh. "Sounds a little optimistic."

"It's called faith, Nick. You remember that."

Nick received the barb as it was intended, and swallowed hard.

"You sure you don't want to preach?" Dan asked. "I know you're hoarse and your throat hurts, but I can't help thinking that getting back in the saddle will do you more good than harm."

Nick thought it over for a moment. He was jealous of his pulpit, and never liked to have anyone take his place. Maybe he'd feel differently by then. "I don't know," he said. "Maybe I could come up with something."

Dan leaned forward and put his elbows on his knees. "Look, Nick, I know you're depressed. I know you're upset and feeling defeated, but we need you, man. You're our leader, and we need for you to lead us. A lot of the congregation doesn't know what to do. They're all distraught. But sometimes this kind of thing makes us stronger, you know? You're the one who taught us that."

Nick let the words sink in. Maybe Dan was right. Maybe God had allowed this tragedy for a reason. They'd been praying for a revival, but he had not expected God to bring it with a fire and a murder. He hadn't expected it to come with so much pain.

He blinked back the mist in his eyes. "Dan, I want to do the right thing. I want to do what God wants me to do. I'm just not sure that preaching is it anymore."

"Why was your call last week so much different than it is this week?"

"Maybe it's not," Nick said. "Maybe I was never called in the first place. Maybe I was just kidding myself."

"How do you grow a congregation from a dozen people to two hundred and not really be called? Nick, I can't believe you're questioning this when it's so clear in my mind."

Nick's eyes softened as he fixed his gaze on Dan.

"Nick, I don't even think you realize what an opportunity we've been given. Something really special might happen because of this fire. And even the murder. You know what they say about the Christian's blood being seed. At the funeral, I just know that Ray and Susan are going to want the gospel presented in some way. They're not going to let Ben die without his death bearing some kind of fruit."

"I wouldn't know," he said. "I don't even know the guy who's preaching it. I don't know what he believes. And the last I heard from Susan, she's not on speaking terms with God."

Dan sighed. "She's upset and lashing out, but she'll come through it. Are you going to the funeral?"

"Probably. It'll be weird not preaching it. There's so much I'd like to say about Ben. He was a good kid." He rubbed his face roughly. "Aw, Dan, I think God's talking to me. Telling me it's time to pass the baton. But I just keep thinking about all the people I never reached. There are still so many I've been praying for. Issie Mattreaux, and some of the other paramedics. Some of the guys at the station. My father . . . He never even heard me preach . . . It's so hard to believe that the ministry is over, just like that."

"It's not over," Dan said. "Nick, you've got to believe that. It's not. God still has a purpose and a plan for you, and for our whole congregation. And our church burning down is not going to take that away."

But somehow the fire . . . and Issie Mattreaux . . . had blurred Nick's vision. Nothing was clear anymore.

Chapter Thirty-Three

● ● ●

Jake hadn't expected to be at the hospital so long. The emergency team started Benton on an IV of antibiotics and cleaned and stitched up his leg. It had taken hours for the bag to empty so that they would release him.

Benton had crutches by the time they left, but was so weak that he could hardly walk on them. As he got into the car, he held up a hand for Jake to high-five. "We did it, man. Pulled the wool over their eyes."

Jake wasn't so sure. They had asked a lot of questions and caught them lying about their names. When they'd finally demanded identification before they would treat them, they'd realized they were both minors. They had called Benton's dad, and the man had taken his time getting there. He'd been steeped in hang-over pain, and refusing to believe their story, had cussed Benton out for tangling with anyone who had a knife. When he hadn't been needed anymore, he had taken off, leaving Benton to ride home with Jake.

If Jake knew Benton's old man, he was probably planning to stop off at the nearest bar.

Jake was worn out by the time they got back in the car. "That's it," he said, starting the car. "I'm sick of Cruz. Look what he did to you, man."

"I'm okay," Benton said. "He didn't mean nothin'. We were all drunk."

"Well, he could have killed you. I'm going back to get my drums, that's all. I'm quitting."

"Man, you can't quit. It's my grand-mother's house they're practically living in! I'm stuck. You're the one got me into this. I don't want to hang with them if you're not."

"Then throw them out."

"Oh, right," Benton said. "I'll just hobble up on my crutches and threaten them. They'll be runnin' scared, all right. Are you crazy? Besides, what I did to that kid last night makes me part of them whether I like it or not."

Jake knew he was right. "He's not gonna be happy that we went to the hospital. But at least maybe he'll be afraid to do anything to us. The thought that anyone knows anything might stop him. We can say that we didn't tell them anything, but that we're afraid they're on to us now, that they need to find another place to meet just to be safe. Then, after they move all their stuff out, we can just phase out."

"It won't be that easy, man. What if they use me for a scapegoat and tell the cops what I did?"

Jake knew he had a point. He tried to turn it all over in his mind as he drove. "All right, then. Let's just face this head on. We'll go back to the house and tell Cruz we went to the hospital. We won't say anything about them being onto us, because you're right, they'll get even. We'll just hang on for as long as we can until we make sure he doesn't trash the house. And I need to find out about Issie. I'm worried about her, man. I tried calling her all night."

"She's dead," Benton said. "No way Cruz let her get away."

Jake slammed his hand on the steering wheel. "Don't say that! She *can't* be dead. She can take care of herself. She's tough, man. We would have heard if he got her."

"Then why wasn't she home all night?"

Jake shook his head. "I don't know."

"If they didn't kill her already, they will."

"Shut up, okay?" Jake said. "Just shut up!" He rounded the curve leading to Benton's grandmother's street, and caught his breath. Police cars lined both sides of the street.

"They're onto us," he said. "They found the house." Still far enough away that he might not draw attention, he made a U-turn and headed back the other way. "Man, I can't believe this. They're going through the house. Maybe they arrested Cruz and the others."

Benton started to sweat. "You think they know about me? What I helped do to that kid?"

"I don't know. But your old man probably woulda said something, if they'd been looking for you. Don't you think?"

"We can't be sure." He twisted in his seat and tried to see if anyone was following them. "I can't go home," he said. "I can't let them arrest me, Jake. They'll try me as an adult, and I'll never make it in prison. Man, I can't go down for *murder.* What was I thinking? Why did I let her talk me into that? I killed a guy to impress Jennifer, and now I'm going to prison . . ."

Benton was getting on Jake's nerves.

"Where can we go? We can't just drive around all day."

"The compound," Benton said. "If they weren't arrested, that's where they'll be."

He thought of Cruz's grandfather's deer camp, which they were converting into a secure compound where they could all live. It was far from ready. The water had been cut off, and there was no air conditioning or electricity. He couldn't imagine them staying there. But he didn't have any other ideas.

"I can still get out of town," Benton said. "I can just run."

"With what? You don't have any money. You're sixteen. What will you live on?"

"I can do odd jobs on the road."

"Get real, man. You're gonna take off by yourself, with that leg?"

Benton wiped his face, then slammed his hand on the dashboard. "You think Cruz can keep us safe? Hidden? You think we can trust him?"

"*No*, we can't trust him. Are you crazy? He cut you with a switchblade, Benton!"

"But he was just overreacting. Most of the time he's a great guy. And if all that stuff Jennifer says about him is true, about coming into his kingdom . . ."

"Give me a break! I'm trying to find him for one reason, and that's to find out where Issie is, and what's going on with the cops. He is not some messiah, and I'm not going to follow him!"

"But he's the only one who can save us," Benton was rambling. "He's the only one who knows and understands the cause and has our best interests at heart and . . ."

Jake was beginning to sweat, too, even though his air conditioner blew out as hard as it would. He wished Benton would shut up. He turned down the dirt road leading to the deer camp, and navigated his way through the trees and over a shaky bridge, until he came to the rotting old structure that Cruz was going to turn into Fort Knox.

He saw two pickup trucks backed up to the door. Cruz, Jennifer, Redmon, and Graham were carrying chairs and mattresses out to the truck beds.

"There he is, that jerk!" Jake slammed the car into park.

"What are you gonna do?" Benton asked. "You're not gonna get out waving your fists and cussing them out, are you? Because you ain't speaking for me."

"Fine," Jake said. "Then speak for yourself." He got out of the car and slammed the door. Cruz and Graham dropped the mattress into the truck bed and turned to look at him. "Where's my aunt?" he demanded. "What did you do to her?"

Jennifer came around the truck. "You mean, what did *she* do to us?" she asked. "She shot at us, Jake. She's crazy. She almost killed me." She pulled her hair back and showed the bandage on her forehead.

"Then she's alive?" he asked.

"Of course she's alive," Cruz said, in a maddeningly calm voice. "What did you think I'd do? Kill her?" He smiled that charismatic smile he had that disarmed people so quickly, but he didn't disarm Jake.

Jake wasn't sure he believed him. "Yeah, actually," he said. "Call me crazy, but when you chased out after her waving your shotgun, I couldn't help thinking that."

"Well, I didn't, okay? But she turned the cops onto us and they're looking for us. So now we have to set up a hiding place. We've got a place. They'll never look for us there, but we needed the mattresses and chairs that are in this place."

"They're swarming all over Benton's grandmother's house," Jake said.

"I know," Cruz said. "They've been hounding our mother, but we hid out last night in an old hiding place my granddaddy and his Klansmen used to use."

Benton got out of the car and balanced on one leg. Afraid he was going to step on his bad leg and burst the stitches, Jake angrily opened the door of his car and jerked the crutches out of the backseat. He thrust them at Benton, daring Cruz to ask about them.

Benton looked at them as if Jake had somehow betrayed him.

"Where'd you get those?" Cruz asked.

Benton gave Jake a sick, frightened look.

Jake was ready. "Man, this morning Benton woke me up moaning, and he was practically delirious. He had a fever so high I thought he was gonna croak on us. Leg was swollen up like a tree trunk."

Cruz looked suspiciously at Benton's leg. "So what did you do?"

"Took him to the hospital in Slidell. Don't worry, we didn't tell them how it happened. We made up a story."

"They bought it?" Cruz asked.

"Yeah, man," Benton said, wobbling weakly. "Not like it's a gunshot wound or nothin'."

Cruz's face softened, and he looked down at Benton's leg. "Man, I am so sorry. I owe you big time. You're a hero, man, for what you did last night. Now that Jenn has explained your part in things, I can't believe what I did to you."

Benton shot Jake a surprised look, then brought his bloodshot eyes back to Cruz. "Man, it's no big deal."

"No big deal?" Jake spouted. "Benton, this guy *stabbed* you!"

Benton looked torn in two. "He didn't mean it, Jake. I'm gonna be okay."

Cruz's jaw popped as he brought his dull glare up to Jake. "I'm sensing a lack of commitment from you, Mattreaux. You ain't thinking about turning on us like your aunt, are you? Because you should know that they're looking for you, too. They're trying to round all of us up today. You're as guilty as any of us."

"Hey, I didn't kill anybody."

"But you were part of the group that did. Now, we have a new hiding place if you want to stick with us. We have a new plan for getting ourselves out of all this, and you, too. If you decide to stay with us, no hard feelings."

"And if I don't?"

Jennifer came closer, her eyes as hard as Cruz's. "Don't bolt, Jake. It wouldn't be wise."

"Is that a threat?"

"You could say that," she said. "Yeah, that's just what it is."

"So why do you want me with you?" he asked, knowing that they didn't care if he lived or died, as long as he didn't talk.

"Maybe we want to keep an eye on our potential turncoats," Cruz said. "Or maybe we think you've got the kind of backbone we need. Maybe we're ready to bring you in."

"Bring me in where?"

"To the inner circle. No more secrets from either of you guys."

Jake thought of that inner circle — Cruz, Jennifer, Graham, and Redmon. They were the very ones who had committed the first murder. Now that Benton had killed, too, were they going to honor him with this? "Benton killed an innocent black kid last night to please Jennifer," he said. "He's already *in* your pathetic 'inner circle.' "

"Everybody has to pay their dues," Cruz said.

"So what are the dues?" Jake asked. "How many bodies?"

Jake's tone made Cruz angrier. "Either you're committed to our cause, Mattreaux, or you're not. Make up your mind."

Jake squinted. "So what *is* the cause again? I forget, since the first one was about getting that preacher, and the second one was about throwing the cops off."

Cruz's lips grew taut over his teeth. "I don't like your tone, man."

Jennifer sashayed closer to Jake in that way she had, and slid her arm around his shoulders. "It's a holy war, Jake. Superiority of our race. God's fight. *Rahowa.*"

Jake stepped out of her reach. "It's not 'superior' to kill a thirteen-year-old kid who didn't do anything wrong. And what kind of statement did Ben Ford's death make? I mean, if you want it to change something, what did it change? Are you expecting the blacks to line up in a convoy and leave town? All that guy did wrong was go get something to eat late at night. You waylaid him in the parking lot, beat him to a pulp, put a bullet through his brain, and left him to burn in his own church. For what? Man, you *know* you just wanted to get at that preacher."

Cruz was getting angrier now, and he

came over to Jake and put his face intimidatingly close to his. Jake's cheeks mottled with heat, but he didn't step back. "You know what your problem is, Mattreaux? You're not a visionary. You're a follower. Leave the planning to me, and you just do as I say. I'm the one who sees the whole picture. I'm the one with the plan."

"Okay, fine," Jake said through his teeth, finally backing away. When adequate distance was between them, he asked, "So . . . just explain to me how Ben Ford's death helped the cause."

"There's one fewer mud person walking around. The world is automatically a better place."

Jake wanted to throw up. But why, he wasn't sure. He wasn't a brotherly love kind of guy, and it wasn't his style to champion a principle. Was he truly concerned about Ben Ford, or about the lies being told to keep them all committed? Or was it fear of prison, or bitterness about what they had done to Benton? Maybe it was all of it together. "I guess I'm just wondering why you picked Ben Ford, and not some drug addict or pimp or loser who beats his wife and kids? Why Ben Ford, who was educated, worked, minded his own business?"

"Because he was there," Cruz said. "And he was black. Those were the only two reasons I needed."

"So how many more are you going to kill?"

"However many I need to."

They all grew quiet, and Jake realized all eyes were on him. They were assessing him to see if he was worthy to be called one of them. He told himself he was not. "Well . . . I didn't come into this group to commit capital murder and wind up on death row. I came to play drums. That's all."

"The band is just the cover, man," Cruz said. "It's the advertisement for our cause. The means of recruitment. But it's not who we are. There's a lot more to us than that." He pulled out his knife, switched it open, and ran his finger along the dirty blade. "This is serious business, and we don't take it lightly. Life or death. You get to choose. You can be for us, Mattreaux, or you can be against us. Life or death."

Jake just stared at him for a moment.

Cruz slapped the flat of the blade against his palm. "Choose, Mattreaux."

Jake looked up at Benton and saw the fear in his eyes. Jake swallowed but didn't answer.

"I'm with you, man," Benton said quietly. "And Jake is, too. He's just emotional because of his aunt and all."

Cruz didn't take his eyes from Jake. Jake knew he was in too deep to get out now.

"Are you with us or not?" Cruz asked again.

He sighed and looked at the loaded truck bed. Maybe if he just went along, it would all be over soon. Maybe he could figure out a way to thwart their next plan and make sure that they left Issie alone. They weren't likely to let him walk away.

"I guess I'm with you," he said, and the words made his stomach burn.

"Fine. Then help us get the rest of the mattresses out of here."

Jake swallowed and ambled back into the house. He saw the filthy mattresses lying on the floor and lifted one. As he loaded it into the truck, he wondered if he was kidding himself about stopping them, or if there was really a chance that he'd escape *both* death and prison.

Chapter Thirty-Four

● ● ●

The funeral service for Ben Ford was held in the Methodist church on Gaston Boulevard.

Nick limped into the building, nodding to those around him who acknowledged him. Pushing through the quiet crowd in the foyer, he offered a nod to his church members milling in the foyer and headed around to the side of the building where he knew the family would be. He found them in the fellowship hall sitting quietly with family and close friends.

He saw Ray and Susan in a corner with Vanessa, who leaned dismally against the wall. Susan's eyes were puffy and red, and it was clear that she had been crying most of the night. He wondered if she had slept at all since Ben's body had been discovered. Vanessa, too, looked as subdued as he'd ever seen her. The teenage girl had on too much makeup, as if it would cover the sorrow and sleeplessness on her face.

Ray just looked angry. He stood there with his hands in his pockets, a taut look on his deeply lined face. Slowly, Nick approached them.

Susan got up and greeted him with a hug. He held her tight, wishing he had words to snuff out her pain. When he'd let her go, he reached for Ray's hand. "You okay, Ray?"

Ray nodded without speaking.

What now? Nick wondered. "Lot of people out there," he said. "Ben was loved."

"Why did he do it?" Susan asked, her eyes boring into Nick's as if to nail him with the question. "Why did God take him?"

He searched his mind for wisdom, but found none. "We may never know this side of heaven."

Susan scrunched up both fists and looked at the ceiling. "I'm so mad!" she said. "It ain't fair!"

She put her hand over her mouth and headed for the bathroom in the corner of the room. Nick turned to Ray. "You're not blaming God too, are you, Ray?"

Ray shrugged. "I blame the hateful no-good slugs who did this, Nick. And like I told you and Stan, if I get the chance, I'll kill 'em myself."

Ray's words knocked the wind out of Nick, and he didn't know how to respond. He searched his store of Scripture verses and experience but found nothing to help. What was wrong with him?

A group of relatives came between them, and Nick went to the sanctuary and took a seat in the back of the room.

Several quiet moments passed, during which he struggled with the tears threatening to pull him under. He hoped no one would sit next to him, that he would be left alone. If he was forced to say anything to anyone, he would lose it for sure. His heart felt battered and bruised, as if it had been damaged along with his ribs and shins.

He saw someone pause at the end of his pew, and he looked over. Issie Mattreaux stood there, wearing a black skirt just above the knees, black stockings, and a black sweater that was a tad too tight. He started to look away, but she slipped into the pew and came to sit next to him.

"Hey, Nick," she whispered. "Do you care if I sit with you?"

He swallowed and shook his head.

She kept looking at him, and he knew she was taking in the tears in his eyes and the emotional struggle on his face. "Hey, are you okay?"

He nodded.

"You just look . . . a little shaken up."

"I'm fine."

She kept looking at him, and he fixed his eyes on the coffin at the front of the room, covered with flowers that Allie had probably made at the Busy Bee Florist. That was what he'd failed to do, he thought. He hadn't sent flowers. There should be a spray at the front with his name on it. He should have expressed his love that way.

But then he realized that it wouldn't have changed anything. What was wrong with him? Did he think a few flowers on a stand would assuage a mother's grief?

"How are your burns?" Issie whispered.

He shrugged. "Fine."

"You're still mad at me, aren't you?"

"Mad? I wasn't mad, Issie."

She looked down at her hands. "I'm sorry for acting that way last night."

He ran back over the frustrating thoughts that had kept him awake all night. "It's okay," he said. "I don't hold grudges."

He glanced at her and wished she didn't look so nice. It was hard to remember why he had rejected her last night, when her hair shimmered in that way it had, and she was by far the best-looking woman in the room. No, he had no business being a preacher.

The organ started to play, and latecomers hurried to take their seats. He watched as the family processed in, Ray and Susan and Vanessa clutching each other for support. The unemotional funeral director pointed the family to where he wanted them to sit. Nick watched the tears, the hugs, and the leaning and comforting and grieving. His own eyes filled with tears again, and he closed them to hold it in. But he wasn't successful.

Issie put her hand in his, and he found himself closing his fingers around hers. It was some comfort, even while it made him feel guilty. He needed the contact. He needed someone to be there for him, someone who wasn't someone else's wife treating him like a brother. He needed to feel, for this one moment, as if he had someone of his own.

He opened his eyes and looked over at Issie. She had tears on her face, as well. He marveled at how soft she looked with tears in her eyes, so unlike the tough paramedic who wrestled grown men when it was required. She wiped her face with her free hand and breathed in a broken sob.

Like him, she was probably second-guessing her actions when they'd found Ben too. She was probably remembering Ray's anguished cries as he realized his son was dead. She was probably thinking about the second kid she hadn't been able to save.

The desire to comfort her eclipsed his own private pain. He let go of her hand and put his arm around her, pulled her against him. She buried her face against his shoulder, and he held her tight as he felt her shaking with grief. The fact that she didn't pull away, didn't seem repulsed by his comfort, melted him even more.

There was something strangely soothing about holding Issie. Her hair smelled of some perfume he'd never known before, and he knew it would haunt him at night when he tried to forget. It was soft against his face, silky, and he stroked it with his fingertips. He couldn't stand to see her cry.

The service began as Susan's uncle took the pulpit, and Nick slowly let Issie go. She pulled back, took in a deep, cleansing breath, and wiped her face with both hands. He knew better than to touch her again.

They listened as the man spoke of Ben's love for Christ, and the things he would have wanted them to know about salvation and heaven, and where Ben was today. Nick found himself praying that Issie would hear. And as he did, he questioned his motives again. Was he praying it for himself, because of the fierce attraction he felt toward her? Did he think a conversion on her part would make it possible for him to think seriously about her? Or did he honestly care about her soul?

Both, he admitted to himself. He wanted both.

The funeral went on as some of Ben's friends from high school and LSU stood up to give eulogies, and others sang. He watched Ray and Susan sobbing at the front, and wondered why people thought funerals provided comfort. In this case, he thought Susan wasn't going to make it through. It was just too hard. Some things required too much.

◆ ◆ ◆

Issie rode with Nick to the little cemetery where Susan's parents lay.

When the service was over, and the family had gone to the black limousines, he and Issie headed back to his car.

They didn't speak until they were in the parking lot. "Tough day," Issie said finally.

He squinted into the breeze. "Yeah. Not my favorite way to spend it."

She turned and looked up at him. "Would you mind giving me a ride to Aunt Aggie's? I don't have a car . . ."

"Of course," he said. "How did you get to the church?"

"Steve Winder dropped me off. I could get somebody else to give me a lift if you'd rather not be alone with me."

He smiled softly and opened the car door for her. "Get in," he said. He closed her door and limped around to the driver's side. When he had started the car, he shot her a grin. "I'm not afraid of you, Issie," he said.

"Good," she whispered.

As he drove out of the parking lot, he realized that it was himself he feared the most, whenever he was close to Issie.

Chapter Thirty-Five

● ● ●

Issie's insurance company pronounced her car totaled. Steve Winder loaned her the pickup truck he drove for hunting, complete with rust and caked mud and bondo where he'd tried to make some body repairs years ago. She was just glad to have transportation.

Knowing that Cruz was still at large, she decided she had to talk to Mike and Lois. She'd heard from some of the cops she knew that they had questioned her brother and sister-in-law about Jake's whereabouts, so she knew they were anticipating his arrest and were probably sick with anxiety.

But when she showed up at their door, they treated her as the enemy. "How could you do this?" Lois demanded. "How could you turn our son in when he didn't do anything? Make him out to be a murderer? You know Jake wouldn't kill anybody!"

"I didn't know what he had done," Issie

said. "All I knew is that there are two kids dead and two churches burned to the ground. Jake's friends were involved, and they tried to kill me last night. My smashed-up car with bullet holes in it is in Sam Slater's salvage yard to prove it."

"But you could have told us first. You could have come to us."

"I had no choice but to go straight to the police to save my life. And believe it or not, I was hoping to save Jake's too."

"See, that's just it, Issie." Her brother stormed at her like he had when she was a kid and he wanted her out of his way. "If Jake was involved, nobody would have been shooting at you. He loves you. You're his favorite relative. He would never have done anything like that."

"I didn't think so either," Issie said, "but you don't know how much a kid can be influenced by his peers. I don't know what he's capable of."

"Not murder!" her brother shouted.

"How do you know? You don't even know his friends. You don't know that he hasn't been to school in over two weeks and doesn't intend to go back. You don't even know about the compound they're planning to build and the fact that Jake intends to live there with these people."

"You're lying," Mike shouted. "If those things were true, you would have told us sooner."

"I've been too busy dodging bullets!"

"Why should we believe you?"

"I don't *care* if you believe me. The plain simple truth is that if Jake knows something, and I *know* he does, he needs to tell the police. If he's involved, then he needs to be punished, and you don't need to stand in the way."

"That's just fine for you to say," her brother said through clenched teeth. "It's real easy for somebody who's not a parent to say, 'Just let him suffer the consequences. Let him go to prison. Let him go down for a murder he didn't commit. He'll learn his lesson.' But he's not your son!"

"Look," she said, clutching her aching head. "The last thing I want is for Jake to go to prison. That's why I didn't say anything when I first started suspecting his friends. But last night he called me to patch up Benton after he'd been stabbed. Does this sound safe to you? Do you want to shelter your son so he can be trapped under the influence of someone who's reckless with a knife?"

"You should have come to us then!" Mike said. "We had a right to know!"

"Well, which is it, Mike? Was I supposed to keep my mouth shut, or blow the whistle? You can't have it both ways!"

"You could have told us without telling the police," Lois said.

"Right. And then his pals would have come after you instead of me, when you tried to intervene. It's not that simple! So don't yell at me for going to the police, the only ones who can really stop this madness. Yell at me for waiting too long to do it. Has it occurred to you that he could be dead?"

"No!" Lois shouted on a sob. "Mike, tell her —"

The blood seemed to drain from Mike's face as he stood over her. "If he's dead, it's your fault. Look what you've done, Issie."

"Me?"

"Yeah, you. If they're as dangerous as you say, they may have taken your snooping around out on Jake."

"I told you, they called *me!* And I begged Jake to leave with me, but he wouldn't." They weren't listening to her. She wasn't even sure they could hear her through their pain and confusion. There was no use trying to bring them around. "Look, I came here because we have to find Jake. Whether he's in trouble or just hiding . . . or something worse . . . we've got to find him."

"Tell us about it!" her brother shouted.

"He was home last night," Lois said. "His bed was slept in. We didn't see him, but he was here. That's a good sign, isn't it?"

"Maybe," Issie said.

"It is," Lois insisted. "He's a smart kid. He'll be okay." She ran into her husband's arms, and he clung to her.

Issie would have given anything to be a part of that comfort they exchanged. But her brother had never been affectionate with her. She was part of their family, yet she was as alone as she had ever been. "I'm gonna keep looking," she said. "I haven't given up on him."

"If anything happens to him," Lois said, "we'll never forgive you."

"I know," Issie said. And knowing there was nothing more to say, Issie hurried out to her car.

Issie worked the three to eleven shift that day. Aunt Aggie had given her a key to her house, knowing she was working late. She wondered if Aunt Aggie would make Nick stay there again tonight. Would he lock himself away from her again, even after he'd held her at the funeral? She couldn't stand the thought of his avoiding her as he had last night.

So she headed to Joe's Place, knowing that some of the medics would have congregated there by now, and that she would be welcome among them.

She walked into the haze of smoke and noise, and vaguely wished she could get them to turn off the flat, nasal Zydeco music blaring on the speakers, and instead play something soft and slow, more compatible with her mood. She found her medic friends at their usual table in the corner. Karen Insminger was there, looking tired and pensive, and Bob Sigrest looked as if he'd already had too many as he dissolved into loud laughter at something Issie couldn't see. Frenchy and Twila were trying to quiet him.

"What's so funny?" Issie asked as she took a chair from the next table and turned it around.

"He's drunk, that's what's so funny," Twila

said. "Maybe you can shut him up. He's making a scene."

"I was just telling them about the fat woman I treated today for low blood sugar, who had all these rolls on her hips."

"Rolls of fat?" Issie asked.

"No. *Dinner* rolls." He burst into laughter again, and dropping his head on the table, almost toppled it.

Issie didn't feel much like laughing, so she gave him a slight grin and rolled her eyes. She looked at the others, who had apparently already heard the story.

"What's wrong with you?" Bob asked. "Don't you get it?"

"I get it," she said.

"Then why aren't you laughing?" he demanded. "Come on, she had dinner rolls in her pockets. *Dinner rolls.*"

"Yeah, Bob. I said I got it."

"Well, you don't have to get an attitude."

"I don't have an attitude," she said. "I'm just not feeling like giggling myself silly, okay?"

Frenchy frowned at her. "You okay?"

She thought of telling them about her talk with Mike and Lois, and her fears about Jake, but decided against it. "Yeah, I'm fine. I just need a drink."

"Well, you're gonna have to go to the bar to get it. We haven't seen a bar maid in over an hour. I think Bob hassled her so bad she quit."

Bob spat out laughter again, and they all joined in.

Issie got up and headed for the bar. She slipped onto a stool, and looked around at the faces of those who were here. The usual clientele filled the place, sitting in their favorite places like their names were carved on the chairs.

She ordered her usual, then looked around, wondering how wise it was for her to be out alone at night. If Cruz and his gang were watching her, waiting for another opportunity to kill her, this was probably the first place they would look. Hadn't her tires been slashed here?

Down the bar, in his usual place on the end, sat R.J. Albright, still wearing his police uniform. He always came here when he got off duty. She wondered if she should consider him protection. Maybe she should just go on to Aunt Aggie's now.

But she didn't want Nick to think she was anxious to see him. No, she thought. She had to stay here until she'd had a couple of drinks to chase her depression.

She could get R.J. to escort her out when she decided to leave, and ask him to follow her to Aunt Aggie's. If he balked, she could offer to pay him something. Men usually didn't mind protecting damsels if there was something in it for them.

The thought that she would have to go to such lengths for protection broadsided her, and when Joe brought her her drink, she downed it quickly.

Haunted by the thought that her brother had turned on her, she took inventory of the men in her life and found that there were none. Her mind drifted back to childhood, when her appendix had ruptured and her mother had barely gotten her to the hospital in time. She had been there for over a week, but her mother had not been able to stay with her at night because she'd had to work her shift at the bar. Her father had been called about her sudden illness, but he hadn't shown up to see if she was all right.

He had sent her a card with a kitten on it and some Hallmark verse about getting well. She still kept that card in her top dresser drawer. She wasn't sure why.

"Another one, Joe," she said as he passed, and he refilled her drink.

She looked down at it, struggling to hold back tears that she had no intention of crying. She had dealt with the absence of her father, she told herself. She was beyond the lonely little girl who pretended that her daddy was away on important business of national security, pining away for his little girl and carrying her picture close to his heart.

The fantasy reminded her of Brenda Hamilton, a close friend of Issie's in the fourth grade. Brenda had almost drowned in Lake Pontchartrain as she and Issie played in a forbidden part of the lake, but it wasn't the trauma of her near-death that ached anew now. It was the desperation of Brenda's father as he'd tried to rescue her. He had fished her out of the water and done mouth-to-mouth resuscitation, breathing his own life into her to keep her alive until the paramedics had come.

She had gone to the hospital with them and waited in the hall as Brenda's father paced back and forth, back and forth, weeping for his little girl one minute and working as her advocate with unconcerned nurses the next. She remembered him chewing out a doctor who seemed to have given up on her. And then he had gotten on the pay phone and called every drowning expert in the country until he'd found one with a treatment that gave him hope.

Issie had sat in a cold metal chair and watched as Brenda's white knight fought her battles for her. Issie had never had a white knight, and from the depths of her soul, she had longed for one.

She threw back the alcohol now, and swiveled her stool to look for any white knights who might be looking for a damsel in distress. But it was just the same old faces. Bob had had enough, and Karen waved as she walked him out. One by one, she bade Twila and Frenchy goodbye, too.

She turned back to the bar and told herself that she was on her own. No white knights in her future, and certainly none in her past. The men she chose were only mirror images of the father who'd sent her a card without even a note when she'd been suffering in the hospital. They were not the knights, and she had to wield her own swords to protect herself from the pain they brought with them.

Her mind drifted to Brenda again. She had eventually come out of her coma, had gotten up and gone home. She had never quite been the same, but her father doted on her as if she was his special gift.

Issie had been so jealous of that love as a child, and had even wished that Brenda's dad would look up one day and notice Issie sitting there, and love her like his own, and offer himself as her advocate and her protector. But when her appendix ruptured, he had not come, either.

Joe refilled her drink again, and again, and again, as she replayed the tapes in her mind. One of these days she would find some shining knight who would swagger into Joe's Place and sweep her off her feet. He would be a man who came when she was hurt. A man who fought for her when she was threatened. A man who wept over the thought of losing her.

A picture of Nick Foster flashed through her mind, and she banished it quickly, telling herself that he wasn't the one who could rewrite her ending. She was more attracted to the ones who were unavailable, the ones who couldn't commit, the ones who were hard to get.

The ones like her own father.

Why was that? she asked herself. Did she really think the ending would ever change?

She finished off her fifth drink, and as Joe filled it again, she began to get tired . . . so very tired. She was tired of being alone, tired of fighting her own battles, tired of the reputation and the expectations and the disappointments.

She was tired of knowing that the white knight would never come.

"Fill me up, Joe," she slurred, banging her glass too hard in front of her. "I've been empty too long."

Joe filled her glass, but she remained empty.

Chapter Thirty-Six

● ● ●

When Issie passed out cold at the bar, with her head down between her arms, Joe was surprised. "What she doin'?" he asked R.J. Albright. "She ain't never done this before, passed out cold right here at the bar."

"Did she drink more than usual?"

"Maybe," he said, "but Issie can hold her liquor, *sha*."

R.J., who spent as much time at Joe's Place as Issie did, got up and waddled around the bar, tapped Issie on the shoulder. "Issie, wake up. Come on, darlin', wake up."

She didn't budge.

"So who I'm gon' call?" Joe asked.

R.J. shrugged. In a conspiratorial cop voice, he said, "Well, don't say I told you, but when she wrecked last night, she called Nick Foster."

"The *preacher*?"

"Yeah, and he come as fast as we did. Stayed with her the whole time."

"Awright, I'll try Nick." Joe picked up the phone and called information for the preacher's number. He got the number and it rang, then clicked as it forwarded the call.

He waited through eight rings before the old woman answered. *"Hola?"*

He pressed a finger to one ear. "Who's this?"

"Aggie Gaston," she said. "Who d'you want, *sha?*"

"Aunt Aggie, ya got Nick Foster there?"

"Who's this?" she demanded.

"Joe, over to Joe's Place. He there, or ain't he? It's an emergency."

"Yeah, he's here, awright. Just you wait." He heard her put the phone down and shuffle off.

◆ ◆ ◆

Nick Foster was sound asleep when Aunt Aggie woke him up knocking on his door. He groped in the darkness and only found a lamp, then felt his way to the switch and turned it on. It was one A.M.

He must have been in a dead sleep. His sleeplessness of the night before was catching up with him. "Yeah, Aunt Aggie," he said, getting to the door. "What is it?"

"Phone for you," the old woman said, clutching the collar of her robe to her throat. "Joe over to Joe's Place."

Issie, he thought. Something had happened. He hurried out and grabbed up the phone. "Hello?"

"Nick, it's Joe. I got Issie here passed out on my bar, *sha.* I need somebody to come get her."

"Passed out?" Nick asked. "What do you mean, passed out?"

"I mean she's out cold."

"Well, that doesn't sound like her," Nick said. "Does it? Does she usually pass out like that? How much did she drink?"

"She been puttin' it away tonight too fast for me to keep up."

Nick looked at Aunt Aggie and waved that everything was all right. The old woman padded back up the stairs. "Well, okay, I'll be right there," he said.

He hung up and stood there for a moment trying to get his thoughts in order. He looked up and saw Aunt Aggie staring down at him over the banister. "Issie in trouble?" she asked.

He nodded. "Sounds like it. I have to go get her, but she'll be all right."

As he got dressed, he wondered why Joe would have called him. How had he known that he was staying here with Issie? If he knew, Cruz might know too.

He drove as fast as he could drive without breaking the law, and was in the parking lot of Joe's Place just moments after the phone call had come. He felt ridiculous walking through the door of the notorious bar that his church had picketed when it had gotten its license years ago. He knew that every person in the room would feel either self-conscious or amused that the preacher was there. He didn't even want to look around and see how many of his church members were in here boozing it up.

Awkwardly, he stepped inside and saw Issie there with her head flat down on the counter. Dreading the confrontation, he limped over to her and touched her hair. "Issie, wake up. Come on, Issie."

She didn't budge.

He shook her. "Has anybody tried to wake her up?" he asked Joe.

"R.J. tried," Joe said. "She didn't want to come around."

He pulled her hair back and felt her neck

for a pulse. It was slow, but still beat against his fingertip.

He put her arm around his neck and tried to raise her up, but her legs were limp and her head hung heavily in front of her. He pulled Issie back from the bar and tried to lift her head. Her eyes half opened and she looked up at him, then tried to lay her head back down.

"Come on, Issie," Nick whispered. "People are staring."

He managed to get her to her feet and pulled her arm around his neck. Her legs didn't offer much support at all, but he managed to get her out to the car. He propped her up against the back door, then holding her there, fished in his pocket for his keys, unlocked the passenger door, and slid her in. She immediately wilted over onto his seat.

He lifted her shoulders up and got in. Her head fell against the door. He started the car.

"Issie, wake up," he said. "Come on. Wake up. I'm taking you home." But she was out cold.

He thought of bypassing Aunt Aggie's and taking her to her apartment, since he didn't want to start any gossip when the old woman saw her condition. But then he realized she wouldn't be safe there, and he couldn't stay there all night watching her. Deciding Aunt Aggie's was his best hope, he drove back to the old house.

When he got to Aunt Aggie's garage, he tried to rouse Issie again. When his efforts failed, he carried her up the steps. What had gotten into her?

He'd heard a lot of things about Issie, things about her promiscuity, things about her binge drinking, things about her reckless behavior, but he had never heard of her passing out in public before.

He got her to the front door and pulled her inside, flipped on the light and looked around, praying Aunt Aggie was sleeping soundly and wouldn't come down to check on Issie. He lifted her in his arms and carried her up the stairs to her bedroom and laid her on the bed. She curled up in a fetal position.

Worried, he bent down beside the bed and put his face close to hers. "Issie, can you hear me?" She didn't stir. "Issie, wake up."

She wasn't responding, so he took her

pulse again, found that it was slow, weak. He went to the easy chair in the corner of the room and sat down, trying to think clearly. Should he take her to the hospital to get her checked, just in case?

After a few moments, he got up and went to the bed again. She had balled even tighter, and he realized she was cold. He looked in the closet and found a handmade quilt, then covered her with it.

What now? Should he go back down to the guest room, far away from where Issie slept, and trust that she would wake up in the morning with a horrible headache and little memory of what had happened tonight?

The thought of leaving her here like this seemed unacceptable to him, so he decided to lean back in the chair and try to relax. Maybe she would stir soon.

As he sat alone in the room, he looked around at the meager belongings she had brought here with her. Just some clothes, a bag of makeup, a toothbrush. Nothing that revealed anything about her.

That seemed to be the story of Issie's life. Nothing personal. That string of one-night stands she'd been known to have was nothing personal. Her nightly visits to Joe's Place were nothing personal. Even the passion she showed in her job was nothing personal. And the flirtations she showed him on rare occasions . . . Again, nothing personal.

He couldn't explain it, didn't know why it happened, but suddenly his heart ached for her, and he wanted very much for her to know something personal, something that could change her life, fill it up, give it purpose.

He decided to pray for her instead of sleeping or fleeing. One hour passed, then two as he laid this whole confusing mess on the altar of God.

Suddenly, she sat up and bolted off the bed, staggering toward the bathroom.

"Issie?" She disappeared, leaving the bathroom door open behind her. He stood there and waited, wondering if he would be needed . . .

Then he heard her retching into the toilet.

He went to the door, not knowing whether to offer her help or stand back and let her have this time alone.

"Issie, it's me. Are you all right?"

"Come in," she said weakly.

He looked behind the door and saw her

sitting in the corner on the floor next to the toilet, her knees drawn up to her chest. Her face looked ashen, and dark circles underscored her eyes.

"I don't feel so good," she said.

He eased down the wall — careful not to hurt his legs — until he was on the floor across from her in the tiny bathroom.

"Joe called me," he said. "Do you remember my coming to get you?"

She shook her head, then winced as if the movement caused her great pain. "I'm so embarrassed," she whispered.

"Don't be. It's just me."

"Jus' you?" she slurred. "Jus' the preacher." She shook her head and slid her fingers up through the roots of her hair as if clutching her head together. "Head feels like it's gonna explode."

"I could get you some Tylenol."

"No, I'll jus' throw up again."

"That might be a good thing," he said. "You probably need to get it out of your system."

"No," she said, reaching out for him. "Help me up."

He reached for her hands. She was shaking as she took his. He tried to pull her to her feet, but her legs were too weak. Then she got that sick look on her face and dropped back to her knees. In seconds she was heaving over the toilet again.

He backed out of the room, trying to give her some privacy as she retched. He hadn't bargained for this. This was too intimate for him, something he hadn't expected. What would people say if they knew he was in the bathroom off of a bedroom in the middle of the night watching Issie heave into a toilet?

Then he chided himself for putting the approval of men before Issie. It made little difference what people thought. His church was burned to the ground. Soon they would have his resignation and his congregation would be scattered and it wouldn't matter what people thought of him anymore. It was what God thought that mattered, and God had put him here with this woman for some reason he couldn't fathom, and he had drawn him into this bathroom where she was sick. How could he walk away without helping her?

He had to stay, if for no other reason than to let her know she wasn't alone. It seemed critically important that he get that message through to her.

When she finished throwing up, he stroked her hair again. "Issie, do you want to go back to the bed?"

She nodded, and he helped her up. When she almost fell again, he steadied her and walked her into the bedroom. He helped her onto the bed, covered her with the quilt, then backed away.

"You gonna be okay?" he asked.

She didn't say a word, just closed her eyes as if she was sleeping again.

He tried to kneel beside the bed, but the pain in his shins stopped him. Instead, he bent down and touched her face with the back of his fingers. "I'm going downstairs," he said. "But you call if you need me. I'll be right here, okay?"

She nodded but didn't speak. Slowly, he left the room, but left her door open so he could hear her.

Chapter Thirty-Seven

● ● ●

Word about Issie's condition at Joe's Place spread like pollen, coating the conversations of everyone in Newpointe by noon the next day. And even greater news was the fact that Nick Foster had been the one who'd come to get her.

Issie had been the subject of gossip before and tried to ignore it the best she could. But as always, it did bother her. She hated herself for making such a spectacle of herself, and wondered what had made her do such a stupid thing. The fact that Cruz hadn't come along when she was vulnerable was sheer luck, she told herself. If she kept it up, she wouldn't be able to get Aunt Aggie or Nick to help her anymore.

Jake still hadn't been found, and Cruz and his buddies were still at large. Despite her hangover, she couldn't stay at home, not with somebody out to kill her and nothing to do about it. She might as well be working. Her seven-to-three shift came too early to endure with a hangover, but she managed to function. Steve was bad about swapping shifts to accommodate his softball games, his hunting, and his fishing. Some days he wanted to work late, others he wanted to work early. Issie tried to keep her schedule matched with his, because they were so used to working together.

Fortunately, today was a slow day. Forced to sit in their rescue unit at the Walmart parking lot — a central location in town from which they could reach most locations quickly — she and Steve usually passed the time listening to music and making up stories about the people walking by.

But today, Steve was more interested in Issie's story of the night before. "So what are you trying to do?" he asked. "Ruin the preacher?"

She shot him a look. "What do you mean?"

"I mean everybody in town knows that he practically spent the night with you last night."

"He did not spend the night with me," she said. "We were both guests in Aunt Aggie's home, on separate floors, for Pete's sake."

"And you just happened to be drunk, and

you want me to think that you didn't throw yourself at him?"

"Throw myself?" She wanted to get out of the rescue unit and hitchhike home, but she knew she had to stay. "I can't believe you said that."

He leaned his head back on his seat and stared out the windshield. "Issie, I know you love living dangerously, but stay away from the preacher. A lot of people value him in this town. The last thing those people need after losing their church is to lose their preacher too. Or even their respect for him."

"They're not going to lose respect for their preacher," she said. "He's a nice guy. He was helping me."

"Find somebody else to help you, Issie."

Issie fought the anger boiling inside her. "You know, you really ought to mind your own business," she said. "This has nothing to do with you. It's not even your church. He's not your preacher so you don't have to defend his honor."

"All I'm saying is that I know how you work. Nick Foster is not who you need to be chasing."

"What makes you think I'm chasing him?" she asked.

"The rumor is that he's the one they called to come get you last night."

"Well, I didn't have anything to do with that decision."

"There's also a rumor says you called him yourself when you got shot at and had that wreck."

That was true and she couldn't deny it. "I felt like I might be dead by the time the night was over. You'd call a preacher too."

"I just hope you don't have anything up your sleeve. Remember Mark Branning?"

"Nobody's ever going to let me forget that! I don't have anything up my sleeve, Steve! Who did you want me to call? You? You were probably at home watching the *Brady Bunch* with your cute little wife and your darling little children. You probably would have checked the caller ID and seen that it was me and decided not to answer."

"I wouldn't do that," Steve said.

"Of course you would," she said. "Every time I've ever called you at home I've gotten the machine."

"I'm a busy guy."

"I called someone that I thought would be home and I thought would respond. And I was right. He did help me. He stayed with me the whole time and solved the problem of where I was going to stay. What's wrong with that?"

"What's wrong with it is that Nick Foster has enough problems without you in his life right now."

His scathing indictment crushed her. She tried not to cry. "So what am I, a piranha?" she asked.

"No offense," he said, "but a lot of people do think of you that way."

"Oh, give me a break," she said. "I thought you were my friend."

He stared at her, silence passing between them, then finally he said, "I am your friend, Issie. That's why I'm giving you good advice. I hope you'll take it."

"I don't need your advice about Nick."

A call came through on the radio, and they both came to attention. There was a wreck on Jacquard Boulevard and someone was claiming whiplash.

Steve started the unit and radioed that they were on their way. There wasn't more time to talk, and Issie decided to push her anger to the back of her mind. She didn't have a defense after all, and she knew that Steve was probably right.

Besides, there was nothing like working an accident to get her mind off of her own problems.

When they got to the scene of the accident, Issie was surprised to see Nick there. She hadn't expected to see him there with those bandages still on his legs. But there he was, dressed in complete uniform, helping Mark, Dan, and George assess the damage to the car.

The passengers were all standing on the sidewalk, and it was clear from her first glance that no one was injured. Still, she got out of the unit with Steve, found the woman who claimed her neck was sore, and began to evaluate her symptoms.

When she'd gotten the neck brace on her, she looked up and saw Nick watching her. She hadn't seen him this morning. He'd been gone when she'd gotten up, and now she had trouble looking him in the eye.

"How do you feel?" he asked.

She shrugged and stood up. "Oh, a little mortified. And my head feels like it's been run over fourteen times." She looked up at him, trying to change the subject. "What about you? I didn't think you'd get a medical release until your lungs and burns healed."

"I'm just on office duty," he said. "I came on the call in the capacity of chaplain. There are some things I can still do."

"Well, you be careful," she said.

"I will. But what about you? You're not planning a trip to Joe's Place tonight, are you?"

She blinked back the mist in her eyes and looked into the wind. "Nick, I don't even know what to say. I'm so sorry. And no, I'm not going back tonight. I'm ashamed to show my face."

He just stared down at her as if processing that thought, and she wondered what he was thinking. Dan called from the fire truck a few yards down the road, and Nick waved.

"Well, guess I'll see you a little later. You take care, okay?" He dipped his face to her ear, and whispered, "And next time call me *before* you get into trouble."

She looked up at him, and their eyes met and held for a moment, a moment that was full of unspoken words. Issie wondered if his thoughts were anything like hers. She was getting too attached to him, and that was dangerous. As Steve had said, the last thing Nick Foster needed in his life was Issie

Mattreaux. Maybe she needed to do what he said and back off. Maybe the greatest act of gratitude she could offer him was to cut all ties with him before her heart was any more entangled.

Then she told herself that she was kidding herself if she thought Nick had given her a second thought. She wasn't his type, and she never would be. Nick was one of those rare white knights, but white knights never went for damsels like her.

◆ ◆ ◆

As the firefighters drove back to the fire station, Mark, Dan, and George were quiet. Nick knew what they were thinking, but he didn't want to give them the chance to voice it.

Finally, as they pulled into the truck bay at midtown station, Dan looked back over his shoulder. "You're playing with fire, Nick."

Nick had seen it coming, so he didn't flinch. "Dan, there's nothing going on."

"I *saw* something going on," Mark said. "I saw the way she looked at you. Don't underestimate her power, Nick. She's trapped me with it before."

"Oh, man!" Nick said. "You trapped your-

self. You got wrapped up in lust and started going to the bar with her and the next thing you knew, your marriage was on the rocks."

Mark looked at him as if he couldn't believe he had said those words. Nick had never been that bold with him. There had been many conversations between them about lust and temptation, but Nick had never looked Mark in the eye and told him he had been to blame.

Instantly, Nick regretted it. "I'm sorry, Mark. Look, I know you never had an affair with her. I know you rectified things before they got out of hand. But I'm just telling you that it's not all her fault. She's been a victim some too."

"I thought you didn't believe in victimhood," Dan said. "If I recall, you've said that people make victimhood an excuse for sin."

"I don't believe in overlooking sin so that we can justify anything we ever choose to do," Nick said. "But I've prayed a lot about her. I've wanted to reach her. I've never been able to. And lately she's been through a lot. For some reason, I'm the one that keeps getting called to help her. Now, you tell me. As a preacher, as a Christian, as a human being, what would you do if someone called you and told you they were in trouble?"

"If it was Issie Mattreaux," Dan said, "I think I'd pass."

"Well, I can't pass," Nick said. "I've thought about what people would say and what they would think. And then I've realized that I have to care more about her soul than my reputation. And if people want to think the worst about me, then they might as well go ahead. It's not like I have a lot to lose."

"Of course you have a lot to lose," Dan said. "You're still our preacher. We didn't fire you."

"No, but someone fired the church," he said. "It's not there anymore, guys. Wake up."

"There's still a church," Mark said. "There are still people who want to worship. They want you to lead them in that. You're our shepherd, Nick. Don't let her lead you off in another direction. You aren't immune just because you're a man of God."

Nick didn't say anything. He just got out of the truck and slammed the door as he went into the station.

Chapter Thirty-Eight

● ● ●

No one expected to see Ray drive up that afternoon and go into his office without saying a word to anyone. They hadn't expected him back for at least another week.

Nick stood at the edge of the truck bay, looking out at the trailer parked between the fire department and police station, and wondered if he should go talk to Ray. Dan came up behind him and set his hand on Nick's shoulder. "He needs to talk, man."

Nick nodded. "I'm not sure he needs to talk to me. I never can think what to say when I'm around him. It's like all my experience goes out the window, all the Scripture, all the wisdom God's ever given me, and I just stand there, speechless and angry that Ben is dead."

"Man, I do even worse than that," Dan said. "You're his preacher, his chaplain, and his friend."

"I'm also the one who found Ben's body."

"He knows you tried to save him."

Nick nodded, hoping that was true. He slid his hands into his pockets and walked slowly across the freshly cut lawn to the door of Ray's office. He knocked, but there was no answer, so Nick turned the knob and pushed the door open.

Ray sat in the dark at his desk. "I didn't say come in."

Nick came in anyway. "I just wanted to tell you it's good to see you back."

Ray rubbed his face and nodded wearily. "What are you doing here?" he asked. "I ain't seen a medical release."

"Well, I'm not officially back," Nick said. "Just office duty. I figured with you out, I could take up some of the slack. I didn't have anything to do what with the church gone and all. Plus, I figured with the two murders, somebody in protective services might be needing a chaplain."

"Well, I better not catch you fightin' a fire. With those injuries you're liable to get in somebody's way and cost 'em their life. We've had enough death." He dropped his hands to the desk. "How are you feelin', anyway?"

"I'm okay. Getting better all the time."

"I've had burns like that before, Nick. You ain't kiddin' nobody. They don't heal up in four days."

"Well, I appreciate your concern." He looked down at his feet and sought to change the subject. "Have you heard about the church service we're having Sunday out on Aunt Aggie's lawn?"

Ray nodded. "Heard somethin' about it. I don't know if we'll be there."

Nick felt that personal stab of failure again. "Ray, don't turn your back on God. You need him now. Susan and Vanessa need him. Come back and let us help you heal."

"I don't *want* to heal." His voice broke, and he covered his face.

Nick didn't know whether to get up and go to him, or let him suffer alone. He cleared his throat. "I know," Nick told him. "That's a common feeling. You just want to grieve, you want to feel the pain, you want to hang on to it because it's kind of like hanging on to the person."

"Don't tell me what I feel," Ray said. "You don't know what I feel. I don't know *any-body* who knows how I feel."

Nick's mouth trembled as he tried to say

the right thing. "You're right. I don't. There's no way I could."

"He had his whole life ahead of him, Nick!" Ray bellowed. "His whole life. He was gon' *be* somebody."

"Ray, he *is* somebody. In case there's ever been a moment's doubt in your mind about Ben's salvation, I mean . . . I want you to know that I've prayed with him, talked with him myself. He cared about the Lord. I know he's in heaven."

Ray broke down again, and finally Nick got up and came around his desk. He leaned over his friend and put his arms around him. Ray fell into him and cried the tears of a broken man. "You can do this, Ray," Nick said. "We don't grieve as those who have no hope. This is not the end for you and Ben."

"Feels like the end," Ray said.

Nick just held his friend and let him grieve as he hadn't been able to do before.

Chapter Thirty-Nine

● ● ●

Nick was emotionally spent by the time he left Ray's office just after three, so he decided to go home. He got out of his car and looked across the street to the church that had been such a fixture in his life for so long now. It was odd to see the rubble piled on the property that had once been donated by someone who loved the Lord. He couldn't believe it was all wasted now.

He crossed the street and went to stand in the center of his scorched foundation, around the place where he estimated the pulpit had been. Had he taken his pulpit for granted? he wondered. He'd always thought it would be there, as if it had some hedge of protection around it and the Lord would never let harm come to it. He supposed it took losing it to realize how significant it was.

He sifted through the rubble and came to a pew that was still intact, though it was black from the fire. He sat down on it, testing it with his weight. It held him up, so he relaxed and looked around at the things that were scarred and soiled from the fire.

Some of the elders had met with the insurance agent, and he'd already been out to look at the damage. He hoped the church would get enough to rebuild. He hoped they had the energy to start again.

He covered his face with his hands as the despair of the last few days rose up inside him, and as he began to weep, he began to pray, asking God to show him what his purpose was in this, what it could possibly mean, and what he was to do with it.

A rattling, rusty old pickup truck pulled up to the curb, and he wiped his face quickly. It wasn't until the car door closed that he saw that it was Issie.

She stood there in uniform, just off work, but she looked weak, pale, still ailing from the night before. He couldn't believe she had come here instead of going back to Aunt Aggie's to rest after a hard day on the job. She came to the scorched pew and sat down next to him. "Hey," she said softly.

"What are you doing here?" he asked.

She sighed. "I don't know. I saw you

coming out of Ray's office awhile ago, and you looked kind of upset. I thought I'd come by and just see if you were okay."

He couldn't think of a response to that so he just sat there.

"What are *you* doing here?" she asked.

"I don't know," he said. "I thought I'd come over and just look at the place. Every time I look this direction I'm shocked. I can't believe the building's not still here, that my pulpit's not standing, that there aren't pews everywhere, that people can't come and go."

"But you know insurance will take care of it and you can rebuild."

"We can't rebuild Ben," he said. "We can't rebuild the sense of security and peace that we had in this building."

"You sure don't put much confidence in your congregation," she said. "I mean, it seems to me if this was such a great church, that a few problems like this wouldn't ruin everything."

She was right. He didn't have much confidence in the church. Most of the time he felt he was pushing an eighteen-wheeler uphill, heavy with the cargo they needed to bear fruit in God's kingdom, but they just never felt like turning the ignition on. Now he feared what energy they did have would die out completely, and he didn't know if he had the strength to keep pushing.

He didn't want to talk about it anymore, so he looked at her, assessed her face and her eyes. "How's the hangover?"

"Better," she said. "Thankfully, we didn't have any major trauma today."

"So have you had your fill of Joe's Place yet?"

She looked across the street at the trailer Nick lived in. "It's not Joe's fault. It's mine. Next time I won't drink so much."

He shook his head. "Issie, what's it going to take?"

"For what?" she asked.

"For you to wake up and realize that that's no kind of life."

"Hey, good people get hurt and killed too. Ben was at your church every time the doors opened and he's dead now. So living a high-and-mighty life doesn't guarantee safety."

"No, but the risk is higher when you pass out in bars and thumb your nose at the people trying to kill you."

"I didn't thumb my nose," she said. "What are you talking about?"

"You shouldn't have gone anywhere alone last night," he said. "You should have kept as low a profile as possible. Why would you go about your normal routine when Cruz is looking for you?"

"I don't know. I was depressed. My brother had all but thrown me out of his house because I turned Jake and his friends in. I guess I wasn't thinking clearly. I was upset and worried, and I needed a drink."

"You never *need* a drink."

"I *needed* to relax, get my mind off things." She looked frustrated as she groped for words. "You could never understand. You live some kind of unreal life, and I don't know how you do it, but I'm not like you. You've probably never had a vice in your life."

"Hey, I had plenty of vices before I became a Christian," he said. "I gave in plenty. I know what I'm missing, Issie. I'm missing a lot of heartache, a lot of turmoil, a lot of anxiety, a lot of remorse, a lot of self-indictment, a lot of guilt. I'm missing those feelings of waking up in the morning and running the night back through my mind, trying to figure out if I did or said anything that I was going to regret today."

"You?"

"Oh, yeah, me. The miracle is that God could take somebody like me and use me. I mean, he didn't just transform me into a new creature. He literally made me into something he could use."

"Well, that's you, Nick. You're a useful kind of person. He could never use me."

"Of course he could."

"Not with my past," she said. "You don't know all the stuff I've done."

She looked sadly off in the distance, and he reached for her chin and turned her face back to his. "Issie, look at me."

Those dark eyes came up to meet his.

"You have no idea how useful you could be. God has a plan for you. He's had a plan for you all along. You just wouldn't follow it. But if you started following it, you could do amazing things."

Her expression seemed soft, vulnerable, and for a moment he thought he might be getting through. Her eyes were stricken as they locked into his, and he thought he saw a fine mist painting the inside edge of her lids, but then that hard look came back and she was skeptical again.

"When I think of God's plan for my life, I

picture me in a black church suit with ugly pumps and my hair pulled back in a bun. I picture me going around with a fifty-pound Bible, waving it in people's faces and quoting Scripture every time I open my mouth. It doesn't sound like much fun to me."

"Issie, you know a lot of Christians. Do they act like that? Do they look like shells that are going around repeating robotic phrases?"

"No," she said, "some of them don't. But some do. They talk about Christ and righteousness, and in the next breath they're declaring themselves superior to Jews and blacks and gays . . . and anybody who's not like them. Even Cruz and his group are Christians. They don't drink or smoke or do dope, but they kill people. And they think it's okay because they figure if they hate somebody, then God must hate them too."

"Issie, they're not us."

"They say they are."

"They're liars. They're using the banner of Christianity to camouflage their hate. They're defining who we are, Issie, but they're defining us wrong. Don't buy into their lies. Go to the Bible and see what God says. And look at the ones who follow that

Bible, the ones who love and pray and cope and help people in need. The ones who think not only of themselves, but of others, no matter how different they are. The ones who hate sin but love sinners enough to rescue them, just as surely as you rescue people every day."

She looked down at her hands, turning his words over in her mind.

"Issie, Christians are not a bunch of clones without personalities. God doesn't want that. He needs all kinds."

She swallowed. "Well, I could be wrong. I have been before."

"Well, if you're wrong about this," Nick said, "then your eternity will be affected by it. I don't want that for you, Issie. I don't want you to miss this."

She breathed a laugh. "I don't particularly want that, either."

"Then come out of the cell."

Her smile faded. "What cell?"

"The one on death row. There's someone waiting to take your place. Your pardon is waiting. Until you take it, you're in bondage, Issie. You're trapped. You think you're free but you're not. You've just constructed your own prison."

"Oh, yeah?" She was starting to get angry. "And what exactly am I trapped by?"

"Sin," he said. "You hate it and you don't want it, but then every night you go back to Joe's Place and you drink and you pick up a man."

"Okay." She got up from the scorched pew and held up her hands to halt his direction. "I do *not* pick up men," she said. "But even if I did, it is not a sin to attract a man."

"No, but it's a sin to lust after them, make them lust after you, and take them home with you." He hated saying it. He didn't want her to turn on him, but if he let it end like this, he might never have another chance to be this honest with her.

"How dare you?" she asked. "Just because things aren't going great for me does not mean that I'm some kind of hell-bound sinner."

"You said there were things in your life that God wouldn't be able to accept," he said. "What do you call those?"

"Well, so what? Maybe they are sins. But you don't have to paint me to be some kind of harlot who prowls into the bar every night looking for her latest victim. I'm not like that. I go there to unwind, to talk to my friends."

"Oh, I know you're not like that," he said. "You're not a hunter. I think you're the hunted."

Her mouth fell open. "And who is hunting me?"

"Lots of people," he said. "They're all looking for a pretty girl with a big heart who just wants to be loved."

She rolled her eyes and shook her head and looked into the wind. It whipped her hair around her face, and she shoved it behind her ear. "I know what I'm doing, Nick. I'm in perfect control. I'm the driver in my life."

"You're contradicting yourself all over the place, Issie."

Again she shook her head with disbelief. "Okay, so I am, but you're confusing me."

"I'm confusing you because you're not making any sense."

"So the only sense to be made is that God has a plan for me and I'm supposed to follow it, and all his rules, and live like you live, constantly depriving myself of everything in the world that I want?"

"Well, see, that's the thing that's different," he said. "If you gave your life to Christ, you'd want different things."

"The other night you admitted that you don't," she said, lifting her chin defiantly. "You admitted that you're tempted just like I am."

"I'm tempted," he said, "but in my heart I want what God wants for me, and that's why I take that escape when he provides it."

"Well, maybe I don't *want* that escape," she said. "Maybe I *like* the so-called prison you say I'm in. Maybe I don't want to walk through the door that he's opening for me to get out. Maybe that's because I don't see it as a prison."

"No one ever does," Nick said. "That's what's so sad."

She groaned and combed her hands through the roots of her hair. "You make me crazy, you know that? You drive me right up the wall."

"Yeah, I've been known to do that."

She looked suddenly very weary, and he remembered her crouched like a little girl next to the toilet last night.

"I'm tired, Nick. I'm going to Aunt Aggie's. I just came by to check on you, see how you were doing. I guess you're getting back to normal, throwing your punches." She got up to leave.

"I'm not throwing punches, Issie. I'm trying to throw a life raft." Nick followed her, stepping over some of the rubble on the way to the pickup.

She reached the truck door but didn't get in right away. Instead she stood there and looked up at him.

He wondered if Mark was right, if she knew exactly the power she had over men. He didn't want her to have that power over him. Still, he stood there looking down at her, stricken with how his heart rate escalated when she looked up at him. Even when she wasn't at her best, there was something about her eyes that drew him in, something that had always made his heart jolt.

"I worry about you," he said. "Last night, I sat by your bed and prayed for hours."

He couldn't define the poignant expression that passed over her face. It was something between shock and sorrow, and for a moment, he thought she was going to cry. "No one's ever prayed for me before," she whispered.

"I have," he said. "I've been praying for you for years."

She looked down at the key in her hand,

her eyes stricken. "My advocate," she whispered.

He frowned. "Your what?"

She swept her hair behind her ear. "Nothing. I was just thinking." Those tears filled her eyes now as she looked up at him. "Thank you for worrying about me."

He smiled. "You act like I'm doing it on purpose when, in fact, I just can't help myself. I guess it's this built-in protective mechanism that I get whenever I see a lady in trouble."

Her smile faded. "A damsel in distress, you mean?"

"It's not a sign of weakness, you know. Vulnerability and weakness are not the same things."

She tried to smile again, but quickly that smile faded and tears seemed to rim her eyes as she looked up at him. "You make me feel safe, Nick. I like to be around you. That's the real reason I came looking for you today."

A lump lodged in his throat, and he tried to swallow it back. "I'm glad," he said. "You deserve to feel safe."

She looked up at him again with those honest probing eyes, and as he regarded her, he wondered what it would be like if he reached out and slid his fingers along her neck, up her jawline, into the roots of her hair. He wondered what it would cost him if he leaned down just a few inches and grazed her lips gently with his.

It was almost as if she read his thoughts. "I wish I was different, Nick," she whispered.

"What would you do if you were different?"

"I'd probably pull out all the stops and chase the only white knight I know," she whispered.

He felt the blood coloring his face.

"Can you imagine Issie Mattreaux going after the preacher?" she asked, teasing.

He wondered if it was his imagination or if she was moving closer, testing him with her proximity. He didn't move back. Instead, he just looked into her eyes, glanced down at her lips. He was breathing harder than he meant to.

"Can you imagine the preacher falling for Issie Mattreaux?" he whispered.

She looked at his lips then, and he wet them, thinking how easy it would be just to dip down and touch hers.

"What would people say?" she asked.

"I don't know," he whispered.

They stood there like that, stricken and paralyzed as the cool breeze teased around them. Finally Nick opened her truck door. She took his cue with a disappointed look, got in, and started the engine.

"Feel free to call me if you get scared before I get over to Aunt Aggie's," he said. He leaned down, putting his face even with hers. His eyes were serious as he locked into her gaze. "No kidding, Issie. I have a few things to do at home, but you let me know if you need me."

"I will," she said, and that smile came back to soften her lips. "Thanks, Nick."

He closed the truck door, stepped back, and watched her drive away. He crossed the street and went into his trailer, turned on a lamp, and sat down in the chair that someone from his congregation had given him. He pulled his feet up and stared at the shadows on the wall.

What was it about Issie Mattreaux, he asked himself. Why was she on his mind so often, and why did she keep turning up in his life? He closed his eyes and confessed that to the Lord, told him he felt like Hosea falling for a prostitute. But in Hosea's case, God had ordained it. He knew better than that. God had not led him to Issie Mattreaux, because she was not a believer. He couldn't think of anything more miserable than being married to someone who didn't have the same values, the same goals in life, the same purpose, someone who didn't know where to turn in times of trouble, someone who didn't know the value of her life. Simply because of the blood of Christ, God would never put him with Issie. It just wasn't possible. These feelings he was having, they were lustful feelings. He wanted her because she was the unattainable, and because she was so darned pretty. He asked God to take this desire away from him, to make him stop thinking about her and stop caring. He asked him to make him think of her the way a preacher would think of a lost person, instead of the way a bachelor would think of one of the prettiest women in town.

Maybe he was playing with fire as Mark had said. Maybe *she* was. And then he told himself again that maybe he had misread his calling, that maybe he wasn't pure enough to be a preacher. If he was, wouldn't he be able to put her out of his mind and move on? If he was truly called to preach, why would he be having feelings like this for a woman like Issie?

Maybe God had brought him to the end of his preaching career for a reason. Maybe he was displeased with the thoughts skittering through Nick's mind. Maybe his weakness toward Issie was symptomatic of the weakness in his own faith. Maybe he had no business trying to uphold the faith of others when he had such a hard time fleeing temptations in his own heart. Maybe it was time to resubmit that letter of resignation.

Maybe this time he shouldn't take no for an answer.

Chapter Forty

● ● ●

Saturday morning, Nick woke before Issie did. Nervous about facing an expectant, wounded congregation the next day, he decided to leave Aunt Aggie's and go home to work on his sermon. Aunt Aggie wasn't anywhere to be found, so he assumed she was out walking. He left her and Issie a note, then drove up to his trailer and saw bulldozers on the church grounds. Junior Reynolds sat on one and Jesse Pruitt on another, clearing the rubble. Several dozen other people stood around the grounds in work clothes.

It was as if he was walking into a surprise party as he got out of his car and crossed the street, for the members of his church who had shown up to help began to cheer and holler.

"What's going on here?" he asked.

"We decided to go ahead and clear the land," Jesse yelled from the bulldozer. "That way we can get started rebuilding as soon as possible."

He hadn't had the chance to think of that himself. Instead, he'd been so blinded by the rubble that he couldn't see into the future at all. He looked around at all the faces and all the people in work clothes prepared to spend the day clearing the junk away from the church. There must have been forty or fifty people there. He felt the heaviness of his heart lifting as his mind flitted back to that letter of resignation he was planning to offer them. Maybe he would wait. There was no reason to put a damper on the work they would be doing. Instead, he rolled up his sleeves and began doing what he could to help.

◆ ◆ ◆

Issie woke up a little later, thinking about Nick. She got up and showered quickly, then came out of her room to see if he was up. To her disappointment, he was already gone.

She kicked herself, wondering why she spent so much of her time thinking about the preacher. He wasn't the exciting, tough, alpha-male kind of guy that she usually fell for. Instead, he was sweet, sensitive, safe. So why did her heart pound out of control when she was around him? Why did her hands tremble and her mouth go dry? Why had she stood there at the truck yesterday, looking at his lips and waiting for him to kiss her? Why had she been so crushed when he had stepped away again?

The thought of her feelings for Nick began to make her hate herself. She could never be good enough for a man like him.

She went into the kitchen and found a note that Aunt Aggie had gone to take snacks to people working on the church grounds. She made a bowl of cereal and sat down, hating the thought of being alone today. She wished she hadn't made Nick feel like he had to avoid her. She wondered if that was a sign that he was attracted to her, or repulsed by her.

Still, as she finished breakfast, she began trying to think of reasons to see him today. The church grounds, she thought. Aunt Aggie said they were working on the church grounds. Maybe if she went to help . . .

She cleaned her dishes, then went to the truck and drove to Nick's street. But even as she drove, she realized that part of the reason she was thinking so much about Nick right now was that he was not interested in her. Had he been, she didn't even know if she would have given him the time of day. She felt a little bit like Mark Twain who would never join a club that would have him as a member.

For that, she hated herself.

She pulled onto his street and saw the bulldozer on the church grounds. Dozens of people sifted through rubble, and she wondered if she should keep driving to keep from stirring any further gossip about her and Nick.

But she had no place else to go, so she pulled Steve Winder's old pickup truck into Nick's gravel driveway and sat there idling for a moment.

She shouldn't have come here, she thought. She started to pull out of the driveway when she heard something bang on her truck. She looked out the window and saw Nick standing at the door. She rolled the window down. "Nick, I was going to volunteer to help, but I don't want to cause you any trouble."

"Cause me trouble? Why would you?" he asked.

"Just coming here. I mean, the rumors."

He shook his head. "They're all so busy over there, they don't care."

"What are they doing?" she asked.

"They're clearing the property," he said, "so we can start rebuilding."

She turned and looked out her rear window and saw that women and children and old men and young were all helping. "Looks like they could get it all done today with that kind of a turnout."

"That's what I was thinking," he said. "They planned all this without me. I didn't even ask them to come. I was going to try to find a way to do most of it myself, or scrounge up a committee. I thought I'd have to twist arms and beg and plead. But they turned the ignition themselves, and I didn't even have to give them a shove."

She thought she'd missed something. "Huh?"

"Never mind. I just mean that my job is to equip the saints to do the work of the church, but it always seems like it isn't really happening that way. Today it is. Come on and help, Issie. They're all too busy to speculate about why you're here. All hands are welcome."

"Are you sure?"

"Of course, I'm sure," he said. "Come on." He opened her truck door and ushered her out. She followed him across the street, wondering if this was his way of getting her assimilated into the fellowship of the church. She wasn't sure, but whatever he was doing, it was working, because she really did want to be a part of this effort.

Chapter Forty-One

● ● ●

Allie had stiffened the moment she saw Issie drive up in Nick's driveway. She wondered if the rumors she'd heard about them were true. Had Nick been spending time with the woman who once tried to steal Allie's husband away?

"Oh, great," Mark said, coming up behind Allie and following her gaze. "Don't tell me she's coming to help."

They watched her get out of the car, and Allie turned back to tying up garbage bags. "Looks like it."

"Are you okay?" Mark asked. "We could leave if you're uncomfortable."

Allie tried to reassure him with her smile. She knew that Mark hadn't given Issie a thought in a long time now, and he had managed to rebuild her trust in him as they had built their family. But she wasn't sure she wanted to get chummy with Issie.

Celia touched her shoulder, and Jill approached her too. "Really, are you okay?"

Jill asked. Celia had her blond ponytail pulled up and was covered with soot since she'd been sifting through the rubble for anything they could salvage.

"I'm fine," Allie said. "I forgave Issie a long time ago."

"Then why do you look so tense all of a sudden?" Jill asked her.

Allie turned back to gaze at Issie's truck. "Because I still get uncomfortable around her. I wish I could forget, but I just have problems with her."

Mark saw that Issie was coming into the crowd of workers, and Nick was treating her like one of them. "I'm gonna ask her to go home," he said.

Allie grabbed his arm. "You can't do that."

"But Allie, I don't want you to have to work beside her today and drag up all those memories. This is *our* church."

"No, it isn't," Allie said. "It's Christ's church. And if we can't welcome someone like Issie into our fellowship, even rejoice that she would come, then we're the ones who don't belong here. Not her."

His face softened and he studied his wife's face. "You're right. I know you are. I'm just trying to protect you from my own stupid past mistakes. Plus, I question her motives. I think she's after Nick."

Allie looked up at Mark again. Their eyes met, and she looked away. She had always secretly suspected that Nick had a thing for Issie. She wondered what the appeal was, and if he realized he was on dangerous ground.

Then she felt guilty again. If Jesus had shied away from the woman at the well, or the adulteress who was about to be stoned, just because of who they were . . . well, that would mean he'd have to shy away from Allie for her past sins, and Mark for his, and none of them would ever be forgiven. Suddenly one of her favorite Scripture verses struck her in the heart: "This is love: not that we loved God, but that he loved us and sent his Son as an atoning sacrifice for our sins. Dear friends, since God so loved us, we also ought to love one another."

There it was, she thought. She had to love because Christ loved her. It was very simple, really. Cut and dried. Black and white, with no gray areas. Issie had as much right to her love, as Allie had to Christ's. And it was Allie's job — no one else's — to make Issie feel that she could be accepted here on the holy land where God's house had been built.

Chapter Forty-Two

• • •

They gave Issie a job sorting through a pile of hymnbooks in a box, and salvaging the ones that could still be read, as well as the Bibles that had been in the pews. The fact that anything was salvageable was a small miracle, Nick said. Issie felt an awkward sense that she didn't belong when she saw Mark and Allie working alongside everyone else. She and Allie had had a difficult time speaking to each other ever since she had caused problems in their marriage.

As she sorted Bibles, she was peripherally aware that Allie and Mark were whispering to each other. Was Allie telling Mark to get her out of here? That's what *she* would have been doing. Was she threatening to go home if she had to lay eyes on Issie Mattreaux one more time?

Hours passed and everyone kept working. She worked quietly, not interacting much with anyone else, though occasion-

ally someone spoke to her as if she did belong.

When they'd gotten the building leveled
and cleared and everyone was backing
away as the bulldozer made its last sweep
through, Issie saw Allie heading her way.
She stiffened instantly, bracing herself for
whatever was coming. She wondered if Allie
had waited for the noise of the bulldozer, so
that no one would hear her chewing her out.

But when Allie reached her, Issie saw a
smile instead of hostility. "I appreciate how
hard you worked today, Issie."

Issie tried to return the smile. "No problem. I didn't have anything else to do."

"Some of us are about to go over to Aunt
Aggie's and set up the chairs for tomorrow's
service. Nick wanted me to ask you if you
were interested in coming."

Issie looked up across the crowd and saw
Nick on the other side of the bulldozer. He
could have asked her himself, she knew, but
there was something about sending Allie
over that was supposed to speak to her
heart. She looked up at the woman whose
home she had almost wrecked.

"I don't know. Maybe I'll just go on home."

"Oh, no. We need your help. Besides, I

wasn't going to say anything, but Aunt Aggie cooked a little extra for the firemen today and she said that we could eat when we got to her house."

Issie studied Allie's face and wondered if she was just a good actress, or if she really wanted Issie to come. "Why do you want me to go so bad?" she asked. "I would think you would want me as far away from your husband as I could get."

Allie's eyes saddened, and she looked away. "I have to admit, sometimes when I'm around you bad memories come back. But that's my problem, not yours. The truth is, we're all here cleaning up a church, and there's not a reason in the world that you shouldn't be there working right along beside me if you want to be. Believe it or not, Issie, I forgave you a long time ago."

Issie looked away. She hadn't asked for forgiveness, had never admitted wrong, but denying that she had been seemed like a waste of effort now. Her eyes filled with tears, and she looked down to hide them. "You have every reason to hate me," Issie admitted.

Allie smiled. "Christ has every reason to hate *me.* But he doesn't. So how could I hate you?"

When Allie went back to her husband in the crowd, Issie found herself unable to speak or think. The lump grew in her throat and she tried to swallow it back, but she knew she was going to burst into tears right here in front of everybody and cause another round of gossip if she didn't get out of here. Quickly, she crossed the street and headed toward the rusty pickup that was still parked at Nick's house.

She got in and sat there for a moment, covering the tears that were coming through her lashes. Suddenly there was a knock on the window. Nick stood there, looking in with concern. She rolled her window down.

"Issie, what's wrong?" he asked.

She wiped her eyes and tried to pull herself together.

"I saw you talking to Allie," he said. "Did she say something that upset you?"

"No, no. Not at all."

"What then?"

"She was very sweet," she said, bringing her misty eyes up to his. "And she has every right not to be. She's forgiven me for the way I intruded on her marriage. Thing is, I guess I'd be more comfortable with the hate, because I know how to deal with that."

Nick reached through the window and wiped a tear that was rolling down her cheek. She drew in a deep breath as if jolted by the contact. "I'm not a very nice person, you know," she said. "Even if I wanted to come to your church, be a part of this, I couldn't. I would never fit in."

Nick just kept smiling. "One of my favorite Bible passages is in 1 Corinthians 6," he said.

She gave him a smirk. "Haven't read it lately."

He grinned as if he knew she didn't even own a Bible.

"It says, 'Do you not know that the wicked will not inherit the kingdom of God? Do not be deceived: Neither the sexually immoral nor idolaters nor adulterers nor effeminate nor male prostitutes nor homosexual offenders nor thieves nor the greedy nor drunkards nor slanderers nor swindlers will inherit the kingdom of God.' "

More tears erupted in Issie's eyes. "Well, see there? That keeps me out on several counts."

"That's not my favorite part," Nick said, leaning in the window and getting too close to her face. "The next verse says, 'That is what some of you were. But you were washed, you were sanctified, you were justified in the name of the Lord Jesus Christ and by the Spirit of our God.' "

She looked up at him, her eyes intent on seeing the insights that seemed too natural to him.

"You think you don't belong in that group over there?" Nick asked. "Well, Issie, almost every one of them fits into those categories before they came to know Christ. Some of them just had heart problems. They weren't outward thieves and they weren't going around committing adultery, but they were doing it in their hearts. Others of them did these things openly. Just look at them, Issie. You've lived here long enough to know. You know who has changed and who hasn't. If people couldn't change, then Paul wouldn't have said, 'Such *were* some of you.' God doesn't keep those people out of heaven unless they decide to stay out. He can wash you and sanctify you and justify you in the name of the Lord Jesus Christ. And then you can be just as much a part of this congregation as anybody over there. We're just all a bunch of turned-around people."

"Turned around?" she asked.

"One hundred and eighty degrees. We changed our direction. We're striving toward Christ now instead of toward sin. That's the only difference between you and me."

She leaned her head back wearily on the headrest. "But I have a lot of baggage, Nick. A lot of people in this town have things to hold against me. And if I haven't hurt them, then they have preconceived notions about who I am and what I do."

"Those notions can be changed," he said. "I guess before this crisis with the church, I didn't have a lot of faith in my people. I guess I thought they wouldn't know what to do, how to act, unless I told them. Like they were all a bunch of sheep that would scatter if I wasn't there to keep them all together. But I'm learning differently. They've grown. They've matured. They're wiser than I thought. And they're too wise to think that they're above you somehow. That life of sin is just behind every one of us. We're all sinners saved by grace."

"What does that mean?" she asked. "Saved by grace?"

He drew in a deep breath. "It means we don't deserve it. Not one of us here deserves to be in communion with Christ or to go to heaven. Not a single one of us. But for some reason that no one on this earth can fathom, God looked down on us and saved us from our emptiness. He filled us up, Issie. He can fill you up too."

Someone across the street called to Nick, and he waved. "Come on, Issie. We're headed over to Aunt Aggie's to set up for the service. Won't you come?"

She wiped her eyes with both hands. "You don't need me there, Nick. I'll find something else to do."

"I'd like for you to be there," he said. "Please come. I like your company."

The words spoke volumes and told Issie all she needed to know to persuade her into coming. If it was true that Nick liked her company, then maybe these feelings she'd been nursing toward him were not entirely absurd. Somehow it vindicated her. She drew in a deep breath and got out of the truck. "All right," she said, "I'll come." Then she followed Nick back across the street and into the crowd of church people, climbing into the back of Jesse Pruitt's truck, to be transported the few blocks to Aunt Aggie's.

It took a couple of hours to set the yard

up in such a way that they could worship adequately the next morning, and as Issie found herself getting involved in the plans, she began to wish she could be in attendance. She had never come to Nick's church, had never heard him preach except at a funeral or two.

By the time the chairs were set up and the pulpit had been placed, and they had figured out where they would plug in the microphones, amplifiers, and speaker system, Issie found herself alone with Nick. Aunt Aggie had gone to the fire department to start supper, and the others had headed home. The dip in the land, so that the chairs were seated at the bottom of a bowl-shape in Aunt Aggie's acreage, allowed the hills around it to act as barricades against the breeze. Issie sat on one of the chairs like one of the congregants, trying to imagine whether she would feel out of place if she came. After a moment, Nick came and sat down beside her. "So what do you think?" he asked.

"I think I'm going to have to come hear you preach tomorrow," she said.

He grinned. "Are you kidding me?"

"Nope. I could hardly work this hard to

get everything set up, and then not be here."

"Well, yeah, but you realize *I'm* supposed to be preaching, don't you? Really think you can handle that?"

She breathed a laugh. "It's not your preaching that's kept me away. Maybe it's the church building."

"So you have a paranoia about church buildings?"

She shook her head. "No, I have a paranoia about rules."

"I told you —" he began, but she cut in.

"I know you did. It's not about rules. It's about the heart. I think I saw some evidence of that today." She could see that that pleased him.

"So you're really coming tomorrow?"

"I'm really coming," she said.

"Then I guess I'd better go home and work on that sermon."

"You don't have it ready yet?" she asked.

"No, I guess I've been a little distracted."

She suddenly felt guilty. "I guess I'm the one that caused that. All the rescuing you've been doing."

"No," he said, "it's not that. I've just been a little depressed. I haven't felt like there was any point." He looked over at her with a grin. "But if you're going to be here, maybe there is."

"Glad to be of service," she said.

• • •

That afternoon when Nick went back to his trailer to work on his sermon, he got his Bible and his other study aids and piled them all on his kitchen table. He began to write the sermon that the Lord had laid on his heart today, while he'd been working with his flock to salvage the church. As he was writing, he pictured Issie sitting there soaking in every word, so he wrote the sermon directly to her and prayed while he wrote it that the Lord would penetrate her callused heart so that that empty look would vanish from her eyes, and instead he would see joy and peace like he'd only seen in believers.

The depression since the church fire, the murder of Ben, his own failure in rescuing the boy, his worries about what Cruz and his gang might do next, and his doubts about his own calling all vanished in light of the hope that he might lead one person to Christ tomorrow.

And that person might be Issie Mattreaux.

Chapter Forty-Three

● ● ●

The old furniture warehouse Cruz's grandfather provided for their new hiding place was musty and dirty, and had the peculiar smell of newborn rodents. It gave Jake the creeps, even though he realized it was the least of his troubles. He had noticed a difference in the way Cruz and Jennifer and the others treated him, for they weren't making plans or strategizing in front of him. They were taking all of their planning sessions into another room — LaSalle and Decareaux were now part of the inner circle — and he and Benton were left out, along with the others who hadn't earned that status.

That was fine with him, since he didn't want to be a part of any more of their crimes anyway, but Benton felt slighted. "Man, here I am hobbling on crutches, popping antibiotics and painkillers, and worried about being arrested for murder. I paid my dues, but they're still treating me like I'm not worthy of hearing their stupid plans."

"You're better off," Jake said. "Trust me. I'd leave if I could."

"Why can't you? Nobody's bound and gagged you."

"Not physically, but they sure don't let me out of their sight." He glanced toward the closed door to the small room that had once been an office. Cruz and his confidants were huddled in there for an "executive meeting." Grayson, Drew, and Herring sat near the door, as if guarding it from anyone coming in or going out. The girls — Blair, Meg, and Kaye — worked at a table in the corner, assembling pipe bombs that Cruz said were security measures to defend them. "I want to see what they're gonna do next," he said. "I want to hear if they're planning to use those pipe bombs on Issie."

"Issie *and* Nick Foster," Benton said. "A little while ago, when they were setting up the mattresses, I heard Cruz say they're an item now. Said Issie passed out in the bar the other night, and Nick came to get her. Nick's life already wasn't worth a dime to Cruz, and now the two of them together? Issie can really pick 'em."

Jake looked at Benton as if he was delirious. "Nick Foster, the preacher? You're outta your mind. Issie would never get hooked up with a preacher."

"Ask Cruz," Ben said, as if their leader's word was gospel. "And Cruz *hates* him, man. I'm surprised they didn't burn his trailer down when they hit his church. He lives right across the street from it."

"I think they made their point with the church . . . whatever that point was." He rubbed his face hard, as if to wipe off his confusion. "Man, I *have* to do something." Jake dropped his elbows to his knees. "I bet my parents probably think I'm dead."

"My folks probably *hope* I am," Benton said.

"No, they don't."

"You're right," Benton said. "They probably haven't given me enough thought to care one way or another." He sat down and propped his leg on another chair. "My kid brother's probably freakin' out, though. He worries a lot."

"Maybe you could get a message to him that you're all right. Maybe he could go tell my folks. Maybe warn Issie."

Benton looked toward the room where

Cruz and Jennifer were. "No, I better not. If they found out, they might think I was turnin' on them."

Jake knew they already thought that about him. He was still uneasy about what they might do eventually. First chance he got, he was out of here, and the more he knew when he left, the better. Then maybe he could head off some of the damage they were planning to do.

Chapter Forty-Four

● ● ●

By the next morning Issie had almost talked herself out of going to the church service, even though she had given Nick her word that she would be there. She didn't know what to wear, for she owned very few dresses, but she went home long enough to sift through her various skirts and blouses, and finally came up with something that she felt was appropriate.

Then she worried about how to act. Did they kneel when they started the service? Maybe not out in the yard, she thought. Did they chant things she wouldn't know the words to? And what about singing? Should she just stand there and let everyone know she didn't know the first word — as if that would come as a surprise to anyone — or should she try to hum along and pretend she did? And what if they did something hokey like look at their neighbor and quote some Scripture she didn't know, hug, and say, "I love you"?

She wondered if she would be better off staying home. She found a million reasons to do so as she showered. She didn't feel well. Her muscles ached from her work yesterday. She had some reading to catch up on, friends to visit, a nephew to search for.

Yet tugging equally at her mind were the memories of Nick's excitement yesterday when she told him she would be there. It seemed to mean a lot to him, though she couldn't imagine why. The thought that he might like being around her as much as she enjoyed being with him seemed unfathomable to her. Still, she wanted to explore it a little more, and she remembered the feeling of belonging she had had yesterday working among the people of his church, and Allie's forgiveness and invitation to help set up for the service. She had worked hard. She wanted to see the fruit of her labor.

Finally deciding that she needed a friend to go with her, she picked up the phone and dialed Karen Insminger. It rang four times before the phone was answered.

"Hello." Karen sounded hoarse, and Issie knew she had pulled her out of a sound sleep.

"Karen, it's me, Issie."

"What do you want?" she asked, irritated. "I was sleeping."

"Then you shouldn't have answered the phone," Issie teased.

Karen didn't find that amusing. "This better be important, Issie."

Issie chuckled. "Well, I guess important is relative. I wanted to see if you would go to church with me."

"Church?" Karen started coughing as if the shock had been too much for her. "Excuse me. I thought you said 'church.' "

"I did, actually."

"I'm sorry," Karen said. "I must have really been out of it. I thought you said this was Issie."

"All right," Issie said. "So you don't want to go. All you have to do is say so."

"I don't want to go," Karen returned. "So, what's this all about anyway?"

"Well, it's the church that burned down the other day. Calvary Bible Church. I sort of helped them clear the land yesterday and everybody kept inviting me. And I've gotten to be pretty close friends with Nick Foster, the preacher."

"Issie, you're not after him, are you?"

Karen had heard the rumors, Issie thought. She wondered if all the medics sat around when she wasn't with them, speculating about her love life. "Don't you people have anything more exciting to think about?"

"I've just never known you to be interested in church, that's all. The only thing that could possibly get you there is a man."

"Thanks a lot."

"So, is that it?"

"No," Issie told her. "He's just a nice man. He's helped me. And also there's that community support kind of thing. The church burned down, but it didn't stop them from having services out on Aunt Aggie's lawn, and I just kind of feel like I ought to be there, just to show support."

"Oh, yeah, that's you," Karen said. "Little Miss Community."

Issie regretted calling. "I guess I've got my answer. Go back to sleep."

Karen had hung up even before she'd gotten the word "Bye" out, and Issie wondered why she had even bothered. Then, with her stomach in her throat, she headed out to her pickup to attend church for the first time in her life.

She was a few minutes late for the service, and as she pulled back up to Aunt Aggie's, she found a parking place in an empty lot beside her house. A couple of guys she knew from town waved her into a space.

She sat in her truck for a minute and rolled down her window, listening for any sounds that might clue her not to go to where the congregation was gathered. She heard the sound of a keyboard and a couple of guitars. Guitars in a church service? Then she realized that this was Nick's church. Nick probably had some of his personality tied up in it. Maybe it wasn't quite as stuffed shirt as she had imagined.

She eased out of the car and looked down toward the congregation. So many people had come that they were setting up extra chairs. She hoped Nick was encouraged by that.

She saw that someone was standing up front and singing, a young girl, maybe eighteen or nineteen. Maybe now wasn't such a bad time to go in.

She closed her door quietly, then walked through the cars and made her way down to the yard near Aunt Aggie's house. When she saw that there was standing room only at the back behind the chairs, she decided she would just stay there. That way she could slink out if she felt the need to. But before she had a chance to get used to her position, three different men had stood up and waved for her to come sit in their place.

She started to shake her head, thank them very much and tell them no, that she would stay right where she was, when she met Nick's eyes from the front of the gathering. He smiled at her and waved for her to come up and sit down in an empty seat near the front.

She dipped her head, looking at the ground as she made her way up, wishing no one here knew who she was. She imagined she heard gasps as she walked up the grassy aisle, people shocked that Issie Mattreaux had come into the presence of the Lord. Lightning would probably strike the whole assembly. The sun would be darkened and Nick would be struck dumb. If there was a God, he sure didn't want the likes of Issie Mattreaux in his house, even if it wasn't a house anymore.

She took her seat and looked up to see that she was next to Dan and Jill Nichols.

Jill patted Issie's arm. "Glad to see you here," she said. Issie just nodded.

When the girl stopped singing, Nick came to the front and grabbed one of the guitars. Issie's eyebrows came up as she watched him begin to play a chorus of "Amazing Grace." She didn't know where she had learned it, but somewhere in her past that song had become part of her consciousness. She couldn't make herself mouth the words, but as the others around her sang, she began to hum along.

The familiar sound of that tune was like a soothing balm to her soul. She couldn't imagine why she would respond so to it. She had never really concentrated on the words before, but now she listened, wondering why a song like this would be handed down from age to age, generation to generation, and why it would still be so popular.

She saw some of the people singing it with their eyes closed as if the song itself was a prayer that rose straight to heaven.

Chapter Forty-Five

● ● ●

Cruz and Jennifer had heard about the work done at the church site the day before, and all the people who had turned out for it. They'd heard about Nick Foster working right there along with the others, and the fact that the church burning had drawn the congregation together, instead of scattering them apart. And from the signs posted all over town, they'd learned about the church service on Aunt Aggie's lawn.

"Right up here, take a right," Jennifer said. "Where the cars are."

Driving the black van he'd borrowed from Decareaux, Cruz slowed down as he saw the cars parked on the side of the road. His eyes squinted as he came up beside the bowl-shaped lawn and saw the hundreds of people in folding chairs, worshiping in song.

He stopped the car and rolled his window down. The strains of "Amazing Grace" flew on the breeze. "You believe this?" he asked his sister. "There're more people here than they usually have on Sundays."

Jennifer pointed down to Nick, standing at the front of the crowd. "Look at Nick Foster. Standin' down there like they're worshipin' *him* or somethin'."

Cruz drove on, his face twisted as he tried to think it through. "So the church burnin' didn't phase 'em. They're stronger than ever. Nick Foster wasn't even affected."

"We have to do somethin' else," Jennifer said. "We can't let him win."

Cruz's hands tightened on the steering wheel as he drove faster. "Oh, we're gonna do somethin' else, all right," he said. "We'll show Nick Foster. And this time there won't be one black kid dead."

Jennifer's eyebrows lifted, and her eyes shone with the same light he'd seen in his mother's eyes when they were kids and his grandfather was preparing to go on one of his missions. "What are we gonna do?"

"We'll send people back over to mingle with them when they break up, and find out what they can about their next service. And then we're gonna be there to surprise them."

Chapter Forty-Six

● ● ●

When they had ended "Amazing Grace," Nick led them into a chorus of a faster song that Issie had never heard before, and those around her clapped their hands and sang along.

There was joy here, she realized, even though their building had just burned down and one of their families had lost a son. How could they find joy after that? She had expected a service of mourning, a service full of guilt, but instead, she felt the love of the people around her.

When it finally came time for Nick to give his sermon, he put the guitar on its stand and headed to the microphone at the front of the group. For the first time in her life, Issie Mattreaux heard the gospel of Jesus Christ presented in a way that couldn't be denied.

When he ended the service with a prayer of repentance and acceptance of Jesus

Christ, she felt her spirit fighting her mind for control. She wasn't ready to pray with him, because she wasn't sure she believed it could all be that easy. But she listened to every word, contemplating what it meant. And just before Nick led them in the amen, Issie whispered a prayer to Christ. "I don't know if you're there, but if you are, you're going to have to prove it to me."

She knew it was probably blasphemous, probably something that didn't please God. She knew that people said he wasn't a God to be tested, but she wasn't sure he was God at all. How could she be sure he wasn't just some figment of these people's imaginations that they clung to because they were weak?

But as she looked up at the congregation which had already burst into song again, she realized that she was the one who was weak, and these people had a rare strength that she had scarcely seen in her life. Something inside her yearned to have that kind of strength.

She didn't know why tears came to her eyes at that very moment as people around her were singing and praising God, but she found them rolling down her cheeks, and she wiped them away as quickly as they came. She saw that Jill had noticed she was crying, and she looked as if she didn't know what to do for Issie.

Issie thought she had to get out of there, had to get in her truck and drive away where she could cry in peace, or wipe from her mind whatever it was that had started her crying in the first place. She reached down for her purse, but Jill touched her back.

"Don't leave," Jill whispered. "We're having lunch right out here after the service. I really wish you'd come."

Issie wanted to ask her why, but something made her really want to stay, so she let go of her purse and sat up straight. She told herself she would just have to fight the tears and get through this morning. Something told her it would be worth it.

• • •

As the church service broke up, Nick found Issie in the crowd. He tried to get to her so that he could invite her for lunch, but people kept coming up to him and giving him hugs, telling him it was going to be all right, that they didn't need a building to worship the

Lord. The Holy Spirit's glory had not abandoned them.

He needed to hear those words, but he also needed to get close to Issie to make sure she stayed. She needed to be wrapped in the fellowship of these people. She needed to know what it was to be around those who trusted in Christ.

But the real reason he wanted to get close to her was to see if she had prayed the sinner's prayer with him. He had led the congregation in it just for her, but he'd had no indication that she had prayed it with him. It was suddenly very important that he find out if she had.

He cut through the group and found Issie standing with Jill and Dan. He was surprised that she hadn't made her way out yet. "Issie, I'm so glad you came," he said, in his best preacher voice. "I thought for a while you weren't going to."

She smiled up at him. Her eyes looked wet, red. He had seen her crying, and it had given him hope. "Sorry I was late."

"So, give me your best shot," he said. "How was it?"

"Not as bad as I thought," she said.

He looked wounded. "Is that all?"

She laughed softly. "You'd know what a compliment that was if you knew what I'd been expecting."

"Is it something about my personality that told you I was a terrible preacher?"

"No, not the preaching," she said. "I just hadn't been to a church service before. The only time I've even darkened the door of a church is when I went to a wedding or a funeral."

"Well, we'll have to keep you coming long enough to darken the door of ours when we get it built," he said. "So how about staying for lunch?"

Issie shrugged. "I was thinking about it, but I didn't bring a covered dish or anything."

"Don't worry about it. Aunt Aggie made enough for a dozen people. In our whole history of covered dishes, we've never had a shortage."

"All right," she said. "I guess I'll stay."

Issie forgot the tension with which she had approached church this morning, and as she ate lunch and fellowshiped with the people, most of whom she'd known all her life, she found that there was no judgment or condemnation among those who surrounded her. A few snubbed her, but overall, she didn't get the general impression that people were asking what a woman like Issie Mattreaux would be doing among them.

Finally, she realized there were so many people there that most had probably not noticed her. She sat on a lawn chair that Nick had brought for her to use, and tried to fight the feeling that she was special, that the preacher had singled her out to pay special attention to. But that was silly. It wasn't as if he was singling her out because she was an attractive woman. It had a lot more to do with her soul than she wanted to admit.

She scanned the crowd looking for people who might be whispering about her, when she saw two young faces milling in the crowd. She had seen them before. They had been there when she treated Benton's leg the other night. Her heart tripped into race mode, and she sprang up and started toward them. They must have seen her coming, for they put their backs to her and started to walk away. She broke into a trot, but they went faster, threading through cars and getting far away from the crowd. Finally, she caught up to them. "Hey, you!"

The boys turned around. "Yeah?" They were both wearing jeans and wrinkled T-shirts, and she knew they hadn't been in the service or she would have noticed.

"You were at the Benton house last night. You know my nephew. Where is he? Where's Jake Mattreaux?"

"I don't know any Jake Mattreaux," one of them said.

"You're lying," she told them. "I know you're lying. Where is he?"

They both stared at her, their faces suddenly serious. A chill went through her, and she realized she shouldn't have gotten so far from the crowd, not when their group had tried to kill her just days ago.

"I'm warning you," she said, stepping into her paramedic personality and approaching them as she would if she were in uniform. "I want you to listen to me. If anything happens to my nephew, so help me, I will spend the rest of my life searching for you and making you pay. Do you understand me?"

They didn't seem amused at her bravado, yet she knew they had not taken it seriously. But without another word, they both turned and walked away. Quickly, she searched the parked cars for the truck she'd been driving and ran to get into it. She could follow them. She could follow them and let them lead her to Jake.

She pulled the truck out of its place, then made the block and saw the two boys in a white Ford Escort. They were pulled over to the side of the road a couple of blocks from the church, and two other kids were getting in.

Where had they all been? Why had they been at the church? What were they up to?

She hung back, staying out of their sight, until they were on their way. Then she followed them, hoping they would lead her to Jake.

Chapter Forty-Seven

● ● ●

The arsenal of guns that Cruz and the group were bringing in clued Jake that they were planning something even worse than the church burnings. As he and Benton sat in a corner of the moldy warehouse while Cruz plotted in another room, he began to wonder if there was something he could do. "Somebody needs to turn these idiots in," Jake told Benton. "How many more people are gonna die?"

"At least two, if we try to turn them in," Benton said.

"Well, maybe we're both just cowards."

"Maybe we are."

He watched Benton devour a bologna sandwich as if he hadn't eaten in a week. "How's your leg, man?"

"Sore," Benton said. "Really sore. But I'm not feeling so weak anymore. Antibiotics . . . good stuff."

Jake tried to see through the glass door

to the room where Cruz and the group sat. "All those cameras they had, and the Polaroids they brought back . . . what are they taking pictures of?"

"Who knows?"

He looked at his friend again. "Benton, you know we gotta do something, don't you? We can't let them kill any more people. Not if we ever plan to look ourselves in the mirror again."

Benton dropped the last bite of his sandwich, as if the words had stolen his appetite. "Hey, I can't look myself in the mirror now, after what I did."

"Then undo some of the damage by helping me figure out what they're up to, so we can stop them."

The door to the office room came open, and Cruz, Jennifer, and the others came out. Benton got to his feet. "I'll see what I can find out."

◦ ◦ ◦

Issie followed the car at as much distance as she could, trying not to be seen as they rounded curves and turned corners, heading into the warehouse district of Newpointe. They led her to one old warehouse set back from the street, with garbage filling a ditch out front, and about six cars and pickups in front of it.

Was this where Jake was?

She watched them all go in, then left her truck some distance down the street and got out to walk the rest of the way. She went to the window of the building and peered in and saw the pile of guns in the middle of the floor, and Jake's dangerous friends encircled around them. But she didn't see Jake.

He was in there somewhere, and something told her he was in trouble. Maybe he was in a back room, hurt. Maybe he needed her.

She went to another window and looked in, trying to determine if there was some way to get in and look for him. There was an open window on the side, and it opened into a dark room that was separate from the room where they seemed to congregate. She managed to lift herself into it, and dropped down into the room.

She looked around. There was a table, and it was covered with papers and snapshots. She went closer to study them. They were pictures of this morning's worship service, she realized, pictures of the congregation sitting in Aunt Aggie's yard. They looked as if they had been taken from the street down — into the bowl-shaped yard. Had there been more of them there, hidden on the hills surrounding Aunt Aggie's property, standing back in the trees where no one could see them?

She wondered why anyone would have taken pictures like this, then she realized that it had to have been the two boys she had spotted and followed. Was that why they had come?

She looked through the small window in the door, and saw them still huddled around a pile of firearms. They were planning something, and it involved Nick's church . . . and lots of guns.

She went back to the table and picked up one of the papers under the snapshots. It was a diagram of the grounds at Aunt Aggie's, the house and trees surrounding where they had placed the chairs, and on the hills surrounding the worship area, she saw stick figures with guns pointed threateningly at the crowd.

Her heart jolted. Quickly, she folded up the paper and stuck it into her purse. She had to get out of here. She had to take this to the police and warn them. She slipped back up to the windowsill, but as she did, her foot caught on a hubcap leaned against the wall, and it toppled and fell with a clatter.

She dove out the window and bolted toward her truck, praying that no one had heard. But behind her she heard someone yell, "It's that woman again!"

She saw Cruz explode out of the warehouse, and she ran with all her might to reach her truck.

Chapter Forty-Eight

● ● ●

Jake shot out behind Cruz, trying to stop him long enough for Issie to get away. But Cruz was gaining on her like a linebacker foiling the winning touchdown. He caught Issie and knocked her down.

"Let her go, Cruz!" Jake shouted. "Let her go!" He threw himself on top of Cruz, but three others descended on him and wrestled him off.

He tried to knock them loose, flailing his arms and kicking at them, but Cruz clamped his arms around Issie, and she kicked and bucked and tried to shake him free. "Jake, help me!"

Cruz wrestled her to a rusty blue Subaru. "Open the trunk!" he shouted, and Jennifer popped it open.

Jake fought to get away, but someone pulled him into a choke hold, immobilizing him. The harder he fought, the tighter the arm clamped against his throat. He drove his fingernails into the arm squeezing the life out of him, but couldn't break free.

He heard Issie scream, and Cruz lifted her and stuffed her into the trunk. She kicked and fought to get out, but Cruz hit her across the face, and it knocked her back into the depths of the trunk. Before she could fight her way back up, he had slammed the trunk shut.

Jake could hear her fighting inside, banging and screaming, but Cruz backed away, and turned, red-faced, to Jake. Jake kicked behind him, his heel tearing into the knee of the person holding him, and his captor cursed and let him go. Jake ducked out of his grasp.

He had to get help. He had to get out of here and somehow get to a phone. He started running, and heard feet behind him on the gravel. Cruz yelled, and he heard Benton telling Jake to run.

Jake headed for the woods and leaped over a log, tore through a cluster of bushes, and slid down a hill covered with dead leaves.

He heard a gunshot, and someone just behind him yelped and fell. He looked back and saw Decareaux in a heap at the top of the hill he'd slid down, and Benton standing with a shotgun in his hand. "Go, Jake! Keep running!"

Jake crossed a stream, then ran up the other bank, clambering to get out of sight. Another shot rang out, and he swung around and saw Benton standing hand to chest, a look of shock on his face. He stood there for a moment. His eyes met Jake's, and he mouthed the word, "Run." Then his friend dropped and slid limply down the hill. Jake turned and ran.

Somehow, Benton had thrown them off, and he heard them running in another part of the woods, footsteps and cursing and gunshots shooting without aim. He kept running in the opposite direction, pounding the dirt and the dead leaves and leaping over logs and branches.

When he thought he was far enough away, he hoisted himself into a tree and rested on a branch, waiting to make sure he was clear before he tried to help Issie.

◦ ◦ ◦

The car began to move, and Issie lay trapped in the black compartment. She banged on the trunk door and screamed until her throat was raw. They drove for several minutes on the road, and then she felt them pulling off. She heard gravel beneath the tires and was jerked from side to side as Cruz drove the car into a place where she knew no one could find her. Would he kill her when he got her there? Was this how it would all end?

She screamed and banged against the trunk, using all the strength she had to make noise. Someone along the way might hear, maybe at a stoplight, and call the police. But all her efforts seemed futile.

Finally, she heard the engine cut off, heard the door close, heard other car doors slamming, then an engine driving away.

Silence. They were leaving her here, trapped in the trunk of a car in a place where no one would ever look.

Then she heard a car door again, voices, and the Subaru engine starting. She felt the car moving. She screamed and kicked again, to no avail.

They drove for twenty minutes or so, when finally she felt them crunching back through gravel, heard the scraping and scratching of trees. Then the car stopped, and she heard them getting out, heard another car behind them . . . doors closing. The other car left.

The silence screamed out her hopelessness.

Meanwhile, Jake's friends were planning to ambush Nick Foster's church the next time they met together. People would be killed. Perhaps even Nick.

She wailed again and screamed, banging with her shoulder and elbow and trying to get out, but there was little hope.

⋅ ⋅ ⋅

Jake waited for over an hour before he dropped out of the tree. They weren't after him anymore, he felt sure, but panic still raged in his heart. What had they done with Issie? And was Benton dead?

He had to go back. He had to see if the blue Subaru was still there, or if Benton had been taken care of.

He tried to retrace his steps back through the woods, careful not to be heard. He had done a lot of hunting with his father and knew how to remember landmarks. He passed the log he'd almost tripped over earlier, the dead oak, the wasp's nest . . .

Then he came to the spring and ran along

it, looking for the place where Benton had fallen. He went carefully, stopping and listening every few feet, waiting to see if it was a trick. But there were no sounds except those of the mockingbirds in the trees, the woodpeckers drilling out their holes, the crickets and frogs and wind.

Then he saw his friend still lying at the bottom of the embankment, as twisted and broken as when he'd first fallen. Jake's throat constricted as he raced toward him and fell at his side. "Benton!" he whispered. "Benton!"

There was no response, so he shook him hard. He saw the bullet hole through his back, and as terror rose up in his throat, he turned him over. The exit wound had taken most of Benton's chest.

"Benton, come on, man. Come on, get up!" He reached for his arm and tried to find a pulse, but there was none.

He sat there on his knees and tried to muffle the sob screaming out his throat. He had brought Benton into the group. He had led him into this trouble, and Benton had died trying to keep Jake from being caught.

"I'll kill them myself," he said through his teeth. "Don't worry, Benton, I won't let them get away with this." He left his friend on the dirt, then climbed up the embankment, intent on making someone pay. He slowed as he got to the top and looked carefully toward the warehouse. All of the cars were gone.

They had bugged out, just like a military unit whose security had been compromised. The blue Subaru was gone, and Issie was in trouble.

They were taking her away, locked in a trunk, and he didn't know where he could send anyone to help her. Still, he had to get help. He would have to forge ahead in the woods, hoping to come out somewhere on the other side, or find a hunter or someone else who could help him, and rescue Issie.

He got up and stumbled into the brush as fast as he could, knowing that death could catch up to him at any moment.

Chapter Forty-Nine

• • •

Nick was worried about Issie. He didn't know why she'd taken off the way she had, but an hour later, she still hadn't returned. He was getting nervous.

When Steve Winder, Issie's partner, called around three, he had even more reason to worry. Issie hadn't shown up for work.

"I was wondering if you'd seen her," Steve said. "I know you two have been together a lot lately."

He decided not to comment on that. "Well, no, I haven't seen her, not since our picnic this afternoon. She left in a big hurry. She hasn't come back."

"Well, she was supposed to be on duty at three," Steve said. "She didn't show up. It's not like her."

Nick frowned. "She didn't call or anything?"

"No," Steve said, "and I've been trying to call her apartment and nobody's home. I even called over at her brother's and he said he hasn't seen her."

"Has this ever happened before?" Nick asked.

"No way," Steve said. "I've been her partner for a couple of years now. She's never even been late."

Nick felt sick. Something had happened to her. "Look, I'll see if I can catch up with her. I'll get back to you."

"Thanks."

Nick hung up the phone and sat staring at the wall for a moment, trying to separate panic from concern. Where would she have gone so quickly? Who might she have seen? He grabbed his cell phone off the counter and rushed outside. He got into his car and set out to find her before it was too late.

♦ ♦ ♦

Jake managed to keep running through the woods, desperate to get help. He was lost and it was getting dark and he didn't know how far he had to go to get out on the other side. All he knew was that he couldn't give up now. He had to get to someone who could help Issie before she wound up like Benton.

He reached the bayou and stood for a moment, panting and sweating and trying to figure out which way he needed to go to get out of the woods.

He took off running along the bank, hoping that he was right in determining that it would come out next to the place where the new post office sat. Then he could get to a phone and call the police. Maybe it wasn't too late to save Issie.

He'd never been so thankful in his life as when he heard cars up ahead and knew he was getting near civilization. He ran faster, harder, thickets and thornbushes tearing at his pants legs and his arms.

He crossed the street and went to the drugstore where a pay phone sat at the corner of the parking lot. He dug through his pants pockets, got out the money for the phone, then stood there a moment, trying to decide whom to call first.

He put the change in and started to dial his parents but realized that might be a mistake. They would want to come get him, but home was the first place Cruz would look for him, and he couldn't risk having them find him there.

No, he thought. He needed to call the police. They were the only ones who could help Issie. He didn't know the number so he dialed 911 and waited for the dispatcher to answer.

"Nine-one-one, may I help you?"

"Uh, yeah," he said. "Uh, I'm calling to report a crime." His voice was shaking and hoarse. He could hardly get it out.

"What crime?" the dispatcher asked.

"Uh, kidnapping, sort of. Issie Mattreaux. You may know her. The paramedic."

"Yeah, I know Issie," the dispatcher said.

"Well, she's sort of been kidnapped. A guy named Cruz has her. I saw him put her into the trunk of a car, and he drove away with her. I don't know where they are, but you might still catch them in the blue Subaru."

"Can I have your name please?" she asked.

His mind started reeling, and he thought she wouldn't send help until he gave her what she wanted. "Keith," he lied, "Keith Jones." That seemed to satisfy her, and she got off the subject.

"Keith, can you tell us where they were headed?"

"No," he said, "I have no idea."

"Was there some kind of fight, some kind of argument?"

"Sort of," he said. "She had kind of stumbled on some evidence and ratted on them. They want revenge."

"What kind of evidence?"

"About the church burnings and the murders. Also, a guy got shot over by the old Mayflower Furniture warehouse. He's in the woods, down an embankment. I'm pretty sure he's dead."

There was silence for a moment. He pictured her frantically trying to get a message to the cars she was dispatching. He started to realize that his call could be traced. At any moment now police cars could descend on him, and in moments he'd have handcuffs snapped on and be on his way to jail.

He hung up.

He started walking toward the edge of the woods, hoping to stay in the shadows enough that he could get away from this place in case they had traced the call. And as he walked along, he tried to rack his brain for a place to go. None of his friends could be trusted. He didn't want to put his own parents in jeopardy.

Nick Foster. The name came to him out of the blue, and he remembered hearing that Issie and Nick might be an item. He knew Nick would want to know that Cruz had it in for him, that the first fire and killing had to do with revenge against him.

Maybe Nick could help.

He knew that Nick lived across the street from the church that had burned down, so he headed that way, just a few blocks away, and hoped that Nick would be home.

It took him half an hour to reach Nick's trailer, and when he did, he realized there was no car there. He peered across the street to the place where the church had been and saw no sign of Nick. Where could he be?

Maybe he was at the fire station, he thought. What if he was there all night and Jake couldn't reach him without giving himself away? He stumbled onto the front porch, a weather-beaten structure that was in need of repair.

He walked up the rickety steps, wishing for the cover of darkness, though it was only five P.M. He sat down in a corner and leaned back against the rail. He didn't know how long it had been since he'd slept. Most of the people he'd been living with only fell asleep when daylight hit.

He closed his eyes and tried to relax, wishing that Nick would come home soon. If not, he supposed he'd have to sleep here all night, but he would have to leave before daylight. Maybe the police would take the information he gave them and find Issie by then, and then they could arrest Cruz and Jennifer and the rest of the gang before they did any more harm to churches or people, or Jake's own relatives or friends.

● ● ●

Nick searched everywhere he thought Issie could be but didn't find her, and as he drove, he felt the growing sense of panic that something had happened to her. She was in trouble. He knew better than to think she had just been irresponsible by not showing up for work. He had contacted everyone he knew who was a friend of Issie's, but no one knew her whereabouts.

Almost to the point of despair, he decided to head back home, get on his knees, and pray for Issie as hard as he could. It was the only thing he knew to do.

He drove back to the street where the

church had burned and pulled into his gravel driveway. His headlights lit up the front of his porch, and he saw the shape of something he hadn't expected on his porch. Had someone left something, he wondered, or was that a person hunched in the corner waiting for him?

Issie, he thought suddenly. She was here, waiting for him to get home. He should have known. He stopped the car, lunged out, and raced up the steps.

"Issie?" But when he got to the front he was shocked to see that it wasn't Issie at all. Instead, a young man was hunched in the corner. Could this be Jake?

Startled out of sleep, the boy sat up straight. It took a second for him to orient himself, then as if he realized where and why he was here, he grabbed both of Nick's arms and pulled himself to his feet.

"Nick, Issie's in trouble!"

"Where is she?" he asked.

"I don't know," Jake said. "She was snooping around the warehouse where we were. I think she followed somebody there, and she went in. They must have heard her, because she ran out, and then Cruz went wild. He put her in his trunk and drove her off somewhere. I don't know where they went."

"In his trunk?" Panic almost stopped Nick's breath. Issie might not live through this. He pictured her somewhere locked in the trunk of a car. Was she dead or alive?

He unlocked his front doors and bolted inside, Jake on his heels. "We've got to call the police," he said.

"I already did," Jake told him. "I don't know if they believed me but I tried. I described the car, and I told them who was driving it. Maybe they can find her."

Nick dialed the number of the police department and asked for Stan's desk. Stan wasn't in, so he talked to Sid Ford.

"Sid, Nick Foster. Have you heard anything about Issie?"

"We've got an APB out on that same blue Subaru right now," Sid said, "but we ain't found nothin' yet."

"Come on, Sid!" Nick yelled. "This is a small town. How many places are there to look?"

"They coulda left town by now," Sid said. "They could be anywhere between here and the south shore. There's woods all around, man."

"Sid, he's got her in her trunk. He could kill her if he hasn't already!"

"I understand that," Sid said, "and we're doin' the best we can. We've got dogs out, and a helicopter, and everybody's looking for her. But we can't do more than that. Not unless you've got some more information that would help us."

"What do you need?" Nick asked. "You have the make and model of the car. You have the name of the person driving it."

"We're workin' on it," Sid said, "and when we find somethin' out, trust me, you'll be the first to know." Sid hung up, and Nick sat staring at the receiver in his hand. He slammed it down, almost breaking the telephone, then he turned on Jake.

"They're your friends," he said. "Now you tell me where they might have taken her!"

"I'm telling you, I don't know," Jake said. "I'm on your side, okay? She's my aunt. I've known her all my life. I don't want anything to happen to her. That's why I came here. I've been out of the loop on everything for the past couple of days, and then they killed my friend Benton. Shot him through the back, and he didn't deserve it. He killed a kid for them, all just to throw the cops off of Cruz. And look how they reward him!"

Nick felt sick. "Do you know where Benton is?" he asked. "Are you sure he's dead?"

"Absolutely dead," he said. "He's out by the warehouse, only everybody's gone."

Nick's mind raced. "Jake, it would be a good idea to take the police to him. Come on and get in the car."

"No!" Jake said. "They'll arrest me, man. Lock me up! Then who's gonna look for Issie?"

"I am," Nick said. "The cops are."

"But I *know* places," he said. "I *know* some of their hangouts. There's Cruz's deer camp . . . Besides, I already told them where he is near the warehouse. They'll find him there."

Nick tried to think, and he rubbed his temples with shaky hands. "So she was still conscious when he got her into the trunk?"

"Yes," Jake said. "She was conscious all right. Banging and kicking and screaming. It's a wonder he'd ever keep her in that trunk."

Nick hoped that was true. Maybe her rage and her emergency training and her strength would get her out of this. He was shaking, sweating, and his mind was having trouble following a logical train of thought. "Okay, Jake, we have to do something." He sank down on to the porch step next to Jake, still rubbing his face. He let his fingers slide slowly down his cheeks. "Jake, how do I know this isn't some kind of trick? I don't know you. I don't know what you've been up to. For all I know, you may have killed Ben Ford."

"No, I didn't," Jake said. "I knew they killed him, but I wasn't there. Man, I was stupid. I bought into everything. Cruz thinks he's God or something, and we all thought he was too. He had the Bible memorized, and he had this plan for us to build a secure compound and live together and grow our own food. It felt good to believe in something and have a goal."

"So you let them kill people and you sat by and didn't do anything about it?"

Jake looked down. "I know it's stupid. But I'm telling you the truth. By the time I got wise that he wasn't who he said he was, I knew they'd kill Benton and me both if either of us tried to get out. Plus Issie was getting involved where she shouldn't have, making a lot of people crazy, and I decided I'd better stay with them just to make sure they didn't get to her, 'cause you know they slashed her tires and they broke into her apartment and left a dead cat on her bed. *I gave them the key and let them do it! I'm such a jerk!*"

"Why didn't you call the police?" Nick asked.

"Because I was messed up," he said. "And I was scared. And to tell you the truth, I was worried that I would be the one going to jail. I didn't know what would happen."

"So your staying out of jail was more important than saving your aunt's life?" Nick asked. He could see the self-hatred on Jake's face.

"What can I say? I'm a coward. I admit it!"

Nick groaned and rubbed his eyes hard. He let out a heavy sigh. "At least you came now."

"Well, it's not going to do her a lot of good if she's already dead," Jake cried. He smeared his tears away. "How could I have trusted those guys? I knew they didn't care about anybody but themselves."

"It wasn't a matter of trust," Nick said. "It was a matter of you getting something out of it. You were having fun. You didn't have any restrictions on you. You had the freedom you thought you wanted. But just like all the freedoms we think we want, they wind up becoming a prison instead. You might have been trying to keep yourself out of jail, Jake, but you're in a cage as surely as if the police had put you there."

Jake didn't deny it. "I can't undo anything I've done," he said. "All I can do is try to find her, try to help *you* find her."

"Then think," Nick said. "You mentioned a deer camp. Can you take me there?"

Jake tried to calm down, and it was clear his mind was running through all the possibilities. "Yeah, I could find it easy."

Nick got to his feet and pulled his keys out of his pocket. "Okay, let's go."

They piled into the car, and pulled out of the driveway. "Which way?" Nick asked.

Jake pointed the direction he needed to turn.

"You know, this guy, Cruz," Jake said. "He's a lunatic. Really. He's insane. He stabbed Benton in the leg because he was kissing Jennifer or something. It was like he blacked out and went into some kind of rage. Didn't even make sense." He gestured to the next turn. "Up here, to the right."

Nick drove, the streetlights flashing then darkening his face as they passed.

"So what's your relationship with Issie anyway?" Jake asked. "I know she doesn't go to church, but you and her are the talk of the town. Even Cruz and them know you got her from the bar the other night."

Nick was quiet for a few moments. "We've gotten to be good friends lately."

"Well, if you don't mind my saying so," Jake said, "it doesn't seem like a match made in heaven to me."

"It's *not* a match made in heaven," Nick said. "We're just friends. I've been worried about her. She knew she could count on me, for several things," he said. "For coming out and looking for her, for rescuing her, for praying for her."

"Issie needs a lot more than prayer right now," Jake said. "Up here. Turn into this dirt road."

Nick turned onto the dirt road, feeling as if he might be driving into a trap, but he had to try. He put his headlights on bright and drove down the dirt road, weaving back and forth among the trees, till finally he came to an opening and saw an old, inactive oil rig in the middle of the property. There were no cars to be seen.

"Aw, man," Jake said. "We came here once with a keg of beer, so I thought they could have parked her here."

Nick slammed his hand on the steering wheel. "Then where are they?"

"I don't know," Jake said, "but there are a few more places that they've been known to go. I'll take you to each one of them. Just turn around and go back out the same way you came in."

Nick did that, but as he drove, he realized how hard this was going to be. Issie could be anywhere, and it might already be too late.

● ● ●

Chapter Fifty

Issie was bleeding. She had a cut across her cheek where Cruz had hit her, and a gash down her arm where she had wedged it between the trunk and the car, trying to keep him from closing it. As he'd wrestled her into the trunk, her calf had caught on a sharp metal corner, ripping open her pants and slashing her leg. She lay cramped in the darkness, folded in a fetal position.

The rough carpet beneath her was wet with her blood. She wasn't sure which was bleeding harder — her face, her arm, or her leg — but she couldn't maneuver enough to get to any of those places to apply pressure. She tried to turn or wiggle free so that she could move more easily, but she was wedged.

Pain shot through her leg, throbbed on her cheek, and the cut on her arm rubbed against the hard carpet as she tried to turn over. Her head ached, but worse than all that was the realization that if she didn't get out of this car and days passed, and Nick Foster's church met at Aunt Aggie's for the midweek service, they could all wind up dead, right down to the preacher himself. There was no one to warn them.

She wailed, then screamed for help again and banged on the metal roof. But no one came, and she feared no one would. Where had they taken her? They had driven for some time. They could be out of town, far away from Newpointe, way back in the woods where no one would ever find her.

She wondered if Jake had told them what had happened, if they were even looking for her, or if he had wimped out and decided to go back to his gang. Or had they killed him? She had heard several gunshots.

She managed to squeeze her arm free and began to reach above her head where she couldn't see, feeling around for the few items Cruz had left in his car. She found some greasy jumper cables and a tire gauge, but nothing else.

Was God trying to get her attention, or had he only turned away?

She closed her eyes and tried to take inventory of what had brought her here. She had to admit that her own influence over Jake might have led him to his association with these people. She hadn't shown him any reason not to get involved in evil.

Everyone was good, she had told him, because good was a relative term. She had told him that we defined our own good and evil. It was whatever you thought it was. But now she knew that wasn't true. There were clear lines between good and evil, lines that Nick understood, and all the people in his congregation did as well. It was only beginning to become clear to her.

What had brought her here? she asked again. Was it generations of a family who followed their own path? She wondered if her brother would even look for her, or if he'd simply drown his worries in a bottle of wine. That was how their family handled crisis.

But now it all seemed to have caught up with her, as if God was trying to get her attention. She wept harder and yelled out, "You've got it, God! You've got my attention now! What do you want me to see?"

She thought of Mark Branning and Allie, the forgiveness that Allie had shown her, yet the way that Mark avoided her as if she would bring plagues on him. She thought of how happy Dan and Jill were, and Stan and Celia, in spite of all the trials they'd faced.

She had never seen them go out and get drunk just because things went bad. She hadn't sat around the table with them at Joe's Place reliving the cases they'd gone out on that day. They led quieter, cleaner lives, lives that she had considered boring until she'd found herself locked in the trunk of a car.

She had even considered Nick to be boring at one time, but something in her spirit had changed. Lately he had seemed like someone safe, a point of refuge in which she could hide. She didn't know why she had been so attracted to him lately, why she'd gravitated toward him in every situation, why he was the first person she thought of when she needed to call for help. But now *his* life was in danger, and she could do nothing about it.

She banged on the roof again, trying to get the trunk up, but it wouldn't budge. She was getting weak. If she didn't do something soon to stop the bleeding, the life might just bleed right out of her.

She groped down around her legs, and

touched a towel that seemed stiff and greasy. She took the towel and bit until it tore. Then she ripped a strip and managed to bring her leg up as far as she could. Wiggling her way down, she was able to touch her calf. She inched the strip of cloth around it, tied it tightly to stop the blood.

"Please, God," she whispered, "don't let me die here. Get me out of here so I can tell them before they kill everybody."

She didn't care about herself anymore, or her past sins or her very soul. She didn't care what was going to happen to her in the future. All she knew was that Nick and his congregation were in trouble, and she could help them if she could just get free.

She tore off another strip and wrapped her arm, bandaged it as tightly as she was able in the small space she had. Then she wadded another piece of terry cloth and laid her face down on it. The pressure would stop the bleeding, she hoped, but it wouldn't stop the pain. And every time she moved she was liable to start it again.

She closed her eyes and tried to picture God watching over her from somewhere up in the sky too far away to reach her and unlock that trunk.

"I know you don't have anything for me, God," she said. "I'm not even worth your time. I'm probably so repulsive you can't even stand to look at me. But that's okay. You can turn your face from me . . . But those people at that church, they're your people. And Wednesday night when they gather for their service, Cruz is going to be waiting. And there's not going to be any place for them to run." She started to sob.

"Please, God. I don't want Nick to die. I don't want any of them to die. You've got to stop them or you've got to help me so I can. Do whatever you want with me. I don't care. I deserve every bit of it. But they don't."

She wasn't sure if the bleeding had stopped, and she almost didn't care. She felt the life drifting out of her as sleep pushed its way in. Finally, she drifted into a state of rest, weary from tears, fighting, and the loss of her own blood.

Chapter Fifty-One

● ● ●

Cruz drove the black van to the edge of Aggie Gaston's property. They had circled the block until her bedroom lights had gone off, and now they felt safe pulling up to the ridge circling her property. There were two of them — Redmon and Graham — besides himself and Jennifer, four guerillas brave enough to risk their lives to support the cause. They would make their mark. They would scatter that congregation and knock down their high-and-mighty preacher, and make a name for themselves even better than their grandfather's.

And if all his fame was postmortem, he supposed that was preferable to going to jail. He had always known he would lay down his life. He pictured himself walking through the pearly gates, rifle in hand, and seeing only the faces of Caucasians who cheered him like one of the heroes of his faith. God himself would greet him like a messianic prince and crown him with a jeweled crown, and take him to his new point of power, where he would rule the underclass with an iron scepter.

And Nick Foster would learn not to mess with him.

They got out and headed to their respective posts around the perimeter of Aunt Aggie's property. It was just a drill, a practice session to make sure everyone knew where they were supposed to be. They had to do it under cover of night to make sure no one saw them.

He chuckled lightly as he headed for the tree that he would stand behind on Wednesday evening before the sun set, and as this mixed congregation sat and prayed together, probably about rebuilding the church that had no business linking itself to God, they would rain hell and brimstone down upon them.

That is, if Jake didn't ruin everything for them. He thought of the kid again, somewhere out there waiting to make trouble. That was why he'd kept Issie alive. He hoped that one of the team he'd sent looking for him would find him, and Issie's life would be enough incentive to keep him from talking.

His only disappointment was that he hadn't been able to talk more members into following him in this mission. Jennifer was with him, because she had grown up as he had, and knew what it was like to experience the thrill of a mission well-planned and executed. But he'd had to be careful with the others. He'd kept his plans exclusive to his inner circle, and asked for volunteers who had the courage to finish this church off once and for all. Until they did, their plans for the compound would be on hold, and they would have to wait for critical new recruits with money who could finance their plans. Vengeance was the Lord's, he told them, and until he wreaked that vengeance, God's blessing would be withheld. He'd had a vision, he told them, and had received the clearest of orders.

So far, only Redmon and Graham had agreed to be a part of this. He knew they didn't quite understand why he was doing it — after all, Nick Foster had insulted and implicated him and Jennifer, not the others — but they had such a fascination with the other shootings across the country

that he suspected they just wanted the no-
toriety. Both of them were detached from
their families and outcasts among their
peers, and had little to lose. Their commitment to him and their holy war was exem-
plary.

He saw that Jennifer, Harris, and Graham
stood in their positions at the other corners
of Aggie's property, with perfect shots down
to the bottom of the bowl that was her land,
where the chairs had been set up Sunday
morning. He shone the flashlight on his face
again and gave the signal for which they
were all watching. He heard a series of pops
produced by their mouths, as if they were
kids pretending to shoot guns. But Wednesday night there would be no pretense.
Wednesday night before the sun set, the
bullet fire would be real.

Chapter Fifty-Two

● ● ●

Issie's throat was dry, and the gashes on her face, arm, and leg ached. Her muscles had gotten stiff, and she could hardly move. Her head throbbed with all the force with which she'd been slammed into the trunk.

Her eyes had adjusted to the dark, but she still couldn't make out everything in it. At least her bleeding had stopped and the carpet beneath her face had dried crisp.

She tried to squirm free so she could turn and see what was behind her in the trunk or what was at her feet, but it was too tight and she couldn't move. The air was getting stale, thin, and she was having trouble breathing. She was drenched with sweat.

It had been a cool October for Louisiana, but tonight it seemed sweltering. She wasn't going to make it. She would die of thirst if not hunger, or her wounds would get infected.

She reached up and tried to feel the junction between the trunk lid and its bottom, and felt the rubber strip that kept it sealed. If she could just peel back that rubber strip she'd be able to get some air. Maybe she would be able to see out in case anyone came. If she had warning, maybe she could scream and yell, or surprise Cruz with a counterattack.

She picked at it and pulled until part of it tore, and then she began to chip it away where the heat and age had made it flake. After a while she had a little slit where air was coming through. She saw that the car was in some kind of shed. It was still dark outside, and she wasn't able to see much of anything, but the cool air on her face was welcome.

She started to think of her mother, the woman who had died just two years ago. Issie had grieved even though their relationship was lacking.

Sarah Mattreaux had once had a dream of being a singer, but according to her, she'd never had a break. She hadn't finished high school, for she'd quit early to follow a boy in a rock band that she thought was going to make her a star. Instead, she had wound up singing from band to band in the seventies, never lighting long enough to get a real job.

It was during that time that Issie's brother

had been conceived. Sarah had never told the name of his father, and he had taken her maiden name. Issie wondered if she even knew who the father was. Years later she'd had Issie with an alcoholic who felt no familial responsibility at all.

She started to cry and wished she could call out for her, the mama who had so rarely been around to bandage her wounds and nurture her spirit. Her mother had always worked nights for tips. She and her brother had practically raised themselves. She wondered if her mother had died with regrets.

She wasn't bitter, she thought, trying to keep her mind occupied as she sought out the good memories she had of her mother. They had attended a Saints game together when Issie was thirteen, she recalled. She had thought it was something that her mother had chosen to do with her, but halfway through the game she'd realized that her mother was there because she'd met one of the Saints players who happened to be married at the time, and had gotten free tickets in exchange for her agreement to meet him after the game.

Fortunately, they had lost and the married football player hadn't been in the mood to spend time with the barmaid, who wasn't as pretty in the light of day as she'd been in the dim lights of the bar. Issie wondered what she would have done if the man had been interested. Would she have left Issie in the hall outside the locker room or locked her in the car?

She searched her mind for other good memories. Christmases, Thanksgivings . . . But she only remembered a lot of drunkenness, strange men in and out of the house, cursing and anger and blame. But she wasn't bitter, she thought. She had turned out all right. She didn't need a nurturing mother, any more than she needed a father.

She thought of Nick's sermon yesterday, of the way he'd referred to God as a loving father. That wasn't a concept that Issie had ever known. She couldn't quite grasp it. To her, the word *father* meant abandonment and neglect. It meant turning one's back, forgetting you ever existed. It meant pain and heartache and absence. No, she couldn't imagine any good coming from her thinking of God as a father.

She heard a car engine and wheels on the gravel, and peered through the slit trying to get a glimpse. It was impossible to see in the dark shed.

She waited until she heard the shed door open, then she began to bang and kick on the hood of the trunk, praying it wasn't Cruz.

"Help me!" she screamed. "Help me! Somebody, please come help me! I'm in the trunk."

She heard a key in the lock on the trunk, heard it turn, and the trunk sprang open.

Cruz stood over her as she raised up.

Double doors opened to the night, and a van idled there with its headlights shining in, blinding her.

"So you ain't dead yet?" Cruz asked.

She thought of trying to run for it but knew her legs wouldn't cooperate if she tried to leap from the trunk. She would wait until he had her out, until she was standing on her feet. He cocked his pistol and held it to her head.

"I've been tryin' to decide whether to finish you off or to wait till we find Jake. I'm thinkin' he might do everything we say if he knows your life is in my hands. Besides, Wednesday ain't that far off."

The significance of Wednesday shot through her brain with the velocity of a bullet. "You're planning to kill all those people, aren't you?" she managed to croak out.

He smiled. "Oh, that's right. You're Nick Foster's latest project, aren't you? I heard about him draggin' you outta the bar the other night. Like to drink, do you? Bet you're thirsty now."

"Please . . . ," she whispered.

"Sorry," he said, snapping his fingers. "I plumb forgot to bring you anything. So how's your sleeping quarters? Are you comfortable here?"

She took the opportunity to look around her in the trunk, now that there was light. She saw a two-liter bottle lying sideways in the wheel well where her feet had been. Next to it was an oily rag. There was nothing else there of consequence, but at least she knew that water might keep her alive until someone came. If he locked her back in, she would have to make sure that her head was near the bottle.

"Let me out, Cruz," she said. "Please. I won't tell anybody. I won't get in your way again. You don't want to kill me. I haven't done anything to you."

"We practiced tonight," he said. "We waited till Aggie Gaston was in bed, watched her turn her light off, then we went to the trees surroundin' where the church

will be set up Wednesday night. And we
practiced. Do you know what our signal is?"
he asked.

Closing her eyes, she shook her head.

"Soon as I pull the trigger and kill the
preacher, the others are gonna start firing."

She closed her eyes. "He hasn't done
anything to you. Why him?"

"Because he thought he was better'n me,
comin' to New Orleans and snatching away
my army. Tellin' them that God loves
everybody, that he died for the gays and
the blacks and the Jews and the Indians . . . He's dangerous," he said, "full of
lies and blasphemies, and I'm just makin'
myself a vessel to be used of God for his
own vengeance."

"You're insane," she whispered.

He grabbed her by the hair and ground his
teeth. "I don't like it when people call me insane." He put his face up close to hers. She
could smell his breath. She had the image of
rotten meat hanging between his teeth.

"These gashes look pretty bad," he said,
stroking his thumb along her torn cheek.
"You're going to have a nasty scar there.
That pretty face'll never be the same."

She slapped him away, but it only made

him angry, and he grabbed her by the hair and pulled her up out of the trunk. Her chin hit the metal and she almost fell headfirst, but she managed to get her legs out and catch herself.

She took a deep breath and decided the moment she could get upright she was going to bolt. It was as if he was testing her, toying with her, wanting to see what she would do. She felt like a rat in a science experiment.

He pulled her straight, turned her around until she was face-to-face with him. She felt faint, felt the waves of dizziness and blackness washing over her as if she would drop right here on the concrete. If so, what would he do with her?

She couldn't faint. He could kill her. Or worse. No, she told herself. She would have to get away.

She tried to summon all her strength, as if by sheer will she could muster the energy to run . . .

But he wasn't going to give her the chance.

He pushed her to the ground, then kicked her in the chin with his knee. She thought for a moment that he had broken her jaw and possibly knocked out some of her teeth. She fell back.

He pulled her back to her feet, turned her away from him, and pushed her as if giving her his blessings to run, but she was too dizzy, still reeling from the agony. She took a step and stumbled, caught herself with her hands, skinning the pads of her hands.

"Go ahead, Issie. Run," he said. "Let's see how far you can get."

She scrambled to her feet and tried to take a step, but he knocked her down again.

"Tag. You're it," he said. He pulled her back up by her hair, put one arm around her waist, and dragged her back to the trunk.

"Please don't put me back in there," she managed to cry, but he picked her up and slammed her down inside. Her head was at the wrong end. She wouldn't be able to reach the bottle, so she got up on her knees and tried to fight him before he could close the trunk. Though she knew she could never win, she managed to get her body situated where her head would be on the other side, and finally she gave up and sank back in.

The trunk slammed shut. She wept until she heard the doors to the building closing, and the car leaving again. He was gone, and she was still here.

It felt as if the wound on her leg had reopened, and she knew there were bloody places on her knees and hands. But at least she had water.

She reached for the two-liter bottle and saw that she could stand it upright in the small compartment. Why had Cruz had it here? she wondered. Was it in case his engine ran hot? Or was it even water?

She unscrewed the top and brought the lid to her mouth. A little of it spilled onto her face and down her neck and chest, and quickly she stood it upright again, making sure that no more was wasted. Yes, it was water, she thought. Real water. She screwed the top on. It might have to last her for days. She would have to be careful with it.

She let the water stay in her mouth, wetting all of her taste buds, and after a while she swallowed and felt the sweet sensation of it going down her throat. Then she lay there weak and in pain, and cried out, "Where are you, God? Can't you see that I'm locked away in this box and nobody's ever going to find me?"

She had a sense that God was listening,

that he heard, that he saw her trapped in this little compartment that no one else could locate. What if there *was* a God, a Father watching over her, looking down on her, waiting for her to call on him? Nick was convinced that God loved even her, that Jesus' death on the cross had been as much for Issie Mattreaux as it had been for Nick Foster.

Issie had doubted that was true. Why would a pure and blameless God give his life for someone as miserable and dirty as she? But just as that thought came into her heart, another one followed.

"While we were still sinners, Christ died for us." Nick had read that in his sermon yesterday.

And on its heels came the words he'd said to her the other day about slanderers and swindlers and adulterers and idolaters . . . and the sexually immoral. She couldn't remember all the sins he had listed, nor the order in which they had come, but she did remember one thing: "That is what some of you were."

It hadn't sunk in when he'd said it before, even though he'd explained it like she was a little child. He'd wanted her to understand that that verse alone showed that even people with filthy sins in their lives could be cleaned up and changed.

Was it possible that that could happen to her too? She closed her eyes. She might never find out. She might never get out of this trunk alive and prove to God that she could be different.

But yesterday, Nick had said there was precedent for that too. There was a thief on a cross hanging next to a crucified Savior. "Today you will be with me in paradise," Jesus had said. He hadn't expected the thief to get down from that cross and go clean up his life. He had known there would be no chance of turning around. He just knew his heart.

Maybe God could know Issie's heart as well. Maybe that was why he had allowed her to be locked in a cramped trunk where no one could find her. Maybe it took that to get her to the point where her heart was ready to call out to him.

"Save me, Jesus," she cried. "You don't have to get me out of here. But whatever happens, I want to know that you're my Father, that you haven't left me, and that I can call on you. Even if I die here, that maybe today I'll see you in paradise."

A peace like she'd never felt before fell over her, and she filled up with an emotion so deep that it brought tears to her eyes, tears unlike the ones she'd been weeping since she'd been locked in here. Tears that seemed to come from the very bottom of her heart, cleansing tears that seemed to wash away the sins that had eaten at her for years, sins that had become a curse on her family for generations, habitual sins that had a hunger of their own.

Could it be that God could see her as a clean person now? Could it be that all the cycles of sin in her family could be broken in her through Christ?

The trunk didn't miraculously open the moment she prayed the prayer. Her wounds did not miraculously heal. She didn't hear a siren coming up the dirt road to her rescue.

Her situation was not different. But her heart was. And as she lay in the cramped dark trunk, she felt less fear than she had felt before. Her Father was watching over her, unwilling to abandon or forsake her.

She closed her eyes, and sweet sleep fell over her.

Chapter Fifty-Three

● ● ●

By ten o'clock Jake had run out of places to look for Issie, and Nick was growing frantic with the search. At one point he had called the police station to see if there were any updates, and Sid told him that she hadn't been located yet. Benton had been found where Jake told them he would be, however, and he was, indeed, dead.

Nick had broken the news to Jake, and watched him cover his face and begin to weep. Somehow, the kid had been holding out hope that his friend had made it.

He looked over at Jake as he drove. "Jake, I think you need to go home now."

"I told you, I can't. It's too dangerous. They're looking for me."

"You need to at least tell your parents where you are. When they hear about Benton, they'll think you're dead somewhere too."

Jake thought that over for a moment. "I

want to. I really do. But I can't figure out how to do it without giving myself away."

"Well, how about if I call your parents and have them meet us somewhere? If anybody's watching your house, they won't know where your parents are going."

"What if they follow them?"

"I'll tell them to stay aware of it. They'll know. If they're looking, they'll know if someone's behind them."

Jake looked out the window for a moment, then turned back to Nick. "All right," he said, "but I hope this doesn't get anybody else killed."

Chapter Fifty-Four

● ● ●

Nick didn't tell Mike Mattreaux anything more than he had to. He asked them to meet him and said he needed to talk to them about Jake. Quickly, Jake's mother had grabbed the phone.

"Do you know where our son is?"

"Please, just meet me," Nick had said, "and be careful. Don't let anybody follow you. If you think they are, then turn around and go back home and call me on my cell phone."

Now he and Jake waited at the old abandoned gas station on the east side of town. As they waited, Jake leaned his head back against the seat. Nick could see how tired he was. He wondered how long it had been since the kid had had a good night's sleep.

"So what are you to Issie, really?" Jake asked him as they waited.

Nick was getting tired of this line of questioning. "A friend, I guess."

"No, you're more than a friend."

Nick met Jake's eyes and saw that he was searching. He hoped the kid didn't see more than Nick wanted to reveal.

"You two have something going, don't you?"

"No, we don't. We're cut from different cloth," Nick said.

"You can say that again."

Nick stroked his lip with a finger and gazed out the window. "Why are you so interested, anyway?"

"I just heard about you taking her home from the bar the other night. And everybody's saying that you two are getting to be an item."

"Oh, I wouldn't say that," Nick said. "I like Issie. There's something about her that's really special."

"Then you two do have something."

Nick didn't want to talk about it anymore. In fact, he didn't want to talk about anything. He just wanted to rack his brain for other places he should look for her, and get down on his knees and pray as hard as he could that God would hear his prayers . . . and hers if she was praying . . . and get her out of the mess she was in.

They saw headlights coming up the road, and Jake stiffened. The car turned in.

"My parents," Jake said.

Nick looked beyond them and saw that they were alone. "Nobody with them, nobody following."

"Good," Jake said. He got out of the car and stood beside the passenger door. The moment his parents saw him they slammed on brakes and lunged out of the car. Lois was already in tears.

"Jake, we've been looking all over for you! Where have you been? Are you hurt, son?"

Mike was more reserved as he came closer to his son. "Jake, you're not involved in anything criminal, are you?"

Jake evaded the question. "I got Issie in a lot of trouble, and right now we don't know where she is, but Cruz took her and, Dad, I think he's going to kill her. He'll kill me too, if he finds me."

Mike's face went pale. "Have you called the police?"

"Yes," Jake said, "they're looking for her. But they haven't found her yet, and it's been hours."

Mike turned his desperate face to Nick. "What have you got to do with all this?"

"Jake came to me," he said. "And I've been out looking for Issie."

"Have you been hiding him all this time? Keeping him from us?"

"No," Nick said. "He just came to me tonight."

He swung back to his son. "How did Issie get involved in this?"

"She's been involved all along, Dad," Jake said. "She snooped around where we were and saw things, and then she turned us in."

"They already tried to kill her once," Nick added. His voice cracked as he went on. "I'm worried about her, Mike. They're capable of anything."

Mike looked sick as he ushered his son into the car, and then he turned back to Nick and asked him what was being done. When he'd updated him, Mike drove off to hide his son.

Chapter Fifty-Five

• • •

Nick headed back to the police station, got an update on the search for Issie, and learned that she still had not been found. Every available police officer was looking for her, he was told, and off-duty cops were coming in to help with the search. They all took her disappearance personally, since they considered her one of their own.

But the all-out effort to find her had produced no results.

Frustrated and not knowing where else to look, he headed over to the fire station to ask for prayer. Mark and Dan were on duty, and George Broussard was filling in for Nick. Nick found all three of them in the kitchen, and he shuffled in. "Hey, guys."

They all looked up from what they were working on.

"Hey, Nick," Dan said. "I tried to call you awhile ago. I heard Issie was missing."

Nick came into the kitchen and plopped

down at the table. Mark set his hand on his shoulder. "You okay, man?"

"No, I'm not okay," he said. "Her nephew said that his pals threw her into the trunk of a car and took off with her."

"You're kidding me," Mark said.

"No, she's in a lot of trouble if she's even still alive." Tears burst into his eyes, and his mouth shook as he tried to hold back his despair. "Look, I came by tonight to ask if you would pray for her."

"We have been," Mark said. "You can count on us."

"So what has Issie gotten herself into?" Dan asked. "Does this have to do with the killings and the church burnings?"

Nick nodded. "She knows who it is, and she gave Stan the names. It was exactly who I thought."

"That Cruz kid?" Dan asked.

"You got it. And so help me, if I could get my hands on that kid . . ." He rubbed his mouth to cover his emotion. "But see? That's what's wrong with me. I took the wrong approach with him from the beginning. If I'd treated him like a fertile lost soul instead of a false teacher, maybe he wouldn't be so dangerous. Maybe I could have gotten through to him. I had the chance, but I blew it."

"You were protecting our own youth," Dan said. "What could you do? He wasn't going to listen to you."

"He might have if I'd tried getting to know him instead of chewing him out. Now two people are dead, and Issie could be the third." He drew in a deep breath and brought his tired eyes up to Mark's. "I need your help, guys. I can't preach at the service Wednesday night. I'm too distracted, and I don't feel worthy of leading that congregation in anything. Would you two lead the service for me?"

Mark and Dan looked at each other. "We could give our testimonies or something, or kinda give a pep talk to the congregation," Mark said.

"Sure," Dan told him. "We can work it out." Dan pulled out a chair and sank down, looking intently at his pastor. "You're pretty shaken up, aren't you?"

Nick let out a deep sigh. "I can't stand the thought of her out there in trouble with a bunch of thugs . . . imagining what they could be doing to her, if she's even alive. And to think of her locked in a trunk . . ."

"Issie's strong," Mark said. "She's tough. I once saw her fight a delirious wrestler. She can handle herself."

"And I'm sure the police are doing everything they can," Dan threw in. "I heard they're treating this like they would if she were a cop. She's one of our own in protective services. They'll find her."

"They're not doing enough." Nick buried his face in his hands and shook his head hard.

Dan and Mark were quiet for a moment, then finally, Dan spoke. "Man, you really have a thing for her, don't you?"

Nick looked at him over his fingertips. For a moment he was quiet. Then finally, he whispered, "I know what you two think of her. Her reputation. Even the experiences you've had. But she's a special person. I've seen her brokenhearted over accidents she's had to work. I've seen her cry over pain that little kids have to suffer. I've seen her work until she was about to drop to try to revive somebody who'd flat-lined. Even now she's in trouble 'cause she was trying to save her nephew."

He looked up at both of them, pleading for them to understand. "I know she's not right for me. I know we're unequally yoked and all that. I know that it's pretty pathetic for a preacher to let a girl like Issie get under his skin, a girl who spends more time in the bars than she does in church. I know all that. But I didn't plan this. I know you think it's one of those damsel-in-distress kind of things, that I want to rescue her so I'm starting to think I have these feelings for her. Transference, or whatever . . ."

"It crossed my mind," Mark admitted.

"It's not that," he said. "Issie's gotten to me for the last couple of years. I don't know what it is about her. Just something. Maybe because she's so wrong for me. But I think I understand her better than most people do. She didn't have a good childhood, you know. She never knew her father very well, and her mother's value system was pretty messed up. She was never home. Issie and Mike practically raised themselves."

"It's not like you, Nick, to make excuses for sin."

"I'm not trying to make excuses," he said. "She's responsible for her behavior and for who she is and what people think of her. But I'm just saying that she's deeper than that. There's more to it. When God looks at her, he sees more." His voice broke off and his face twisted again, and he looked up at the ceiling. "God can see her right now. He knows where she is. Why won't he tell me?"

"You want us to pray with you, buddy?" Dan asked.

The tears spilled over Nick's cheeks, and he wiped them away quickly as if he couldn't let his friends see him this upset over a woman. "Yes, please pray with me," he said, and together they all bowed and began to pray.

Chapter Fifty-Six

● ● ●

As he finally drove home, Nick had another bout with his tears. He brushed them away angrily and asked God why he couldn't just tell him where she was, why he couldn't lead him right to the car and get her out of that trunk if she was still there.

He didn't understand why God would take a woman who was so close to turning to him, who had given Nick opportunities to share with her in a way that he'd never had before. Why would he let him get so close, only to snatch her away?

She couldn't be dead, he thought. She had to be alive. This couldn't be the end of her.

As he pulled into his driveway and his headlights lit up the front porch, he looked to see if there was any one slumped there, as Jake had been earlier. Maybe she was hiding, waiting for him to come home. But he saw nothing.

He turned off his headlights and sat in the car, staring at the dark house. What was he doing? he asked himself. Living in a parsonage, acting as a shepherd to the flock that was without a house? Was he tainted because he'd fallen in love with a woman who didn't know the Lord? Did that disqualify him for service to Christ?

"I want to do your will, Lord," he whispered. "I don't ask that she and I get together. All I ask is that you lead me to her, help me to find her. And if not me, somebody else. Lord, please help them to find her before she dies." He closed his eyes as tears squeezed out. "I'm giving it up, Lord," he said. "The calling. I know it wasn't real. I thought it was but I *can't* be called to do this. You're trying to tell me something, and I just don't know what it is. As soon as I find her, as soon as we know what's happened to her, I'll give up my church and you can bring in whoever you have called to that position. Someone who can lead them, protect them. Somebody strong, somebody who doesn't make so many mistakes."

He suddenly felt like a dismal failure because he hadn't led Issie to Christ. She might be giving up her spirit at this very moment. If so, he would never forgive himself, and he'd never get over it.

He got out of the car and went into the house, miserable and knowing he wouldn't sleep. He would call the police station every hour and check to see if they'd found her yet. He wouldn't rest until he saw her again.

Chapter Fifty-Seven

● ● ●

Issie woke up hungry. The hunger was a deep pain in the pit of her stomach, crying out to her loudly, demanding that she fill it. But there was nothing to eat. She didn't know if she would ever eat again.

"Is there food in heaven, Jesus?" she whispered, like a curious child who'd just been introduced to heaven as a new concept. Then she remembered hearing something about the marriage feast of the Lamb, how all the believers would be invited one day.

Would she be there, adorned like a bride at her own wedding? Would she be among all those in white? She couldn't picture herself in white. Scarlet, maybe. Yet the sense of cleanliness, of newness, washed over her as it had last night when she'd whispered her prayer to her Savior. She knew without a doubt that he had heard, and that he had accepted her, as she had accepted him.

"Me a bride," she whispered. "Imagine that." She hoped he would clean up her wounds, take the swelling away, heal the bruises. She didn't want to meet her Maker looking like this.

She reached for the bottle of water, unscrewed the top, and carefully took a sip. It went down her throat, filling her, nourishing her.

"Thank you, Lord," she whispered. She knew that she needed to ration it out, but she had a feeling she wasn't going to live long enough for it to matter. She was just so grateful that it had been there when she needed it. She had no doubt that God had prompted Cruz to put it there, probably weeks ago, then forget that he had.

Her head still ached and the gash on her leg had begun to swell. She suspected it was getting infected. She was thankful that it wasn't August, but even in the middle of October the heat sweltered in the building and turned the trunk into an oven.

Eventually the heat itself would kill her, if not the hunger. She hoped she could sleep until God saw fit to take her life.

But then she realized that something terrible was about to happen. The shooting was going to take place. When? What was today? Monday, Tuesday? She honestly wasn't sure. The hours had blended together, and the darkness had made it hard to mark the time.

Wednesday, Cruz and his thugs were going to show up at Aunt Aggie's and try to do away with the people of Nick Foster's church. Nick would be the first to go, and there was nothing she could do about it.

She began to weep again. "Lord, take me if you have to, but please don't take him. That church needs him. Oh, Lord, stop them somehow. Expose them. Let them all be locked up before the day even comes."

But God didn't always answer prayers the way she thought he should, which was why she was bent up like a rag doll stuffed into the trunk of her car. She didn't know how God would answer her this time. All she knew was that he would . . . somehow . . . in a way that fulfilled his will.

◆ ◆ ◆

Nick spent the next two days looking for Issie again, and made the rounds to every place he could think of. He navigated his way to every fishing hole he'd ever heard about, both in and outside of Newpointe, and drove for hours and hours searching for any sign of her.

Finally, he called the elders of his church and asked them to come and pray with him for Issie tonight. He didn't know where she was or what he could do for her, but God did, and they needed to go to him.

Ten men showed up and sat in a circle in his living room, praying from deep in their hearts for the woman who wasn't even a part of them, because it was becoming increasingly obvious that Nick cared deeply for her.

He didn't even try to hide it anymore. His feelings were as obvious as the tears on his face.

Chapter Fifty-Eight

● ● ●

By Wednesday morning Nick knew the meaning of "praying without ceasing." He didn't remember if he had slept or not last night, for he'd spent so many hours praying for Issie. He was beginning to despair of ever seeing her again, and he felt sure she had never come to know the Lord. He considered it his own personal failure. He would never see it as anything less.

When Mark and Dan and some of the other elders of the church came to get him so that they could set up chairs on Aunt Aggie's lawn for that night's service, he didn't have the energy to go. But reluctantly, he allowed them to take him to the old woman's house. Aunt Aggie seemed as distraught as he at Issie's plight, and hadn't been able to cook for the firemen since Issie disappeared.

When all was done, he found himself alone with Dan. "How do you feel, Nick?"

his friend asked. "If you can't preach tonight, somebody else can do it."

"No," Nick said. "I can't stand up in front of these people and tell them everything is going to be all right. All my preaching about suffering purifying the church . . . I don't care if it purifies the church. I don't care if it purifies me. I just want Issie to be found, and I don't understand why she hasn't been."

Dan sat down across from him and stared out into the breeze. "I wish I knew what to say, buddy. Some way to help."

"If it was me who had to suffer," Nick said, "I'd do it gladly. And the church . . . if God's trying to purify us . . . okay, we prayed for revival. But Issie's not one of us. She doesn't even know where to turn." He got up and looked down at Dan. "What if she died not knowing the Lord? What if I had all those opportunities to tell her and I never made her understand?"

"Nick, you did tell her," Dan said. "You told her so many times you probably can't even count them. She wouldn't listen."

"She *couldn't* listen," Nick said. "She just didn't have the ears to hear."

"Who has to give her those ears?" Dan asked. "You?"

Nick shook his head. "No. I know only the Holy Spirit can do that."

"Then why are you beating yourself up, man?"

"You make it sound like it's simple," Nick said, "like all I need is a little assurance to soothe my conscience, then just wash my hands of her and forget she ever existed. But I can't forget! She might still be alive. And I don't know where she is!"

Dan looked down at his feet. "I've been praying for her day and night, Nick. I know you don't believe that. You think we have some kind of vendetta against Issie. But I've worked with her for years and I feel pretty close to her. I don't want to think anything happened to her. I'm still hoping for the best. Issie's tough. Don't forget that."

"Yeah, real tough," Nick said wryly. No one knew how vulnerable she really was. For some reason, she had only revealed that to him.

He looked at the men across the lawn from him, still setting up chairs. "Tonight after the service I'm going to give them my letter of resignation again, Dan. And this time I'm not going to take no for an answer."

"No, Nick!" Dan said. "You need time. You *can't* do that!"

"Watch me," Nick said.

Chapter Fifty-Nine

● ● ●

Issie didn't know how long she'd been here now, but if she was guessing right, it had been three days. She had seen daylight come and go, had tried to mark the dark hours, but the days were running together and her hope was running out.

Her body ached with the effort of lying still in this cramped position, her bruises and gashes were sore to the touch, and she was almost out of water despite her efforts to ration out her drinks. Her hands had been shaking so badly today that she had spilled half of what was left. She only had a little water left.

Her head throbbed and her joints felt as if they had been pulled apart. She was having chills and knew that she must have fever, for even in October it was still warm enough that she should have been sweltering in the trunk.

She tried to peek out where she had

pulled the rubber back, but the building was dark and she couldn't tell whether it was late afternoon or evening. If it indeed was Wednesday, then this was the day that Cruz and his evil friends would be dispersing around Aunt Aggie's property, aiming their guns at the congregation of Nick's church. She wondered how many would die.

She closed her eyes and began to pray, knowing that she was probably never going to get out of this trunk in time to stop the madness. But God knew where they were. He knew what they were doing. Would he allow the shooting to proceed?

She thought of Nick's sermon Sunday about how suffering sometimes brought revival, how tragedy purified the church and made it more vibrant and alive. It had made no sense to her then. Now she wondered if it would work that way. Was God going to allow evil to have its day? Was he going to put these people through suffering that they'd never experienced before? Could they endure it?

She thought back on the shooting that had happened at a Fort Worth church not that long ago, and recalled the article she had read about how that church had become even more effective than they had been before, how it had bonded them more closely to each other and to the Lord, how it had brought them all to their knees and made them turn to prayer as a significant habit of their lives.

Had God used that evil for good? Had it rippled out from that church into the community, reaching people like herself and drawing them in? Could God make good of even this?

She tried to find peace in that hope but still couldn't stop thinking that if she could just make her way out of this place she would be able to go and stop them. She would be able to warn Nick before the first bullet fired.

There had to be other ways to suffer through, to purify a church, she thought. Surely the church burning was enough, and Ben's murder. But then she wasn't God and she didn't know what he knew.

She recalled the words she'd heard so many times but never really in context, not until she'd spent time with Nick. "Thy will be done." Could one really pray that even on the cusp of tragedy? she asked. Then quickly the answer came.

Yes, trust me.

"I do trust you," she said, "but please don't take Nick. Please don't take him. They need him."

She shivered with the chills coursing down her spine and wondered how long it would be before she would drift out of consciousness and into oblivion. She wondered if God would wait a while before taking her to heaven, or if he would come for her immediately.

It didn't matter much. Either way, the next time she opened her eyes she would see Jesus. The thought thrilled her. She couldn't believe it. She had never been that sure of anything before, yet some part of her longed to stay here, to explore what life could have been like if she had embraced it God's way. She'd love to try that again.

"Lord, I'll be the thief on the cross if you want me to," she said. "I'll be the one who never has the chance to come down and clean up his life. I'll be the one who will see you today in paradise. Or I can get down off this cross and walk back into Newpointe and let you change my life the way Nick says you can. I'll be a walking testimony, the bad girl turned good, the one who couldn't do it on her own but who finally figured out she didn't have to."

Either way was okay with her. God's hand was on her life now, and it was on her eternity. For the first time in her life she felt the peace of knowing that everything would be all right, however it turned out.

Chapter Sixty

• • •

The congregation started arriving for prayer meeting at five Wednesday afternoon. Aunt Aggie, still disturbed about Issie's disappearance, had not made her characteristic smorgasbord. But members brought covered dishes which they set up on rented tables.

They milled around the grounds as they ate and fellowshiped, none of them aware that their gathering made them prey for the hunters waiting to take them down.

ı ı ı

From her state of half-consciousness, Issie Mattreaux thought she heard the sound of a car. She tried to peer out the little slit she had created by pulling the rubber away from the trunk, but all she saw was the daylight peeking through dirty boards in the building.

She told herself that she needed to cry out, needed to kick on the trunk and beat the top of it and scream so that someone would hear her. But she had so little energy left.

She kept her face on the carpet beneath her. She had to find the energy to cry out, she thought. She had to make some noise. She groaned, tried to make herself heard, but her throat was dry and it barely croaked out.

She hit the trunk with her fist, kicked against the metal. "Help!" she managed to get out. "Somebody help me!"

She heard a car door slam, then the doors to the small building were opened. Cruz, she thought. He was back, probably to speed her death.

Any minute now he would open the trunk and torture her a little more, dangle freedom in her face, then slam the door shut again.

She heard him doing something to the car, then heard the sound of water running. After a moment, the trunk opened. Blinded by the sudden burst of light through the open doors, Issie tried to raise up, but was too weak.

Just as she suspected, Cruz stood over her.

"Not dead yet, huh?" he asked. He saw

the empty two-liter bottle lying next to her and pulled it out. "Where'd you get this?"

Her lips were cracked and parched. She just looked at him. The acrid smell of gasoline rose on the stagnant air. He leaned over the trunk and looked Issie in the face. "Have you ever thought of hell, Issie?" he asked.

Her mind raced for an escape. If she could grab him by the throat, pull him down, pull herself out of this trunk, maybe she could get away.

"'Cause in a few minutes," he said, "just a very few minutes, this car is gonna be on fire, and you're gon' be in the middle of hell. And then me and my friends, we're gon' go to where Nick Foster and his church are meetin', and we're gon' blow them all away. Most of them are already there, in place."

She reached up, tried to grab his collar, but he knocked her hand free.

Come on, Issie, she told herself. *Get up. You can do it.*

She reached up again, this time clawing his face. With as much adrenaline as she could summon, she threw herself up and tried to bolt out, but his fist came down across her face, reopening the gash on her cheek and knocking her back in.

The back of her head hit against the rim of the trunk, and she screamed out in pain. Before she knew it, he had her back in the trunk and darkness closed over her again.

The smell of gasoline fumes made her nauseous and she gagged, but there was nothing in her stomach to throw up. Had he doused the car with fuel? she wondered, panicked. Was he about to set her on fire? Was it almost over?

The words kept dancing through her mind as the pain in her head overtook her. *Today you will be with me in paradise.* The words gave her a strange comfort, and she let herself slip away.

Chapter Sixty-One

● ● ●

Cruz parked in the designated area where they had decided to leave their getaway cars. They had a plan to use pipe bombs to distract attention so they could get away, so he'd stuffed two into his pockets and pants legs, so he would be able to toss them when he was ready. As he got out of his car and headed through the woods that would come out at Aunt Aggie's property, he felt the thrill of knowing that soon his plans would pay off.

He got to the edge of the property and saw that Jennifer was already in place behind a cypress tree. He looked across the dip in Aggie's land for Harris and Graham on the other side.

They were ready.

From his position, he tried to see around the tree. He saw a plume of smoke drifting above the sky and knew that that was the old stable he had set on fire. The whole structure would go — from the wall he'd doused with gasoline, to the other old, brittle walls — and eventually the car would catch the flames. She was probably dead by now. Nothing was going to stop them now.

He checked his rifle, which one of his disciples had stolen from his father's gun cabinet. Satisfied that it was ready to go, he waited until the right moment.

Chapter Sixty-Two

● ● ●

The crowd milled toward their seats as Jesse Pruitt started playing his harmonica at the front of the assembly, leading them all in a chorus of "Blessed Be the Name of the Lord."

Nick's head throbbed with the ache of urgency as he walked to the back of the congregation and sat down. His people filled in around him, and as they did, he pulled his letter of resignation out of his pocket and quickly read over it again.

He hoped they wouldn't be too hurt by this. They'd had enough loss lately. But God was doing things in his life that he didn't understand. He didn't know how to work around them or through them. All he could do was follow what God wanted, and right now it looked as if he wanted him out of ministry.

As his congregation sang praise songs to the Savior, Nick's soul felt heavier than it had ever felt. He cried out in his heart to God, praying that he would lead him to Issie, that somehow she would be okay, that in spite of all the odds and all the fears and dreads that had coursed through him, that somehow God would bring her through this.

Are you still listening, Lord? The question came from an honest quadrant of his heart, pleading for an answer.

Then suddenly he opened his eyes and lifted them up to the heavens, and he saw a plume of smoke coming from somewhere miles away, over the trees. He got slowly to his feet.

He wondered if the fire department had been called. He tried to think where that smoke might be coming from, and realized there was nothing in that area but woods. Maybe someone had left a campfire, or a hunter was making his meal . . . Or maybe after the dry summer they'd had, a spark had caught into a giant conflagration. Or maybe . . . just maybe . . .

Someone was in trouble.

Issie! He knocked his chair over with a crash, leapt over it, and bolted toward Aunt Aggie's house. He pushed past her on the porch and headed inside.

"Where you goin', *sha*?" Aunt Aggie asked, following him inside. "T-Nick!"

"I saw smoke," he said. "There must be a fire back up in the woods."

He picked up the phone and dialed the number for the station. Junior Reynolds picked up the phone. "Midtown Station."

"Junior, there's a fire over on the northeast corner of Newpointe, back up in the woods, probably near Hamp Carlson's deer camp. Have you had any calls?"

"No," Junior said, "none at all. Does it look bad?"

"Not yet," he said, "but we gotta get over there before the whole forest catches. And I'm thinkin' that maybe it's where Issie is."

He hung up the phone and hurried back out to his car. He didn't even notice the attention he caught as he jumped in and skidded away.

In seconds, he heard the sirens coming behind him. If only he could find the smoke, maybe it would lead him to Issie.

Chapter Sixty-Three

● ● ●

Issie smelled the smoke as it began to seep in through the one hole she had to get oxygen, and with her hand she tried to cover it up. But the metal was hot, and she recoiled. She remembered the oily rag she had seen in the trunk and groped around in the cramped space until she found it. Quickly, she stuffed it into the hole. The smoke stopped seeping in. Despite her fever chills, she felt the heat being turned up around her. She closed her eyes and knew that it was almost over.

Soon her spirit would leave her body and it would float into heaven where she would be with Jesus in paradise . . . just as he had promised the thief on the cross. That was the option he had chosen for her, and it was all right. "Just please, Lord," she whispered weakly, "please protect Nick and his congregation. You must have angels that could take care of them. You must have ways."

She heard the fire crackling around the car. Soon the fuel tank would ignite.

She hoped it would be over quickly.

♦ ♦ ♦

Cruz was a little thrown when he saw Nick running from the area, jumping into that car, and skidding away. And then he heard the sirens and that had shaken him as well, but the emergency vehicles had flown right past Aggie Gaston's house. They weren't coming here.

The possibility occurred to him that they might be going toward the fire. He cursed, realizing he should have ignited the car instead of just the structure hiding it. He had chosen that way to give her a slow, frightening death, in which she felt the heat rising by degrees, and had a long time to think before the car actually went up.

She was probably dead by now, anyway. She had probably died from smoke inhalation, and the fire had probably already claimed the car. If they were about to find her, it was probably too late.

He looked from Jennifer to Harris to Graham, and knew they were wondering when he would give the signal. But Nick Foster was gone. There was no use scattering the flock unless he could take the shepherd too. He wanted to wait just a few more minutes. Maybe Nick would be back.

He gave them the signal to wait, then he checked his watch and decided he'd give it ten more minutes. The service would go on for at least another hour. They had plenty of time.

Chapter Sixty-Four

● ● ●

The smoke was like a beacon as Nick got closer, and he felt as if the Holy Spirit was leading him just like the cloud over the Tabernacle when the Israelites were in the wilderness. It was telling him which way to turn, how far to go into the woods . . .

Behind him the fire truck forged through. The closer he got, the more certain he was that this was something to do with Issie, but he had a terrible feeling that they were getting there too late.

As the cloud of smoke thickened and made it impossible for them to see, he kept driving until he saw the blazing stable up ahead. Then he saw the flames and realized that it was the car inside that was engulfed. He jumped out — ignoring the pain in his legs — and headed for the flames.

Behind him the firemen leaped off the pumper truck and began unwinding the hose. He saw Junior Reynolds, Cale

Larkins, and Ray Ford, the chief, working quickly. They ran the hose up to the building and began dousing the flames.

As they pushed the flames down with the water, Nick opened the door. A blue Subaru sat at the center of the building.

"Issieeeeee!" He bolted in with the hose spraying alongside.

"I've got to open the trunk," he shouted. "Issie may be in there!"

They kept dousing the flames as Nick ran back to his car for a crowbar, then in just a few deft motions, was able to disengage the trunk lid. Coughing and gagging on the smoke, he threw it open. And then he saw Issie.

She lay limp inside the trunk, her lips dried and cracked, and her face bruised and cut. "Issie!" He lifted her out.

Just then he heard the sirens of the rescue unit and he rushed her toward it. He didn't even wait for the gurney. He just climbed with her in the back of the unit, and Steve Winder immediately began hooking her up to oxygen while Karen Insminger, the medic filling in for Issie, put a mask on Nick.

As soon as she could breathe, Issie's eyes came open. Nick came into her focus and she tried to rise up. "Issie, you're going to be all right. You're okay," he said. "Can you hear me?"

She tried to grab the mask off of her face, but he fought her to keep it on.

"Come on, Issie. You've got to breathe with the mask."

She shook her head and tried to say something, but the words wouldn't come out. "Please," she whispered. She pulled the mask off again. "How many did they kill?"

"How many did who kill?" Nick asked her.

"At your church," she said. "Wednesday night?"

"It's Wednesday night right now," he said. "What are you talking about?"

She managed to partially sit up. The urgency in her eyes was startling. "Nick, you've got to stop them."

"Stop who?"

"Cruz and all the thugs that burned your church down," she managed to say. "They have a plan . . . They're at Aunt Aggie's . . . they're going to kill everybody!"

Steve slowed his ministrations and shot a look up at Nick.

"Issie, just relax. Just calm down and rest a minute."

"No!" she cried. "You've got to stop them! Don't you see? That's why God led you to me. It wasn't to save me. It didn't *matter* if you saved me. You have to save the church."

"The church is gone," he said. "It burned down."

"Not the building!" she cried, grabbing his shoulders. "The people! Cruz is going to kill them. They have guns . . ."

Her words rang too true, and he stood there, frozen at the horror of it. "Please, Nick!" she said. "Please go!"

"Issie, are you sure?"

"Yes!" she cried. "Oh, Nick. Be careful!"

He got out of the rescue unit and saw Stan Shepherd getting out of his car. Nick ran to meet him.

"It's Issie, isn't it?" Stan asked. "Is she —"

"Yeah, she's alive," he interrupted. "But she says they're about to have a shooting spree over at Aunt Aggie's."

"The prayer meeting?" Stan asked.

"You got it," Nick said. "We better get over there."

Stan was already grabbing for his radio mike as Nick got into the car with him.

Chapter Sixty-Five

● ● ●

They had waited too long already, Cruz thought, and he was getting uncomfortable. Darkness was beginning to fall, and soon he wouldn't be able to see his targets well. Jennifer, Redmon, and Graham were getting impatient.

The person giving his testimony tonight droned on and on. Cruz knew the minute he quit, they would begin to pray. Once they did, he didn't know how much longer they would have. Soon they would break up and go home. He couldn't let it happen without doing what they had planned, even if Nick Foster wasn't here.

It was time. He nodded to Jennifer, who nodded to Redmon and then to Graham. They all raised their weapons and got their targets in their sites. Cruz got out a pipe bomb and held it under his arm.

He moved his finger to the trigger and fixed his gun on the one at the front, hoping that would be signal enough to get the others to shoot. His heart began to triple-beat as adrenaline rushed to his head. His finger closed over that trigger.

He heard a click at his ear.

He swung around and saw the barrel of a gun pointed at his head. That same black cop who had detained him the other night stood there with barely restrained rage in his eyes.

"You the one killed my nephew?" the cop asked. The barrel of the gun nudged against Cruz's face, and he almost dropped his weapon. Instead, he got his finger close to the trigger. If he could pull it, the others would shoot and it wouldn't matter that this man had a gun to his head.

"Might wanna drop that gun, scumbag," Sid said.

Cruz didn't even have to aim the gun. It didn't matter if he hit anything. All he had to do was make the noise, send the signal. He got his finger around the trigger and squeezed.

Bullet fire coughed across the property and he heard screams. And then the others went off and there was gunfire everywhere and people screaming and fleeing for their lives.

Sid grabbed Cruz's shirt, pulled him down, and wrestled the gun away from him. Before Cruz could defend himself, he was handcuffed behind his back.

◆ ◆ ◆

Nick Foster was already running toward his congregation when he heard the first shot and screamed, "*Get down!*"

He threw the six-year-old Hampton twins to the grass and tried to cover them with his body.

He heard shrill, piercing screams around them as more bullets fired, and he prayed out loud, not even sure what he was saying. He saw Dan and Mark racing for their wives, Celia trying to cover her toddler, choir members scattering. He didn't know how many guns were aimed on the congregation, but it sounded like warfare.

And then a sharp pain shot through him, knocking him from the children. He lay there for a moment, trying to utter one last prayer, before all went black.

◆ ◆ ◆

Cruz lay with his face in the dirt, waiting for the battle to be over. The count of fatalities would be worth whatever he had to pay for this. He had accomplished his mission.

His grandfather's lawyer would keep him out of jail, and he would win.

A bullet fired past him, startling him, and he realized someone was trying to knock off the cop to give him a chance to get away. Cruz got his knees beneath him and raised up, preparing to run for it.

People kept screaming as more bullets fired, and Sid turned to fire back.

And then a bullet jolted Cruz, and cut through his leg. He yelled and fell forward again, and realized that the bullet had ignited a pipe bomb.

He tried to stop the wick from burning, but locked in the cuffs, his hands couldn't reach. He let out a bloodcurdling yell. Sid turned and saw the sparkling wick on the side of Cruz's bloody leg, and dived away to take cover.

The explosion that followed sent further terror shattering through the crowd, as everyone saw Cruz dying by his own weapon.

Chapter Sixty-Six

● ● ●

One by one, Stan Shepherd and the other police officers captured the gunmen and disarmed them. In the wake of the gunfire, people were wailing and screaming and groaning.

Stan waited to make sure that there wasn't another guerilla hiding in the trees waiting until they least expected it. Finally satisfied that they were all accounted for, he headed down the hill.

He looked around at the bleeding people one by one. Eddie Neubig had a gunshot in his hand, and Andre Bouchillon looked as if he was clutching a bloody ear. Louis DeLacy, the town's judge, was sitting up, but he was clutching his knee. Stan could see that it had been shot.

He kept looking around, taking inventory of the wounds, but he saw no one bleeding to death, no one who looked lifeless on the ground, no one unconscious.

And then his eyes came to Nick. He was lying on his back and looked as if he'd been shot in the left side.

"Nick!" he screamed, and several of the men scrambled to their feet to help.

Paramedics rushed down the hill with a gurney and started triage. Stan surrendered Nick to them and tried to see who else was critical. Nick seemed to be the only serious casualty.

He heard sirens coming and saw that other rescue units from surrounding towns were arriving on the scene.

He heard a yell and saw Ray Ford at Nick Foster's side. "Save him!" Ray was yelling. "Get him outta here, *now!*" He ran along beside the gurney, and Stan followed. "Stay with us, man!" he yelled at Nick. "Come on, man! You gotta stay with us! We need you. This church needs you. We can't do without you, man!"

Stan saw Nick open his eyes.

"There you are," Ray said. "You're with me, ain't ya?"

Nick managed to speak. "I'm with you, Ray. I'm with you."

"You gon' be all right," Ray said. "You

gon' bounce back. Me and Susan, we gon' be prayin' for you."

"Speaking terms?" Nick got out.

Ray was crying. "Yeah, man. We're back on speaking terms. God knows what he's doin'. You taught us that."

Nick managed to smile. "Appreciate that, man."

Stan watched as they loaded Nick into the rescue unit. Then he set about trying to help with the triage scene that had emerged around them.

Chapter Sixty-Seven

● ● ●

The waiting room outside the ICU at Slidell Memorial Hospital was full of people from Calvary Bible Church waiting to see if their pastor was going to live or die. Word was that he'd been shot in the left side near the kidney.

Allie and Mark, Stan and Celia, and Dan and Jill huddled together in a corner praying for their friend and spiritual leader, and for the doctors who would save his life if it was going to be saved. Other groups huddled in various parts of the waiting room. Some cried over the trauma that they had all endured; others chattered nonstop with a nervous energy that couldn't be assuaged.

When Ray and Susan came in, a hush fell over the room. They said their hellos to various people, then crossed the room and sat down with their closest friends.

"How is he?" Susan asked.

Allie looked up at her with red, swollen

eyes. "It's touch and go, Susan. He may not make it."

"Well, he has to," she said. "He just has to." She burst into tears and Celia pulled her into her arms and held her. "What will our church do without him?"

No one had an answer for that.

Susan wiped her face and pulled back. "I had a dream," she whispered. "Last night, it was so vivid. I saw Ben."

Jill's face twisted in pain for the mother.

"He told me he was fine, just fine. That he was havin' a big time up in heaven. That he wouldn't come back for the world, not even if they let him. He tole me we would see each other soon . . . that it might seem long, but it really wasn't." She wiped her face and breathed in a sob. "And he tole me I needed to go back to the church, stop blamin' God. That death was the best thing ever happened to him." She broke down and began to weep, and Celia pulled her back into her arms.

They all clung together and wept, then prayed some more. Finally Celia got up. "I think I'm going to run and check on Issie," she said. "Somebody needs to tell her about Nick."

"Nobody told her yet?" Ray asked.

Mark shook his head. "Well, none of us. We've all been kind of preoccupied."

"You know, she's the one who saved the day," Ray said.

"How?" Allie asked.

"When we got her out of that trunk, the first thing she told us was that they were planning to ambush the church. If it wasn't for her, there's no tellin' how many would have been dead. Sid woulda never stopped Cruz, and those others woulda emptied their guns."

Silence fell over them as they realized how close they had come. Allie shivered. "Then we owe her a thank you," Allie said, "a big one. I'll go with you."

"I'm going too," Jill said.

Before they reached the door, Mark had joined them. "Wait for me," he said.

Dan was behind him, and Stan brought up the rear. Together they marched up the two flights of stairs to Issie's room. They found her lying in bed with cuts and bruises and an IV feeding nourishment into her body. Her brother and sister-in-law sat on the couch near the bed talking quietly.

Allie was the first to knock. Issie's eyes opened partially.

"Issie?" Allie asked, tentatively stepping inside. "Feel like company?"

Issie nodded. "Come on in, Allie."

They all came into the room, filling one side of it. Slowly they made their way around the bed until they surrounded her. She was pale as death and had dark circles under her eyes. Bruises and a gash colored one side of her face and both eyes. Her lips were cracked. Allie put her hand over her mouth.

"I saw the news," Issie whispered. "Said nobody was killed."

"Thanks to you," Allie said, beginning to cry again. "Oh, Issie, it was awful. We were running, but there was no place to go. If the police hadn't stopped them, there would have been fatalities." She stopped on a sob, unable to go on.

"We owe our lives to you," Jill said.

Celia took her hand. "Our children, people we loved." Her voice broke off, and she caught herself in tears. Swallowing hard, she said, "I really appreciate what you did, Issie."

"I didn't do anything," she said. "I just told the truth. I just wish I could have done it sooner."

"Are you okay?" Celia asked.

"Oh, yeah, I'm gonna be fine," Issie said. "Just sore and tired. I'm going to have to have a little plastic surgery to clean up the cut on my face, I'll be on antibiotics and fluids for a while, but I'm going to be okay."

She managed to open her swollen eyes and looked up at Jill and Dan. "Where's Nick? He was really worried about me when they pulled me out of the car, but he hasn't come by to see me."

Jill pushed the hair out of her eyes. "Issie, Nick was shot."

Issie sucked in a breath. "Oh, no. I knew it. I knew it."

"He's in surgery," Allie said, "but we don't know how bad he is."

"We'll let you know as soon as we get word," Mark threw in.

She began to sob, and her brother got up and came to the edge of the bed. He tried awkwardly to calm her with a pat on her hand, but she wouldn't be comforted. "Why Nick?" she wailed. "Why Nick, of all people?"

None of the others had an answer, so they just stood there, weeping along with her.

"I don't get it," she cried. "I didn't know it was going to be so hard. I thought after I gave my life to Christ that things would get easier, not worse."

Everyone just stared at her through their tears. "You gave your life to Christ?" Mark asked.

"Yes, in that trunk. And God kept me alive so I could tell them. But why didn't he spare Nick?"

"We don't know," Allie said, "but all we do know is that accepting Christ doesn't mean you're instantly immune to suffering. Look at all of us, Issie. We've all been through it."

Issie looked at Mark and Allie and thought about the killer that had gone after Allie two years ago. Mark had even been shot trying to defend her. She looked at Stan and Celia and recalled the poisoning that had almost killed Stan and how Celia had suffered in jail for weeks trying to prove her innocence in the crime.

And then there was Jill and Dan, and it had just been a few months ago that Jill had been held hostage by a man considered a terrorist, and had fought for her own life and Dan's while she tried to help justice be served.

No, she couldn't say that they had been immune to suffering. Even the very church that she had thought was so protected had taken its share of pain. Now it appeared that there was more suffering to be done.

"Then what good is it?" she cried. "What good is it to be one of God's children if you're not taken care of?"

"Oh, but you are taken care of." Allie leaned over the bed, putting her face close to Issie's. "Issie, you are. Because even if something happens to Nick, we know we'll see him again."

"It doesn't make it easier," she cried. "It makes it a lot harder."

"But we don't have to despair. God has his reasons, and they're bigger and broader reasons than we could even imagine."

If the words had come from anyone but Allie — the woman whose husband she had once tried to steal — they might have been intolerable. But she was aware that Allie knew the hard way.

"I know this is silly," Issie said, "but I was in love with him. I know it's ridiculous, somebody like me, falling in love with someone so unattainable. A preacher, of all things."

"Issie, I think Nick's had a thing for you for a long time," Allie said. "Maybe God does have a plan for you two. It's not over yet."

"We have to pray," Issie said. "It worked before, when I prayed that God would protect your congregation. And he did. He really did. Prayer works."

She struggled to sit up, and they raised the head of her bed. "Come on," she said, reaching for their hands. "Everybody, please. We've got to pray."

They all held hands and stood around the bed of the bad girl of Newpointe, who had been washed and restored and changed, and prayed with her that Nick would be all right.

● ● ●

Chapter Sixty-Eight

It was almost an hour later when they stopped praying, and Allie realized that Lois and Mike had had their eyes closed. They had been praying with them. They heard movement at the door and saw that Ray had come in sometime during the prayer. He had stopped in the doorway and waited for them to finish. "He's out of surgery," he said quietly. "It's a miracle."

Issie sat up straight in bed.

"The bullet missed his kidney," Ray went on. "It hit part of his intestine, but they took care of that. They've got him stabilized."

A cheer went up around the room, and Allie threw her arms around Issie. "I want to see him," she said. "Can I go see him?"

"Issie, you can hardly get out of bed," Lois told her. "Come on, lie back down."

"No!" she said, "I need to see Nick."

"He ain't awake yet," Ray said, "and

when he does wake up they're gon' have him in ICU."

"I *have* to see him," Issie said. "Would you find out when the first visiting time will be? It's important, Ray."

Ray nodded. "I'll do it, Issie, and I'll come back and let you know."

As Ray left the room, the others laughed and cheered again. The Lord was with them, Issie thought. He had answered their prayers. Maybe there was hope after all.

Chapter Sixty-Nine

● ● ●

Nick wasn't sure he wasn't dreaming. He opened his eyes and tried to focus on the woman standing over him. Issie, he thought. But what was she doing here? She faded in and out of his consciousness, then came into clear focus.

"Nick," she was saying. "Nick, can you hear me?"

"Issie," he whispered.

She smiled and he saw the redness of her eyes, the bruising on her face, the gash, reminders of what she'd suffered at the hands of a madman.

"Nick, we thought we'd lost you!"

"I think they told me I was going to live," he whispered. "Unless I was dreaming."

"You better live," she said. "I have a lot to tell you."

He squeezed her hand and stroked the soft skin there. He couldn't believe she had been locked away in a trunk for three days.

It was like being in the belly of a whale. He wondered if she felt anything like Jonah.

He blinked back the tears in his eyes. "You saved my church," he whispered. "You saved all those lives. You saved me."

Tears burst into her eyes again, and he saw the way her mouth trembled as she tried to hold back her emotions. "Not me," she whispered. "God."

A tear fell. "I'm glad you see that. I'm glad you understand. He was watching over us, wasn't he? My church was not a building, but I had forgotten that until I heard those bullets flying and people dropping to the ground. Those people are the church. Not a bunch of wood and bricks. The church is the people who inhabit it. It's the God who inhabits them. God didn't take my church away from me."

Emotion welled up in his throat, and he swallowed it back and closed his eyes. When he looked up at her again, she was crying too. Their eyes locked into each other's, and he felt an intense connection with her. He couldn't remember ever having that kind of connection before.

There was something about her, he thought, something that had always gotten to him, under his skin and into his heart. And it was still here, stronger than ever. Even when he had resolved never to be unequally yoked, when she bent over and hugged him, he couldn't help wrapping her in his arms, holding her close to him.

But they were unequally yoked. Then it occurred to him. She had agreed that God had saved the church. And if she understood that, then maybe . . . He let her go and pulled her back enough to look into her face. It was only inches from his, and he could see the little golden flecks in her dark eyes, the pink rims, the redness of her nose.

"You said that God saved the church," he said. "You believe now."

Those tears came even faster down her face as she nodded her head.

"You've accepted Christ?" he whispered, astounded.

She only stared at him for a long moment, and in that moment he convinced himself that she was going to say no, that she hadn't gone quite that far. Maybe she had a cursory belief in God, understood that there was a supernatural power directing things around her. But a relationship with Christ was another thing.

"I have accepted him," she whispered, and his heart took wing. He tried to get up, but she made him lie back down. "That's not the amazing thing. The really amazing part is that he's accepted me."

Nick's mouth opened. He couldn't think of words that adequately expressed the joy soaring inside him. It was a miracle, an even greater miracle than God stopping the shooters from killing anyone in his church. God had saved Issie Mattreaux.

Overcome with the miracle of that grace, he framed her face with his hands and pulled her closer. Their lips met, and he kissed her hard and long with all the joy and sadness and grief and anxiety and desire that he had felt for her for so long. And he could feel in her kiss that she felt it too.

She didn't see him as a big brother, or a protector, or even the preacher who barraged her with customized sermons. No, she was kissing him like a man.

They heard someone in the doorway of the ICU, and a nurse's shrill voice cut across the moment. "Time for you to go, honey. Visitation is only fifteen minutes."

She nodded to the nurse, then turned back to Nick, her eyes swimming with tears.

"I love you, Nick Foster," she whispered.

He was so shocked he couldn't speak as she sat back down in her wheelchair and allowed the nurse to push her out. As she disappeared from his sight, he began to weep with relief and joy and hope like he'd never felt before.

Was God going to give him permission to pursue his relationship with Issie? The thought that that might happen overcame him as he closed his eyes and began to pray. And for the first time in a long while, he began to realize that God's plan for him might be even better than he expected.

Chapter Seventy

● ● ●

The courtroom was full of reporters from both national and local stations, all waiting to capture the arraignment of each of Cruz's followers. Thanks to Jake's testimony, the police had rounded up everyone involved in the murders and the church burnings.

Sidney Clairmont, Cruz and Jennifer's grandfather and the grand wizard of the KKK, hired his own lawyer from New Orleans to represent his surviving granddaughter. He marched into the courtroom with a suit that looked like it had fit ten years ago, and with a smug grin on his face that said this was a minor setback in their lives, but they would clear it up before long.

Jennifer sat in an orange jumpsuit with dirty hair and a gray cast to her skin. She had stopped eating since seeing her brother killed by the pipe bomb he had meant for the church. She was going to follow her martyred brother, she had declared, and didn't care whether she did it from jail or from home.

Judge DeLacy, who had been on the grounds of Aunt Aggie's when the shooting had occurred, and who had even had his kneecap shattered by a bullet, had excused himself from the case and had the hearing moved to Slidell so that another judge could handle it. Still, he sat in the courtroom, hoping the whole group got all they deserved.

When their case was called, Jennifer came before the judge.

"What do you plead?" the judge asked.

"I don't care," Jennifer said, her eyes fixed on the floor in front of her.

"You *have* to give me a plea," the judge said.

Her lawyer whispered something in her ear, and finally, she brought her dull eyes to his. "Not guilty by reason of insanity."

"Insanity," the judge repeated distastefully. He leaned up on the bench and glared down into their eyes. "Since you're so insane, you won't blame us for lockin' you up. Just to make sure you don't have a mental lapse again."

"Your honor," the attorney said, straightening his tie and shuffling papers as if this was a routine case. "She's just a kid."

"Not according to the law, she isn't."

"But we both know that she is," the attorney said. "She just lost her brother, and she hasn't been well. Their mother is a fine, upstanding Christian woman. Let her keep this young lady at home and get her through this bad time until the trial."

"We all know who her mother is," the judge said, "and who her grandfather is. Thank you, but I b'lieve I'll stick with my original order. She will be held in custody pending the trial, and I don't care if she eats or not."

Jennifer gave no response, but her grandfather got to his feet.

"Your honor," the lawyer said, "I'd like to have her mentally evaluated to see if she's even competent to stand trial."

"She's gon' stay in jail, Counselor."

"Judge, when you hear how this child was abused by her daddy for most of her life, you'll understand her instability. Jennifer here was sexually abused, and her brother was beaten repeatedly throughout his life. They were both exposed to repeated acts of violence throughout their childhoods, acts that seemed normal to them. I'd like a mental evaluation to prove —"

The judge banged the gavel again. "I'm sorry for their past history, Counselor. But thousands of people who were abused as kids live decent, law-abiding lives every day. They don't kill people. The victim defense won't work in my courtroom. I'm sick to death of hearing people come up with excuses for committing horrendous crimes. I don't care about excuses. I care about seeing that justice is done." He looked at his bailiff. "Next case."

Jennifer was compliant as the bailiff led her out.

Chapter Seventy-One

● ● ●

Six months later, the new sanctuary was filled to overflowing with people who had come to dedicate the building and listen to Nick preach the first sermon in it. Nick gave an invitation that day asking anyone there who wanted to walk the aisle and profess their belief in Jesus Christ to come to the altar.

Issie, whom he'd baptized in Bayou Lafayette as soon as he had recovered a few months ago, walked the aisle with her brother, Mike, his wife, Lois, and her nephew, Jake.

For the past several months she had been in a Bible study group that Nick had led in his home, and he'd found her to be an enthusiastic student of the Word of God. She soaked up the things he taught her with a hunger that surprised him, and gradually he saw the emptiness in her heart being filled with Bread of Life and Living Water. He saw her father-longing satisfied as she learned what it was to be embraced by the paternal arms of the One who loved her enough to die for her.

He had seen joy in her like he'd never seen before, and he'd seen purpose, for now she knew why she was here. As far as he knew, she hadn't been back to Joe's Place since the night he had rescued her from herself.

When the service was over, Nick took them to a room in the back and talked to Jake and Lois and Mike about their salvation. And then he deferred to Issie as she began to explain the simple concept of grace to her nephew, who had trouble believing he could be forgiven for some of the things he had been a part of. Awaiting trial for being an accessory to murder, he knew he would serve time in jail. How could God forgive him when the justice system could not?

Nick was proud of her, so proud that he could hardly stand it. And even as he listened to her teach those she loved about her own salvation, he found himself struggling to hold back the tears.

Later as she and her family left the

church, he watched them walk out to the new parking lot and get into their car. He stood at the door, moved by what he had seen here today, the fruit she was bearing, the burden she had for telling those she loved about Christ.

He heard footsteps behind him and glanced over his shoulder to see Mark, Dan, and Stan come up behind him. Stan put his hands on Nick's shoulders and shook him roughly, affectionately.

"So what are you waiting for?" Mark asked.

Nick looked over at him, saw Mark leaning against the doorway's casing, his arms folded and a smug grin on his face.

"What do you mean, what am I waiting for?"

Dan grinned and nodded toward the car driving out of the parking lot. "It's pretty obvious that you and Issie are made for each other," Dan said.

Nick grinned then, understanding. "I've been waiting for a lot of things," he said. "I wanted to make sure I wasn't taking advantage of her in her vulnerability. A baby Christian, struggling to walk. I didn't want to get in the way of that, or interrupt it in any way.

And I didn't want to wonder if she was trying to be something I wanted, or if I was trying to be something she wanted. I wanted to watch her for a while, make sure her salvation was real, and disciple her."

"She's bearing fruit," Mark said. "That looks like a good sign to me."

Dan shook his head. "She's not the same party girl that she used to be. She's really getting into this church thing. Her heart is different."

Nick nodded. "Yeah, her heart is different." But he hoped it wasn't too different, for he couldn't forget the words she'd whispered to him in ICU months ago.

I love you, Nick.

Since then, they'd dated frequently, but he had deliberately taken things slow. He didn't want to rush her, didn't want to get in the way of God's work in her life, didn't want to interrupt her healing.

But he didn't know how much longer he could wait.

He grinned as they all watched him watch her drive away. "I think she's getting better looking all the time too," he said.

They all roared as if their favorite team had just made the winning touchdown, and all of them patted him on the back and hugged him roughly.

They headed back into the church.

• • •

Mike took Lois and Jake to the restaurant they had chosen for lunch, so that they could hold a place in line while he took Issie home. She wasn't hungry, she said. She wanted to go home and be alone for a while.

She rode in the passenger seat of her brother's car, her gaze fixed on some invisible object outside the window.

"So is Nick coming over for lunch?" he asked.

"No," she said. "He didn't mention it."

"Then why don't you want to eat with us?"

She shrugged. "He said some things in his sermon today. I want to go home and look them up, and put them in context, and study them while they're fresh on my mind."

Mike grinned. "Man, you've changed."

"Not enough," she said. They rode in silence for a while, and finally, she looked over at him. "Mike, I've been thinking a lot about Dad lately."

"Dad?" he asked. "Why?"

"I don't know," she said. "The concept of God being my Father sort of keeps it coming to mind. That didn't sound like a good thing to me, you know? To me, fatherhood meant neglect, indifference, absence . . . I didn't get a warm, cuddly feeling when I thought of God as that."

"I can relate to that," he said.

"But lately, with Nick, I've felt that security and that love and that sense of being cherished . . . all the things that fathers are supposed to give to their children. All the things I missed with every single man I ever dated, because I never knew that I didn't just have to rewrite the last chapter in my relationship with our dad. I didn't know that I could rewrite the entire story, and start with a different type of man, one who had all those paternal traits that I wanted so much."

"So that's what Nick is to you? A father figure?"

"Not exactly. I'm just now understanding that maybe what I need in a husband is a man who can love me as a wife, cherish me and enjoy me, and be attracted to me and flirt with me . . . but also nurture and protect me with that fatherly security I never had. It changes everything, Mike. I wish I'd known it before, when I was choosing rogues and rats to go out with. I wish I'd known that I could have what I always wanted. But I didn't know. I thought I could find what I wanted by choosing unavailable men like Dad, and through my wiles and my looks, capture them into falling for me. But men like that never do fall that hard for a woman, and they're never more available than Dad ever was."

Mike frowned as he let her thoughts sink in. "I should have been that for you. I was your big brother. I was supposed to take care of you."

"But you were as neglected as I was. How could you know any better? We were two kids bringing ourselves up. You did the best you could with what you knew."

His eyes misted over. "What if it doesn't work out with Nick, Issie? What if he never asks you to marry him?"

Her gaze drifted out that window again. "I'll be disappointed, but not broken. Because Nick will have given me something pretty important. He'll have shown me, just for a while, what God's father-love for me is all about. And I know God can take it from there."

• • •

The next afternoon, a huge portion of the town turned out for the drill that would help the emergency personnel of the town prepare for another disaster. They staged a hurricane with tornadoes, and mock casualties lay all over the school grounds.

Attired in his turnout gear and his mask and tanks, Nick helped with the triage operation that the paramedics were involved in. They ran from actor to actor assessing invisible wounds.

He saw Issie across the bodies, watched her pretending to administer care to a victim.

Nick found it hard to concentrate. He'd been trying to ask her to marry him for the last week, but every time he got close to her, his heart raced and his palms sweated, and he found himself gazing into her eyes and forgetting any rational thoughts he'd ever had.

He knew he should just come out with it, tell her he loved her and wanted to spend the rest of his life with her, but some part of

him feared that she would say no. He didn't
want it to end just yet. He'd been carrying
the ring every day in his pocket, and he had
it on him now, but he didn't know when he
would get the chance to ask her.

He looked around for where he was
needed and saw that the firemen were almost finished with their work. The paramedics had the wounded under control.
They were nearing the end of the day, and
he knew the drill had been successful.

He went back to the fire truck and took off
his mask and cap, hung his tanks on the
back of the seat, opened his turnout coat.
Issie came around the truck, hurrying to put
her crash cart away in her own rescue unit.

She winked at him as she passed. "Kind
of a fun day, huh?"

"Yeah, fun." He reached down and
grabbed her arm, pulled her back. Her eyes
brightened into that flirtatious look he loved,
as she looked expectantly up at him.

He leaned back against the fire truck.
"You know, it's not so easy being around
you, keeping my thoughts to myself."

She smiled. "I know the feeling."

He leaned down and kissed her. The fact
that she didn't recoil, that she always let

him come close, continually surprised him. "So what are you going to do after this?" he whispered.

She slid her arms under his turnout coat and around his waist, and threw her head back to look up at him. "I don't know. I thought I might rent a movie, invite a nice man over to watch it with me. A preacher type, maybe. You know anybody like that?"

He shook his head. "I wasn't talking about today."

"Oh?" she asked.

"I meant what are you doing for the rest of your life?"

Her eyes grew serious as she gazed up at him, unable to answer.

"That's my stupid way of asking you if you thought maybe you'd like to spend it with me."

For a moment the shock on her face was hard to read. He wasn't sure if she was thinking of a nice way to let him down easy, or if she was so stunned that she couldn't think of a way to say yes.

Then she burst into tears. He let her go, suddenly ashamed and full of remorse. It was too soon to ask her, he thought. How could he have been so stupid?

But then she threw her arms around him again, raised up on her toes, and kissed him with all the heart and enthusiasm that he had hoped for. Pulling back slightly from his lips, she whispered, "The thought of being your wife is just one more example of grace in action," she whispered. "That in my wildest dreams, you would pick somebody like me."

"I could never pick anybody else," he whispered. "Then you'll say yes?"

"Yes!" she cried. "Yes! Yes! Yes!"

She threw her arms around him again and he lifted her up and spun her around. Others started to come around to see where all this noisy joy originated.

None of them had to ask what had happened. Everyone knew. Some things were just meant to be.

Afterword

• • •

Last night as I was trying to relax and fall asleep, I began reflecting on the 23rd Psalm and all the riches layered in that passage. And I came to the phrase I've repeated and read many times before.

He restores my soul.

Always before, I dwelled on the verse before it, about his leading me beside the quiet waters. That is, after all, a wonderful thought in such a stressful, noisy world. And I've pondered the verse after it, about the Lord guiding me in paths of righteousness. That's particularly important to someone like me, who has no sense of direction.

But this is the first time I've lingered on his restoring my soul.

And I realized that he does, in such a merciful way. He has restored my soul when I've beaten it and bruised it through my careless actions and terrible choices. He has restored my soul when I've allowed it to run empty, and he's restored it when I've filled it up with things it wasn't made to hold. He has restored my soul when others have crushed it. He has restored it when there was no hope for restoration.

And I wondered what my life would look like now, if I had never allowed that restoration. What if I had pushed God away when he reached down for me like a daddy reaching for his toddler? What if I had not reached up to him, allowing him to lift me? What if I had not laid my head on his shoulder?

Where would I be if I'd had to take the punishment I deserved for the sins I committed, and if I'd had to walk through life without that perfect, unconditional love? What if I'd had to face a future eternity with only hopelessness and fear?

Thank God for Jesus Christ, who loved me so much that he took that punishment for me, cleaned my slate, restored my soul . . .

I can't wait to see him face-to-face.

About the Author

● ● ●

Terri Blackstock is an award-winning novelist who has written for several major publishers including HarperCollins, Dell, Harlequin, and Silhouette. Published under two pseudonyms, her books have sold over 3.5 million copies worldwide.

With her success in secular publishing at its peak, Blackstock had what she calls "a spiritual awakening." A Christian since the age of fourteen, she realized she had not been using her gift as God intended. It was at that point that she recommitted her life to Christ, gave up her secular career, and made the decision to write only books that would point her readers to him.

"I wanted to be able to tell the truth in my stories," she said, "and not just be politically correct. It doesn't matter how many readers I have if I can't tell them what I know about the roots of their problems and the solutions that have literally saved my own life."

Her books are about flawed Christians in crisis and God's provisions for their mistakes and wrong choices. She claims to be extremely qualified to write such books, since she's had years of personal experience.

A native of nowhere, since she was raised in the Air Force, Blackstock makes Mississippi her home. She and her husband are the parents of three children — a blended family which she considers one more of God's provisions.